Above the Glebe

A Farming Family's Heartbreak during the American Revolution

PAMELA GILPIN STOWE

ABOVE THE GLEBE
A Farming Family's Heartbreak during the American Revolution

iUniverse books may be ordered through booksellers or by contacting:

iUniverse
1663 Liberty Drive
Bloomington, IN 47403
www.iuniverse.com
1-800-Authors (1-800-288-4677)

ISBN: 978-1-4917-7828-9 (sc)
ISBN: 978-1-4917-7827-2 (e)

Library of Congress Control Number: 2015917521

Print information available on the last page.

iUniverse rev. date: 10/28/2015

To my granddaughter,
Iris Hope Stowe
and her parents,
Nathaniel & Heather

Glebe (glēb) n.

1. A plot of land belonging or yielding profit to an English parish church or an ecclesiastical office.
2. Archaic The soil or earth; land.

[Latin glēba, clod.]

http://www.thefreedictionary.com/glebe

The town of Fishkill, north of the busy port of New York, was their home. It was part of the British Colony of New York, between the Hudson River and the Colony of Connecticut, an area referred to as Middle District.

The Holmes were a typical, late-1700s colonial family. Most people in Middle District at that time were planters, men and women of the land, of the glebe, the soil, the dirt they cherished. And it was that land, that clod of dirt on which they farmed, fished, toiled and buried their dead, that nourished them as it did the people that preceded them. The soil brought forth a bounty of vegetables, fruit, nuts and grains; it all came from what was under their feet.

The rich dirt provided them with life itself. Whether one was above the glebe or below the glebe, it was a part of them and they were a part of it.

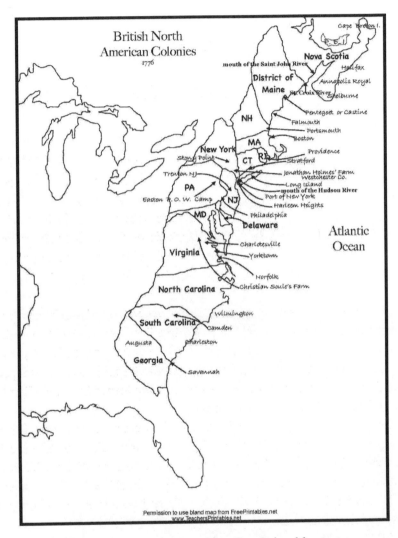

British North
American Colonies
1776

Nova Scotia

mouth of the Saint John River

Halifax

District of
Maine

Annapolis Royal

St. Croix River

Shelburne

Pentegoet or Castine

Falmouth

NH

Portsmouth

Boston

MA

New York

Providence

Stony Point

CT RI

Stratford

Jonathan Holmes' Farm
Westchester Co.

Trenton NJ

Long Island

PA

mouth of the Hudson River

Easton P. O. W. Camp

NJ

Port of New York

Harleem Heights

Philadelphia

MD

Delaware

Atlantic
Ocean

Charlottesville

Virginia

Yorktown

Norfolk

North Carolina

Christian Soule's Farm

Wilmington

South Carolina

Camden

Augusta

Charleston

Georgia

Savannah

Cape Breton I.

Permission to use map from FreePrintables.net

Chapter 1

April 1758: British Merchant

Virginia had made her deliveries of baked goods to the King's Inn and finished her visit with her friends, sisters Parthenia and Helena Salem, who worked in the Inn's kitchen. With her basket filled with empty pie plates, she skipped across the grass to the long drive to head back to her Aunt Sophie and Uncle Joost. She thought about how much she loved her life and how someday, like her sister, she too would meet a man and marry. But she was in no hurry for marriage, of that she was certain.

Along the road, an array of wildflowers seemed to speak to her and she slowed her pace. The beauty of Mother Nature filled her heart with warmth. There was no doubt about it; the world was one great and wonderful place. Virginia decided to pick a big bouquet for Aunt Sophie. As she stepped toward the flowers, she saw a vague shadow. She turned her head slightly and noticed, not too far behind, a man.

Virginia was at first surprised, and then grew unsettled, to see a stranger walking in her direction. Most people were either on horseback or carriage. She took another glance. He was just a short distance behind. Although he was a nice-looking man, she decided not to pick flowers, recalling what Uncle Joost had told her. He had always cautioned her not to speak with strangers.

"With the liberty we give you," he said, "comes responsibility."

She walked a little faster and heard the stranger say something. She acted as though she had not heard him. With a gentle British accent, the handsome stranger called to her. Thinking only of what Uncle Joost told her, she continued on her way, walking almost as fast as her heartbeat. The stranger picked up his pace and finally caught up with her. He tipped his hat to her and gave her a charming hello.

Virginia blushed, her eyes down. He introduced himself as Mr. Colter. Virginia returned the greeting without making eye contact. He kept pace and they went a short distance past a grove of white birch. Near the birch, she spied a large patch of her favorite flowers, lily of the valley, but she thought it best to continue walking. She remained quiet, although the man was very complimentary.

"Let me be of some help to you," the stranger said. "Why not let me carry that heavy basket and you can go pick some of the flowers."

The young man's offer relaxed her somewhat, and she dropped her eyes and offered a modest smile. "Oh, no, thank you, I can manage."

Her eyes were on her basket when she felt him grab her arm. Startled, she saw his face had suddenly turned dark and she struggled to shake herself free. His grip tightened as he pulled her off the road toward a thick wooded area. Virginia panicked; she kicked and screamed. She almost shook herself free while the basket and pie plates flew into the air. He punched her in the jaw, then in the eye. With her free arm, she hit him in the head and dug at his face with her fingernails. He then took control of both her arms, dragged her across a bed of lily of the valley, and hit her again in the face.

Virginia's screams became weak and her body even weaker. She was overpowered but she was determined to save herself. She again screamed for help. He stopped dragging her, pulled her up and told her to be quiet or she would end up dead. He wrapped one arm tightly around her waist and with his other hand firmly covering her mouth; he shoved Virginia to the ground. He was on top of her. Filled with terror, she tried to get up, tried to push him off. He laughed in her face. He told her she had asked for it. He stood up and she saw evil, although he was smiling as if it were a sport, some kind of sick game. He spat in her face. Then he kicked her in the head.

From that moment, she faded in and out. He ripped off her jacket and pulled up her skirt and woolen petticoat. She remembered begging him to let her go as she tried to wiggle free. The full weight of his body was crushing her. When she screamed weakly, his fist slammed into her mouth. She tasted her own blood. Her vision became blurry and she found it difficult to breathe, unable to fight back.

She felt his groping hand under her petticoat, touching inside her thigh, She became hysterical, and as he covered her mouth, she sunk her teeth deep into the flesh of his hand. He punched the side of her head, leaving her unable to hear. But she could smell him and his whisky breath. She continued to bite down on his hand, and he placed his other hand tightly over her nose. As she struggled to breathe, she became lightheaded.

Aware that he would not hesitate to beat her to death, Virginia resigned herself. He immediately thrust into her, penetrating her with such force she thought her body was being ripped apart. She felt a combination of numbness and pain from her head to her feet. The crushing weight of his body, the repetitive thrusting and the smell of his breath were the last she remembered.

৩

Earlier that day, Virginia's world was in perfect harmony. She woke to the festive singing of several birds perched on the branches of a large willow tree. She closed her eyes and listened. She smiled as she lay in bed and thought about the wonderful years she had shared with her aunt and uncle. She realized how fortunate she was.

On her hands, she counted the years since she had left her family home in Scarsdale. It was hard to imagine it had been nearly ten years. She laughed to think she would be twenty years old on her next birthday. Her teen years had passed so quickly. She put her feet on the cool floor, stretched her arms as she glanced out the window. She got dressed in anticipation of a busy day.

The comforting smell of bread fresh out of the ovens greeted her as she went down the back staircase to the bakery. She made herself a pot of tea and thought she had never been happier. Aunt Sophie brought her sliced cheese and bread. After her light breakfast, she packed the order for the King's Inn, including pies, breads and biscuits.

Making deliveries for the bakery was her favorite part of her working day. Sometimes she made deliveries as far as a mile away, but the King's Inn was about half that distance. She enjoyed her walk, while carrying sweet-smelling baked goods. Because it was April, wildflowers in patches of yellow, white and blue, lined the dirt road like the silver border of a dark cloud. She wanted to pick some flowers for Aunt Sophie but that would have to wait until after her delivery. She had a deadline to meet.

Wildflowers always caught her fancy, and her mother taught her how to press flowers between pages of her Greek myths. Some of her favorite

3

flowers were pressed neatly in the family Bible on the page where her parent's marriage was recorded. The thought of her parents made her smile and she looked to the sky and said, "You are both so loved."

She continued walking, taking in as much of nature's beauty as she could. She smiled to think of the abundant freedoms she enjoyed. She was the daughter of a Scarsdale cloth merchant, Edmund Poore, and Virginia and her older sister Magdalene were raised in a comfortable home on a small farm, where they raised chickens and a small number of cows and goats. Their peaceful home life came to an abrupt end when Virginia was eleven. Her father died of fever, and two weeks later, her mother died.

With the loss of both parents their lives changed dramatically. Magdalene married Jonathan Holmes and settled in Fishkill. Virginia went to live with her aunt and uncle in New Rochelle. Even though she was only eleven, Virginia enjoyed meeting people and going places. New Rochelle offered much more excitement with theaters, tearooms, daily print news, and shops galore in a town not far from the busy ports of New York.

The other big draw to live with her aunt and uncle was their bakery business. Virginia was eager to learn about it and Joost and Sophie were eager to teach her. She imagined herself with a white baker's apron filling pie shells, kneading rolls and breathing in the aroma of bread baking in the stone ovens. To be out socializing, meeting new people and hearing about their adventures was her dream.

It was not common for a young woman to be out alone, but Virginia had a job to do. The Dutch culture was more relaxed than the British way of doing things. Women were given more freedom and people tended to be more accepting of change and less fearful. For that Virginia was thankful. British tradition, she thought, was too restrictive toward women. A balance between the genders was an accepted way of life for the Dutch. In Virginia's mind, she was free to make her deliveries and make friends.

As she got closer to the King's Inn, she thought about sharing a glass of lemonade with her friends, Helena and Parthenia Salem. When Virginia arrived, Helena was busy cleaning and chopping vegetables for the guests' evening meal. Parthenia, the older sister, oversaw the work in the kitchen and kept an eye on the food preparation. The sisters were unusually attractive mulattos. They were articulate and gifted with a sense of humor. They never failed to make Virginia laugh. Once they got her laughing so hard that she cried and nearly wet her bloomers.

It was mid-afternoon when Virginia walked up the drive leading to the

King's Inn. She knocked on the back door of the large kitchen and entered to the joyful laughter and hellos of the Salem sisters. Together they placed the baked goods onto the worktable.

The King's Inn was a country place, a local tavern that offered tidy rooms and meals to travelers of all kinds. The inn did a brisk business all year, and it was a frequent stop for Virginia's deliveries. The inn was not far from the harbors of New York, and the clients who stayed at the Inn often checked in one day and checked out the next. The fast turnaround was like the frequency of ships coming and going out of the New York.

The Salem sisters once told Virginia that even though their father was white, they were former slaves from Richmond, Virginia. They received their freedom when their owner, who was also their father, gave up on colonial life and returned to Great Britain. Virginia was surprised when the sisters said he required that they both learn to read and write before granting their freedom. She was certain that it was not the usual requirement, but he knew they would have a better chance at a good life if they could read and write.

Parthenia and Helena often sat on the back porch, in the warm sun, snapping off ends of green beans or washing turnips, potatoes or other root vegetables. The sisters did not know their real birth dates. More often than not there were no birth records for slaves. They felt fortunate to know their father. They never really knew their mother, who died shortly after Helena was born. Before they were given their freedom, they were told an approximate year each one was born. With that information, they selected their own birth date after reading about astrology.

During most visits to the King's Inn, Virginia and Parthenia would talk about the events in the colonies. The French and Indian War overshadowed other news. It was a war the British were confident they would win and the colonists were invaluable in helping the British. Most of the sisters' information about the war was several months old and came from the men who visited the Inn. Those overheard conversations, laced with rumor and exaggeration, were about how the British and Colonial forces were preparing for numerous assaults against French forts and cities of Eastern Canada.

Other talk at the Inn was about the British plans once they won the war. With the defeat of the French and their comrades, the Indians, some guests with British accents would boast about North American territorial gains. Parthenia was often among the first to hear about news, rumors and events of the war. Whatever the news, the latest French surrenders or a major British defeat, it came to the King's Inn by way of well-traveled guests.

While Helena and Parthenia did their daily chores at the inn, cleaning rooms, sweeping hallways or polishing the ornate banister, guests and their conversations would surround them. Often, Parthenia would hum a song so as not to give the impression that she was listening. The "what ifs" of the French and Indian War was a hot topic of debate. "What if France was finally run out of North America? Would King George make the thirteen colonies pay the war debt?" On that topic guests were widely divided. Jokingly, Helena predicted the war debt debate would likely lead to another war.

The fresh pies were now sitting on a ten-foot-long worktable made from thick planks of oak, worn smooth from all the years and the work done on it. The table was the hub of cooking activities. Food items piled on the table awaited washing, cutting, rolling, wrapping, kneading or carving while other foods were boiled, roasted, steamed, baked and grilled. Finally, when the food was ready for serving, they placed it in covered stoneware and pewter. Then, they brought it to the even larger dining table where hungry guests gathered.

With a smile Helena offered Virginia a glass of lemonade. Virginia quickly drank the entire glass and laughingly held out her glass for more. Helena and Parthenia giggled at Virginia's unladylike manner. Even though it was she they were laughing at, Virginia's reaction to their giggles was her own laughter. Then, with a light heart and a hop-skip, she twirled around, grabbing the basket with the empty pie plates, and shouted a gleeful goodbye.

The sun was beginning to shine on the morning dew when Helena and Parthenia walked to the King's Inn for another day of work. They were both tense; the previous evening they had received word that their dear friend had not returned home from her delivery. They hoped she had arrived home later than usual. As they walked along the dirt road, Parthenia noticed what appeared to be a white cloth in the thick of a woods. She pointed it out to her sister and they both stood still, as if frozen, fearing what they were about to find. Holding each other's hand, they stepped toward the white cloth. As they got closer, horror overcame them. It appeared to be a woman's body.

The two sisters ran through the brush toward the body. They could not identify who it was because the woman's face was badly swollen and disfigured. Parthenia fell to her knees to see if the woman was alive. A chill rushed through Parthenia as Helena gestured toward a basket and broken pie plates nearby. The Salem sisters knew it had to be their beloved friend, Virginia, who lay before them like a rag doll.

Parthenia placed her hand on Virginia's chest hoping to feel a heartbeat. She turned to her sister and shouted a directive, "Helena, run and get help! She is barely alive."

Helena immediately ran off in the direction of the King's Inn. As Parthenia knelt over Virginia, covered with dried blood on her face, neck and legs, she was nearly hysterical and tried to speak calmly to herself. Not since her life as a slave had Parthenia seen violence of this magnitude committed against a woman.

Parthenia gently picked up Virginia's head, placed it on her lap, and put her fingers into Virginia's mouth to be sure her airways were clear. Her hair was crusted with blood. Tears began to fall from Parthenia's eyes. Horrified and overwhelmed with fear, she began to hum a melody she had learned as a child. She hummed the tune close to Virginia's ear, hoping she could hear the soothing song. Parthenia took off her shawl and cradled it around her friend.

She then whispered, "Virginia, please wake up, please wake up, Miss Virginia."

A fast-moving flatbed wagon carrying the innkeeper, his wife and Helena came to a halt on the road. They quickly lifted Virginia onto the wagon bed and took her directly to the doctor in the village, with Parthenia, unable to stop weeping, clutching Virginia's hand. The doctor checked her breathing and her heart. With a hopeful expression he turned to the Salem sisters.

"It is fortunate that you two young women found her. She is alive, although badly beaten. She would not have lived much longer on the damp ground in the woods. However, she is not out of danger yet. Some people don't wake from a coma."

The innkeeper's wife told Parthenia and Helena that the inn had a room available for Virginia if the doctor didn't keep her. "A British businessman, Mr. Colter, had a room reserved for two weeks, but with much abruptness, the gentleman had to leave town."

The doctor suggested someone go to Joost and Sophie's bakery to inform them of Virginia's whereabouts and that she was in critical condition. The innkeeper volunteered to let them know.

⟡

After several days, Virginia was still in a coma and not showing much improvement. She remained in the doctor's home for another two weeks. Eventually, the doctor expressed doubt that Virginia would survive. He suggested it was time for her to go to the inn. The Salem sisters had asked the innkeeper if they could care for Virginia there. The doctor said he would stop at the inn each day to check on her. He was worried about Virginia's weight loss, fearing she might starve to death, but he kept that to himself.

Behind the inn was a small building with several rooms that were no longer being used. Helena had spent two weeks preparing one of the rooms for Virginia. The Salem sisters knew she loved the sunlight so they chose a room with a southern exposure. With everyone's help, the once bare room now had a bed adorned with three fluffy goose-down pillows and a comforter that resembled whipped butter. They placed fresh flowers on the wide windowsills.

Helena and Parthenia took turns nursing Virginia without neglecting their other responsibilities at the Inn. Parthenia boiled water to bathe her. She was sure a warm cloth would feel good on her battered body. Helena brought a small jar of a healing balm made of beeswax and herbs to sooth Virginia's bruised and broken skin. Within a week, she was more recognizable, even though the swelling in her face was slow to leave. The ongoing coma had become worrisome, as it did not appear Virginia had any response to voice or touch. Regardless, the Salem sisters remained hopeful.

Joost and Sophie stopped in regularly to check on their niece. Joost remained distraught, blaming himself for Virginia's situation. Joost told his wife that he should have known better than let Virginia go on deliveries. He had been told the town had been changing since the start of the French and Indian War. He read about how that war, even though far to the North, had brought an increase in travelers to the town.

In late April, three weeks had passed since the assault on Virginia. The morning air smelled like lilacs and Helena opened the window. She sat next to Virginia's bed, held her hand and began to hum, then quietly sing. The sound of her own voice comforted her and she was hoping it would comfort

Virginia as well. As she gently held her hand, she felt Virginia's fingers move, ever so slightly. Helena saw a twitch in her eyelid, and then Virginia attempted to open her eyes. Her lips parted ever so slightly and she let out a soft moan. Helena, full of disbelief, hoped it was not a dream. Virginia was returning from the mythical place where she had found comfort.

Helena smiled at Virginia and whispered, "Welcome home, my dear Virginia."

Six weeks passed, and Virginia was finally able to return home with her Aunt Sophie and Uncle Joost. Virginia's daily routine included bed rest, healing balms and herbal teas, prepared by Parthenia and Helena. Virginia was beginning to eat small meals and slowly started to gain strength. The doctor felt a full recovery was promising, even though her mind was forgetful. It was not as keen and full of zest as it was before the assault. Virginia noticed that the usual welcoming smell of early morning baking was making her feel ill. Bread baking in the oven was one of her favorite aromas and now it was causing her to vomit. This left Virginia perplexed.

The Salem sisters visited Virginia almost daily. They brought fresh cut wildflowers, herbal teas and more beeswax healing balm. To both of them it appeared Virginia was improving but in Parthenia's mind, something was not in balance.

After one visit, Parthenia told Helena, "Virginia's vomiting just does not fit into her recovery. Neither does her moodiness, as she swings from a somber mood to a radiating glow of happiness."

"I agree," Helena replied, "but we must remember she suffered a tremendous assault."

With her sister's comment, an alarm bell went off in Parthenia's head and she felt the blood drain from her body, she knew exactly what was going on with Virginia and exactly why she was not in balance.

෴

It had been nearly nine months since Virginia's body was found on the forest floor. A cold December wind blew through New Rochelle as Virginia's labor pains increased with intensity. The Salem sisters continued to care for her during her entire pregnancy and were there now to act as her midwife. Outside, wind and hail pounded everything in its way while Parthenia lifted a healthy baby boy into Virginia's arms.

As Virginia took her baby from Parthenia, she began to cry. Virginia's face filled with confusion; almost as if she did not know from where this baby had come. Then when she heard her baby's cry and looked at his face, her doubts turned into sheer happiness.

With her baby in her arms, her eyes filled with love for her son.

"I wish to give my son the name, Salem," she told the sisters. "It would be an honor if this is okay with you." Both Parthenia and Helena hugged each other and smiled down on Salem and his mother. The Salem sisters, by saving her life, had saved the life of her baby too.

Salem's birth continued to be a mixed blessing. She loved her baby but at the same time, the baby came to her by such a horrid event. She did not know how to sort it out. Even with the unconditional support of her aunt and uncle, she still suffered enormous shame.

She quietly ached from the comments of busybodies. Some people in the village said she was promiscuous and others said she was a prostitute. Daily she was reminded of her shame, an unwed mother. At times, she felt full like a hermit in her uncle's house. She often wondered if the cruel looks of others had become more painful than the rape and beating. Her self-pride was lost. Everyone in the town knew what Virginia had endured that April day, but a few twisted the story to fit their pernicious theories. In her mind, the rape was not her fault. However, she lived with unbearable humiliation and dishonor. She grew increasingly depressed and often wished she had not survived.

Once Salem was born, she returned to help in the bakery, greeting customers and taking orders. Daily, Virginia seemed haunted by looks and stares of disapproval by women who whispered, pointed and shook their heads as if she were on trial and they were the jury. People were judging her without knowing the truth, she thought.

Interrupting her sleep nightly was not the cries of her infant son but her own tremendous distress. Questions dwelled heavily on her mind. Would she and Salem become outcasts? How would Salem, an innocent child, react to the demeaning looks once he was old enough to understand? Would her son be forced to live a life scarred by his mother's rape? Would mother and child need to go separate ways? Virginia did not share her anguish with anyone. She harbored it inside and she began to cry herself to sleep at night. She grew more morose and the shame hung on her like an insidious dark creature.

She felt cursed and then there was sweet Salem. Did she know what the people were saying about him, calling him a bastard child?

Often, during the night, Virginia would wake in a sweat, thinking the weight of her blankets was her attacker. In her sleep, she would kick and toss as if someone lay so heavily on her that she could not breathe. She began to fear falling asleep. Her nightmares of being pinned under this monster were too horrific and real. She smelled the whiskey on his breath and she would awake retching.

Once awake, she recalled Parthenia's advice for calming herself—take deep breaths, and slowly let each breath go. She recalled Parthenia telling her to imagine each exhale was cleansing her body of all the bad memories. With each exhale went the bad and with each inhale came the good.

Finally calm, she would pick up her baby, hold him close, snug in her arms. Quietly she would sing him a lullaby, a child's song in Dutch, just as her mother sang it to her when she was an infant. Gazing at her son, she would wonder how something so beautiful, so perfect and loved, could be the result of such a grotesque act of violence.

Nonetheless, day after day, as a nineteen-year-old unmarried mother, she grew increasingly isolated. Her sister, Magdalene, was nearly a full day's ride away. Her parents were both dead, and her aunt and uncle were trying hard to fill their shoes. She felt they might be being more charitable than loving. She feared she was a burden. She began to question her good fortune.

Her struggles with overwhelming despair and feelings of helplessness grew with each setting sun. She went to Aunt Sophie's kitchen garden to inhale some fresh air. She fixed her eyes on the dirt mounds of squash, melons and cucumbers, and shuddered with dread. She thought these mounds seemed like infant burial sites. Everything in Virginia's daily life was beginning to appear unnaturally morbid.

Her aunt and uncle were doing all they could to offer Virginia and her infant son a secure and loving home but with every passing month, Virginia became more withdrawn. She hardly spoke and did not even care to go outside. She seemed to be drifting into a realm of hopelessness, haunted by her own ghoulish thoughts. She told herself she was unfit to be a mother, unfit to raise her son.

The more Virginia withdrew from her baby, aunt, uncle and the Salem sisters, the better she felt. She imagined running away, going where she was totally unknown and starting a new life. Somewhere that she would be treated as a respectable young woman, somewhere that she could find peace of mind. She often thought about Magdalene, but the last thing she wanted to do was burden her with her tortured mind.

Aunt Sophie would sometimes overhear Virginia weeping. Finally, she shared her concern with Parthenia and Helena. All three women understood that sometimes after giving birth women experience extreme sadness. In addition, of course, Virginia had also lost her parents and was dealing with the memory of a brutal rape. They decided to gather around her, listen to her and provide her with herb teas that might help her.

Helena knew just what plant might cure Virginia's woes—Alchemilla mollis, also known as Lady's Mantle. She told Aunt Sophie about the medicinal powers of the plant and its use since the Middle Ages for relief from a variety of feminine ills. The Salem sisters were confident that this plant would remove the dark cloud from Virginia. At their modest home, Parthenia and Helena had an apothecary of lotions, potions and drying herbs to soothe the soul and ease almost any pain. Time, however, was not on the sisters' side.

Without talking with her aunt or uncle, Virginia connected with a local Anglican minister and arranged to have her infant son adopted by a middle-aged couple. The couple, the Gates, had no children of their own. She was confident she was making the right choice and she was sure it would be her son's only opportunity to have both a father and a mother. She loved her baby and wanted the best for him. She wanted to give Salem a fresh start. Virginia wanted her son to be in a family and be free of labels, rumors, and all of the haunting, shameful history of his conception.

Virginia sat at a writing table painstakingly putting her love into words that forever would be on paper. In one letter, she explained to her son why she was giving him up. Virginia dipped the pen into the inkwell and began to weep. Her teardrops fell on the linen paper, causing a smudge here and there in the dark ink. She completed four different letters to Salem—letters for him to read when he was old enough to understand. She folded the fourth letter into quarters and placed it into a small blue satin bag that was a gift from her parents. On the front of the satin bag was embroidered her initials: V. P.

She knew it was time to leave her aunt and uncle. Virginia lifted Salem from his cradle. In just five months, he had gotten so much heavier. As she took him in her arms, his eyes opened wide and he smiled. She wrapped him in a soft blanket trimmed in silk, and with her free arm; she placed some items in a bag and hung it over her shoulder. She had a warm feeling as she saw the sun beaming in the window. While holding Salem tightly against her breast, she placed the satin bag under the blanket near her baby's heart and left her room, quietly closing the door.

Her aunt, busy in the garden, did not see her leave. Virginia exited the yard, closed the latch to the gate behind her, and walked down the street in the direction of the Gates farm. They were on the outskirts of the town, a thirty-minute walk. As she approached their farm, she was reminded of the new and better life that Salem could have. She mustered all the inner strength she could, kissed Salem on his nose and began to sing the old Dutch lullaby her mother had sung to her.

Standing on the street, she felt frozen. In front of her was her son's new home. Quietly under her breath, Virginia whispered, "We are at your new home, Salem, where you will have a father and a mother who will love and protect you. They will love you almost as much as I do."

Her voice quivered as she walked toward the Gates' front door. Before she could knock, the door swung open, startling Virginia. Standing in front of her was a kindly looking middle-aged man and woman. The woman wiped tears from her eyes and her husband stood by his wife's side with his arm around her shoulders. Virginia, holding her son close, gently kissed him goodbye. As she pressed her lips to his blond hair, he smelled of all things good and innocent. She handed Salem to his new mother who smiled down on him, warming Virginia's sad heart.

After a pause of silence, the couple invited her in. Virginia declined, saying she did not have time to visit. She took the small blue satin bag from under the baby's blanket and holding it in her trembling hand, she gave it to Mr. Gates.

"I have two wishes," she said. "Will you be so kind as to please share these letters with Salem when he is old enough to understand?"

The couple looked at each other and Mr. Gates replied, "Of course."

Virginia continued, "Second, will you please let him keep the surname Poore?"

The Gates nodded their heads with affirmation. Mr. Gates said that he would be sure to follow her wishes.

No one knew Virginia had decided to give her baby away, not the Salem sisters, not her aunt or uncle, and not even her own sister, Magdalene. No one knew the severity of her sadness. Virginia, unable to keep her tears back, said goodbye to the Gates and turned and walked away from her son's new home. She wanted one last glimpse of her beloved baby; she wanted to turn around for one last look but she forced herself to resist the temptation. She willed herself to turn the page, closing that chapter in her life forever.

Once she got to the main dirt road, Virginia walked in the opposite direction of her aunt and uncle's home. Virginia was not in any hurry to go anywhere. She had a mixed sense of who she was, of grimness, and thoughts of despair hung in her mind. If only I could fly, she thought, I would go far away to another place where I could find peace.

She struggled to ignore her thoughts. She began to dwell on question after question. Would Salem grow up thinking that she abandoned him? Would the Gates forget to save those letters for him? Is my son with the right people? Will they care for him as I would and protect him from harm? Her confusion grew as her thoughts became grimmer and she repeated those questions over and over again, as if a punishment. She felt hollow, longing to hold her baby. She wanted him at her breast, near her heart. Was she being cruel to both her baby and herself by giving him to the Gates?

She continued to walk, her head down and her mind trying to push the array of emotions away. She wanted to feel peace, to feel complete and whole. Finally she came to a realization that she had saved her son from disgrace, but could she save herself? She did not think anything in her life would turn out right and her baby was best without her. She now knew what having no hope felt like, and it was a pain she could not bear.

A small bridge was in her sight, about fifty yards down the road. Once on the bridge she could see the river flowing freely below her feet. She did not hear the multitude of songbirds joyously singing. She did not feel the warm summer breeze blowing gently through her hair. She paused. Virginia did not hear the beautiful sounds of nature surrounding her. She could only hear what the whispering of the gentle breeze told her.

She continued to stand on the wooden bridge and listen to the one sound that seemed to be calling for her, quietly reciting her name. Soon the rush of the clear water, joined with the soft breeze, spoke to Virginia in a soothing tone. She was beginning to feel the sun's warmth on her face. That warmth of sunshine combined with the rush of the river cradled her trouble of anguish and despair. In an odd way, she was ever so slightly feeling better and wanted to sit at the riverbank, closer to the flow of the water, which seemed to enchant her.

She left the bridge and walked down to the river. She came upon a clearing and there was a small path leading down to a sandy riverbank.

She nestled herself on the warm sand, like a hen on her nest. Magically her mind felt free and she began to feel happiness.

She watched the penny-bugs dart about the water's crystal clear surface. As a child, she was told that if you could catch a penny-bug, bury it in the sand, then come back next year and dig it up, you would find a penny. She smiled at the thought of something so silly. Virginia sat and enveloped herself with the sound of serene waters flowing into the current, the swirls captivating her imagination. The river was a peaceful kingdom and large tree branches arched over the river.

From where she sat, she saw a chapel of tranquility, far away from the misery and anguish that occupied her soul for so long. The relief she was feeling caused her to feel woozy and lightheaded. She walked to the water's edge, rested on her knees to splash some water on her face and then cupped water in her hands to drink. That was when she could not help but notice the river's surface, appearing like a mirror, reflecting the heaven above with fluffy clouds, deep blue sky and the blazing sun. She sat closer to the water and took another handful to drink. Even the taste of water helped to soothe her.

She closed her eyes and rested while her hands fiddled with some small stones. She felt the smoothness of each stone, picking it up and feeling its warmth, then carefully placed each one in her pockets. She felt miles away from all misfortune and miles from disgrace. The horror of rape, the giving up of her precious son, Salem, was all behind her. By now her pockets were full of her chosen stones, a treasure she would keep.

Lost in thought, she carefully got to her feet. She smiled as she listened to the welcoming calls of the rushing water, a clean and relaxing sound. She dipped her toe into the river. It was crisp and renewing as she walked into the water up to her knees.

The bottom was sandy, soft to her feet and she now felt a satisfying sense of security. With each step she took deeper into the water's current, she felt a heightened sense of well-being. The rushing water embraced her fragile body and soothed her every pain. Her feet no longer touched the river bottom. Could she really be flying in the flow of water or was she flying in a burst of wind? On the other hand, maybe she was one of the penny-bugs, darting joyously. She had beautiful wings to take her away. She had found her abode, a place filled with peace.

കൗ

Magdalene watched as her husband rode up the drive, returning from his trip to town. He entered the kitchen and handed her a letter from her Aunt Sophie and Uncle Joost. It was just about time to have tea and before opening the letter, she filled the teapot with hot water. As the tea steeped, she began to read how they could not locate Virginia.

Magdalene had a mixture of confusion and panic. "Jonathan, I don't understand. Aunt Sophie said Virginia is missing! What is she talking about?" Magdalene handed the letter to him as she sat down in the chair.

Reading the letter, Jonathan said, "Aunt Sophie writes they have heard Virginia has given her son, Salem, to some family."

Magdalene did not hear Jonathan because she was still thinking about no one knowing the whereabouts of Virginia. "I don't understand why Virginia would be missing? She has gone through enough. Are they looking for her?"

"Yes, they are," he replied. "Several volunteers from New Rochelle and people from the King's Inn are all asking if anyone has seen her." Jonathan quickly read the letter to himself, put it down and poured tea for his wife and himself. He saw his wife's anguish.

"Jonathan, why didn't she say something to us? Did you say she gave Salem away?"

Jonathan nodded and handed her the letter.

"This letter is not about Virginia; it can't be. I know she would never have given her child away and just vanished," Magdalene's voice was quivering, "Virginia loved Aunt Sophie and Uncle Joost, and the life they had provided for her. She loved her baby boy and she never would have done this."

A week went by and still nothing more about Virginia. Finally, another letter came from Aunt Sophie. The news was not good. They found Virginia's body caught in tree limbs and small branches downriver from the bridge over the Wanacook River. Magdalene was grief-stricken. In addition, no one knew the name of the family who had Virginia's son. She and Jonathan, speechless, embraced each other.

Stepping back from Jonathan's embrace, Magdalene cried: "It is my fault. I have not been there for her. I have been selfishly enjoying my good life with you and the children and have not thought about Virginia." She dropped her head, her voice becoming a whisper. "I am ashamed of myself.

How could I be so selfish? I was thinking about my children and myself. I was not there to comfort her during the difficulties she quietly endured." Magdalene wondered why her sister did not want Salem to come live with them. They would have loved to bring Salem into their family.

Jonathan listened to her and did not say a word. He understood she needed to express her deepest fears and regrets. There were many questions but no answers. Magdalene requested her sister's body come back to the Middle District for burial. She knew Virginia would find peace near the peach trees next to her parents, in the Holmes family cemetery.

On the first day of May 1759, Virginia's body was laid to rest. With the sweet smell of freshly dug soil in the air, Jonathan Holmes stood next to his wife and held in his arms their eight month-old son, John Roger, who soon would get the nickname, J.R. Magdalene, once again a visual expression of fertility, was pregnant. She maintained a stoic appearance while her heart mourned for her only sibling, who at the young age of nineteen, took her own life and left many questions.

On Virginia's coffin was a burst of colorful wildflowers. Magdalene's eyes settled on the brilliant purple, blue, yellow and delicate white flowers and asked herself: Why did this happen? Was Virginia so unhappy? Why did she not contact me and let me know of her pain? Magdalene knew she would be asking herself these questions until the day she died.

Nothing made sense; no one could give her an answer. She wondered, does death have a meaning or is death an absolute when the body simply goes back to enrich the soil, as oxen or trees would? She dropped her eyes to a pile of freshly shoveled soil and thought it was beautiful. The May sun beamed down on the family and Magdalene's eyes clouded with tears.

The touch of her husband's warm hand around her shoulder brought her back. In front of her were her four fair-haired children, two sons and two daughters, all under the age of seven. Soberly, the young family watched while the coffin was lowered into the earth and covered with soil. The cycle of life continued. The soil nourished her and she gave nourishment back. The ground on which we stand, hunt, fish, farm, fight, live and die is the dirt beneath our feet. This piece of earth, clump of clod, this piece of glebe is sacred, whether you are above the glebe or six feet under.

Magdalene's children had lost an aunt, the only one they had. Her children would never have a chance to know Virginia. They would never see Virginia's dimple in her left cheek when she smiled. Young Obadiah shared the same dimple. They would never see their aunt's stunning blue eyes that Magdalene's daughters had inherited. Her children would never come running at the sound of Virginia's voice or listen to her tell a story about mystical characters from far-away countries.

Magdalene waited while her son looked up at his grandfather, Obadiah, who held John Roger as his head rested on his grandfather's shoulder. Two granddaughters stood on each side of the old man. Magdalene smiled at the image of a small pair of bookends holding up a great big old book.

Jonathan wrapped his arm around her shoulder. She knew how fortunate she was; her life on the farm with her husband and four healthy children were all she could ask for. With her handkerchief, she lightly dabbed her eyes and then came a sudden warm rippling sensation inside her womb, her unborn child moved, a gentle reminder of all things good and a promise of life intricately infused with the mournful reality of death.

In her grief, Magdalene forgot about Virginia's infant son, until the gentle ripple of her own baby brought her back to reality. She dropped her head to her chest and stopped herself from crying so loud it might even wake Virginia. A gentle tug on her skirt brought her back to the purpose of the moment. She saw John Roger wanting her attention; he was determined to be picked up and held by his mother. Her youngest son had a gleeful, but determined expression, and she smiled and thought of her good providence.

Magdalene and Jonathan walked from the family cemetery, their young children following close behind. Grandfather Obadiah was trailing them all, carrying J.R. and taking time to smell the budding peach blossoms. Magdalene took solace in knowing her sister was here with her on the 400-acre Holmes farm. Virginia would never be apart from her again.

As the years flew by, Magdalene's two daughters, Elizabeth and Sarah, often reminded her of when she and Virginia were children. Her daughters played with corncob dolls and told stories to one another for hours on end. She often told them about the fun she and Virginia had, whether it was playing hide-and-seek in the hayloft or making up games so their chores would be more enjoyable.

One afternoon, as Magdalene stitched up a torn shirt, she thought about the power of memories and her fond thoughts about Virginia helped her gradually accept the tragic loss. Hardly a day would pass when she did not have thoughts of her sister that would make her smile.

On the other hand, she hardly ever thought about Virginia's son, Salem. Perhaps it was because she never held him in her arms. The adoption was a mystery and no one in the family knew of Virginia's intent to give her baby away.

After Virginia's burial, an entire year passed before Magdalene got word that a good family, found by the church, had adopted Virginia's son. The boy was with two loving parents who had been childless. The news helped Magdalene feel better. Magdalene thought Virginia wanted her son raised by these people as an only child. She thought it best not to involve herself even though she never understood why she was not chosen to raise her sister's son. She resigned herself to accept Virginia's wishes.

Magdalene wanted to see Salem but feared her involvement would only lead to him asking questions. He needed to have his own life, his own identity and his own destination. Magdalene hoped, by not getting involved, it would protect him from the painful truth. She was unaware of Virginia's letters to her son, stored in the blue satin bag.

Chapter 2

June 1775: Weddings and Rebellion

Time waits for no one and Jonathan and Magdalene often noticed how quickly the years had passed. They now had five sons, Obadiah, John Roger, Elijah, Jacob and Joseph, and nearly all were now young men. Their two daughters had begun to think about marriage and family. Sarah and Elizabeth both were tall with a soft feminine appearance and a glimmer of elegance. They were also smart, with a strong sense of self, which they did not hesitate to make known. Both attracted many young men who wished to court them. Sarah, the oldest, had accepted the marriage proposal of Beach Beardsley.

Magdalene and her daughters planned a festive wedding in June. For a number of reasons it was a favorite time of year for Sarah. Almost every flower of Middle District was in bloom, the sun was reaching its highest point in the sky, the days were longer and sunnier. Sarah's grandfather, Obadiah, now passed, used to tell her that everything came to life during the month of June. Not only the flowers, but the birds and the insects were full of life. Even the brook sang in June with its swift flowing waters and gentle pools.

Sarah and her handsome groom radiated a glow of hope. Magdalene and Jonathan asked the local Anglican reverend, Beach's uncle, to perform the ceremony. The entire day was nearly perfect. The sun shone brightly over the jubilant occasion. To provide plenty of room for the large Beardsley family, Sarah and Beach wanted to marry outdoors. A steady flow of Beardsleys arrived by carriage, flatbed wagon and on horseback. Young Joseph wondered how anyone could have so many relatives.

Most of Beach's family traveled from the eastern side of Dutchess

County and a few came from as far away as the colony of Connecticut. The Beardsley clan initially came from coastal port towns in Connecticut. In all, sixty Beardsley men, women and children came to wish the young couple good health, many children, and a long life together.

As her younger sister Elizabeth watched and listened to Sarah and Beach say their wedding vows, she saw an expression of contentment on Sarah's face. She saw her sister and Beach as a perfect fit and she thought about her own wedding day. Elizabeth glanced at Beach's younger brother Nathaniel—their eyes met with a spark as she blushed and quickly turned her head to avoid embarrassment.

After the marriage ceremony, praise and expressions of congratulations for the young couple filled the air, only to compete with the aroma from all the foods that found their way to the large table. The wedding quickly changed from formality to celebration—a party.

At just about that time Elizabeth's eye captured another glimpse of Nathaniel, who did not see her because he was busy talking with Beach and Sarah. Elizabeth loved the way he looked and then suddenly Nathaniel turned to look at her and their eyes locked again. Elizabeth felt uneasy and her eyes then darted to Sarah who waved Elizabeth to join them. Elizabeth walked over to her sister and Beach. Beach introduced Elizabeth to Nathaniel. Full of confidence, he took Elizabeth's hand, shook it gently, and said he was pleased to meet her, especially on such a beautiful day. Nathaniel was thrilled, he knew they shared a certain feeling.

✧

One year later, the Holmes and Beardsley families again got together for another wedding. The two families had an enduring bond between them. Their ancestors had known each other from the late 1600s. They met when they immigrated to the British colonies of New York and Connecticut. A century later, the families were strengthening their bond. This time the bride and groom were Elizabeth and Nathaniel. An addition to the guest list was Beach and Sarah's baby, Magda.

Nathaniel and Elizabeth stood proudly in front of the Reverend Beardsley of the Anglican Church. Her mother thought that they looked like a prince and his princess. She burst with pride and gave her husband's hand a squeeze.

Magdalene had prepared enough food to feed all the king's men: baked

21

oat and rye bread and rolls, sliced cold meats along with smoked meat and sausage, both cheddar and Gouda cheeses, freshly churned butter, last fall's peach and apple jams, the most favorite lemon curd plates. The Beardsley family brought smoked meats and smoked fish along with two large barrels of fermented cider.

A short time after placing the platters on the table, Magdalene noticed some were in need of refilling. She went about her work making sure there was enough food for everyone. No one had ever left her home hungry and today would be no exception. While she replenished the cheese, meats and butter plates, she overheard a conversation between two men. They were talking about King George's "unreasonable" acts against the colonies and the turmoil of boycotts and demonstrations in Boston.

The men expressed hope that the Continental Congress would open both the King's and the Parliament's eyes.

"You might not feel so hopeless about bringing change to the colonies once you read the pamphlet," one of the men said. The two men were discussing *Common Sense*, a pamphlet that had been published anonymously.

"What is written in the pamphlet is thought provoking and motivating. It is a well-thought-out argument for why men should be free of monarchies," the man said.

The second man asked, "How did you get your hands on this revolutionary material? Aren't you worried the British will find out and you will be thrown in jail?"

"Oh, that won't happen," the first man said. "My uncle, in Connecticut, gave me his copy of *The Courant*, which included the entire pamphlet in its February issue. And, as far as I know, the men who printed *The Courant* haven't been arrested."

The conversation Magdalene overheard caused her to shiver with angst. How could men talk so openly about revolution? Could they actually support a revolt against King and country? She knew these ideas could lead to the accusation of treason. She recalled that a year earlier the King had published a proclamation for all British subjects, including all of the colonists, to help put down the rebellion. The King was clear—any act to support the rebellion was an act of treason, punishable by hanging.

Then Magdalene was horrified. She recognized one of the voices. It was Beach's voice, and he was full of enthusiasm for freedom from the King. Then she thought perhaps she had misunderstood. He would have to be crazy to challenge the British Monarch, the ruler of the world's largest empire.

Beach continued speaking about General Washington, Commander of the Continental Army, who he called a man of tremendous vision, courage and guts." Then Beach added about the man who authored *Common Sense*, "I hear he plans to donate some of the funds made from this publication to the Continental Army!"

Magdalene heard the excitement in Beach's voice as he spoke about the call for independence and having the right for one's own destiny. She had not mistaken what Beach had said. Rattled, she dropped one of her large platters. It hit a stone and smashed into small pieces. Beach heard the crash and immediately went to Magdalene's rescue, catching her as she began to fall on the shattered dish. Beach took Magdalene to a bench shaded by a horse chestnut tree, then returned to the broken platter and picked up the shards of glass.

Beach returned to Magdalene, placing a cool cloth on the back of her neck. It felt so refreshing and she took his hand, smiled and thanked him. She sat in the shade and closed her eyes for a moment, listening to a small group of men who brought their fiddles and a flute. Once they began to play, the music spread over Magdalene like a blanket of comfort. She asked herself if she really heard Beach say he intended to enlist with Washington's army.

Magdalene felt a warm touch on her hands. It was Sarah, full of smiles, holding three-month-old Magda. Sarah sat next to her mother.

"Mother, I am glad you do not have any more daughters to marry off. The weddings have taken a toll on you. Please sit here and I will see to things."

From where Magdalene sat, she could see all of the people who came to celebrate Elizabeth and Nathaniel's marriage. The yard was full of wedding guests, happy chatter, music, smiles, pats on the back and wishes of good will. She could not imagine why some colonists wanted to revolt. Life in the colonies was good. They lived peacefully, surrounded by abundant resources. Their farms produced more than enough food for their large families. The extra would be sold or traded for cloth, leather, wood, spices, and tea.

Hardworking colonial families shared a fruitful life, just as they did when Magdalene's ancestors came to New Netherlands as traders and merchants in the booming Dutch colony. She recalled stories her grandmother told—stories about the freedoms of Dutch women. Those freedoms were not available to the women of England or France.

She recalled her grandmother's many stories of how, at one time in New Amsterdam, Dutch women could own property and keep their family name after marriage. They also had equal rights to operate a business and possess money. They had the same rights as men. Women could freely go into a tavern, discuss topics, and enjoy a brew with others. Magdalene understood why she had a strong confidence in herself. Sadly, she thought those freedoms were taken away when the British took New Netherlands and New Amsterdam for themselves. She smiled and thought that if anyone might have a bone to pick with the King of England, it would be the women.

Her thoughts kept returning to Beach, her daughter's husband and the father of her darling grandchild. Was her daughter destined to be a widow? She watched Beach's mother walk across the lawn toward her. She was an elegant woman. She sat next to Magdalene and they talked about the joyous day. They talked about the here and now, not about the past and surely not about the future.

Obadiah watched his mother, and once Mrs. Beardsley left her side, he went to her. He suggested they walk around and mingle with the guests. That was when he noticed his mother trembling. Without drawing attention to her, he slowly walked her toward the house.

"Mother, are you okay?" he quietly asked. Obadiah noticed her face was drained of all color. He wrapped his arm around her shoulder then nestled her in a comfortable chair near an open window so she could listen to the music and merriment.

Jonathan Holmes caught a glimpse of his wife as she went into the house and he followed. He was not surprised to see Magdalene totally worn out.

"My dear wife, it is no wonder with all the excitement and preparations for our daughter's wedding, you must be exhausted." He sat with his wife; her hands, soon securely wrapped in his. Her head rested on his shoulder. He thought about the day they were married. He touched her wedding band and twirled it around her finger.

Jonathan smiled at her. "Remember our wedding day?" Magdalene smiled. "You were the most beautiful bride in Middle District. Well, no, that's not true … you were the most beautiful bride in the Colony of New York! Now, you are the most loving mother of your two happily married daughters." Jonathan gave her a quick kiss on her cheek and said with a sparkle in his eye, "My lady, you should be proud, of your daughters and yourself."

Outside, the merriment continued. Jonathan thought that if the Beardsley family was not already one of the largest families in the colony, the Holmes and Beardsley marriages would make sure they were the largest. Magdalene listened to cheers and laughter outside. She thought about all the changes that had taken place in the year since Sarah and Beach married. It was painfully clear Elizabeth's wedding day was unlike Sarah's. Elizabeth's wedding day was entwined with a youthful unrest, a questioning of authority. Only heaven knew what 1777 would bring. On a positive note, she could hope for more grandchildren.

Magdalene loved and respected Beach and Nathaniel and hoped Beach would change his mind and not get involved with the dangerous rebel cause. With much determination, she directed her thoughts toward her husband. She noticed how Jonathan was a touch wistful to see his two girls, now both married women, going to their new homes with their husbands. Both of his daughters would now be living on the eastern side of Middle District where much of the Beardsley family lived.

"Did you know Beach hopes to eventually relocate to Connecticut where his grandparents and great grandparents were born?" Jonathan asked.

"He has a lot of family in Connecticut coastal port towns and cities," Magdalene said. The Beardsley ancestors had settled in and named the town of Stratford.

"Yeah," replied Jonathan, "He recently told me the civil unrest, the growing conflict between some British colonists and the Crown gave him concern, and he may need to delay the move to Connecticut."

"What sort of conflict?"

"Connecticut coastal towns have become targets for the British naval fleet and these port towns and cities are being fired upon and one by one set aflame." Jonathan could see the bewilderment in Magdalene's eyes. "Most paramount are Beach's concerns for his wife, Sarah and their baby, Magda. He would never expose them to danger."

Magdalene tried not to say a word, but she could not hold it inside any longer. "Jonathan, I cannot agree with you. Beach would indeed expose his family to danger. After all, he wants to join Washington's army!"

Initially speechless, Jonathan tried to defuse any hysteria in his wife. "Beach is a smart, ambitious young man, we must have confidence."

25

Magdalene smiled at Jonathan. They sat cherishing each other's company away from the saber rattling of the youth. She tried to convince herself she had misheard or misunderstood what Beach had said. In Magdalene's mind, Beach's support for the rebels could not be possible. In her heart and for the sake of her two daughters and their husbands, Magdalene hoped the love and devotion each couple shared would be more powerful than the conflict at hand. On the other hand, she feared the turmoil might splinter these young families.

Soon everyone gathered to say farewell to the bride and groom. Mrs. Beardsley and several of her sisters and daughters cleared the empty platters from the table. The day of such emotional ups and downs, thought Magdalene, was coming to a close. Interrupting her thoughts, she saw Obadiah bringing a small oak barrel from the root cellar.

"This is the last barrel of grandfather Obadiah's peach brandy," he announced, and a group of men cheered. Mingling among the guests, Jonathan noticed that the conversations were about the latest oppressive acts of the King and that the spreading discontent dominated the conversations.

Several Beardsley men began to express their enthusiastic support for independence. Jonathan heard the conviction in their voices and it grew stronger with each sip of brandy. The men claimed to have read many of the pro-revolutionary papers and pamphlets coming out of Boston, Philadelphia and other cities.

Jonathan was surprised when his son-in-law, Beach, began to talk with vigor about ridding them all of the King. Jonathan dismissed Beach's enthusiasm for independence to the peach brandy. Nonetheless, Jonathan thought hard about the writings. He held a belief it was every man's right to be free and especially free from the tyrant King George, but he believed bloodshed was not the way to go about it.

The Holmes family read some of the printed propaganda being disseminated across the colonies and they were familiar with various newspaper headlines encouraging rebellion. Educated men, masters of the written word, aroused a growing disdain for the Crown. Many colonists saw the King's use of taxation as an obstacle to their own financial security. The King was a barrier to reaching their goals and pursuing their own happiness. Jonathan admired the Beardsleys blazing desire for independence. They were sharp thinkers with well-groomed reasoning skills. Beach and Nate did not come from a wealthy family. They did not have social position. They were proud farmers and planters. Their souls were in the soil,

One month after the marriage of Elizabeth and Nathaniel, an organized group of men who called themselves the Continental Congress traveled to Philadelphia to represent their colonies. In the process, they made a written declaration to King George. They announced to the world their independence from the Crown. This action was earth shattering to many who lived in Middle District, where most people did not see revolution as a way to solve their problems with the Parliament or the King. To Jonathan what was first seen as reckless rumors and dangerous declarations was now a bone-chilling reality with unforeseen consequences.

Jonathan would spend evenings by the hearth fire with his five sons. They would talk about what they had read that day in the print news.

"I think, along with the Congress' declaration for independence," Obadiah said, "there came a thunderbolt, a line dissecting revolutionaries from non-revolutionaries." He paused. "Now there is talk about forcing everyone to sign an agreement stating they support the ideas behind the impending revolt, a coerced pledge of support!"

"The way I see it," Jonathan said, "most colonists do not want war for a variety of reasons. First, some people do not give a damn about the matter. Second, there are those who wish to remain neutral."

"I can't blame anyone for wanting to be neutral," J.R. said.

His father continued, "Third, would be the large number of people in the colony of Pennsylvania whose religion is against war of any kind."

"The idea Beach and Nate would consider enlistment with Washington is nuts!" J.R. said.

"Those two don't have to enlist to risk hanging from a noose," Obadiah said. "Their fervent belief in revolution and their talk of enlistments would mark them as traitors!"

"I don't know what they could be thinking," sighed J.R.

ᥱᤁᤁ

The winter solstice, the shortest day of the year, was the day J.R. first met Abigail. Her father, Mr. Brouwer, was coming to the Holmes farm to buy a horse, and as his carriage entered the yard, J.R.'s father asked him to grab his coat and keep an eye on it.

As J.R. left the house, he was surprised to see a young woman in the Brouwer carriage.

"Please let me introduce myself and my daughter," Mr. Brouwer said.

"I am pleased to meet you, Miss Brouwer." J.R. said.

She smiled and nodded. "You may call me Abigail and your name is …?"

"My name is John Roger, J.R. is my nickname."

The sun, low in the sky, was perfectly placed behind her red hair as if a halo encircled her head. J.R. was captivated by Miss Brouwer's wholesomeness, her calm voice and confident attitude.

The two fathers strolled to the stable where they viewed the horses and discussed price. While in the stables, the two men shared their concerns about the political upheaval in Boston along with the battle at Brooklyn Heights.

Mr. Brouwer sighed: "My only son was killed during the Battle of Brooklyn Heights this past August. It was the worst news a man can get, his only son dead. I think our grieving may never end."

Jonathan was saddened. This was the first revolutionary death he had heard about from someone he knew. "I am unable to imagine the pain you and your family are suffering," he said. He did not know what to say. How does someone give sympathy for such an unimaginable loss? He did not want to say too much or too little.

Mr. Brouwer briefly highlighted how the fighting was disrupting the once peaceful and productive British colonies. The news from Boston was not good. Fighting between the British and the rebels was moving into Connecticut, closer and closer to their own British protected Middle District. "Hundreds of families wanting to be far from the conflict are moving, relocating. It is said Washington and his army are encouraging kids to steal horses, weapons and money for the Continental Army. We could no longer live in Trenton, I lost eighteen of my finest horses; stolen by rebel raiders."

Mr. Brouwer paused, wiped the corner of his eye, and continued. "In simple language, we feared for our own safety. Trenton has become a hotbed of unrest. Washington's army was encamped across the river in Pennsylvania, likely waiting to pounce on Trenton. My wife had suffered enough with the loss of our son. I had no choice but to leave our farm. Those who call themselves revolutionaries are destroying whatever they touch. It has become a lawless town succumbed to mob rule."

Jonathan, wide eyed, listened in disbelief. "How can this be? Are there no laws, no consequences, no law enforcement to stop horse thieves?"

Mr. Brouwer dropped his head to his chest, stared at the ground and in a quiet voice replied, "There were no arrests, no fines, no jail time for these hoodlums. I have this one horse and carriage. I hope I can sell the farm in Trenton. We moved in haste to Middle District because we know we will be safe here because of the British presence."

As Mr. Brouwer checked over a gelding that Jonathan and his son Joseph raised from birth, Joseph came into the stables and introduced himself. Mr. Brouwer said, "Joseph, you certainly do have a fine selection of horses." He checked the gelding's hooves, legs, patted its nose, and spoke in a gentle tone to the horse.

He smiled, turned around and said, "This is the one. What do you want for this fine gelding?" They quickly settled on a price and Joseph walked to another part of the stable to clean a stall while listening to the conversation.

Jonathan did not want to appear too nosey but asked: "So what are your plans, will you stay in Middle District?"

"We love Trenton. My family has been farming the Trenton land for nearly 150 years, since before the British defeated the Dutch, taking New Amsterdam for themselves. It was about that time my ancestors moved to Trenton. You can't imagine how difficult it is to abandon property your ancestors cultivated. Their blood and sweat are literally mixed with the soil. We all eventually became part of the rich dark dirt which nourishes us, all living things."

Mr. Brouwer abruptly stopped talking, to compose himself. "I must apologize to you, Mr. Holmes, for taking up so much of the morning."

Jonathan assured Mr Brouwer, "This fighting will come to an end and we may then return to our normal lives. I believe the rebellion will get worse before it gets better, but those anarchists can't defeat the greatest military in the world."

"Yes, I suppose I agree with you on that point. The British Crown has the military strength to suppress the rebellion in a day. The question remains, will they use it?"

Jonathan thought about Mr. Brouwer's remark. He felt confident the British would use every military strategy and weapon in their arsenal. Why wouldn't they?

Mr. Brouwer sighed. "For me, right now, much depends on the sale of our Trenton farm. Currently, I am renting a small house here in Middle

District, and will continue to do so until a buyer comes forth for the home in Trenton."

"You don't think you will be going back to Trenton?"

"I think the chances of my family ever getting back to Trenton are slim at best. We don't know where this rebellion will take us; it is beyond our realm of influence. The Trenton property is priced at half its value and I wouldn't be surprised if someone torched it simply because our son fought for the King."

ᘓ

The clouds of war hung heavily over the northern colonies. Battles between rebel fighters and the British increased with frequency. To Magdalene the war was sheer madness, nothing more, nothing less. She did not have true loyalties to the King and if it were known, she never had any fondness for the British monarchy. She attributed that feeling to her Dutch heritage but she did know her ardent position against war. It caused such grievous turmoil and it was the wrong way to solve disputes. Negotiation and compromise was her motto.

Magdalene realized none of that mattered when, in late December, Obadiah enlisted with the Loyal American Regiment of New York. Soon after Obadiah's enlistment, Jacob and Elijah came home with the news they too would be wearing the uniform of the Loyal American Regiment. In spite of every comment and claim to the contrary, Magdalene held fast to her belief that rebellion against the King was fool-hardy at best, and she had no doubt the rebellion would be short-lived.

As weeks passed, her optimism waxed and waned. Then suddenly, her greatest dread came true. In a letter from Sarah, she learned Beach and Nathaniel had enlisted with Washington's army. This news put the entire Holmes household in shock.

Magdalene entered a period of denial. She was confident the fighting would end by harvest time. She thought the rebel fighters would tire of their cause and their families would insist they come home. Their spouses would tell them to give up their crazy ideas, the reckless notion of independence and freedom. She shook her head and asked herself: Who has time for a revolution? Everyone has a farm to manage, a family to feed, seeds to plant or a business to operate.

She thought her three sons and her two sons-in-laws would be home in time to cut the hay, pick the apples and harvest the acres of potatoes, oats and barley. Magdalene was convinced, and she told her husband of her end date.

"I hope you are right, my dear," he said. "The war finished by fall would work out well for everyone."

Jonathan, on the other hand, followed the printed news and listened to what was being said by others. The talk about confrontation between Washington's forces and British troops made it seem more like war with the passing of each month. Increased tensions spread through each of the thirteen British colonies.

With every new edict from the King and his Parliament, the well-organized revolutionaries reacted with their own law—a law dismissing the King's powers. Some colonists were stunned by the bold reactions of the rebels toward the King's mandates. The lack of force shown by the British Empire left many colonists asking why.

Magdalene spent many evenings clearing the dinner table, washing dishes and thinking. As she poured hot water into the basin filled with plates and silverware, steam rising from the basin felt soothing on her face. As she washed and rinsed each plate, she tried to think of nothing, but tonight it would take more than warm steam to relax her. She could not stop thinking about the reports of men dying in fierce hand-to-hand fighting. Troubling too, were the reports of soldiers returning after the battle to put their bayonet into the hearts of their enemies who lay on the battlefield with wounds.

Magdalene traced her paternal and maternal heritage to the Dutch settlement of New Amsterdam. Even though the Dutch and British were often at war with each other, Magdalene had a sense of loyalty for the British monarch. All her sons who enlisted to save the colonies, not necessarily the Crown, adopted that same loyalty for the Monarch.

If she had one complaint about the King, it would be his oppression of women. As soon as the British took control of New Netherlands from the Dutch, they denied women many rights they had when the Dutch ruled. Once a woman married any of her property became her husband's. A woman had no right to operate a business or to sue an abusive husband.

Under Dutch law, things might have been different for Virginia. In fact, her sister would have had the right to take the man who raped her to court, free of disgrace. Dutch law would have enabled Virginia the right to sue that man. Under British law, there was no such protection for Virginia. All of the protections were for the perpetrator.

Magdalene wiped tears from her eyes, telling herself, that this was the law of the land for which her sons could give their lives. She shook her head and laughed. Bewildered, she dropped her head to her chest, then lifted her chin, taking deep breaths, one by one, until she began to feel grounded and the last dish was dried.

Chapter 3

January 1777: Unshakable Confidence

During the bitterly cold month of January 1777, General Washington and his Continental Army defeated the British at Princeton. This defeat sent shockwaves through the colonies. Loyalists and the colonists who wanted to stay neutral were distressed. To those who hoped the rebellion would go away quickly, the British defeat was devastating.

J.R. took the British defeat at Princeton with grave disappointment. Word of Washington's victory increased morale and added thousands of recruits to the Continental Army. Now with the victory at Princeton, the rebels were fired up for independence. J.R. thought one victory by this group of soldiering misfits was one too many. The consensus in Middle District was how could this band of rebels defeat the mighty British? It seemed impossible. The British forces were the most sophisticated army in the world!

About to turn nineteen, J.R. was young, impressionable, and on the verge of visiting a recruiter for the L.A.R. (Loyal American Regiment). He did not want to enlist, but in the wake of the defeat at Princeton he began to think about the need to put an end to the revolution. It was becoming a time to pick a side, to support the King or the revolution, and neutrality was not an option. He weighed the pros and cons, including his responsibility to help suppress the rebellion and to rectify the lawlessness consuming the colonies.

The rebel victory at Princeton also helped Washington's army achieve two other enormously helpful events. First, it boosted morale for the Continental Army. Second, the French grew much more likely to increase their support. The French Empire was beginning to like what it saw. Battles and bloodshed were becoming commonplace. War had begun. The blood, bodies and body parts of rebels and Loyalists were being absorbed into the coastal lands, rivers, woods and fields. The soil of every colony would soon be soaked with blood.

J.R. was aware of the direction the young British colonies were heading. The so-called gentlemen rebel rousers, some educated in Boston, where once they wore cravats, were now risking a noose. The king ordered hanging for anyone who took arms against the throne. J.R. tried to ignore newspaper reports of British troops shooting defenseless Bostonians. Such treatment was not in the realm of anyone's imagination. J.R. was sure something else was going on and there must have been more to the story. The conflict between a minority of British colonists and British authorities was making less sense. He asked fewer and fewer questions, helping reduce his own awareness of the growing strife. J.R. was becoming unquestioningly obedient to the Crown.

The massacre in Boston happened when J.R. was twelve, seven years earlier. The rebel propaganda referred to it as the "Bloody" Boston Massacre. J.R. remembered the horror he felt when he heard that British soldiers in Boston had fired their guns on unarmed protesters in the street. Since that horrible day, protests had increased and boycotts of British goods were having an impact on England's trade. The King's laws against the colonists had become more punitive.

The Parliament refused to see any error in their way of rule. They had a huge war debt from the French and Indian War and the colonies were to foot the bill. It was simple. After all, the colonists were the great benefactors of defeating the French and their Native American allies.

Outright rebellion was evident by 1774 when Parliament made a final attempt to get the colonies under control with tyrannical laws. The British government hoped that brute strength would force the colonies to put down their muskets and pitchforks and become dutiful, complying subjects of the King.

Now, at Princeton, the Continentals had experienced their first true, measurable victory. The rebellion's longevity seemed to be more promising with each British defeat, large or small. The rebels were gaining power and self-assurance. They established their own Congress and their own army. As the American colonies drifted further from the Parliament's authority, the King's demands became more oppressive.

The number of colonists opposing the Crown's control was steadily growing in number and in determination. Dozens of towns established their own arsenal and colonial militia. The King had long required every male in the colonies to own a musket and every town to have a militia. Men across the colonies with their muskets, lead balls, and gunpowder were ready and willing to join the rebel cause and fight against King George.

The Middle District was not far from the British-dominated port of New York and was secluded in a Loyalist stronghold. J.R. and his family were not directly exposed to rebel protesters. This group was highly energized by extremists like Patrick Henry of Boston. His speech, *Give Me liberty or Give Me Death* became fighting words for the rebels. Ultra-revolutionary philosophers and talented writers worked tirelessly to turn public opinion toward ideas of freedom and independence and away from the Crown.

Radical thinkers in the Boston area began to band together to carry out acts of cruelty against those who supported the King. Nothing was safe, not their homes, farms, businesses or families. Roaming gangs, calling themselves Sons of Liberty, singled out the Loyalists. Gangs bent on theft and destruction raided the homes where Loyalists lived. Along with taking valuables, these gangs hoped to take away the Loyalists' allegiance to the Crown, with a weapon of terror.

With the many acts of rebellion, the year proved there was no doubt in the mind of those revolutionaries they were spearheading change. With unshakable confidence, these rebels composed, signed and sent a declaration to the King, proclaiming the colonies were independent from England. This was a first; no other British colony ever claimed that in a written document. Meanwhile the size of the local militias grew, and Sons of Liberty gangs intensified their terrorist raids against Loyalists.

During the years the colonies were growing and testing British authority, J.R. was growing and learning the occupation of being a farmer, planter and cultivator. He was sad to see his love for farming coming to an end, but the rebellion was forcing him from the farm to be a soldier for the Crown. He would soon replace his sickle and pitchfork with a musket and powder horn. He would learn what it takes to be a soldier and try not to forget what it takes to be a planter. He had self-discipline, was a self-starter, could read and write, and was physically fit for any action. Although his loyalty to the King was complicated, that loyalty was never questioned by him. It was simply a given.

❦

Bull's Head Tavern, a thirty-minute ride on horseback, was a gathering place for the Holmes brothers. The tavern, five miles from the Post Road, was a meeting place for farmers and tradesmen, where they would share conversation and news. A mug of ale or a shot of Irish whisky brought laughter and hearty debate to the crowd. Each visit to the Bull's Head enabled everyone to become current on the events in Boston, New York and Philadelphia.

While Obadiah and J.R. were was enjoying jars of ale with their two brothers-in-law, Nathaniel and Beach, a man entered the tavern and sat beside him. The traveler appeared to be friendly enough. J.R. could not recall just how it began, but the topic of the King came up and the traveling man made several strong remarks about the Crown. Beach reacted to the traveler, and J.R. could not believe what Beach said.

J.R. understood there would be many different casualties as a result of the turmoil, but he never imagined one of those casualties would be the Holmes-Beardsley family bond. He listened to Beach Beardsley describe the havoc the British had been causing in numerous Connecticut and Rhode Island coastal towns and seaports. The Beardsleys, a highly respected family like the Holmes, were from Middle District, but had left the area to relocate to Connecticut.

Nathaniel, who was the quieter, deeper-thinking brother, added fuel to the fire by going into detail about the Intolerable Acts. Nathaniel became even more vocal about the Parliament making it illegal for towns to have town meetings.

Obadiah attempted to change the subject but had little success. Nathaniel was talking about fair representation and ending oppressive measures dictated by the Crown. It appeared Nathaniel was grooming himself to be a town leader. It was, however, a short-lived quest, because of the ban on town meetings, dictated from thousands of miles to the east.

"I hope the rebellion ends quickly with a decisive victory of independence," Beach said.

The Beardsleys sympathies were in total conflict with the Holmes perspective and J.R. shuddered at the possibility of Beach or Nathaniel joining the Continental Army. What would happen if they became engaged in the same battle? He could see the war dividing their family, two families who had shared so much for nearly a century. He sipped his ale and contemplated the future. What might the future bring? Maybe the war would end soon and none of this would ever happen.

"Beach, are you familiar with King George's *Proclamation of Rebellion?*" J.R. asked.

Beach smiled. "Yes, the King claims we are in a state of rebellion. Good of him to notice we are here and unhappy."

"All colonists who support actions of civil disorder will be seen as traitors. Punishment will be death by hanging. Doesn't that alarm you?"

Beach had a ready response. "King George has made many new laws, rules, and declarations, and has also taken away some of the freedom we once enjoyed. He has gone too far, his actions are punitive. It is my opinion the King has stepped over the line and is now infringing on our rights."

A stranger lifted his tankard toward Beach, saying, "Bravo! Bravo!"

"J.R., to answer your question, I do not believe the King has the wherewithal to carry out his threats."

Like between the Beardsley and Holmes families, the lines of demarcation were becoming clear in the colonies. Middle District was free of rebel control. Several hours south of the Holmes farm, at the port of New York, the British Army had its center of operations for the thirteen colonies. The entire waterfront area of New York was home to many ardent Loyalists.

Washington and his Continental troops now dominated New Jersey and across the river at Philadelphia. Washington's occupation made it difficult for Dutch families there who were not supporting the rebellion. Many of those Dutch families were relocating to Middle District, where they hoped to find peace.

Before the three oldest Holmes brothers, Obadiah, Jacob and Elijah received their orders, they made regular visits to Bull's Head Tavern with J.R. During one visit, the topic of discussion was about the Sons of Liberty.

"Their raids are a new kind of warfare, terrorizing innocent families," Obadiah said.

Elijah added, "Those men are cowards, cowards of the worst kind!"

"It's amazing," Jacob said, "the raiders don't even get arrested for their theft and destruction of property."

J.R. took a deep breath and said, "And, for all we know, men who do midnight raids may be right here in the tavern tonight!"

A stranger at another table stood up, began to throw insults at J.R., and challenged him to a fight. The stranger was obviously intoxicated and as the stranger charged J.R., Obadiah stood up to block the man, Obadiah felt a fist graze his left eye. The stranger lost his balance, and fell to the floor.

The tavern-keeper came over with rope and they hog-tied the man until he sobered up.

"I guess he didn't like what I was saying," J.R. told his brothers.

"I think everyone is on edge." Obadiah said.

"No one knows what to expect next." Jacob chimed in,

"Maybe the guy thought we were talking about him," sighed J.R. "The fighting has everyone feeling restless and tense."

A mercantile salesman named Pagan was a regular at the tavern. He spent his time traveling between Boston and Trenton along the Post Road. Pagan was a good source of news for the men of Middle District. Like clockwork, Pagan could be found at the tavern every other week.

One day, when Obadiah, J.R., and Jacob entered the tavern, they saw Pagan was there. Pagan told the brothers about laws some colonies were passing that would force Loyalists into poverty and bankruptcy. Pagan said the new laws applied only to Loyalists.

"Teachers and lawyers are being denied the right to work," Pagan said. "Shopkeepers are being boycotted and going out of business. The colonies that are under rebel control are not safe for Loyalists to live without being subject to harsh discrimination."

Jacob shook his head in disgust. "Just how far are the rebels going to push us? They ignore the laws from Parliament."

Pagan interjected, "Loyalists are being subject to public humiliation, physical attacks and confiscation of property."

The Holmes brothers were baffled. The laws passed by the rebel leaders in Boston seemed harsher than the acts coming from the King.

Elijah, who had just arrived, said: "The rebels praise freedom and praise the rights of man with one side of their mouths and out of the other side comes laws that are destroying men and their families, just because they think differently."

J.R. hung his head and sighed. "We seem to be living in a troubled time. We are a British colony and we are British subjects, but now we could be forced to follow the laws of a group of illegitimate leaders and deal with mob rule! I am curious to know how the Parliament is reacting to these bogus laws." He could see the bottom of his ale mug, but he dismissed the idea of ordering another. "What do you think, brothers, time to head home?"

After saying their farewells, the four of them left. The sun had set and J.R. could hear the peepers in a boggy area. The peepers were so loud, even they sounded as if they were complaining about the King. J.R. thought the hatred toward the British was springing up faster than the weeds in the Holmes' fallow fields. He often used his knowledge and understanding of sowing, tilling and reaping as an analogy to the discontent of those who called themselves revolutionaries. The rebellion, like unchecked weeds, would soon dominate and destroy everything good in the colonies.

ᘓ

Jonathan's words broke the sound of the trotting horses as he and J.R. rode to Bull's Head Tavern. "It's difficult to imagine two years have passed since the first muskets were fired in Lexington and Concord."

J.R. nodded. "Two years of fighting with untold numbers of dead and wounded. At times I wonder how we got here." He paused. "Nothing has changed. No one is willing to negotiate or come to a compromise. God help us when the French come to the aid of Washington and his men." Discouraged, J.R. lowered his voice. "The Crown has no time to waste. The French will join in the conflict and more likely sooner than later."

Jonathan was dismayed. If this happened, many were certain the war would continue, maybe for years. "It is hard to imagine, but if Washington and the French work together to defeat the King's forces in the colony, who knows, maybe the British Isles would be the next target."

"Well, father, I guess stranger things have happened."

"The second Continental Congress plans to meet again," Jonathan said, "and I can only imagine what outrageous move they will make next. I don't think they can top their declaration of independence." The rebel congress was meeting in Philadelphia while the British were building up their fleet from the shores of Long Island to Chesapeake Bay.

"I am glad I am not a betting man," J.R. said. "I couldn't guess what the next year might bring."

J.R. believed that with every passing day the fate of the colonies was more uncertain. The social fabric was beginning to tear apart. Thread by thread, the cloth that united the colonists from the District of Maine to Massachusetts to south of the Carolinas, was unraveling.

"You know father, with all this civil disorder and death, the men of the Continental Congress continue their discussions and debate in comfortable rooms, enjoying three meals a day and a warm bed at night. These men call themselves revolutionaries. They represent each colony making their laws, writing their declarations and sowing their seeds of propaganda. There is no doubt they are organizing the smuggling of guns and cannons and fattening their bankrolls. No surprise, with no King in the way, that some of these men would become wealthy as a direct result of this seemingly endless war."

"What makes them tick?" his father asked.

"What makes who tick?" J.R. replied,

"What makes men so determined to rise up against one form of governing to replace it with another? How can they be so sure mob rule and total chaos won't take over?" Jonathan asked.

"Look, father, these rebels have no capital city, no country, and no common currency."

"Yes, son, but they have determination. Their efforts are no longer a feeble attempt, but a dangerous attempt to usurp the Crown's influence. Remember son, all of these men are risking their neck and they know if they don't succeed, they will all be hanged."

They arrived at the Bull's Head Tavern, their mouths dry from talking and their minds ready for good conversation.

Jonathan told his son, "You know, in the opinion of many Loyalists, the self-appointed congressional committees who are meeting in Philadelphia are conducting an overt act of treason." Jonathan lowered his voice. "Be careful, son, what you say in public. You can never be too careful."

The sentiments expressed most strongly at the Bull's Head Tavern were of how the conflict would come to a speedy end. A man at a far table said as much. "This conflict won't last long. The British military just brought closure to the long French and Indian War in North America and the seven-year war in Europe. Our British troops are ready for battle. And they are the best trained in all of Europe."

As J.R. sat at his father's side in the tavern, he thought about how he would soon be confronting the events that could change him forever. His single reality would be the war, a reality that could alter his young life in ways he could not imagine. The rebellion, led by renegade British subjects who put themselves in charge of local militias, continental armies and printing presses, could consume J.R. and his family.

For the Holmes family, March began with the enlistments of Obadiah, Elijah and Jacob. All three had joined the L.A.R. Their enlistment represented their commitment to save the colonies from civil disorder. British officers came to local taverns for the sole purpose of recruitment, and young men were excited about the challenge.

The enlistments were carefully planned. While young men waited for their orders, they were able to remain at home to plow the soil, and plant the year's crop before reporting for duty. Many of the men enlisting expected to be back on the farm by harvest time; exactly what J.R. figured.

That night the four oldest sons took their usual places around the hearth to share thoughts, stories and ideas. They talked about activists from Boston and Philadelphia who were stirring feeling of nationalism, while talking up the rights of all men. They also wrote about freedom and self-determination. The authors made complex new ideas simple for all to understand. Obadiah had been able to find a copy of one of the pamphlets.

Jonathan entered the room and saw the pamphlet Obadiah was holding. He took the pamphlet and read the bold print on the cover, "*Common Sense. Does this Englishman have a name?*"

"No, well, yes, he must have a name," Jacob said, "but we have no ideas what it is."

Jonathan handed the pamphlet back to Obadiah. "All of this sounds rather interesting and I would like to hear more about what this Englishman has to say."

Obadiah continued reading from the work.

Then Jacob suddenly asked, "Having this pamphlet in our home may make it seem we support the rebellion. Could we be hanged for having this in our possession?"

"I would hate to say yes," said J.R., "but this would likely be considered traitorous material."

Elijah had a look of panic on his face. His father quickly added: "Son, we are reading this to gain a broader understanding of what people in the colonies are thinking. And let us hope in this effort of ours to understand, we are not accused of supporting the rebellion." Jonathan paused, looked at Elijah and added: "I know where your loyalties are, son, no cause for concern."

"But father, from what Obadiah has read thus far, it is treasonous talk against the King!"

"Only treasonous if you act on what you read, son,"

Obadiah interrupted. "Can I get back to my reading? I think we left off on the second section, *Of Monarchy and Hereditary Succession*"

J.R. was thinking while Obadiah read aloud. He thought about the numerous writings, speeches, protests and the impact of propaganda, all of it hardly diminished by the King's acts of retaliation.

By then, Joseph had joined them. "It seems as if the King wants the colonies to revolt, it seems as if he thinks the only way to settle this rebellion is with war. And you know he might be right!"

"And what if he is wrong, what if he is dead wrong?" Elijah asked Joseph.

Obadiah became frustrated with all the interruptions. "We can certainly see how threats by the King deepen the rebel anger, and how the resulting social upheaval has escalated. That is why I enlisted. I want to be a part of the solution."

Elijah and Jacob nodded in agreement.

J.R. felt his family was in the middle, between the colony they cherished and the empire to which they owed their good fortune.

Chapter 4

Spring 1777: Enlistment

J.R. and his kid brother Joseph saddled up for the thirty-minute ride to Bull's Head Tavern. J.R.'s decision to enlist in the L.A.R was not easy; he had hesitant voices echoing in his head. J.R. tried to hide that from Joseph. Ultimately, J.R. decided to enlist to help put an end to Washington's victories. No matter how he felt about the war, J.R. wanted to be part of the solution to stop the fighting. As they neared the tavern, J.R. pushed away his doubts. The rebellion had to end.

Joseph was thrilled and honored to join his older brother. He, unlike his four older brothers, was too young to go to Bull's Head Tavern for drink and conversation. Being just thirteen-years-old, he spent much of his time on the farm.

As they tied their horses outside the tavern, the buzz of activity startled them. There were a couple-dozen horses already tied and numerous officers were walking about inside and outside. All the activity transformed the tavern into a hive of red jackets. J.R. gave Joseph a wink as they entered the tavern. The sun gleamed through the small, square windowpanes, casting shadows on the wide, worn floorboards. The large room was furnished with long tables and a combination of chairs and benches for seating. There was a higher and larger table where the keeper of the tavern stood to serve customers ale, cider and whiskey. J.R. noticed that several other men from Middle District were signing up.

The officers were using three tables for enlistments. Two of the tables were inside the tavern and one was outside under a tall maple tree. Inside the tavern, J.R. could smell spilt ale and whisky, an odor that seemed to never go away. In the large hearth, the early morning fire was now a pile of cinders and ash.

He was about to show his loyalty to the King who, in many ways, had made life secure for colonists. How could we, as Loyalists, forget the British forces had defeated the French in 1763? With that grand defeat, the territory of the thirteen colonies had more than doubled! It was the King's army and many colonists who secured France's vast Canadian land for the British colonists to settle.

J.R. crooked his head to look at Joseph, gave him a quick smile as he began to wait in line for his turn to enlist. With the robust enlistment interest shown, J. R's confidence grew. All indications were good that the rebellion would be short lived. As J. R's place in line moved closer to the table, he listened to the conversation of the King's officers. They talked casually among themselves and appeared to have not a care in the world. They simply acted like British gentlemen enjoying an afternoon at their club. J.R. smiled, thinking this was a good sign.

In another part of the tavern, the impressionable Joseph was mesmerized by the officer uniforms. Wide-eyed, Joseph scanned each officer from head to toe, starting with their curled hair, the pigtail tied with a black ribbon and the gorget with a large pendant worn like a necklace near the throat. Each was delicately engraved with King George III's initials. Joseph was captivated by the glitter and shine as his eyes dropped to the shiny buttons on the double-breasted scarlet jackets. Each officer wore white leather breeches stopping just below the knee. At their waist was tied a scarlet sash. Below their knees were white gaiters, or knee-high stockings. Finally, his eyes went to the shining black riding boots. Joseph thought the officers were indeed impressive.

The scarlet jackets and other embellishments transformed each officer into an object of power and grandness. Joseph mused that these men were the King's warriors, and they seemed invincible with their swords of silver and brass, their pistols, muskets and bayonets. Joseph was spellbound as he watched the men circle the room. He had never seen such pomp. He could not imagine the clothing made them better fighters. He laughed to himself while he tried to imagine how in the world these men could win a war wearing such outrageous clothing.

J.R. finally reached the front of the line. His mouth was dry and he felt his heart beating faster. He provided his personal information to the enlistment officer, while out of the corner of his eye he watched Joseph follow a group of men outside.

One officer looked at Joseph and asked, "Young man, are you here to enlist?"

Joseph, stunned by the officer's remark, replied, "Me? Oh no sir, I am too young. I came here with my older brother, J.R. Holmes. He is enlisting!"

The officer examined Joseph up and down and asked, "What is your name?"

"Joseph Holmes, sir."

The officer radiated a friendly manner while saying, "You would make one very fine young soldier, Joseph."

Joseph, flattered by the officer's remark, hoped he was not blushing. It was stunning to have an officer chat with you, but for an officer to complement him, saying he would make a fine soldier, brought a huge smile to Joseph's face.

Meanwhile, J.R. completed his enlistment paperwork. They informed him his orders would be delivered to his home by courier on the first day of April. When he received his orders, he was to report to Captain Randall's Company in a borough of New York. There, he would be trained. Randall, also from New York, had a fine reputation as a military leader. The Randall family was among the first British settlers to the area. The family had built a thriving import business at the port of New York. If the rebels succeeded, his family would have a lot to lose.

J.R. searched for Joseph and saw him outside carrying on a conversation with some of the younger officers. J.R. chuckled to himself. J.R. caught Joseph's attention and waved for him to join him. J.R. was harboring a strong thirst. He ordered a pint of ale for himself and one for his brother. Joseph sipped his ale silently while J.R. listened to the volley of conversations about the war and how ultimate victory would, without a doubt, belong to the British. Joseph felt like an adult; he could not believe he was having ale at the Bull's Head Tavern, just like his father and brothers.

Once J.R. finished his ale, they left behind the recruitment noise and returned outside, where they mounted their horses to ride in the direction of their farm. About 15 minutes into the ride, J.R. yelled to Joseph, "Let's take the shortcut through the fields."

The horses left the dirt road, carefully descending a steep grassy knoll and splashed through a clear brook. On the other side of the brook, the horses climbed a small embankment to an endless field of green grasses spotted with yellow and purple flowers. As they galloped across the extensive tract of flat land, they anticipated no harm would come their way. They rode on with a strong sense of freedom and with the knowledge the war would end soon, and they would be back to the life they had known and loved.

Even at thirteen, Joseph was an excellent horseman and soon overtook J.R. Their horses were fast, the best in Middle District. Joseph was known as far away as Connecticut as an exceptional rider and trainer.

Joseph had been on horseback before he was walking. His four older brothers taught him how to handle horses and how to ride. Along with Joseph's own keen interest in the animal, he was one of the most knowledgeable horsemen in the area and diligently made a study of the best treatments for horses when they became sick. He used local herbs to help cure them from whatever might ail them. He also used simple things like packs made of mud or even molasses and mustard. Those who owned horses in the Hudson River Valley were thankful for a kid like Joseph.

"Remember when we would come out to this spot and dig for arrowheads?" J.R. asked Joseph.

"Certainly. Once you brought me here to dig for arrowheads on my birthday! I think I was turning nine. I will never forget the arrowhead I found that day; it was a beauty! Its color of white quartz gave it a magical quality." J.R. listened to his brother and thought about his own treasured arrowhead collection and how, someday, he would give it to Joseph.

J.R. had one other collection besides his arrowheads. This was a unique selection of hearty seeds. Every fall he gathered seeds from the best and most hearty grains growing in the fields. He observed how over a couple of years, some of his crops appeared healthier and gave increased yields. He carefully selected and stored the seeds of those parent plants. After each harvest, the select seeds were stowed away in woven flax sacks and sometimes in small wooden boxes. Everything was carefully marked with labels and put in a cool, dry room. J.R. took great pride in his seeds. He knew this practice would eventually increase the yields of his fields.

The two brothers rode their horses hard through the shortcut and in no time were able to spot their farm in the distance. They arrived at the barnyard and their horses were sweaty and tired from the vigorous race home. They dismounted, removed the saddles, horse blankets and bridles, before leading them into the stable.

For Joseph, the stables were his second home; he spent most of his time caring for the horses from the time they were born to when they were sold. Joseph loved his horses. He would train them and care for them from nearly dawn to dusk. When horse owners needed advice, they came to young Joseph Holmes.

They began to wipe the sweat from the horses' bodies, then brushed each horse down. Next, they gave them water and finally led the animals to their stalls. J.R. turned to his kid brother, put his arm around his shoulder and gave him a tight squeeze.

"Hey, Joseph, since we got back you have become very quiet. What's on your mind?"

"Not a whole lot, but as we got closer to home, I was reminded of how much I love this farm and my family."

"You've got that right, little brother. That goes for all of us!"

"What I mean is, I would miss this place if I had to leave it for any amount of time."

"Joseph, luckily you don't have to give that possibility a second thought! I do understand what you are saying because once my orders arrive I will have to leave the farm for the very first time in my life." J.R. paused, realizing the impact of what he had done. His orders would soon be on their way and he would leave all that surrounded him. Trying to sound upbeat, he said, "Hey Joseph, let's go see what mother is cooking!"

∞

Magdalene stood at one end of the long table in the center of the kitchen. She vigorously mixed the flour and water until the dough was dry enough to tumble out of the large wooden bowl onto the freshly floured breadboard to knead. Once back in the wooden bowl, the large clump of dough was covered with a cloth and placed in a warm cupboard next to the kitchen hearth.

Next she grabbed a handful of washed vegetables and chopped them with speed and precision. She turned to the hearth and using a long wooden spoon stirred the corn meal and molasses pudding. Next on her to-do list was to prepare the chickens for roasting. That morning, Elijah had killed the foul and plucked their feathers.

She turned her head toward the hearth. Flames were dancing between the hot coals and an array of large and small black pots and kettles. The fire began spitting as fat dripped from the roasting chicken on the skewer. Water boiled in another pot, rolls began to rise, and the pudding baked as sounds and smells swirled around the hearth. Magdalene took a break, wrapped herself in her lambs-wool shawl and walked into the dining area to survey the table. She was pleased; all was in order. For a moment, she took a seat in the rocker before returning to do the final prep for their celebratory meal.

With her shawl around her shoulders, she opened the kitchen door, stood on the porch but saw no one. Were John Roger and Joseph still on the way back or were they in the stables? She took a moment to reflect on all the goodness that surrounded her and her family and she smiled and listened. The sounds of the peepers in the swamp were early that night. She felt a gentle breeze and breathed in the aroma of nature. She was thankful and content with life. She was reminded daily of her good fortune, having a compassionate husband and seven children, all gifts she cherished more than life itself.

That night's supper was to acknowledge John Roger's enlistment. J.R. was the fourth son to join the L.A.R. Each enlistee was a proud American, born in the Colony of New York. Some of the members of this regiment were fourth- and fifth-generation American colonists.

Magdalene beamed with pride for her enlisted sons. Her seven children thrived on her happy, confident disposition as well as her cooking. What her grown children did not know was her mastery at hiding her worries and concerns. With a war breaking out and four sons enlisted, her fears for their safety were all-consuming. War was not constructive, she often thought. War was riddled with what ifs and how comes.

With her fourth son enlisting to help bring order and civility back to the colonies, her depth of worry deepened. Magdalene never stopped reminding herself to show her children confidence; to let them see her pride for them and not to see her anxiety. She particularly did not agree with her sons' sense of urgency to enlist but in spite of her own strong feeling about the rebellion and the Crown, she would not allow it to show. She had a hard time accepting the conflict, let alone her sons enlisting to fight.

She was thankful for one thing. Her youngest son, Joseph, was not going anywhere. Joseph was only thirteen, too young to go off to war, and for that, she was relieved.

Her oldest son, Obadiah was twenty-five. He was the first to enlist, joining Captain Finaly's Company of the L.A.R. Obadiah was tall like his two sisters and his strongest trait was his curiosity about the world around him. He was an orderly young man who kept a journal, logging weather conditions and details of the civil unrest consuming the colonies. Obadiah was single with seemingly little interest in marriage, but he once had his eye on a woman named Charlotte, until she married his closest friend, Charles Chambers, the man with whom he enlisted.

Next to volunteer were two of her middle sons, Jacob, seventeen, and Elijah, fifteen. They enlisted with Colonel Beverly Robinson's Company of the L.A.R. Jacob, small compared to most boys his age, was given the rank of drummer. Elijah would be trained as a foot soldier.

Magdalene reached for the hemp rope dangling from the dinner bell. With an effortless tug, she rang three claps of the bell, sending the message it was time to leave the fields and head home for dinner. Jonathan, Obadiah, Elijah and Jacob had been in the fields all day. With the sound of the bell, they stopped work and returned the animals and tools to the barn and shed. Next, they gathered around the well to wash up. Jacob dropped the wooden bucket down until it splashed, filled it with cold water and pulled it up. The last one to wash up had the chore of fetching a bucket of water for the dinner dishes.

Meanwhile, Magdalene saw J.R. and Joseph coming out of the stables. She waved to them and returned to the boiling pots hanging over the fire. She drained the water from the boiled potatoes; saving the water for a batch of potato rolls to make the next day. She drained the carrots saving the water for soup stock. Her youngest, Joseph, all smiles, entered the kitchen and she turned and gave him a kiss on the cheek, a wink and a pat on his behind. Jacob followed.

She whispered to Jacob in a quiet, but proud motherly tone, "Tonight J.R. is the guest of honor at dinner. He is an intrepid young man to volunteer, just like you, Elijah and Obadiah."

Jonathan sat in his usual chair. His eyes surveyed the length of the table while a cavalcade of images flashed in his mind, memories of his marriage, the hundreds of gatherings there with his seven children, the weddings of his two daughters, and finally the enlistments of Obadiah, Elijah, Jacob and now John Roger. In his and Magdalene's house, the dining table had become a place for heartfelt occasions, gatherings of gratefulness and a place for nurturing both the body and the soul. It was also a place for good-byes. Finally, the table offered a safe place for expressing differing opinions. This is where they learned fair debate.

Magdalene, the last one seated, sat next to her youngest son, Joseph.

Obadiah, Jacob, and Elijah took their seats and J.R. sat at the opposite end of the table from his father.

Once they all had taken their seats, Jonathan raised his cup of cider, cleared his throat and announced, "I would like us to recognize J.R. He has joined the L.A.R. and his mother and I are bursting with pride." Jonathan looked at each of his five sons and continued, "Your mother and I are proud of all our sons."

With the words, "Dig in," the hungry family began to pass around the steaming bowls, platters and covered dishes. They reached in many directions across the table. Bowls and platters of food took flight. Everything was in motion, passed around and around. The table was an arena of aromas, a feeding trough topped with everyone's favorite boiled potatoes, seasoned carrots sprinkled with dried dill, hot applesauce with freshly grated cinnamon, nutmeg and a pinch of ginger along with two roasted chickens smothered in French thyme.

A sudden relative stillness hung over the table, as the serving bowls lay still and the knives and forks chattered on the plates while everyone enjoyed each mouthful. Magdalene lifted the carrot bowl which had a few carrots remaining. She gestured to Joseph, and he finished them. Jacob jokingly told Joseph to eat his carrots because they would put hair on his chest and his chin. Jacob grinned and Joseph smirked.

Joseph, being the youngest, had to develop a good sense of humor and a thick skin. When it came to his older brothers, there was no telling what practical joke they might play on him next. Joseph grabbed the remaining carrots and inhaled them. Then he checked to see if he had grown any hair on his chest and felt his chin for stubble. Joseph knew how to make them all laugh.

Toward the end of their dinner Magdalene said, "I hope all of you have room for peach bread pudding and hard sauce." The room was filled with nodding heads.

A black pot was placed on the table directly in front of Jonathan and a smile came over Joseph's face. He thought that this was the time. He waited a moment for his mother and Obadiah to seat themselves. Joseph stood up.

Magdalene turned to Joseph and asked, "Did we forget something?"

Joseph replied, "No, of course not, mother." His eyes circled the table slowly, meeting each member of his family.

Elijah was puzzled. "Sit down Joey, you best eat your pudding before I get my hands on it!"

Joseph smiled but ignored Elijah's comment. He continued to stand. Joseph's heart began throbbing as he searched for his voice. Why was he so nervous about what he was to share with his parents and brothers?

Finally he said, "Everyone, I too have grand news to share with you."

Magdalene smiled at Joseph thinking his sense of humor was getting the better of him, but she sat quietly deciding to play along. Joseph's words began slowly and became even slower as he expressed his good news to the family. He looked at his father, a symbol of strength, and then at his mother, a woman of natural goodness. Their puzzled faces began to appear worried.

"I too, am a soldier of the King's army," he announced, "I will proudly defend our King's honor, our colonies and our way of life." He stood solid, shoulders back, chin up.

A silence came over the room. His parent's reaction was disbelief, confusion and shock. His father's face was white and his eyes vacant. After several moments, Magdalene, without saying a word, slowly began to stand next to where Joseph was still standing. She placed her hand firmly on the table for strength. She hoped the edge of the table would steady her. Joseph gave her his arm and noticed her face was as ghostly white as the linen tablecloth. She slowly turned from the table and within a second, collapsed on the floor.

Jonathan jumped out of his chair and rushed to his wife. He quickly dipped his dinner napkin into Magdalene's water glass and frantically patted her forehead, her cheeks and neck with the wet napkin. Jonathan picked her up with the help of Obadiah and they took her to the adjoining room. They lay her gently on the upholstered sofa and placed a small blanket over her legs. Joseph ran to the kitchen and grabbed her lambs-wool shawl and wrapped it over her shoulders.

Joseph whispered in her ear, "I am deeply sorry to have upset you Mother. I hoped you would be proud of me. I want to defend our way of life, our farm and our family just as my brothers will do."

Magdalene could hear the passion in Joseph's voice and realized he was seriously committed. However, how could he be seriously committed to a cause he knew nothing about? She thought this rebellion was a serious and dangerous affair, surely not suitable for children.

A couple weeks later, Magdalene and Jonathan shared with each other what they had observed in their five sons and two sons-in-law. It was an intense, disturbing, yet curious difference between their sons' ambitions to fight and keep the colonies intact, compared to the determination their sons-in-law exhibited.

Beach and Nate had fire in their bellies. They boldly supported independence. They wanted no more dictates from an unreasonable King, or any king for that matter. The two Beardsley brothers spoke about self-determination with purpose. Every word they said about the conflict was wrapped in their own unshakable determination. It was obvious to Magdalene and her husband that their two sons-in-law were not going to be stopped from taking charge of their own destiny.

They hoped their sons-in-law would not die at the gallows. Nate and Beach's reasons for supporting the revolt were well-rooted and resolute. Magdalene's sons expressed a different attitude about supporting the King's cause. Her sons' ambition to enlist was driven by duty and obligation along with wanting a quick end to the madness. This was in stark contrast to Beach and Nate's belief. The Beardsley clan was an ambitious lot. Clear and simple tenacity drove them. Beach and Nate personified persistence with a definite goal.

When Magdalene and Jonathan were alone, they wondered if the unparalleled sense of determination Nate and Beach possessed might have an impact on the outcome of the conflict. All the while, she and Jonathan dreaded the fast approaching day when their five sons would receive their orders. Any day an emissary from the L.A.R. would ride into their yard carrying five sets of orders for them to report for duty. She shivered at the thought of her sons being in harm's way.

Another burden arrived when Magdalene and Jonathan received a letter from their oldest daughter, Sarah, who now lived in Sandy Hook, Connecticut. Magdalene picked up her pewter letter opener to break the wax seal and began to read. A moment later, she was overwhelmed with anguish. She put the letter down not wanting to read any more.

Beach and Nate had enlisted in Washington's Continental Army. Her daughters' husbands were now active participants, taking up arms against the Crown. She faced a stunning realization, Nate and Beach would be hung for treason if either a British or Loyalist soldier caught them. The King had given his word, anyone who supported the rebellion would be hung as traitors to the British Empire.

With the arrival of this news, Jonathan Holmes grew quiet. He spent much time thinking about what this traitorous behavior would mean for his two daughters, Sarah and Elizabeth, and his little granddaughter Magda.

Jonathan tried to focus, trying to reassure his wife this conflict would end soon. Did he really believe that? No, he knew better, and many dark questions lurked in the pit of his belly. Foremost was the question of whether his own five sons' sense of loyalty to the Crown would be able to compete on the battlefield against the resolute, bold bunch of rebels.

When the rest of the family learned the disturbing news about Beach and Nate, Obadiah struggled to comprehend having to fight against his sisters' husbands, and he feared this could lead to a permanent break in the family. He was bewildered by their decision, and his other brothers began to see just how complicated rebellion could be.

Jonathan lay awake at night wondering how this would affect the fate of his two beloved daughters. He tried to keep an open mind, but he was disappointed with his two sons-in-law. They had made a decision that could dangerously alter their lives and the lives of Sarah and Elizabeth.

Chapter 5

Spring 1777: Harlem Heights

J.R. and Joseph were the last of the Holmes brothers to receive their orders. They were to report to Captain Randall's Company of the L.A.R. at Harlem Heights, a British military headquarters in the Colony of New York.

The night before their departure, they packed their few belongings into leather knapsacks. Their personal things included writing paper, ink and sealing wax. Joseph, unable to find any sealing wax, asked J.R. if he would break his stick of sealing wax in half and share it with him. J.R. was happy to do so. Magdalene reminded her sons not to forget the thick wool blankets she had given them.

Jonathan cleaned and polished J.R.'s musket. Joseph did not need a weapon; no one expected him to see any fighting. They each tied their bedroll and knapsacks to their horse's saddle. Joseph wished he knew how to tie a knot that would ensure things would not come loose on their journey to Harlem. Jonathan Holmes handed J.R. his musket. J.R. took a long look at it and then it hit him: he was leaving home with no idea when he might return. J.R. stood still studying his father. He was a middle-aged man, strong chin, wide cheekbones, with sadness clouding his eyes.

Jonathan and Magdalene stood in their dooryard and watched as J.R. and Joseph prepared to leave. J.R. mounted his horse and Joseph walked up to his father, who towered over him by a foot, and gave him a hug. He turned to his mother with a forced smile and kissed her on the cheek. He told her not to worry and gave her a hug.

With her arms wrapped around her youngest child, she did not want to let him go. Her tears were impossible to fight back. He too was sad and forced himself to step back from his mother. He turned toward his horse, put one foot in the stirrup and hoisted himself into the saddle.

Jonathan and Magdalene were alone for the first time in nearly twenty-seven years. Their five sons were gone, fighting for King George III, and their two daughters were married to men supporting the rebellion. Jonathan put his sturdy arm around his wife's shoulder as they walked back to the house. They already longed for the time when their family would be whole again.

Manhattan, Staten Island and Long Island were securely under the control of the British Command and it was comforting to know that Manhattan, Brooklyn Heights, Haarlem Heights, White Plains and points north along the Hudson River were predominately a haven for Loyalists and British operations. However, just west of the Hudson River, too close for comfort, the rebel army lurked and hoped to take the British by surprise whenever and wherever they could.

As they rode into Manhattan, Joseph peered at the map. "I hope we aren't lost."

"Lost … no," J.R. said. "his map of the Manhattan boroughs clearly show we are on the correct road to our military encampment at Harlem Heights"

"Do you think we will see any rebels between here and there?" asked Joseph.

"No, I doubt it, but if we do, they would have something to worry about, being in the hotbed of a Loyalist-controlled colony. You know, the rebels tried to take this area once and likely learned their lesson. They high-tailed it out of here and ran like scared rabbits to the Colony of New Jersey to hide."

They both remained silent as they meandered south toward the Harlem River. J.R.'s eyes were drawn to the river, the marsh and the flora that grew vigorously along endless wetlands. He noted the land as being predominately a lush meadow.

After a few minutes, J.R. asked, "Do you know about the events that occurred in this area last September?"

Joseph wrinkled his forehead. "No, I don't think I do know, but I bet it had something to do with Washington and his soldiers. Tell me what happened. I really want to know!"

J.R. began to tell Joseph about the Battle of Harlem Heights. "That site is where Washington and his rebel army had an early battlefield victory, and the British had their first battlefield defeat."

"So how did the British troops reclaim this land from the rebels?"

"From what I understand it took the Loyalist troops and British forces about one month until this land was back under British control. British troops coming in from just north of us were hoping to trap Washington and his army on the island of Manhattan, a clever plan. Without much hesitation, the rebels retreated to White Plains."

Joseph was fascinated. "How quickly things happened in war, one minute you have possession of a strategic location and then you don't. How in the world do Washington and his rebels manage to maintain their supplies of food and ammunition while running around between Harlem Heights, White Plains and New Jersey?"

J.R. thought Joseph's question was insightful for his age. "Yeah, you might think maintaining supply lines and feeding an army of men would be a challenge. When the rebel forces took Harlem Heights and then left for Fort Washington, they took food and weapons left by the former British occupants. Next our men took Fort Washington leading to another decisive British victory."

Joseph cleared his throat and in a triumphant tone said: "J.R., you know, I think we have without a doubt, selected the right side to support."

"Yeah, I agree, because it gets worse for the rebels. The Fort Washington commander surrendered to the British, and we got nearly 3,000 rebel troops who became our prisoners. But, what was more important, the entire garrison overlooking the Hudson now belongs to us and the British soldiers."

Joseph smiled. He relished hearing stories about British victories over the rebel's rag-tag army. They rode onward finally crossing the King's Bridge over Harlem River. This was where they encountered their first military checkpoint. J.R. showed the soldier his orders and told Joseph to do the same. They continued south to Harlem.

After a short silence, Joseph asked, "How come you know so much about Fort Washington?"

"Well, I listen to what people are saying and I read all the print news I can get my hands on. I also think Fort Washington might be my military assignment." J.R. smiled at his kid brother, and suggested they spur their horses along to report for duty before the sun got much lower in the western sky.

Joseph had one more question, "Why haven't we, well, I mean the British officers, changed the name of Fort Washington?"

J.R. smiled, and told his brother the question was a good one, but perhaps the British had more important things to focus on, like fighting a war.

ɛᴓ

Within days after J.R. and Joseph arrived at Harlem Heights, things began to change radically for Joseph. Two British lieutenants had taken notice of Joseph's exceptional riding abilities and they told their commander that Joseph would be an invaluable scout. They said the boy rode a horse like no one they had ever seen.

The commander, Colonel Barnes, said he would give the suggestion serious consideration. Barnes reviewed the boy's enlistment information and learned Joseph was barely thirteen years old and could read and write. That combined with his youthful appearance and excellent riding ability made it likely he could ride into an enemy area without arousing suspicion. It was agreed that Joseph would spend his days and nights gathering information by serving his King as a scout. Joseph was thrilled, but he was warned not to tell anyone about his work, even members of his family, who believed he was tending horses in the officers stables.

Joseph was honored to be given such an interesting job. He attending brief but intensive training where he learned to keep to himself, listen to conversations, run coded messages, and observe troops to determine their numbers and where they were headed. He was to do all this while bringing little attention to himself. Joseph felt he was lucky to get a position of such importance.

During the summer, Joseph was informed that all of the boroughs of New York and the lands halfway up the Hudson River Valley were secured by the King's military operations. He learned fleets of British ships waited just beyond Long Island with men and supplies for the next offensive attack. He was impressed when told the British Navy ruled all the oceans of the world, and the navy was highly trained and had thousands of ships in its arsenal. He saw the British as a world power that no one would dare anger.

As June turned into July, Joseph began to attend logistics sessions, led by British officers whose job it was to figure out how to get men and supplies from the port of New York to the ever-changing battle lines in the

57

interior of the colonies. Joseph learned how river access was paramount for the flow of supplies. Fortunately for the British, Fort Washington and Fort Lee, a small garrison on the New Jersey side of the Hudson, were both securely in their hands.

ભ૭

After several days of training, J.R. and other recruits from the Colony of New York mustered out to Fort Washington. He felt good to have the chance to say a quick goodbye to his kid brother, but he thought it odd Joseph did not mention anything about working with the horses or how life was in the stables.

As J.R. packed his knapsack and rolled up his blankets, a mixed sense of confidence and uneasiness entered his mind. He knew Joseph would be safe as a stable boy and he tried to shake off his doubts. By mid-morning his unit began their march north from the encampment at Harlem to Fort Washington.

When J.R. and his regiment came in view of the fort, he was struck by what he saw, a majestic structure built by rebels. His eyes drank in every aspect of the fortress, five bastions, and ingenious structures projecting outward for defense against assault. As the regiment got closer to the fort, he could see the many cannons strategically placed on the bastions. He recalled being told Washington's Pennsylvanian soldiers built the fort to be highly resistant to a British attack. Washington wanted this fort built to protect the Hudson River from British warships. J.R. thought that did not work out too well for them! It was situated at the highest point of land on the north end of Manhattan.

He thought it curious, that the fort and Washington's Continental troops failed to hold off an assault by the British and Hessian troops the previous November. Now the fort was a stronghold for the Crown. J.R. was proud to be on the side of soldiers who had taken such a strategic structure.

ભ૭

At Harlem Heights, Joseph assignments as a scout were exciting. He felt fortunate to ride his horse through villages and towns to secretly observe and ferret out information. Joseph had an excellent memory and did not need to keep notes. His ability to recall the slightest detail was invaluable.

The officers and Colonel Barnes provided Joseph with training that, at times, seemed endless. What he was learning was never dull as he focused on techniques, strategies, locations, behaviors, mannerisms and observation. His numerical ability was highlighted in knowing the number of men, guns, cannons, horses or supply wagons and also knowing where and when they were going. They told him these observations could save many lives and help end the rebellion.

They showed Joseph how to work with maps and how the enemy lines were always in flux. They again ordered him to keep his assignment to himself and that no one, not his family nor even the men he bunked with, was to know about his daily operations as a scout.

Usually Joseph shared almost everything with J.R. and not sharing such an important assignment with his brother would be a challenge, but a challenge he knew he could handle. Time and time again he was reminded his activities were dangerous, and if caught behind enemy lines, his life would hang in the balance.

In training session after training session, a wide variety of topics followed one after another. Especially interesting to Joseph was the speculation about the scouts and spy networks of the Continental forces. Rebel spies sometimes carried on with their everyday lives while passing information, even under the noses of the British. Colonel Barnes explained what might appear to be the most benign action could ultimately cost many British and Loyalist troops their lives. He cautioned that a rebel spy could be almost anyone, even one wearing a British uniform.

Joseph's life was shrouded and his activities became unpredictable. His schedules for every day, week and month would be different. He thought of the day when he could share his secrets with his brothers and tell his own grandchildren how he helped save the colonies from a fearsome rebellion.

When scouting, he always stopped to rest and water his horse at different places and at different times of day. He loved his horse, one he raised from birth on the family farm. Her name was Red, for the color of her coat, a dark reddish brown. He remembered when he trained her to accept a saddle, she bucked and reared. Red didn't easily conform to authority.

Trying to teach Red to be submissive, obedient and docile was a battle. Exhausted, Joseph was nearly ready to give up. As if the horse knew his intent, she stopped being unruly and stopped acting like an anarchist on four hooves. Overnight, Red became Joseph's horse and she would let only Joseph ride her. He laughed when he thought about his efforts to train Red.

Joseph and Red were assigned to ride to certain locations, some of them beyond British control in New Jersey and Pennsylvania. It did not faze Joseph to go behind enemy lines and he quickly became familiar with both Trenton and Philadelphia.

During one of his visits to Philadelphia that summer, there was big news of Marquis deLafayette's arrival in the city. Joseph learned Lafayette was the same age as his brother J.R. And he believed so strongly in the rebel cause and wanted to be a part of this conflict so badly he hired a ship to take him and others to the colonies to meet General George Washington.

Joseph heard numerous rumors about Lafayette. Everywhere Joseph went there was a wide range of reasons given for his visit to Philadelphia. Some colonists thought he was there to draft a secret alliance between the rebels and France against England. Others said Lafayette's journey to the colonies was merely to assess the war situation and provide advice to the Commander-in-Chief of the Continental Army, George Washington. And some people believed Lafayette was visiting Philadelphia because he had a mistress who lived on the outskirts of the city and a second mistress living in Trenton. It was not Joseph's position to judge which of the rumors might be accurate; he was to deliver all this information to Colonel Barnes.

The story that indicated Lafayette was here to create a secret alliance between the Continental Army and France caused an expression of grave concern, almost terror, to come over Barnes' face. If the alliance report was indeed true, and if Lafayette's analysis of the war favored the rebels, France could then decide they would support the rebellion. The need to know more information grew greater with each sunrise.

Colonel Barnes brought a cloth bag to one of the debriefing sessions. Joseph sat across the table from the colonel and watched while he opened the bag. Out came a pair of boots.

Joseph was puzzled. "Colonel Barnes, these boots appear to be rather worn, don't they?"

Colonel Barnes gave Joseph friendly smile.

"Why do you suppose they look worn?"

Joseph grinned. Then his eyes widened, "Oh yes, I get it. A pair of new shiny boots would make me look suspicious." Colonel Barnes was pleased to see that Joseph never seemed to stop thinking.

The colonel explained, "These boots were made to look old. But, look here, the heel of the left boot is false. An empty boot heal is a good place to hide information of grave importance."

Suddenly Joseph's curiosity was piqued, and he watched Barnes remove several nails from the leather heel. The colonel then removed a small folded piece of parchment from inside the heel. Joseph's eyes widened, as if the Colonel were performing magic. Next, he carefully nailed the heel back onto the boot bottom using the same old nails. Joseph's curiosity crested and with utmost attention, he continued to watch the colonel as he reattached the boot heel. Joseph's face revealed that he liked what he had just seen, a most incredible discovery.

"This is a clever way to carry secrets and sketches showing troop movement," Joseph said.

"That is exactly correct," Barnes told Joseph with a firm tone.

Joseph picked up the boots, "When do you want me to wear them?"

"Put them on today and get used to them," said Colonel Barnes.

Joseph struggled to imagine what his next scouting assignment might involve. He had gotten comfortable with not knowing exactly what he would be doing from day to day. Joseph reviewed some of his previous scouting expeditions, hoping they were of value to the King's soldiers, the Hessians and the hundreds of men of the L.A.R. He felt proud to think his work was contributing toward bringing about an end to the war.

The danger of being exposed, caught and hung for supporting the King was a daily reality for him. He felt prepared for anything and everything. If caught, he would deny any accusation of spying. Although, if he was caught while wearing the boots, it would be less likely he could deny being a spy. He thought about it and wearing the boots could be a dead giveaway. He resigned himself to do his job, carefully, wisely and discreetly.

On a bright October afternoon, Joseph had one uncomfortable moment of clarity that scared him. He and Red rode west from Harlem Heights toward the colony of New Jersey. When he arrived, he did the usual lingering and listening in the village. Then he continued north, stopping outside the Lion's Tavern. Joseph dismounted, tied Red's reins to a wooden post and brushed the road dust from his shirt and hat. He yawned while stretching his muscles, then sat outside the tavern on a bench just under an opened window. He stretched again and lay down on the bench pretending to be tired, all the while listening to the patrons inside. They were arguing loudly while drinking ale.

One patron's voice rose above the others. It was a gruff voice full of loathing and he babbled an irate monologue, "What about the Dutch schoolmaster ... one year ago? What have you to say about his terrible fate? He had no trial, no chance to clear himself of those charges. Actions of that nature will only make people hate the British even more!"

Another patron chimed-in, "Yeah, the young schoolmaster, I think from the Colony of Connecticut, an educated man, at Yale, and the British accused him of spying. Then the bastard British hanged the poor man without a trial!" The conversation paused. Every muscle in Joseph's body tensed. His mind was on high alert.

The tavern-keeper interrupted, "It is just over the one-year mark of that senseless hanging of the schoolmaster. Yeah, so the British accused the schoolmaster of spying! Now he is dead. Isn't that what war is about?"

Another voice added, "Whether he was a spy or just someone in the wrong place at the wrong time, who knows? But I do know, young American colonists, not in uniform, are dying every day regardless of whether they rebel or Loyalist. With every death, it is a great loss. If you ask me, it is damn senseless."

There was a long pause and the tavern was oddly quiet. Then, a loud announcement, "I will buy all of you another ale and let's drink to the schoolmaster, may he rest in peace and the British can go to hell!" While the men cheered inside the tavern, Joseph shivered while thinking about the seriousness of the wars' outcome. Each side, at whatever the cost, wanted victory to be theirs.

A cold chill caused goose bumps on Joseph's scalp. For the first time he felt vulnerable. He got up from the bench and walked across the dirt road to be warmed by the afternoon sunlight. Standing alone in the sun's rays, he thought that he was not actually a spy, but a scout, just a scout in service to the King. He thought of himself as similar to the man who delivers the post. He tried to forget about the conversation he had overheard.

Nonetheless, listening to hostile remarks about the British was nothing new to Joseph's ears. He was forever trying to guard against propaganda. For all he knew, the story about the Connecticut schoolmaster may very well have been no more than a trumped-up story to make the British appear ruthless. Joseph figured that had to be the only explanation, the story was just more rumor created by the rebels to make the British officers look inhumane.

Chapter 6

March 1778" Kidnapped

T he wind blew through Joseph's hair as he and Red followed the road north through New Rochelle and the remote farm area of Poughkeepsie then turned in an easterly direction along the Post Road toward Greenwich in the colony of Connecticut. Behind him, the sun would be setting soon. The spring air felt soothing as it caressed his face. Evening fragrances of freshly plowed soil energized Joseph's spirit.

This was his fourth mission of the week and, at times, he thought they could do with a couple more scouts. There was an ever-increasing demand for good intelligence. This time he was to hand-deliver a coded map to a drop-off location, just beyond the border between the Colonies of Connecticut and New York. To ensure that his mission was a success, the coded map was hidden in the heel of his boot.

He longed to visit the Connecticut port towns, and hoped someday he would get an assignment there. Beach had told him he could walk down the street in Stratford or Bridgeport and smell the spices being unloaded and packaged for transport. He wanted to see the majestic homes of the sea captains with the widow walks on the rooftops. He wanted to see the ships, or even a jawbone of a whale. He found it fascinating when he read about sailors who hunted ocean beasts the size of two man-of-war vessels. Someday he would visit those busy shipping ports. But not that day; he was on a mission.

This was an easy assignment, but it would take more than twelve hours riding to reach his destination. Then he would hand over the concealed map, get a bit to eat and ride all night back to Harlem Heights. Joseph and

Red were going due east, toward an area under rebel control, a dangerous place for a Loyalist to be found and a deadly area for a spy to travel.

As he rode his beloved Red, Joseph turned his head to catch a glimpse of the sunset's bold streaks of yellow, orange and red. He forgot about whaling towns and thought of lands beyond the Appalachian Mountains. He wanted to go west someday, too. He figured once the war was over he would go west and maybe have a horse farm on the wide-open spaces just beyond the mountains. He would take the money he earned as a soldier and buy lots of land, just as his Grandfather Obadiah did in New York. He would raise dozens of horses. And people would come from far away to buy them. Joseph was confident it would be a booming business. Once the rebellion ended, he would head west!

He asked Red, "Hey boy, what do you think of that, we can go west and build us a place and raise horses!" Joseph sat with his back straight in the saddle, with hardly a care, thinking of the places he wanted to go, things he wanted to see and most of all, the horse farm he would someday live on with Red.

Joseph knew when he was approaching a town because he saw more walls made of stone. Some were carefully made with each stone fitting in perfectly and other walls were not much more than piles of stones lining the length of the fields. The Post Road seemed to have an endless serenity as the early evening light brought beauty to the fields and forests.

From out of nowhere, a disheveled man on horseback rode toward Joseph. When the rider got closer, the man appeared lost. Maybe he was hungry, perhaps a deserter. The sight of him disturbed Joseph and he attempted to pick up his speed. He then cautioned himself that this could be a spy, disguised as a poor man without a home or food. The rider approached and stopped cold. Joseph also stopped and cautiously offered the stranger a friendly hello. Joseph checked out the stranger. He was in terrible shape, confused, or perhaps drunk. He felt certain the man was not a spy.

Joseph, not liking the feeling he had about the man, was ready to spur Red onward. But suddenly, without any noise, someone jumped on Joseph's back and pulled him off Red. Joseph fell to the road and was quickly overpowered. He realized there were two men. After his initial confusion and shock, Joseph concluded it was an ambush. But why? Joseph surmised that the men must have known who he was and where he was going. He assumed that when they got what they wanted, they would hang him.

Joseph worried about one thing, the map hidden in his boot heel. Joseph decided that no matter what, he would not give out any information or the map. He knew they would kill him anyway. As he struggled with the man on his back he shouted, "What do you want from me, my money?"

Neither man said a word as they tied Joseph's wrist and ankles. With both lifting Joseph like a sack of barley, they tossed him over the back of his horse. The younger of the two men led Red off the Post Road and onto a cart path. Joseph, still reeling from the surprise attack, could only conclude these men were rebel spies and his hours were numbered.

They headed toward a woods and Joseph listened to the two men. He noticed their use of crude slang and words he had never heard. Their vocabulary was limited, and the language they used seemed almost foreign. He bounced around as they rode over rough terrain.

Joseph thought there was no way these two men were spies. Their appearance and smell were foul, their faces unshaven, and their mouths showed broken and missing teeth. If they were spies, their disguises were the best he had ever seen. The only other possibility was that they were common thieves. He grew uneasy thinking that if they are thieves, why did they capture him? Why didn't they just take his money and run? Joseph again asked them what they wanted and he got no answer. The older of the two had a deep scar on his face. He grabbed Joseph's hair, pulled up his head and threatened to scalp him if he didn't shut up.

The younger man laughed and spit as he told Joseph that once they got back to camp he planned to work him over. The remark was followed with more laughter. Everything was funny to these two men, leaving Joseph with a chill.

At their camp, the two men pulled Joseph off his horse, throwing him on the ground, with his wrists and ankles still bound. He saw a third man, sitting on a stump near a campfire, reading a book. Joseph felt a blow to his lower back and heard the same laugh. The shorter man continued to kick him, in his stomach, his head, legs and back. The beating didn't stop until Joseph lay unconscious.

Still laughing, the two searched Joseph's pockets. They found a small amount of money and hastily stuffed the coins into their pockets. The older man then searched Joseph's knapsack and shouted to his younger partner to check the bedroll and saddlebag. He grabbed Joseph's saddleback and proceeded to dump the contents on the ground. With disappointment, they saw a tinderbox, a book, and blank pieces of parchment. Nothing of any interest or value.

After a few minutes, the older man noticed Joseph's boots, which he saw were much nicer than his. As Joseph still lay unconscious, he took off Joseph's boots and removed his own boots that had worn leather soles, tossing them over to where Joseph lay.

The man held his new pair of boots in his hands and smiled, shouting to his buddy, "Ain't these beautiful!" He spit on the end of his shirt to shine the top of the boots before putting them on his feet. He jumped up, dazzling himself with his new footwear and pranced around the fire.

The third man didn't take his eyes out of his book until after the two hoodlums were done with their sport, then he carefully bent the corner of the page he was reading, closed his book and gently put it on the ground. He and walked over to where Joseph lay, then he knelt down, grabbed Joseph's hair and turned his head to get a better look. He wrinkled his eyebrows before returning to the campfire, where he sat down, opened his book and continued to read.

A short time later, the man who was reading shouted to the other two. "You two jackasses better not have killed the kid. You best hope he isn't dead because if he is, you will be next. Go make sure the kid is breathing."

The two lifted Joseph and dragged him closer to the campfire. Blood oozed from Joseph's nose and left ear. The third man's eyes left his book and looked at Joseph. His expression remained indifferent. He returned to reading the thick book he held in his hand.

Hours passed and Joseph regained consciousness. He couldn't see out of his eyes but he could wiggle his toes. He shuddered and thought: My boots, where are my boots? They are not on my feet! Do they know, have they found the map? They must know I am a spy.

He tried to calm himself, thinking that whoever did this would have no idea he was a scout for the British. They would have hanged him if they knew. Joseph tried not to panic about finding his boots. He told himself he had to destroy the map as soon as he could.

One of his captors noticed Joseph had slightly moved his legs. He alerted the younger man and they both jumped to their feet.

The younger man said, "Yeah, he moving his legs. Isn't it good? He ain't dead, this kid ain't no goner."

A couple days passed before Joseph was able to open his eyes. His first images seemed out of focus. Slowly his vision improved, revealing the faces of two men standing over him. One was older with a scar on his face. Joseph began to recall, blow-by-blow, the beating he had suffered. Then, Joseph heard the voice of a third man. This man spoke with an authoritative tone as he told the other two, whose names were Watkins and Pike, what he wanted them to do.

Pike, the youngest of the three, was medium height, thin, with brown greasy hair. He had several missing teeth. He did not appear too bright and could barely speak English. His crooked smile had a stream of discolored saliva dripping from the area of his vacant teeth.

The older man, Watkins, had a large nose, a small face and no chin. He had a noticeable scar in the shape of a "J" on the side of his face. Pike teased him saying his mother had given birth to a nose, and his body grew from the nose.

Unlike the other two, the leader was not referred to by name. He rarely spoke, except to give orders, and he sat away from the others. He spent most of his time reading from a pile of books that surrounded him. Joseph wondered what the leader's story was, was he a deserter?

Joseph was told to put on the boots that were on the ground near him. The boots were badly worn, barely being held together by the stitching. "These are not my boots," he nervously said.

Watkins, the man with the scar, stopped what he was doing. He grinned while he lifting one foot and asking Joseph, "Are these what you looking for?"

"Yes, those boots belong to me. May I have them back?"

"You be mistaken. These my boots."

Joseph got goose bumps at the sight of his boots, but tried to give the impression he didn't care.

A few nights later, Joseph was forced to go on one of their night rides. Nothing that gang of three was doing made any sense to Joseph until that night, when he learned they were criminals who raided peoples' homes.

The next day he thought less about the hidden map in the boots Watkins wore. His head was filled with images of the night ride. He learned the raids were on unsuspecting Loyalists or British sympathizers. Joseph was revolted by what these men were doing and he got physically ill from witnessing the inhumanities the three men inflicted on the families. When they returned from the raids, Joseph was once again forced to sit on the ground with both his wrists and ankles tightly bound with leather cord.

Joseph was unsure how much time had passed since he was kidnapped, but he did remember each raid distinctly. The third man would give Joseph orders to go into a house, wake the family and tell them to get out of the house or they would burn it. Then they told him to hold the family at gunpoint while the three rummaged through the family's belongings.

He noticed the third man never left a home without several books under his arm, and Watkins and Pike destroyed the inside, as if searching for valuables. The feral behavior of the gang seemed to be slowly killing Joseph's own sensibilities. Most shocking was that the three men had convinced themselves that they were doing reconnaissance for the revolution. They believed they were helping the cause for independence.

After Joseph became aware that the reason for his capture was to increase the gang of three to four, the threat of the men diminished. Joseph became a captive member of the group. He grew more depressed with each sadistic raid and it sickened him to see how these three men were convinced that their vandalizing, persecution and plundering of families were acts of glory and of courage.

⌁

At Harlem Heights, Colonel Barnes was anxious. Joseph had been gone for several days without any word from him. Finally, Barnes held a meeting with his two junior officers, Lieutenant Krumb and Lieutenant Worthmore, who had recommended Joseph for the scout position. The colonel explained that if Joseph's drop had not been completed, dozens of men fighting for the King would likely die.

During the meeting, it became clear to Barnes that Krumb was harboring doubts about Joseph. Krumb also appeared worried this would be a negative mark on his military record and thus delay any chance of promotion. He didn't seem too concerned for Joseph's wellbeing. Krumb became increasingly agitated, slammed his hand on the table and shouted, "Why did we put the lives of hundreds of soldiers in the hands of a mere fourteen-year-old farm boy!"

Colonel Barnes interrupted Krumb. "Understand this, Lieutenant Krumb, we can only hope the map and Joseph did not fall into rebel hands. In addition, as far as allowing a fourteen-year-old kid to carry out such important missions, well, perhaps, this is one area that we agree. I think, next time, you will be the best candidate for such a risky and important assignment!"

Krumb's mouth dropped open, panic spreading over his face, and he did not say a word.

That afternoon, Barnes secretly sent a scout to trace Joseph's steps. He was to listen to the local conversations and search for clues that might lead to finding him. The scout returned two days later empty-handed. Joseph had disappeared.

Three weeks passed and still no word from Joseph. Colonel Barnes had no choice but to list the boy as a deserter. Barnes had become fond of Joseph and doubted that Joseph had deserted. But the colonel had to follow regulations, which gave him the status of deserter.

Lieutenant Krumb was sure Joseph had become a double agent, collecting a princely sum for the map. Krumb told Colonel Barnes: "That yob is too smart to get caught. He doesn't fool me for one moment."

Colonel Barnes reluctantly wrote "Deserter" next to Joseph's name in the regiment log, and next to that, he wrote the date, March 1778.

During their next meeting, Lieutenant Worthmore was sympathetic to Barnes' estimation, and figured the kid could have had an accident; he could have fallen off his horse.

Krumb, in his effort to support his position, proclaimed, "Both the British and Continental armies are plagued with desertion. The number of men deserting on a monthly basis rivals the tally of the dead." Krumb paused. "It is not unusual for a soldier to give up and want to go home. When a knave deserts his comrades in arms, suspicion is aroused, fear and distrust shadows him and ..."

Barnes interrupted him. "Lieutenant, I think it best you stop right where you are. You are jumping to a conclusion for which you have no material evidence of support. As your superior, I advise you to watch carefully what you say! I can't emphasize enough, you best think long and hard before you say another word about Joseph Holmes."

Krumb sat and pouted, reacting as if he were being victimized.

Barnes at his lieutenants, saying in a stern voice, "Assessments of this disappearance should be saved for another time and place. Joseph could be in danger. His neck may be in a noose as we speak."

Lieutenant Krumb interjected, "But Sir, we need to explore the possibility that Joseph is engaged in counterespionage. We know Joseph certainly is bright and clever enough to handle it."

Barnes looked at his officers. "Lieutenant Worthmore, would you like to add anything?"

"Yes, sir, in fact, we might convince ourselves quite easily that Joseph is working for the other side. He's an ideal candidate for counterespionage."

Krumb added, "Joseph's young mind is very impressionable and his youthful appearance … maybe he was approached and took the bait."

Barnes was disgusted with his lieutenants. He briskly ended the meeting, turned his back and left the room.

Three weeks turned into six. Still no word from Joseph. In the regiment's logbook, Joseph remained classified as a deserter. In the mind of two lieutenants, Joseph might be worse than a deserter, he might be a counterspy. Colonel Barnes feared the worst for Joseph. He thought he had been taken hostage and beaten until he was willing to share information with the rebel army.

Chapter 7

March 1778: Bull's Head Tavern

Without his sons to help him on the farm, Jonathan Holmes' days were getting longer. After a tiring week in the fields, he made his regular Friday visit to Bull's Head Tavern. Visiting the tavern was a great way to learn about what was happening in both in Middle District and the colonies.

Jonathan read the printed press, but hearing the stories spreading from tavern to tavern gave events greater meaning. Traveling merchants from across the colonies shared their eyewitness accounts with eager listeners. Jonathan found some of the accounts so colorful and so unusual that he had to be alert to separate fact from fiction. Nonetheless, Middle District was a Loyalist stronghold and the majority of people living there were against the war. They felt war was not the way to solve the problems at hand.

When Jonathan entered the tavern that night, it was abuzz with conversation about the French. Jonathan saw expressions of concern. He walked up to the tavern keeper and asked for an ale. The keeper gave him a mug and one word, alliance. Jonathan found a bench near the hearth, sipped his ale and listened.

The rumor that an alliance had been formed between the rebel forces and the French thundered in Jonathan's head. He heard that such an alliance had been signed in early February. The idea of the French empire and the American rebels joining forces was gravely disheartening.

A plump, well-dressed gentleman sitting alone by the hearth looked at Jonathan. "While I was in Philadelphia," the man said, "the word on the street was that the treasury of the Continental Congress had been empty for at least a year."

"Don't you suppose that now the French will fill Washington's war chest and the gold will spill into the pockets of these self-appointed congressional officials in Philadelphia?" Jonathan was rarely sarcastic and he was surprised at his own remark.

The man nodded. "With the hard-fought French and Indian War, the British succeeded in reducing the French holdings in British North America. And now the tables have turned. With a pile of money and weapons, France's influence is stronger than ever."

Jonathan heard a young patron say: "Rebels are nothing more than anarchists. All thirteen colonies are out of control and rampant lawlessness prevails. Where is the law and order that we are due as subjects of the King? Where are those who are supposed to enforce the law?"

Talk at the tavern was heating up with arguments between hotly opinionated patrons. Jonathan watched as two men began to throw punches at each other. The altercation came to a speedy end and the room became quiet. He ordered another ale and tried to tune out the conversations around him.

Jonathan was troubled as he thought about his five sons who proudly wore the King's uniform. He visualized his two sons-in-laws, Nathaniel and Beach, fighting bravely as Continental soldiers under the command of General Washington. He asked himself how things became so complicated. He worried about how the war would change now that the French had come to the rescue of the Continental Army.

He recognized the help from France could not have arrived at a better time for the rebels. Word was, Washington's troops were hungry and they lacked proper clothing. Jonathan recalled that when the war started, the idea of an alliance between France and the rebels was not considered in the realm of possibility. Now it was an eye-opening reality. It would give the Continental Army a huge boost in manpower, weaponry, strategy, money and morale.

A tall, dark-haired man entered the Tavern. He sat across from Jonathan and was a familiar face. A leather merchant from south of Boston, the man stopped at Bull's Head when traveling between Boston and the Colony of New York.

The merchant ordered a mug of ale and after a sip or two, he got everyone's attention. "Would you believe my colony of Massachusetts is attempting to write a law that would force those loyal to the Crown to leave and never return. Simply pack their possessions and leave their homes and leave the colony. The rebel authorities call it the Banishment Act."

Another patron rolled his eyes and shook his head. "I find it hard to believe they are making laws to get rid of us. I have seen it all. These rebel authorities are trying to usurp the King, take control and, would you believe, they are more intolerant than the King himself."

The leather merchant continued: "The Massachusetts Colony is now securely in the hands of the revolutionaries. They continue to intensify their persecution of Loyalists living in that British colony."

Another man sitting across from Jonathan had this reaction: "In Boston, the rebels sound like they have already won the war and have replaced King George III with King George Washington the General."

That remark brought some much-needed laughter. The crowd was thinning as Jonathan swallowed another mouthful of ale. He decided to have a nightcap of a good Scottish whiskey before riding back home.

The tavern had become quieter when the leather merchant said everyone in Boston had to show allegiance to the rebellion. The merchant took a couple gulps of ale and noticed several stunned expressions. A few men got up and moved closer so they could hear what else the merchant had to say.

"If any man refuses to sign an allegiance to the rebellion, the man's entire family is run out; forced to leave their homes, their livestock, their businesses and their land. If they don't sign the allegiance, they will be classified as Loyalists. Their names are added to the list of traitors who will be banished from the colony!"

"I'm not saying that sounds too fantastic to be true," one patron said, "but I just can't imagine that happening."

As he rode home from the tavern, the news and events of the evening tumbled in Jonathan's head. It was alarming! He thought of words like banishment and alliance; they kept the fires of the revolution burning brightly. Jonathan's heart ached about the forced abandonment of family homesteads, farms and land.

Where were the rational thinkers? Where were the men who could solve problems through negotiation? Were these men the first to be run out of town? The rebels targeted anyone who aided the British, and the King's men would hang anyone who supported the rebellion. Jonathan shook his head. There was no winning for the common man on either side of the fighting.

చ్రా

One backbreaking month had passed since Jonathan Holmes last visited the Bull's Head Tavern. He tied his horse, walked in and said hello to the regulars. He ordered his usual ale and sat at his usual place near the hearth fire. There was just a small fire to take the chill off. It was early in the evening and not much of a crowd.

The tavern keeper grabbed Jonathan's attention. The keeper described what he called a "midnight raid" on Loyalist families in Connecticut. This was too close for comfort, Jonathan thought, as he listened to the story.

The tavern keeper said, "We are fortunate to be living in the British-controlled Colony of New York. There is tremendous power behind this weapon of terrorizing people in the middle of the night. This is unheard of!" The keeper stopped to serve several more ales, then he shook his head and said, "Terrorizing innocent people is a powerful weapon in the rebels' arsenal."

Jonathan drank his ale while he yearned for some good news. He listened to other patrons exchange opinions on what they termed propaganda being passed off as news in rebel-controlled publications.

An older planter, who rarely frequented the tavern said, "You know there is this journalist from England; he writes and produces provocative writings. For fear of retaliation, he is hesitant to list his name."

"Most likely, he is a coward," said the tavern keeper.

"Whether is he a coward or a hero of the written word, he is garnering the praise of many from all the colonies," said the planter. "I must say, this man has a talent for harnessing the word and attracting the people to Washington's side. I know it sounds amazing, but it is true." The planter paused, swallowed some ale and added, "If Mr. Washington is falling into another military crisis, this journalist emboldens the people with his writings."

Thinking this sounded familiar, Jonathan remembered that a year earlier Obadiah had several pages of a similar publication.

Jonathan passionately said to the men around him, "Simple rebel propaganda rallies the gangs who carry out night raids, empowers looters and gives encouragement to a 'mob rule' mentality." He hesitated before continuing. He could hardly believe what he had said. "I have to admit, I am more worried than ever about my family's future. If the war is lost, might this be the new normal, propaganda and persecution?" He paused, and no one uttered a word in response. "Gentlemen, the soldiers who are fighting for the right of freedom and the right of free speech are at the same time denying other men those same rights. Could someone explain that thinking to me?"

"Think of it," added the tavern keeper, "Americans who are Loyalists are barred from holding any office, forced to pay double the amount of taxes, and are barred from their professions, be it lawyer, teacher or physician."

"Yes, and any man with a different opinion is disenfranchised," said the planter.

Jonathan added, "If this is how we are being treated now, how might we be treated if they win the war?"

A chilling silence hung over the tavern room. It was clear to Jonathan that in the thick of this fighting, no one was considering that the rebel army could win.

As spring gave way to summer, the sharing of news at Bull's Head Tavern continued with vigor. The patrons learned that the mobs of men who were breaking down doors, confiscating gold and other valuables, burning barns and stealing horses called themselves Sons of Liberty.

One patron said, "Some groups of angry Loyalists carry out acts of horror against the innocent too."

Another interjected, "Well, it is about time we fight fire with fire."

"But," the first man said, "the only difference between the loyalist raids and the rebel raids are the sizable rewards placed on the heads of Loyalists who engage in this sort of scourge against the rebels."

Jonathan added, "When a law is not applied equally to all, when groups such as the Sons of Liberty have complete immunity and no consequence for their ruthless terror, this is not freedom, it is a charade."

"What have the revolutionaries done that has not been unlawful, oppressive or dictatorial?" sighed the tavern keeper.

It was then that a familiar tall, dark-haired gentleman from south of Boston entered the tavern. He looked tired and was not as well dressed as usual. He took a seat. The leather merchant gave voice to how many of them felt: little hope for the future.

"Almost my entire town is being banished," the gentleman said, "and we have but two weeks to arrange transport. I am here in New York to collect on some old accounts. I have been told I can no longer be a merchant of leather. Right now I simply question nothing and just want to get the hell out of this nightmare with my family in one piece."

Chapter 8

March 1778: Hooligans

As Joseph sat by the campfire, he heard Pike refer to the Sons of Liberty in reference to their gang. Joseph was familiar with that name. He recalled Colonel Barnes speaking about them during one of his debriefings. Barnes said that in the cover of night, these so-called Sons of Liberty would plunder Loyalist homes. Barnes referred to these groups as hooligans, bent on terrorizing innocent, non-combatants. Some things the colonel had said about the raiders dovetailed with what Joseph had experienced with the gang. Joseph was getting a better understanding of the gang, but he still had no answers to one big question. How do midnight raiders come to call themselves Sons of Liberty?

His captors referred to him as kid, kept him tied and dictated orders to him. With each new day came a new plan of terror. Joseph kept his ears open and listened. Eventually Joseph learned the leader went by the name of Poore.

Watkins reminded Joseph, "Poore likes things simple. You participate or die. Refusal means you be a traitor."

Poore stared at Joseph. "A traitor to the rebel cause is a traitor to the revolution. Double-crossers will be strung up!"

On many nights, Joseph woke up in a sweat, his heart beating quickly. He was worried about talking in his sleep. What if they found out that he was a soldier in service to the King? Just thinking about how he had spent the last year undercover as a scout for the King's army frightened him. He could feel the noose around his neck.

Neither Poore, Watkins nor Pike used his first name. In Joseph's eyes, the leader seemed to be a very unlikely person to keep company with the likes of the other two. Joseph saw a major disconnect between the literate, sometimes well-spoken leader and the two he bossed around.

Despite Poore's choice of companions, Joseph saw him as a fine-looking man: tall, fair-skinned and at times with a surprisingly gentle demeanor. He reminded Joseph of his older brothers. Poore would spend the entire day reading his ill-gotten collection of literature. He rarely spoke, except for an order or command directed at Pike and Watkins. Joseph noticed he handled his looted books with care and respect, just one of many anomalies in the young man. Poore was mysterious and Joseph was curious.

From the beginning, Joseph noticed that Poore seemed to be plagued with obsessions, be it rage, reading or raiding. He never hesitated to display his bitterness and his scorn on his nighttime forays to the homes of sleeping Tories. As for reading, the topics of Poore's books were impressive; he appeared to have a desire to learn about a variety of things. He read books about history and government, Greek Mythology, the wars of ancient Greece, the downfall of the Roman Empire and sciences and philosophy. Joseph wondered how Poore ended up like this.

✍

From the moment Joseph was abducted, two thoughts dominated his mind. The first was to escape and the second was to destroy the map in the heel of his boot, which Watkins was wearing. Joseph thought that the only possible time he could escape would be during a raid. But that idea eroded early on because Poore kept Joseph within reach. Poore carried a loaded musket and a pistol, and he would put a ball through Joseph's head if he attempted to run for it.

Joseph was frightfully aware that any escape attempt would have to be successful and there would be no room for error. If Pike, Watkins or Poore caught him trying to run, they would surely kill him. Joseph figured he should not even try to escape until he burned the covert message in the heel of boot worn by Watkins. He could not take the risk that they might find the secret compartment.

As his captivity dragged on, Joseph's inquisitive nature remained constant. His interest in Poore seemed to be keeping him sane and from dwelling on his own misery. He mused about his captor and was curious about his surname. Poore was his mother's maiden name and the name of

Dutch descendants living in the British colonies. He doubted, though, that he was kin to this self-proclaimed rebel.

Joseph had an idea. He would ask Poore a question once he was alone with him. The two others, Pike and Watson, often went to town to run errands, haunt pubs, or sell the horses they had just stolen. Once the opportunity was right, Joseph would ask Poore a question, hoping to learn something about the strange situation he found himself in.

⟲⟳

An early morning noise woke Joseph. It was Watkins's voice. He saw Watkins near the campfire, poking it with a stick, trying to keep the fire burning. The coffee pot, hanging over the fire, was coming to a boil. Joseph lay in his bed roll, eyes closed, wishing he was somewhere else, anywhere else. He was discouraged, fearing he would never have the opportunity to escape. In his gloom, he heard Pike and Watkins talk about going into town; it sounded as if they would leave soon. Hearing that they would be leaving meant Joseph might have his chance to ask Poore a question.

Before leaving, Pike placed some coffee on the ground next to Joseph's bedroll. Joseph appeared to be asleep. A somber quiet enveloped the camp. Joseph sat up and drank his coffee while watching Poore, who was sitting by the campfire. Poore stood and walked to where he spent much of his time reading.

His back to Joseph, Poore lifted the lid of a wooden chest he had taken from his knapsack. With his hands and feet bound by rope, Joseph shifted as much as he could to see what Poore was doing. His view was dazzling! He could see the brilliance of gold coins, gold jewelry and precious stones emanating from the chest. Joseph rubbed his eyes in disbelief. He has never seen so much gold in one place at one time.

Poore's fingers reached for the bottom of the chest. Under the coins, gems and jewelry, he retrieved a blue silk bag. He held the silk bag to his cheek then brought it to his nose, to sniff it. To Poore, the bag provided relief from his torment. The bag and its contents, letters from his mother, were his most cherished possessions. The bag was a womb that protected his mother's wishes and love for him.

The letters inside the bag told him a story he never tired reading. A beautifully written narrative from a mother to her son. The letters were the only remembrance he had of his mother. Memories needed for sustenance and solace. When Poore read the letters, his world changed, his pain vanished, if only for a fleeting moment. He would think of how different his life might have been if only his mother hadn't killed herself.

"If only," he said to himself. The sound of those words made him want to seek revenge for his mother's death. He wanted to cry out, loud enough for all to hear. Once he began to read his mother's words, he would hold each word deep inside as if holding his breath not wanting to exhale. He could empathize with her. He too had monumental struggles, although perhaps not as difficult as hers. He too often didn't think life was worth the anguish.

Poore shook his head vigorously, trying to rid himself of the image of his mother's assault. If he ever found the man who destroyed his mother, he would kill him. He closed his eyes, then gently returned the silk bag to his nose. Again he breathed what must have been his mother's fragrance. He had been stunned when he first realized he didn't know where his mother was buried. So much about her was a mystery to him.

Poore again reached into the silk bag, locating a simple band of gold. He sat there, with no expression, simply turning and tumbling the gold band between his fingers.

Poore was unaware he was being watched, his actions studied, and Joseph was astounded to have feelings of empathy for his captor. This man had turned Joseph's life into a living hell. Nonetheless, Joseph realized Poore was in some sort of hell himself. Joseph thought it was time to ask Poore a question. Hesitant, he mustered his voice, but as he heard himself speak, he was not asking the question he wanted to ask. Joseph was asking Poore something altogether different.

"Your mother's wedding ring?"

There was a long, empty silence, Joseph was nervous. That was not the question!

The eerie silence lingered, Joseph's breathing slowed and his heart began to thump. The silence continued.

Then Poore ever so slowly turned his head toward Joseph, his face red and twisted, his eyes like those of a hideous monster, veins protruding in his neck. He sneered and sputtered a flood of malicious expletives. Then, like a huge bull frog, he sprang over the campfire and jumped on Joseph, wrapping his hands around Joseph's neck, squeezing his throat.

Poore yelled, "Kid, you shut your damn mouth, you low-life Tory."

Joseph felt he was about to breathe his last breath.

Poore continued to tighten his hands around Joseph neck. "You best never, ever mention my mother again!" Poore repeated those words while he held Joseph's throat tighter and tighter. Joseph gasped for air. With his hands and feet bound, Joseph could not push Poore away or defend himself. Abruptly Poore loosened his grip and drew back. Joseph's eyes were closed; he lay there, almost too weak to gasp for breath.

Without another word, Poore returned to his position at the campfire. Joseph began coughing and gasping for air, his body weak and trembling. He could not figure out what had happened; he was shocked. The silence that again hung under the forest canopy was broken only by Joseph's coughing and gasping for air.

Then came the haunting words from Poore's mouth, "You little creep, I know who you are. I knew from the moment I saw your bloody face. You look like everyone else in your traitor family. You're a Holmes!" Poore took a deep breath. "You think you are something special, like the rest of them!" Poore dropped his voice and whispered with an edge, "You and your pathetic family and your farmhouse on the hill, you disgust me. You and your brothers are worthless good-for-nothing Tories."

Joseph was trembling, grasping for answers. He tried to work through his confusion. No matter how hard he tried, he couldn't. He began to break down into tears. Joseph heard Poore describe his home and his family. How on earth did he know who he was? Poore sat huddled near the dying embers of the fire. Lifting his head, he faced Joseph. Poore calmed himself, and once composed he walked over to where Joseph lay in his bedroll. Soaked with sweat, Joseph feared Poore had a pistol, and maybe this was the end.

Then Poore cleared his throat. "You blood-sucking lover of the Crown, I am Salem Poore." He calmly articulated each word, each syllable. "I am your bastard cousin."

Poore took a deep breath and continued, "Of all the fools to kidnap, those two losers kidnap you. You! I'm cursed!"

Joseph sat in his bedroll without expression.

Poore lowered his voice, "Did you hear my name? Would you like me to repeat it for you? I said ... Salem Poore, I am your bastard cousin. Your family never made even the slightest effort to find me as if I was dead. Your mother never made an effort to find her sister's only child."

As Poore spoke, his face assumed an almost demonic glow. He began to laugh, softly at first, then louder. As it grew louder, the more insidious it sounded.

Trembling, Joseph couldn't take his eyes off the large bear knife Poore always had strapped on his waist. Joseph wished Poore would just kill him. Joseph was stupefied, unable to find his own voice. He couldn't believe what he had just heard. He couldn't get beyond the word cousin.

Several hours passed, during which Joseph, with his wrists and ankles tied, fell into a restless sleep.

Joseph woke as if startled from a bad dream. He had an urgent need to speak. "You are Sa- ... Salem?" The phrase rang loudly in his mind. You are Salem? You are Salem? The three words seemed to echo through the labyrinth in which Joseph was imprisoned.

Poore casually looked up from his latest book. "You ask if I am Salem? No, I am Commander George Washington, you ignorant excuse of a traitor!"

Salem's sarcasm was unnerving. Joseph trembled, not knowing what might ignite Salem's irrational state of mind. He lay still and his mind raced, his heart pounding. Joseph struggled to think back to when he was at home. He tried to recall if he had ever heard Salem's name mentioned. He knew his Aunt Virginia was buried in the family cemetery plot. Joseph was not mindful of having a cousin. A distant recollection surged into his mind, a vague memory of his mother saying the boys had a cousin. It must be a mistake. How could this demented man be his cousin?

❧

On Salem's thirteenth birthday, his adoptive mother, Mrs. Gates, decided it was time for him to read the letters his mother had left for him. His bright blue eyes widened when she handed him the blue silk bag. The bag felt soft like a mother's hand. It had a scent, a wildflower fragrance that seemed vaguely familiar, a dormant memory of his mother. Was it her perfume or her soap, maybe lavender?

Mrs. Gates sat next to Salem while he read the letters. At that moment, perhaps for the first time, Salem felt all things seemed more complete in his world. He had an aunt, an uncle and cousins.

An affectionate woman with much love for the boy, Mrs. Gates told him how his mother had died, and large teardrops rolled down his face. Mrs. Gates put her arm around his shoulder and kissed him on the top of his head.

Mrs. Gates was the only mother he had ever known. She was a good person in spite of a quick temper. Salem, who was punished sternly, but not often, quickly learned right from wrong. He was clever, hardworking and an active lad. Salem's curiosity and energy were a challenge for his parents, who were old enough to be his grandparents.

Typical of most lads his age, Salem's curiosity placed him in precarious situations. Once, he got his hands on a tinderbox and almost burned down the Gates' barn. On another occasion, he climbed onto the roof of the house and into the chimney, getting stuck. That led to a whipping and a scolding about stupidity.

When not occupied with his farm chores, he spent much of his time working on puzzles. He even began creating his own, pushing himself to find solutions. He soon learned that life was the most bewildering puzzle of all.

One of his puzzles was his mother, Virginia. This puzzle had many pieces, some of which he knew nothing about. Her letters had limited information. He knew she had a sister with the last name of Holmes and she lived in Middle District. He searched and located the Holmes farm in Middle District.

Salem and his horse would disappear from the Gates home for hours at a time but they knew he would return at the dinner hour. Initially he was pleased, almost joyous, to discover that he had family and excitedly watched the activity at the farm. Sometimes he would stop his horse at the edge of the long drive leading to the farmhouse with the blossoming front yard and well-maintained barn, stables and milk house. Salem sat on his horse under the shade of large oaks watching the Holmes boys work and horse around.

Salem was captivated with the antics and activities of his cousins. He would watch them for an hour or two. As he watched them, he would smile and laugh to himself as if he was taking part in the fun. However, he never approached the Holmes family and he was not sure why. Perhaps he was too shy.

Time eventually altered Salem's impression of the Holmes family. His curiosity for the apparent charmed life of his cousins changed to feelings of rejection. He wondered why his aunt had never tried to find him. It seemed odd that they did not want to include him in their family. Maybe they blamed him for his mother's death and her torment and sadness. His thoughts were beginning to poison his mind. His desire to watch the family became increasingly rare and he spent less and less time observing his cousins. On the other hand, his cousins did not know that he was adopted and that his mother had taken her own life because she had been raped and beaten by a British merchant.

Mr. and Mrs. Gates gave Salem a good home and a good life, but it all came to an abrupt end in the spring of 1772 when they died in a carriage accident. Their horse spooked, reared and ran, pulling the carriage off to the edge of the road. The carriage wheel hit an old stump that flipped it over, killing Mr. and Mrs. Gates.

Salem was thirteen, and that night he sat alone for hours, just staring at the door. He hoped that his mother and father would walk through the door to tell him that it was all a mistake. But it was not a mistake and he sat alone crying.

In the aftermath, as the days turned into weeks, Salem's grief clouded with bitterness, anxiety and an anguish that began to consume him. As he saw himself as wretched and unloved, his thoughts of abandonment tormented him. He feared he was truly a bad seed that brought devastation to his mother, the Gates, and now himself. Salem believed that being conceived of rape made him a bad soul, and that perhaps it was he who shamed his mother and caused her death.

Bad fortune continued. The Gates farm was the only place he had known and loved; it was home to good memories, and now the British bank was stealing that from him. Salem knew Mr. Gates had mortgaged the farm to buy seed for planting. He did that each spring and would immediately pay the loan in full after the harvest when the crop was sold. Salem, wanting to keep his homestead, had gone to the bank to negotiate, asking them to put the loan in his name and let him plant the crop. The British bank heard his story and simply denied his request. Later, Salem learned that the British Bank was reducing its debt in the colonies because they could see the possibility of rebellion.

Salem had lost all hope. The bank took the house, barn and acreage for auction. Before the auction began, Salem rode his horse down by the river, the same river that had taken his mother. He stared into the brisk running water where his mother had found comfort. He got off his horse and his blue eyes followed the shoreline to where, in the sand, a beam of sunlight caught a cluster of white flowers. They were a breath of peacefulness and he inhaled the flowers' beauty as he walked to them. He bent down and picked three. The aroma of his modest bouquet smelled clean and full of innocence.

He tossed the bouquet into the river, watching while it gracefully made a soft landing on the fast-flowing water. He continued his gaze as the strong current carried the fragile beauties over rocks and around fallen branches. They flowed onward, twisting and turning with the rushing waters. One separated itself, settling in a still, shallow pool. He shut his eyelids tightly. He was holding back his sadness, his own river of tears, when suddenly they flowed out of control. His cries were loud and full of grief, bewilderment and anger. He was beginning to understand the hopelessness his mother must have felt when she abandoned life, seeking her own solace in the river. But, that choice was not for him.

While watching the water, he had an epiphany, a startling realization. None of this was his fault. But who was to blame? The answer to that question was the bloody British! He would make his enemies pay for their malice. He had suffered and lost everything at the hands of the British merchant, the British bankers, the Tories and the Crown. He despised them and their cruelty, greed and arrogance.

The property auction was scheduled for April. The auctioneer was a small man with a big voice. Salem, confused and in disbelief, gazed at the faces gathered for the bidding. First, some of the house furnishings were put up for bid. Bids were shouted out as the dining table, chairs, and hutch were sold. At that very table, he had first read his mother's letters. At that table, he first learned about his mother's fate and it was there he learned to read, write and make puzzles. Bids were yelled out for the beds, carpets, and wooden crates full of leather and bark bonded books. Then, out came two men carrying Mr. Gates' large walnut wardrobe. Next were Mrs. Gates' fine Irish linens, dishes, silverware, and pottery.

Everything was gone with the bang of a gavel. Farm tools, the plow and livestock, all sold. He continued to watch, forcing himself and hoping he might overcome the torment he felt. Everything was given a monetary value and carried off, similar to Mr. and Mrs. Gates who were taken away, never to return. Item by item, wooden boxes were filled with hand tools. The carnivorous crowd of scavengers swallowed everything. Piece by piece, the few items on this earth that had provided him comfort, sold to the highest bidder.

The only thing that remained was his adopted mother's thin, gold wedding band. The ring found a home with his real mother's letters in the blue silk bag. Finally, for the last time, the gavel sounded for the acreage, barn, house and outbuildings. When all was sold and the auction done, Salem thought the British Bank had recouped their supposed losses tenfold.

Salem tried to shield himself from his pain by reading, hoping his mind would be captured by a faraway place. Extremely well read, he especially liked the topic of disputes between the colonies and the King. With his knowledge grew enthusiasm for rebellion against the hated Crown. His misfortune and loss, along with grief and bitterness put Salem on a path of self-destruction. He felt tormented and, afflicted by the loss of everyone who had ever loved him. His books were his only companion.

Salem got used to living in various towns and sleeping wherever he found an empty barn. His self-reliance was strong, but he hated living with himself and he forbad himself feelings of happiness. He was living for survival and he became restless and incorrigible. Ironically, Salem had found himself going in a similar direction as the British colonies. Like the colonies, he had become defiant, challenging authority and the laws. He taught himself about anarchy and the monarchy. He directed his hate at those in positions of authority, such the Crown and bankers. He had molded himself into a cruel, cold and calculating young man. He knew those traits were his best protection.

At about this time, in the spring of 1773, Salem rode back to the Holmes farm. He halted his horse in his usual spot under the oaks. He tried to imagine his cousins, aunt and uncle welcoming him into their family and he envisioned that he was one of them. He wondered what it would be like, to be raised in such a caring, happy and shameless family. He was asking himself the same questions over and over. Why did his mother give him up? Why didn't she give him to her sister? Did his mother think he would bring the Holmes family bad luck? Salem believed that the Holmes family was deeply ashamed of him being a bastard. His torment grew like a vine around his neck, choking him of rational thought.

Suddenly jolted, he felt hunger rolling in his stomach. Hunger was a harsh reminder of his circumstance. Here he was with his horse, at the foot of a hill gazing at his cousins cleaning up for the dinner and he could not remember how he got there or the last time he ate a meal. He dropped his eyes to the patches on his breeches. Patches and hunger, grim reminders of his unfortunate existence.

A couple of his cousins appearing to be his age were finishing their chores and putting their tools away for the day. He got off his horse and gradually walked up the drive to get a closer look. He noticed a couple of his cousins resembled him; same tall build, light hair and coloring. The closer he walked to them the more he coveted who they were and what they had. Suddenly, their playfulness and happiness made him ill. He climbed on his horse and began to ride away.

A severe stomach pain began to well up inside him. He began to have trouble breathing and felt he was going to suffocate. Salem slowly got off his horse and leaned his weary body against the rough bark of a large oak. Stretching both arms around the tree, he began to cry and became nauseous. Light headed and weak, he turned and slid to the ground and fell into a deep sleep while his horse stood by.

When he woke, it was gloaming; it would soon be dark. His eyes saw his boots were covered in vomit. The sight caused him to retch, all the while he imagined he heard shouts and laughter coming from his cousins' home. With the taste of bile in his mouth, he took one last look at the Holmes farm, vowing never to return.

By 1777, not much had changed for Salem. He continued to sleep in vacant barns or in the woods. He had an obsession to read about the many ways the British bullied the colonies. He could not fathom how anyone could stay loyal to such a dictatorial monarch.

He read booklets that denounced the Crown and encouraged rebellion. He was beginning to feel he had a purpose to his life. Meanwhile, as discontent grew in the minds of many colonists, Salem felt an odd comfort and embraced an increasing sense of control. He wanted to get involved in the excitement. He wanted to be a part of the action, but not on the battlefield. He would not enlist in the Continental Army. No one would give him orders; he was too smart for that. Salem had his own idea of what he would be willing to do to support the rebellion.

Salem believed the British were responsible for all the terrible and tragic events in his life. He also held the Crown responsible for him being a bastard child. Salem was the son of no one and this was the fault of the Crown. Revenge would be his weapon of choice. Someone was going to pay for all he had lost.

Salem cleverly dodged recruitment for the war. He became adept at harnessing his gall into acts of violence. Now in his late teens, he pledged himself to the cause of terrorizing families as a Son of Liberty. He would lead a band of men on night raids, putting horror and pain into the hearts of those families who supported the King and those families who would not state their allegiance to the revolution.

The Sons of Liberty groups were growing in number in each of the thirteen colonies. Salem, like many others had found his purpose. He soon formed his own small group. Their mission was simple; he and his men would plan and incite terror.

Salem idealized many of the masterful Bostonians who had bridled the written word. He admired Samuel Adams, the father of the Sons of Liberty, the conductor of mob rule. Adams, a Harvard graduate, had a keen gift, an ability to arouse and inspire the masses with the written word. Salem found terrorizing intoxicating; he wanted to be a player so he could fill his pockets while taking revenge on everything British.

He had no interest in fighting on the blood-stained battlefields. Cowardly, perhaps, but that was not how he saw it. He saw it as a spark of genius. Why get killed when he could line his pockets by being clever?

Salem masked his cowardly, narcissistic self as a Son of Liberty, a son of Samuel Adams. He finally settled on the well-paid, duty of terrorizing innocent men, women and children. He got his jollies from menacing wives and daughters, although, because of the memory of his mother, he would not physically violate them in any way. He would just frighten them and rob them. Being a Son of Liberty was Salem's answer and avenue to correct all the wrongs he suffered and get back his financial losses. Most satisfying for him was being a son, a son of somebody as revered as Sam Adams, father of the Sons of Liberty.

Chapter 9

May 1778: Tar and Feathers

The evening raid began as Poore had hoped. While the others took Mr. Weeks out of the house, Poore was delighted to find gold coins hidden in his bedroom. The bulk of the gold was in a couple of small bags and Poore stuffed them into his shirt. He had targeted the Weeks family because Weeks sold horses to the British troops. Poore aimed to persuade Weeks to donate his horses to the Continental Army."

To that end, Poore went outside to the front of the house, where Weeks stood, naked. Poore stuck the barrel of his pistol in Joseph's gut and told him to watch. Joseph had been bracing for what was about to happen since that morning, when he began to smell a hideous odor, the pungent smell of pine tar cooking in a large cast iron pot hanging over their campfire. It became clear what was planned when Watkins and Pike returned from town with a cloth sack filled with brown chicken feathers.

As Pike began dumping the hot tar over Weeks' body, Joseph was unable to block out the man's screams of pain. He was sickened by the cruelty.

The plan was to force Weeks' two daughters to cover him in feathers. Poore turned around looking for Watkins and the daughters. Where the hell were they?

Watkins was still in the back of the house. He had his hands full with the daughters. Both girls were hysterical. They were unable to stop crying as they clung to each other. Watkins grabbed and shook the younger girl, telling her to shut up. He slapped her across the face, shoved her to the ground and told her that if she said one more word, he would kill her sister. He then grabbed the older daughter with one hand, pushed her to the ground and slid his other hand under her nightgown. He got on top of her while she struggled to get loose. The more she resisted, the more aroused Watkins became, making him even more determined to have his way with her. Watkins had been eager to "take care" of the two girls since he had seen them shopping in town a month earlier."

Suddenly, the younger girl got to her feet and began to pull Watkins off her sister. Half crazed with sexual desire, he shoved the younger sister with all his might. She flew backward, and as she fell, her head hit a stone wall, stunning her. Watkins returned his focus to the older sister. He was unable to penetrate her because her nightgown was in the way and she continued to fight him, giving him a knee to his crotch. Poore heard the screams and ran to the back, getting a glimpse of the scene. He saw one girl on the ground near a wall of stones. Watkins, with his breeches down around his knees, was screaming bloody murder while covering his privates with his hands.

Poore, angered and sickened by what he saw, knelt by the younger sister. She was bleeding from where she hit her head. Poore then turned to the older daughter. Rage overcame him. Without a word, he grabbed Watkins by the shirt and dragged him around to the front, his breeches still dragging. Poore shoved Watkins' head into the almost empty pot of tar, then poured the last of the tar over Watkins' genitals. Weeks was still moaning on the ground.

Poore, once finished with Watkins, told Pike and Joseph to load some books and silver into their saddle-bags. He then went back to the older daughter. Poore tried to calm her but she fought him off, thinking he was Watkins.

He whispered, "I am very sorry he violated you and injured your sister."

The girl, in shock, was barely able to reply. "The monster was raping me!"

Poore looked into the girl's eyes. "I promise you, this man will be punished for what he did to you and your sister. I will make sure of it; he will pay with his life."

Joseph and Pike quickly packed up the books and silver. Joseph brought blankets for the two girls and helped them back into the house. Within minutes, Poore, Pike and Joseph mounted their horses and rode off, leaving Watkins to follow them later.

⁊◌

It had been four nights since the Weeks raid. Joseph awoke, put his arms up and stretched. Joseph no longer had his hands or feet tied up. He wasn't sure why. In his captivity, he had become accustomed to having his hands and feet tightly bound with rope, then rawhide, leaving his ankles and wrists bruised, cut and bleeding. With his new freedom of movement, he had an odd sense of gratefulness toward his captors.

For several days, both Pike and Watkins had been set out on errands, separately and together. The day after the raid at the Weeks home, Poore was busy writing a letter. Once he finished writing, he sealed it with blue wax and directed Pike to deliver it. Joseph had never seen Poore write and post a letter before that.

Poore gave Pike and Watkins each a list of tasks. Pike's list were all focused around the camp. Watkins's errand would take him to the Colony of Connecticut where he was to deliver a few gold coins to support the Connecticut rebel militia. Pike, green with envy, grumbled about how he would like to go on such an important delivery. As Watkins mounted his horse, Pike jealously ignored him.

Joseph thought it odd that four nights had passed and nothing had been said about the tragic night at the Weeks home. Nothing, not one word. Joseph hoped Poore would do something about it. If Poore didn't, Joseph would, once he escaped. He would report the abuses and the abuser. From Joseph's vantage point, Watkins was handed an important job to carry gold coins to the town of Danbury for the rebel army. It is not like Poore to send Watkins on an errand with a good amount of money in his pocket. Something didn't make sense, but who was he to question Poore's directives.

It hardly seemed possible but Poore had become quieter since the raid. He hardly said a word. He wasn't reading much either, and Joseph wondered if it had something to do with Watkins' assault on the two girls and if this was why they no longer tied him up.

Joseph approached Poore, "Is there anything I can do? Brush down the horses or clean the saddles?"

Poore barely acknowledged Joseph before answering, "Yeah, kid, go care for the horses."

That entire day, Poore attempted to read from his piles of books, but he wasn't able to concentrate. He appeared to be huddled in a shell, where he could be alone.

By nightfall, Pike was puzzled. He was walking around, almost pacing. "Watkins should be back."

Poore, as usual, ignored him.

The next morning, Joseph opened his eyes and saw Pike sitting by the fire sipping coffee with a worried look.

When Pike saw Joseph was awake, he asked, "Should Watkins be back?" Pike lowered his voice to a whisper, "I think Watkins split. He found a ship and going to some island with his gold. He ran for it to get far from this war." Pike was biting his fingernails while nervously pacing.

Joseph shrugged his shoulders and turned away,

Pike's mind was beginning to spin with possibilities about what had happened to Watkins. He followed Joseph saying, "Maybe with that gold in his pocket he made for the closest tavern or maybe he join a ship of pirates. Or pirates kidnap him!

Joseph, fed up with Pike, and said, "Would you please be quiet. Seriously, I don't care if Watkins is gone and I don't care why. He attacked those young girls. There is only one place he should be, and that's at the end of a rope."

A couple more days passed and still no Watkins. Poore did not seem at all alarmed but then not much bothered Poore. One afternoon two men on horseback rode into camp. The strangers were not dressed in uniform, and from watching their mannerisms and the way they talked, Joseph thought they were spies for the Continental Army. Joseph listened while pretending to be reading, trying not to be noticed.

One of the men told Poore, "This man, name I don't know, was stopped by a rebel patrol along the Kings Highway near the Colony of Connecticut. They were searching for British spies. The patrol had received word that a man fitting the description was on his way to Danbury."

Poore listened casually, while showing no emotional response.

The man continued, "As I said, the man was stopped and the soldiers had to forcefully take him off his horse. He refused to cooperate, laughing at our command to dismount. A skirmish with the man followed. We pulled him off his horse, he got his boot caught in his stirrup and the heel fell off. Not only did he fit the description of a man we were warned about, but the guards noticed his boot heel carried strategic troop movement information, which he was going to give to the British. He was carrying a map in the heel." Poore showed no reaction, just listened. The man paused. Joseph glanced at Pike, who was biting his fingernails, fright written over his face.

"With that discovery," the man said, "he was immediately accused of being a traitor to the rebellion."

Pike gasped loudly. The two men on horseback turned to look at Pike.

Pike, shuddered as he said, "Are ya kidding, a spy? That crazy talk." Pike then slapped his hand over his mouth and timidly responded in a muffled tone, "I am sorry."

The men returned their focused to Poore. "He claimed to know you. The way he spoke, he sounds simple or stupid. He might have been putting on a fool's act for us, and you, while he spied for the British!"

Poore nodded, then asked the men, "Since you don't know his name, could you describe him to me? Did he have any scars?"

"Why yes, he had a scare on his face, shaped like the letter J."

Pike's jaw dropped. Joseph listened carefully and put the pieces together. Joseph thought, how clever of Poore!

Joseph now knew why Poore had written the letter for Pike to deliver; it was a tip-off to the rebel patrol. Poore had orchestrated the pick-up of Watkins as a spy.

Before the two horsemen left the campsite, one of them said, "Oh, yes, the guy was hanged within a couple hours of being stopped. We can't waste our time with trials and he carried the look of guilt all over him, but the map was the key piece of evidence."

The second man asked, "If you don't have any questions, Mr. Poore, we will be on our way."

"Wait, in fact I do have a question for you. Do you suppose I may have other spies in my employ?"

Joseph nearly fainted when he heard Poore ask that question.

And Pike yelled out, "Not me, no spy, nope, not me!"

"Mr Poore, we are familiar with your support of the rebellion and appreciate your large donations to the war widows fund." The men told Poore that any money found on Watkins was given to the Continental coffers and his horse was given to the cause as well.

"The boots," Poore asked, "what happened to the boots?"

"Oh, yes, we have the man's boots."

The horsemen left the camp. A silence remained, Pike was biting his fingernails, trembling from both shock of what happened to his friend and fear it could happen to him. Joseph just sat there, acting as if nothing was out of the ordinary. But on the inside he too was full of fear! His mind was swirling. He was done, his cover was broken. The damn boots. Poore knew that Watkins was wearing his boots and he must realize that the map was concealed in his heel. Joseph thought perhaps Poore had known all along. He shivered to think Poore knew he was s spy. Joseph was feeling anxious as he fretted with the hemp cord that held up his breeches. Joseph was determined to look stoic, trying to conceal his utter fright.

With no emotion in his voice, Poore said, "Kid, find something to do."

Joseph feared Poore would see to it that he was the next to be caught by a rebel patrol.

Poore was relieved. He stood up, then stretched as he walked back to the pile of books that were stacked a dozen high alongside his bedroll. Poore was satisfied with the news, but he did not know what they meant about a map. Perhaps it was something the patrol fabricated to have a reason to hang the bastard. But then, Poore thought to himself, weren't the boots that Watkins wore once Joseph's? He thought about it some more, then dismissed any idea that the kid was a spy. He likely stole the boots, or got the wrong boots back from the cobbler after a repair. Poore was only focused on Watkins paying for his crimes against those two girls.

Joseph got busy finding kindling. As he carefully stacked the twigs and branches near the campfire, he could not help but feel leery of what might happen next. He could imagine Poore walking over to him with his pistol in his hand and shooting him at point-blank range. Joseph's mind flowed with "what ifs." That night, once everyone was asleep, he would make his escape. He needed to leave now more than ever. He must get back to Colonel Barnes, back to Harlem Heights. His life was in greater danger than ever before.

Joseph, pretending to be asleep, listened to Poore and Pike, who were sleeping soundly. Joseph very slowly slid out of his bedroll and once on his feet he began to walk toward his horse. He rubbed his wrists as he walked. They were still tender from the open sores caused by the rawhide. He saddled his horse and turned to be sure Poore and Pike were still sleeping. Once Joseph cinched the saddle belt around Red's belly, he lifted himself into the saddle. He heard a shout and without glancing back, Joseph raced out of camp.

Hearing Pike shout, Poore woke up. They both listened to the fading sound of pounding hooves. Poore, confused, saw Joseph's empty bedroll. He shook his head in disgust and lay back down on the cool earth. Under his breath he said, "It is a damn mean world out there. Take care of yourself, cousin."

Joseph rode feverishly without even a backward glance. He kept his face forward, not wanting to check whether Pike was on his tail. He kept repeating to himself, "No looking back, no looking back." He hunched down close to his saddle and rode countless miles in a southerly direction. He led Red off the main dirt road to take shortcuts through fields. He followed shallow brooks or steams so he could not be tracked on his way back to Harlem Heights.

With each gallop, his heart began to beat regular again and slowly his body began to relax. He was feeling free and a sense of relief swept his mind and body. Each gallop put more time and distance between him and the macabre encounter with his troublesome cousin, Salem Poore.. Spending several weeks with Salem Poore had left him with questions that he hoped someday to answer.

Chapter 10

May 1778: Interrogation

Joseph rode south, into the moist haze of the early morning hours. He and his horse, Red, were thirsty, hungry and exhausted, but confident those concerns would be attended to very soon. As Joseph approached the British encampment at Harlem Heights, he felt a monumental sense of relief, safe at last. The sight of the guard post, at the entrance to the camp, relaxed his tense muscles. He could see the tops the tents and the smoke from early morning campfires. Harlem Heights was the most pleasant image he had seen in weeks.

He rode to the guard post where three British guards stood with muskets, bayonets and pistols. One guard greeted him with a stern tone directing him to halt and dismount. Joseph promptly did just as he was ordered, and then the guards patted him down. That was new to Joseph; he awkwardly submitted.

"Identification please," the guard said.

With some hesitance in his voice, Joseph replied, "My identification? No, uh, sir, I do not carry any identification. I am instructed not to carry it with me." Joseph noticed the look on the guards' faces. "Colonel Barnes will verify my identity."

"I want your identification, not a long-winded explanation."

The other guard asked Joseph, "What is your name?"

Joseph responded with his name. That same guard turned and walked to the command post.

It was then that Joseph noticed he was being held at gunpoint. He just stood there with a slight smile, confident that any confusion would be cleared up in a matter of minutes. The wait for the guard's return grew longer. This was the first time Joseph had a problem getting past the guards. He was beginning to feel uncomfortable, something was not right. Still at gunpoint, he continued to stand at the entrance of the British encampment, waiting for the other guard to return, hopefully with Colonel Barnes.

He grew more uneasy, he had just escaped from a rebel gang's captivity and now he was being held at gunpoint. Nothing was making much sense to Joseph. He trusted Colonel Barnes to clear up any issues about his identity. But, what was taking so long? To his relief, Joseph saw an officer walking toward him. He noticed it was not Colonel Barnes, but a junior officer he did not recognize.

The officer introduced himself as Lieutenant Worthmore. Joseph barely remembered a Worthmore, but promptly stood at attention.

Joseph did not let the officer say one word, "Lieutenant, I need to see Colonel Barnes."

The lieutenant was obviously irritated by the question and ignored him.

Joseph made his request again and the officer replied with an impatient smirk. "Young man, at the moment Colonel Barnes is not available."

The lieutenant looked at the guards, then at Joseph. "I understand you want to enter the encampment without any identification. What is your name?"

"I am Private Joseph Holmes, sir."

Lieutenant Worthmore replied, "Is that so, you say Joseph Holmes. Young man, we have questions for you."

Joseph, hungry and tired, thought the lieutenant was referring to his normal debriefings.

"Sir, I have my debriefings with Colonel Barnes."

"Mr. Holmes, I would advise you to stop whining to me. This is not going to be a debriefing; it will be an interrogation. We need answers to questions about your long absence."

Joseph stood in disbelief as Lieutenant Worthmore told him he was under arrest. Joseph couldn't believe his ears. Trying hard not to show his irritability and shock, he asked, "Sir, with what crime do you charge me?"

Worthmore, getting red in the face, impatiently replied, "Holmes, you don't ask the questions, I do. In due time, the charges against you will be noted. For the time being, you are charged with desertion."

"How could that be? I was kidnapped!"

"What?" Worthmore laughed. "You will remain in custody, during which time you will be interrogated and your superiors with decide your guilt or innocence. Holmes, let me warn you of the seriousness of your long absence."

Joseph impatiently said, "Sir, I am in great need of food and water, I have been. ..."

The officer ignored him. Joseph asked again for something to eat.

Worthmore gave Joseph a cold stare. He then called for a couple of new guards, ordering them to take Joseph to the interrogation tent.

Joseph walked in front of the guards and behind Worthmore. The guards led him up a dirt carriage path and across a grassy field to one of a dozen canvas tents skirting the parade field. Joseph was ordered to go inside and wait; the two guards remained outside.

Joseph took a seat on a wooden stool. With each breath he smelled stale tobacco smoke. It was a dreary place with a tarnished oil lantern hanging from the center of the tent. There was so much blackened soot on the glass chimney that it hardly gave any light. In front of him, under the lantern was a makeshift table made from a wooden crate. On the table was a pile of paper, a full inkwell and two quills for writing. As far as Joseph could see, it was early dawn. He sat and waited, wishing for a drink of water.

Joseph thought he left one nightmare and entered another one. He had the chills and could not get himself warm. The tent flap opened and in walked Colonel Barnes. The sight of Colonel Barnes nearly brought Joseph to tears. Joseph noticed the Colonel appeared distracted or preoccupied.

Barnes looked directly at Joseph, "Private Holmes, it is my duty to inform you that your military records list you as a deserter."

That one single sentence nearly jolted Joseph out of his chair. He was dumbfounded. With effort, he opened his mouth, but nothing came out. Again he tried. Slowly, word by word, the young soldier expressed his confusion. "Sir, how could this be, this must be a mistake." His charge of desertion was beginning to edge into full panic. The tent flap opened again, this time Lt. Worthmore entered and took a seat. Joseph's mind finally began to function,

"Colonel Barnes, it must be a clerical error."

Worthmore chuckled at Joseph retort. "No private, this is not a clerical error. Trust us on that, this is a very serious charge that could cost you your life."

Joseph shook his head and tried to think. How in the world could Barnes make such a wild accusation? He was unable to comprehend what was happening. After everything he had endured while in captivity with

Poore, he returned to Harlem Heights only to be charged with desertion, and to be held awaiting interrogation and maybe a hanging.

Barnes repeated his statement, hoping to get some response from Joseph. "Lad, you are being accused of desertion, what do you have to say for yourself?"

Joseph fumbled for words. In a very low tone, hardly audible, his throat as dry, he said, "Sir, I … I …" He paused. He could see Barnes growing impatient with him. Again, Joseph attempted to speak, "Sir, I think … a mistake …" Joseph stopped in mid-sentence, cleared his throat.

With a gruff tone, Barnes said, "Come on Joseph, spit it out. Damn it, say something for yourself! Don't you know we have a war to fight?" Barnes slammed his fist on the table. "What do you have to say? Where in God's name have you been? What have you been doing these past several weeks, and with whom? And, where is the damn map?"

The moment Barnes asked for the whereabouts of the map, Joseph began to sweat. His hands, neck and face felt clammy. Joseph stood and made eye contact with Barnes. Before he could say another word, Lieutenant Krumb entered the tent, followed by a military clerk. Joseph tried to gather his thoughts. He tried to focus on the one question, but he couldn't. His feelings of fear and confusion had invaded his body and he felt crippled. A long silence followed.

After several minutes, Joseph attempted to answer Colonel Barnes' questions, but his throat was too dry. He said he needed some water to drink. He also told them he hadn't eaten for a couple days. The clerk left the tent to get water, bread and cheese for Joseph. A short recess was then taken. Joseph began to feel better after having something in his stomach.

"My record listing me as a deserter is incorrect."

Krumb interrupted him, "Private, that is for us to decide."

"I am a proud scout of the L.A.R. I am one of five brothers who have volunteered to fight for our King and country; to risk our lives to end the rebellion." Joseph paused, cleared his throat, and fixed his eyes on Colonel Barnes; who he knew was his only hope for a fair hearing. I am a man of honesty. If someone is trying to trip me up, if you are hoping I might slip helping you prove your hypothesis, well you are wasting your time."

Krumb's face grew tense. "Private, you play a clever game when you attempt to turn the tables. But, I remind you, you are the one on trial, not us!"

"So, go ahead, question me and you will know where I have been and what I have endured …"

Krumb interrupted again, "Soldier, you are out of order. Your insubordination is duly noted and will only strengthen the accusations and charges against you. Your conduct is unbecoming to a soldier of the King. If I had the power, I would have you hung for the high crime of treason by nightfall!"

With that, Colonel Barnes had all he could take, he stood up and cautioned, "Lieutenant Krumb, I suggest you do not rush to judgement. Your opinions have nothing to do with the charge; you are not the judge and the jury!" Barnes took his seat, noticeably frustrated with his young lieutenant.

Worthmore whispered into Barnes' ear and Barnes said, "Son, records show that you, Joseph Holmes, have not reported for duty in nearly seven weeks. Some of our scouts in the countryside and in rebel-controlled districts of Connecticut have provided us with sworn and signed statements. They have witnessed your full participation in brutal acts against the Loyalists. They describe you as a willful member running with a small group of rebel thugs. Have you participated with these criminals, raiding loyalists' homes?"

Joseph was a loss for words. He feared his defense seemed hopeless. Without giving Joseph a chance to reply, Krumb waved papers in the air. "Speak-up private, what have you to say? Are these sworn, documented accounts of you participating in treasonous activities true?" Krumb paused. "Or, might our own scouts be fabricating stories? Don't sit there as if you are gobsmacked!" Krumb leaned across the table, a foot from his face and asked, "Well, young man, are you ready to explain these accounts?"

Joseph was overcome with doubt and discouragement. He opened his mouth and not a word came out.

Krumb, with a grin on his face, continued, "It appears to me, the deserter is having a mental collapse. It is obvious his mind is gone."

Colonel Barnes angrily interrupted the lieutenant. "Lieutenant Krumb you are not to make such remarks about a prisoner. Conjecture is not what we do! One more callous comment and you will be removed from this hearing."

As Colonel Barnes reprimanded Krumb, Joseph listened to the chirping of birds. But Joseph's temporary tranquility came to an abrupt end with the departure of Colonel Barnes, who left the interrogation steaming with frustration. Joseph saw Krumb was giving him an ice-cold stare.

Worthmore calmly stated a question, "Holmes, tell us, where have you been and with whom? You must have something to say."

"No sir, well, yes sir, I vehemently denounce this charge, none of it is accurate or true. Once I tell you what really happened, I trust these charges will be dropped and erased from my military record." Joseph's voice, the voice of a fourteen-year-old confused kid, began to show some life.

Worthmore responded, "Very good private. I see you have found your voice and I look forward to hearing your account of events."

Joseph saw Krumb smirk and again Joseph fumbled with his thoughts.

Krumb was pleased to see that the kid was intimidated by him, without him even saying a word.

"My account, well, yes," he squirmed in his seat. "I was coerced, kidnapped by this small rebel gang. I didn't participate by choice." Worthmore snickered while Krumb rolled his eyes.

Joseph noticed Worthmore's attitude and became rattled. "From the date I was last at Harlem Heights, I was held captive by a rogue gang. During my captivity I was robbed, beaten and held against my will."

Worthmore asked, "We need to have their names and the descriptions of these rebels."

Joseph paused to calm his voice, took a deep breath and said, "You want their names? I don't know their full names; they called each other by one name." Joseph stopped talking, hoping a pause would help him gather his thoughts. "I was coerced to take part in their hideous acts. When on raids, the group leader threatened to kill me if I did not do as he commanded. When not on raids, I was tied and bound, unable to escape. During a raid, the leader of the group was never far from me and kept a pistol stuck in my belly."

As Joseph answered each question directed at him, Worthmore sat on a stool with an expression of doubt and boredom.

Joseph struggled to answer the repeated questions and was barely able to stay alert.

Krumb continued to roll his eyes, and he began to parrot Joseph's replies,

"Private might you really expect us to believe this nonsense you are telling us!" Krumb paused for a moment and then said, "I think we have had enough for today."

Krumb called for the guard to take the prisoner to his quarters for the night and to bring him back first thing the next morning.

ϲℓϙ

"Private Holmes, you are a disgrace to all soldiers fighting for the King. Your actions have cost men their lives and now you sit here telling us you were kidnapped! Are you aware of what harm your actions have done to the King's efforts to maintain civility in the colonies?" Lieutenant Krumb was full of piss and vinegar and it was clear to Joseph the lieutenant was enjoying himself. As Krumb finished jotting down a few notes, Krumb let a laugh escape from his chinless mouth. Krumb laughed often, and his vulgar breath drifted around the table like a fart in the fog.

Lieutenant Worthmore took a seat at the table He smiled and said, "Joseph you have failed to provide us with proof to support your statement. Private, have you any evidence to support your claim of captivity and being under their control through means of subjugation and coercion?"

Once Krumb heard Worthmore's question, he whispered to Worthmore, "We have that bastard now!"

Joseph sat still and silent. He was discouraged; he did not have any witnesses and he knew these two men had already condemned him. He anxiously wracked his brain, asking himself, what evidence he might have to present. His life depended on evidence and he had none. His thoughts became distracted as he envisioned the innocent people whose homes he helped raid. The images of women and children being dragged from their beds. The images of Mr. Weeks' daughters. At times, those thoughts were even more painful than his ankles and wrists.

Joseph jumped to his feet. Krumb, thinking Joseph was going to make a run for it, pulled out his pistol, and yelled for the guard. A mere moment later, Krumb realized Joseph was not trying to escape.

Standing, Joseph wasted no time rolling up his long sleeves to show the rope and rawhide burns, cuts and sores around his wrists. Worthmore's eyes widened with surprise as he saw the open sores, scabs, bruised skin, and dried blood caked and hardened on his arms. Next, Joseph pulled down his knee stockings and showed both men his bruised and bloody ankles.

Joseph, his eyes, full of pain and hope, told Worthmore, "Sir, these wounds are my proof that I was held against my will." With his voice trembling, Joseph continued, "I was forced to participate in those raids.

They were barbarians and I was threatened. I was ordered to persecute families who were supporting the Crown." Joseph dropped his head and quietly shared some of the horrors. "The terror in which I involuntarily participated will haunt my mind and soul for the rest of my life."

A few large tears fell from Joseph's eyes as he talked. "I have ongoing nightmares and when awake I suffer from the memory of those images and hold myself responsible for my actions. I will never forget the fear I saw in the eyes of innocent women and children as they were forced from their beds in the middle of the night." Joseph became silent.

Worthmore waited for Joseph to continue. Krumb was writing notes. A guard entered the tent with a bowl of tea and some bread for Joseph. His eyes opened wide at the sight of the food and the tea.

To Joseph, it was apparent Worthmore and Krumb thought he was a double agent. After three days of intense questioning Joseph was taken back to solitary confinement while Colonel Barnes and Lieutenants Krumb and Worthmore reviewed the evidence to determine a verdict. As he lay awake, Joseph worried about what the next days would bring.

Joseph was certain Krumb would relish seeing him hung and he feared the odds were stacked against him. All three men had to agree on either innocent or guilty. Would he be free to return to the L.A.R.? Or, would he face court martial and be hanged? He thought how difficult it would be for his family if he were hanged for being a traitor. It was beyond any punishment he could imagine.

It took two days to get the verdict. Finally, two guards marched Joseph to Colonel Barnes' office. Joseph was not ready to hear the worst, a guilty verdict, but it was a possibility. He sat across from Barnes and told the colonel how grateful he was and how thankful he was that the truth would prevail. But, the moment he heard the not-guilty verdict, he was stunned, almost puzzled. How did Barnes get the unanimous verdict?

The colonel stood up and walked over to where Joseph sat, putting his hand on Joseph's shoulder, "Son, I need to tell you, it was not easy to get the three of us to agree. My two junior officers had their own ideas. Remember, regardless of being found innocent, you will continue to be looked at suspiciously by a least one of your superiors, Lieutenant Krumb."

Barnes had to make a deal with Krumb to get a not guilty verdict. Krumb got unlimited access to Joseph's out-going and in-coming mail and a transfer within months to a post he wanted, Fort Royal in Nova Scotia.

Barnes saw no problem with those concessions. In fact, he was happy to transfer Krumb anywhere!

In no time, Joseph was able to rejoin the other enlisted men stationed at Harlem Heights. He was so thankful to be back at the encampment and to be alive! The following day it occurred to him that he had not written a letter to anyone in his family for more than two months. Joseph was informed that Lieutenant Krumb had held Joseph's mail while he was gone. Before giving it to him, Krumb opened each letter and read the contents, making notes. Joseph had received two letters: one from his mother and one from J.R.

Colonel Barnes assigned Lieutenant Krumb to compose the summary report regarding Joseph's return to camp and the interrogation. In that report Krumb supported the initial charge of desertion, and further wrote there was no doubt Joseph was a deserter and a double agent, in short. a traitor.

Joseph returned to duty within a day of his verdict and began an intense preparation, for his new assignment. He was eager to get back to work as a scout for the L.A.R. Somehow, he felt better prepared than ever to help his fellow Loyalists and, more than ever, he wanted to defeat the Continental Army, who he saw as reckless and out of control.

Colonel Barnes, meanwhile, sent his own scout to verify the information that Joseph had given in his defense. By the time Joseph left for his new assignment, Barnes had received his scout's finding, which supported Joseph's story. At that point, Barnes did not see a reason to share the findings. Unknown to Joseph, the word "deserter" remained in his military file. It had not been updated to reflect the not-guilty verdict."

Before he had to leave for his next assignment, Joseph wrote J.R. He so badly wanted to write about his interrogation but was careful not to tell J.R. anything about that. He began his letter by telling him that all was fine and telling some of what he had been doing. However, he could not hold back about Salem Poore, his kidnapping, and his brutal captivity. He described Poore as the gang leader. He also mentioned that a Lieutenant Krumb wanted to nail him.

The letter was posted from the encampment at Harlem Heights, addressed to: Private John Roger Holmes, Captain Randall's Company, Loyal American Regiment, Fort Washington.

While Joseph wanted to share information with J.R., he had no idea who else would see his mail. When Joseph dropped his letter at the post, the young corporal on duty, following orders, took the letter and placed it on Krumb's desk. Krumb carefully broke the wax seal on the letter's flap. He began to read line by line while jotting down notes.

Meanwhile, Colonel Barnes had read the report written by Lieutenant Krumb. Without hesitation, Barnes summoned the lieutenant. When Lieutenant Worthmore interrupted Krumb's reading of Joseph's letter, telling him that the colonel wanted to talk to him, Krumb tossed the letter in his desk drawer, then left the tent.

Krumb entered the colonel's office, and Barnes told him to sit down and gave him a stern and disapproving look. "Lieutenant Krumb, I am going to give you some words of warning about the perils of conjecture. Lieutenant, making guesses impedes the truth, guessing undermines efforts to reach the truth. There is NO evidence that Private Holmes is a double agent." Barnes repeated that point, "No evidence at all to indicate guilt. The limited evidence indicates Holmes was being held against his will. I do not want to hear any more about this topic."

Colonel Barnes paused, not taking his eyes off of Krumb, then in a low voice, almost a whisper threatened, "Krumb have you heard? Word is there is a shortage of lieutenants on the front." Barnes paused again as if for affect. "Lieutenant Krumb, any questions?"

Krumb nervously replied, "No sir."

"Fine then, take back this report and do it over, using the facts, nothing less, nothing more. Have it back on my desk in two hours. You're dismissed, Lieutenant." Krumb stood up, saluted and briskly left the tent. Krumb stormed back to his desk, poured himself a glass of whisky and slammed the flask on his desk.

Chapter 11

Late May 1778: The Letter

Joseph could only imagine the trouble he might be in if Lieutenant Krumb knew that his kidnapping was by a gang leader who was his cousin! Joseph would be walking up the stairs to the gallows. The idea of Poore's identity being known and connected to Joseph was frightful!

A couple days after Joseph posted his letter to J.R., the letter that Krumb had started to read, he was summoned to Colonel Barnes' tent to receive new orders.

Barnes greeted him, "Son, you look to be putting on some weight since you got back. Good for you. You will need it on your new assignment. Please take a seat." Barnes shuffled some papers on his desk and then continued, "Your new orders are not in written form. This assignment is too secretive to be scribed."

As Joseph listened, his anticipation heightened. He paid careful attention, listening to every word. The colonel explained in detail the names of places and people; Joseph committed it all to memory. Joseph was a quick learner, the likes of which Barnes had never seen. As Barnes talked about the waterfront and its possible dangers, he told Joseph about the business of smuggling goods, and in this case weapons. Joseph's interest peaked when he heard the word smuggling.

"There are dangers lurking on the waterfront. It is paramount you do not divulge you name under any circumstance! Your life depends on your ability to maintain your cover. It is the only protection you have. Barnes paused and asked, "Do you have any questions?"

"No, sir." Joseph replied with confidence.

"Very well. Tomorrow you will meet with both Lieutenant Worthmore and Lieutenant Krumb for your final briefing."

Joseph sat on his cot and noticed his stationery under the blanket. He thought about writing his mother before his departure, but he didn't know what he'd say to her, except "all is fine in the stables, Mother, and the officers' horses are fat and happy." He didn't want to mislead her, and he knew that he would not sound convincing, thus leaving his mother to wonder and worry.

⁂

The morning mail call at Fort Washington brought J.R. one letter. He was thrilled to hear from Joseph. It had been a couple of months since he last heard from him.

When J.R. saw the lettering on the folded parchment, he smiled at the chicken-scratch penmanship. J.R. easily broke the wax seal, which did not have the customary "H" imprinted in it. That was when he noticed that two different shades of red wax were used to seal the letter. J.R. did not remember his brother ever being so sloppy, but after all, it was dire times. He refused to worry. After all, a war was being fought and people were over-eager to get things done.

He unfolded the letter, noticing the date with surprise. It was dated seven days ago. He found a quiet place to sit and read the news from his brother. He then noticed the date the letter was written, ten days earlier. He wondered why it took so long to reach him.

May 22, 1778

Dear J.R.,

I must write before I am sent off on my next assignment. I know you wonder how I am and what I am doing. Well, I am fine and staying busy. I am writing to inform you that I am not a stable boy, as Mother and all of you had initially hoped. Please do not share this information with Mother and Father. I am involved with scouting, which is paramount to defeating the rebel troops. I am not allowed to share even this much information with anyone. Forgive me for not going into detail. One other thing, I want you to know that recently, while out scouting in the Northeastern area of Poughkeepsie, almost in the Colony of Connecticut, I was kidnapped and held hostage for several weeks. I was a prisoner held by a gang calling themselves, Sons of Liberty, I am sure you have heard of them. There is a Lt. Krumb here who would like to accuse me of being a deserter. I know you will keep this to yourself.

The young man who led this small gang of three said he was our cousin! Do we have a cousin by the name of Salem Poore? He is about your age and size. From what he told me, I have little doubt this gang leader is indeed our cousin. Why do you suppose I never heard him mentioned by Mother or Father? The young man is bright, but he appears to have demons. He is cruel beyond all measure, a ruthless man. My captivity was filled with the horror of terrorizing Loyalist families in the dead of the night.

By the time you get this letter, I expect I will have departed for my new undercover assignment. For the moment, this is all I can say, and way more than I am at liberty to share. I am fine and will write soon. Be well.

Your brother, Joseph

J.R. sat on a bench, stupefied. He could not figure out what the hell the British officers at Harlem Heights were doing, putting a kid in high-risk undercover situations. They were sending a kid out on the road, alone, to gather information and to lurk around very dangerous men. Those in command of the L.A.R. had assured J.R. that Joseph would be assigned to the stables because of his knowledge and understanding of horses. One sentence jumped out at him. "By the time you get this letter, I expect I will have departed for my new assignment."

He read the letter a second and a third time. He visualized the horror Joseph must have experienced when captured by that group. He could hear the fright in his brother's voice and see the fear in his eyes. J.R. remained on the bench, growing increasingly bewildered and outraged. He wanted to know how something like this could have happened. His brother was only fourteen.

J. R's view of officers changed. He began to see them as men who would do anything, stoop to unethical practice, to win a battle. They had given their word to Joseph's family. Joseph's activities were putting his life in peril. How could they order a fourteen-year-old to run risky journeys all over the colonies on horseback? J.R. tried to calm himself, knowing that he could not say anything to anyone about Joseph's work because it would put his brother's life in danger. J.R. grew furious knowing that his questions could not be answered, because they could not be asked.

After a sleepless night he tried to dismiss the entire concept of Joseph being a spy. It seemed too outrageous to be possible. J.R. began thinking that maybe Joseph was kidding, but no, he knew his brother's sense of humor. Joseph would never kid about something so serious. Maybe Joseph was calling out for help. What the hell happened to his assignment in the stable?

The word scouting and the word espionage continued to haunt his mind. Everyone knew the French were producing weapons for the Continental Army. He had heard numerous reports about the smuggling of guns, bayonets and cannons in British-controlled New York. Weapons were getting by the naval blockade and finding their way to the rebel lines. J.R. shuddered at the possibility that Joseph could be involved it that business.

Execution for espionage was a common event on both sides of the conflict. The horror stories were everywhere and the hanging of spies and traitors was a daily event. One also heard about large sums of gold being lost between its departure port in France and the port of arrival in the colonies. He heard about children being used to carry secret messages while they did daily errands. It was becoming all too apparent that no one was safe from the ugliness of war.

J.R. placed Joseph's letter in the bottom of his knapsack. He wanted to hide the letter where no one might find it. Once it was out of sight, he felt better. It would not see the light of day until he and Joseph were home in Middle District. He thought about leaving his post and going directly to Harlem Heights, but his regiment was under orders. No one was to leave the fort until further notice.

That night, when he finished eating, he went to his tent to retrieve Joseph's letter from his knapsack. In the privacy of his quarters, he decided to read the letter one last time before disposing of it. Holding it in the palm of his hand, he casually left his tent. A few soldiers were making the customary evening campfire and everything was peaceful.

Nonetheless, he felt something strange was going on. To imagine the mention of his misfit cousin in the letter could be dangerous if, indeed, he was involved with the self-proclaimed Sons of Liberty. He recalled his initial opening of the letter; it appeared to have been opened before he got it. Someone opened it, read it, and re-sealed his brother's private mail revealing his past and present activities. If Joseph's letter indeed was intercepted, it showed that someone did not trust him and he was in danger. No matter how hard he tried, J.R. could not make any sense of it. Joseph's letter was explosive with the mention of undercover assignments, the Sons of Liberty, and scouting. Someone knew Joseph had a cousin belonging to the notorious group and they knew Joseph was undercover in New York.

The campfire was ablaze, crackling and popping. J.R. held Joseph's letter between his fingertips; the white linen of the writing paper reflecting the glow of the fire. Just as he was about to drop the letter onto the flames, he jerked his arm back and placed the letter into his pocket. He felt that burning his brother's letter might be a bad omen. He did not see himself as superstitious, but right then he had an overactive imagination. As he walked, he patted his pocket with his hand; the letter inside was the only connection he had with his brother Joseph.

Chapter 12

June 1778: The Spy and the Vulture

With his knapsack over his shoulder, Joseph began his walk to Flushing Bay while recalling his final briefing. Lieutenant Krumb's index figure had pointed to the location, with the map laid across the table, small stones holding it down on each corner. Joseph noticed that Krumb's nails were long, jagged and yellowed, like his teeth.

In a low voice, Krumb gave Joseph an idea of the place he would soon be calling home. "Along the waterfront is the area of Flushing Bay where you will be spending the next several weeks"

Joseph had never had an assignment like this, working undercover on a wharf. "Lieutenant, if I understand correctly, I am to gather information about smuggling?"

"Exactly, you will infiltrate a smuggling ring. In time you will be asked to help the smugglers." Joseph was nearly speechless. He knew this assignment was one that he would tell his grandchildren.

Lieutenant Krumb said, "Hey kid, you best look carefully at this map. You will not be seeing it again." The lieutenant pointed to several locations on the map, saying, "I suggest you memorize the places and names, once you leave here you are completely on your own." Joseph had the ability to carry the exact map in his head and taking Lieutenant Krumb's suggestion, he studied the map from top to bottom.

Then he noticed a large shadow over Flushing Bay. Joseph was relieved to see it was cast by Colonel Barnes.

The colonel said he had stopped in to say good-bye. He also wanted to remind Joseph not to carry anything that might suggest who he was or from where he came. While Krumb waited impatiently to finish his briefing, Barnes reminded Joseph that the smuggling had to stop. It was costing the British empire a well-deserved victory and it was undermining the King's Navy.

The colonel said. "No letters or notes on your body or in your knapsack. Nothing that could identify you or could reveal what you are doing. Son, I wish you safe travels, and do not forget the drop locations; we depend on the information."

"No, sir, I will not forget anything that you have told me or taught me, colonel."

Krumb continued briefing Joseph, telling him how highly skilled and successful the rebel smugglers were with getting muskets, bayonets and canons off the ships and to the Continental Army. He said it was a very sophisticated operation and people were being paid large sums of money.

The lieutenant added, "Many of the men of the so-called Continental Congress are getting rich off the nasty business of smuggling. They are profiting at the expense of young men fighting for something they don't even understand."

"Weapons are coming into Flushing Bay, "the lieutenant said. "then quickly transported to rebel troops in the Colonies of New Jersey and Pennsylvania."

Even with all of the information, Joseph felt challenged. First, he was not familiar with the area of Flushing Bay. Second, and most alarming, was that this duty involved ships, boats and water. Joseph was a good swimmer, that was not his concern, but he knew nothing about boats or ships. He was unfamiliar with the language of the sea and waterfront. He knew nothing about stevedores, wharves, tides, tying knots, or nautical terms. The only words he understood were block and tackle from working on the farm.

He did understand his mission: Show up at the wharves, hang out and make the waterfront home. All the while, he would pass himself off as a would-be stevedore while waiting for a job offer.

"Kid, you will observe ships that are constantly being loaded or unloaded, twenty-four hours a day, one after the other." Lieutenant Krumb said. "Sometimes you can see a hundred ships a week loading and unloading. Since most able men are off fighting, there is a shortage of dockworkers. You are bound to get offered some kind of dockworker job."

As Joseph walked the dusty road to Flushing Bay, he finally found a shady place to rest. He was wearing old clothes; his knapsack was light, almost empty. Under his arm, he carried his bedroll that included the blanket given him by his mother. He needed a haircut, but not a shave; he was still too young to be growing hair on his chin. He ate the remains of bread and cheese packed earlier that day. With his belly somewhat full, he thought that at this pace, he might arrive at Flushing Bay by early sunset. He noticed a haze creeping over the lowlands.

By the time he reached the bay, being surrounded by fog seemed appropriate. He felt literally undercover. As if a long lost friend, the fog tightly hugged the shore. The shabby wooden shingled roofs of the warehouses were barely visible. During inclement weather, it was in these warehouses where Joseph would find shelter.

The first morning at Flushing Bay, he awoke and his hunger forced him to retrieve cornbread and dried fruit from the bottom of his knapsack. The rain that had started in the early in the day was letting up. Without wasting time, he rolled up his bedroll, threw his knapsack over his back and went to begin loitering on the numerous long wooden wharves. He noticed immediately that the waterfront was a mysterious place. It had an assortment of people, the likes of which he had never seen. Some were unusual and others downright frightening!

Stevedores, like farmers, had early mornings. The activity and the number of men loading and unloading vessels astonished Joseph. He had never witnessed anything like this. Some mornings he would hide his bedroll out of sight and meander in and out of the taverns watching and listening while trying to fit in with the others. The more he was seen idling around and asking for work, the sooner he would be hired.

Joseph did not look like a stevedore, a ship's captain, a first mate or member of a crew. Regardless, several days after his arrival, he was offered a job working with the dockers. Between jobs, he found a comfortable place to sit, took out a three-foot piece of rope and practiced tying and untying dozen of knots new knots. All the while, he continued to keep a keen eye open for anyone might be a counterespionage agent or a smuggler. Much to his surprise, he was enjoying his work. He had never known men who made a living related to the sea or shipping. He had never seen men who bore pictures on patches of their skin.

Since first arriving at the waterfront, he was fascinated by the idea of world trade. He read the stenciled letters on crates, boxes of tea from India, spices from China, oils from Italy, cutlery from Persia, sugar and rum from islands far away and whiskey from Ireland. He began to think that someday he might want to get involved in this kind of work.

Joseph ate at a wide number of taverns found on the back streets of the waterfront. In these seedy taverns, he listened to conversations, some he couldn't understand because of the many different languages often spoken by the sailors. Nightly he loitered in the houses of drink having a watery bowl of soup or reading the broadsides plastered to the wall. Going to taverns became part of his daily routine. He thought that was where he was most likely to make contacts with smugglers.

The tavern was a vital part of his life on the waterfront, his single source of what was going on in the colonies. The tavern keeper heard it all. He got the entire rundown of news daily, including battles lost and won, hangings in Albany, Loyalists being run out of the Massachusetts Colony, price of tea, cotton and wood and how many barrels of Scottish whisky the British officers drank in a month. Joseph recalled that it was in a tavern when he first heard about the famous French military leader, Lafayette.

Of the many taverns he visited, the one that offered the most promise and the one he chose to frequent on a regular basis for food and drink, was the Vulture. He felt the Vulture was where he would gain entry into the flow of contraband.

One day, after collecting his pay from the docker, he decided to rest his tired bones for a few minutes on some sacks of seeds. He pulled out a rag from his pocket to wipe the sweat off his face. Then he jumped off the bags of seed, making a beeline for the Vulture. He walked past an assortment of drunks on the boardwalk. Some were begging, others were vagrants, ne'er-do-wells chasing their next gulp of whiskey. Casually Joseph stepped over two tattooed men lying face down in the gutter; by then, not much on the waterfront shocked him.

The work was hard, but the taverns were hallowed ground, especially for sailors. For them the place of drink was everything rolled into one: family, meeting hall, marketplace, and business brokerage.

As he entered the Vulture, he was met by the familiar stench of urine, body odors, flatulence and bad breath. He took short, shallow breaths so as not to retch on his empty stomach. Men filled both rooms of the place and most were bearded and disheveled. With nowhere to sit inside, he found a bench outside the entrance.

He dropped his head into his calloused and blistered hands and was reminded of his captivity by the scars on his wrists. He realized they, like his memories, would always be there to haunt him. He still carried regret, grief and anger. His fingers spread up over his face moving to his head while massaging his scalp. Lifting his chin high, he stretched the back of his neck, tilting his head one way and then the other. As he looked up, he noticed that the wooden carving of the vulture on the tavern's sign appeared almost real. The vulture's eyes saw each patron who entered or left the establishment. Joseph recalled what he had read in a book about birds and wildlife. Some classified the bird as "eaters of the dead" and others saw the vulture as a stealth bird, one that barely made a sound.

Joseph, staring at the looming vulture, whispered, "You can keep secrets forever. Whatever you have seen or heard, no one will ever know." Joseph took a deep breath and tried again to enter the Vulture. The tavern was still crowded but he found a seat. As he scanned the crowd, he noticed new faces. They were J.R.'s age and Joseph felt certain they were not wharf rats. Then he repeated to himself, things are not always, as they appear.

As Joseph listened to the usual talk of espionage and the fate of traitors, he noticed the mariners who were Vulture regulars did not partake in conversations about the war, with one likely exception. That was when the war affected their work related to the sea. They complained about the surge in pirates and privateers. They shared stories about boats taken over by privateers, and brought back to port like Boston and Portsmouth. Otherwise, they only cared about getting cargo to port and getting paid.

While dawdling at the Vulture, Joseph was spellbound by the story of a man named Hale.

A Vulture patron muttered in a low voice, "It happened a couple years past, somewhere right around here at a tavern."

"Was it here at the Vulture?" a man at the table asked.

"No, if it was I would have told you. Anyway this man named Hale was young man who was said to be a schoolteacher. Not far from here, a group of British soldiers circled him and arrested him right then and there." He paused, leaving his listeners in suspense.

"What happened next?"

The British soldiers took Mr. Hale to their officers and young Hale was charged with being a rebel spy! No trial. ..."

Someone interrupted, "Yeah, I remember hearing about that. They hanged him."

The Vulture patron telling the story slammed his fist on the table. "Why did you have to spoil the ending to my story!"

Joseph remembered the first time he had heard the story, about a year ago, thinking it was rebel propaganda. It was when he was scouting with Red.

A docker cleared his throat and said, "I can't believe the British hanged a teacher. You got some wild imagination. They wouldn't hang a young man, without a trial. What the hell is the matter with you? Has the war come to this, we believe almost anything we hear?"

A shabby, bearded man jumped to his feet, yelling at the docker, "You half-wit! Any fool would know this story is true, Hale was a damn good-for-nothing rebel spy. He lurked in Queens to ferret out information on British troop movements."

The bearded man got right in the docker's face. "If you have not noticed, we are at war. Open your damn eyes! What are you, a friend of the rebels? The story is true. We hanged the schoolteacher not far from here."

"You are a sad stupid son of bitch to dare say that to me." The docker puffed his chest out and flexed his arms. Within a blink of an eye, a brawl began with the docker and the bearded man. As they swung their fists at each other, they were attracting other men like a magnet. First, there were two and a minute later, ten men were punching, yelling and cursing.

Joseph was mesmerized by the growing group of men tossing mugs of beer, shouting, breaking chairs. Joseph knew the Hale story. Even though it was hard to believe the British would hang a man without a trial, this was how the King said he would punish anyone supporting the rebellion. He was amazed to hear people still talking about that event two years after the fact. But who really knew; it could be propaganda against the British.

After all the excitement, a regular who appeared drunker than usual, saw Joseph's reaction and yelled loud enough for all to hear, "Hey lad, the story about the school teacher being hanged didn't frighten you, did it?" Joseph acted as it he did not hear him.

"The skinny lad enjoyed that story," the drunk said. "Did you see the expression on his face! Has anyone got another one to tell him? He is about the pee his pants!"

The tavern keeper walked up to the loud mouth and told him to either leave the kid alone or get out. Joseph felt ashamed that he didn't hide his sense of fear. After all his training, he should not have let someone see his feelings. And yet, Joseph thought, maybe being scared isn't all bad. After all, he was only a fourteen-year-old kid and he had to remind himself to act like one.

છે

Everything around him, the sights and sounds, were all new to him but he maintained a lackadaisical disposition so he didn't bring attention to himself. He also kept in mind the warning from Colonel Barnes that at anytime, anywhere, someone might be watching. He was constructing his own warehouse, a warehouse of facts and observations, a mental warehouse, where he stored numerous pieces of information that he could import down the road. During his first few days at Flushing Bay, he learned about things to which he had given little thought, such as the tides and their relationship to the moon. That part of the bay had a seven to eight foot tide. He was astounded to learn that the height of the high tide depended on the phase of moon. Therefore, when the moon was full, the tides were at their highest.

He was enjoying the peaceful sounds of the water, when he was startled by the honking of a large flock of Canada geese. Hundreds flew over him as they headed for a landing at the shallow end of the bay. For a moment, he was reminded of the simple, quiet days before the revolution. In the fall, as the Canada geese were on their journey south, they loved to frequent the recently harvested cornfields where they found tasty morsels of corn. Joseph saw that where the geese landed was near large bogs that offered camouflage, a good location for hiding illegal cargo or a dory.

He decided to sit down and think about what the lieutenant had told him. Disguised ships sporting the Union Jack and knowing the correct code for entrance to the port had gotten by the British blockade. Joseph wondered if he would have the opportunity to untangle the mystery. He did know these smugglers were clever men; the moving and sorting of vast amounts of cargo was full of intricacies such as keeping records, storage, payments and, of course, tariffs.

He began to question himself. Would he be able to spot a smuggler? He knew nothing about smuggling or the black market, except for what Barnes and Krumb had told him. Joseph came to the realization that this assignment might be out of his league. He would much prefer being a scout, riding his horse Red, and feeling as free as the wild geese.

Colonel Barnes said one result of the smuggling was a strong black market. That too, was supporting Washington's troops, eroding the integrity of the King's hopes for his colonies. From what Joseph could see, the men working the wharves, the crews arriving on ships, along with dozens of merchants picking up their products, all appeared legitimate. To find a smuggler would be a challenge.

Joseph grinned when he thought about Pike and Watkins. Those two seemed like regular church goers compared to the men surrounding him now! Some sailors covered their arms, chest and neck with tattoos, some shaved their heads, others had numerous body piercings and some sailors wore earrings and necklaces. He laughed as he recalled J.R. telling him that the Mohegan people wore earrings and necklaces too. Some of these sailors were missing limbs and missing teeth; some had a stump of wood for a foot. One sailor at the Vulture tavern had but one eye. He wore a patch over the empty eye socket.

Sitting on bags of grain, Joseph dozed off and was startled when he woke. He checked the sun's position to figure out how long he had slept. He felt rested and he began to be a bit more optimistic about what he was doing. He recalled Colonel Barnes saying how smuggling had the power to tilt the balance of power over the colonies. If the British Navy lost the vital ports along the New York waterfront and if they lost control of the mouth of the Hudson River, it could mean victory would belong to Washington and his rebels.

Espionage was prolific on both sides of the conflict. Many carried on their task of spying while appearing to be upstanding, everyday businessmen, whether the person was a tailor, grocer or blacksmith, Joseph reminded himself to be cautious. What might look innocent could be informers running messages or using secret codes, signs or symbols. A seemingly harmless gesture, such as wearing a particular piece of clothing, or the way in which clothing hung to dry, could provide information to change the outcome of a battle.

He walked back to the wharf and noticed the largest shipment of small barrels he had seen. His jaw dropped at the sight of hundreds of barrels of Irish whisky, scotch, brandy and rum, keg after keg of distilled alcohol. The barrels were stacked four high on the wharf.

Joseph was startled by a loud, gruff voice, resembling a dog's growl. "Hey kid, what you doing?"

Joseph turned, suddenly face to face with a burley sailor. He was a huge man with long hair, his body covered with a design of ships, dogs and another creature he couldn't make out. Maybe it was a sea monster. With his big hands and thick arms, the man grabbed Joseph's shoulders. Joseph noticed a large knife hung from the man's belt.

"I am looking for a job, sir. Might you need help with unloading your cargo?"

The sailor shoved Joseph aside and barked, "Get lost, kid, and stay away from these barrels. My captain would not take kindly to some kid snatching any of his whiskey! Don't even think about it if you don't want to be sleeping with the fish!"

A majority of the cargo coming into Flushing had to do with the war, including distilled alcohol. There was a tremendous demand for rum, whisky and all spirits. At the top of list for distribution were the British officers. Tavern keepers and other merchants were next in line. The rebels coveted distilled spirits too, and they had to be smuggled in for them, while at the same time creating a profitable black market.

British ships came from ports all over the British Empire carrying cargo to help stop the rebellion. Wooden crates full of knapsacks, canvas for tents and ship's sails, tent poles, blankets, muskets, bayonets, flintlock pistols and many other items flooded the wharves daily. Dozens and dozens of flatbed wagons picked up the cargo, clearing the wharves, only to start all over again with the next ship.

Each day blurring into the next, Joseph kept busy working with the other dockers. Lucky for him, there was a shortage of labor. He recalled Colonel Barnes' warnings of how ruthless the waterfront could be. Joseph saw first-hand that it was a cutthroat place. Knives were carried by every sailor, stevedore and docker. A knife's primary purpose was to cut rope to hold cargo in place A knife's secondary purpose was for self-defense. Working along the wharves was a deadly business in normal times; the war had increased the dangers.

Every waking moment Joseph listened and learned; every evening there was always a new story, true or false, told at the Vulture. One evening the tavern keeper was telling about a so-called Secret Committee. The topic grabbed Joseph's attention, and much to his dismay, he found this story more disturbing than the hanging of spies and traitors.

"I have heard that this rebel committee's purpose is not all that clear," the tavern keeper said softly. "Something having to do with secret information and how to manage secrets, things being said or things being done, like the smuggling of arms for rebel soldiers and the black market for contraband like distilled spirits."

"Sounds like a dangerous business, how do they do that?" asked one patron.

"Easy, I guess one could say. Rebels and rebel sympathizers are doing the smuggling for good wages."

"Yeah, high wages for the very high risk," said the patron.

Joseph listened closely. This was the very activity he was sent to infiltrate.

The tavern keeper appeared uneasy talking about the Secret Committee, but he continued, "These privateering ventures of smuggling are filling the coffers of those men who call themselves leaders of the revolution." Did he mean the smuggling was organized by a committee appointed by the revolutionary congress in Philadelphia?

The patron smiled and said, "I'm not surprised; someone is always out to make money any way they can."

Joseph, becoming dry in the mouth, sipped cider while he sorted out what he had just heard. Some leaders of the revolution were lining their pockets with money made from smuggling weapons. He began to realize that personal gain was a part of war. How could he infiltrate a complex operation overseen by rebels at the top?

Joseph was learning that the revolution was full of complexities. There was profiteering, spying, propaganda and black markets to keep the front lines supplied. He began to see how both sides have self-interest and selfish motives. He hoped he had joined the better of the two sides. Going undercover brought the complexities and the hypocrisies of war up close. The only thing that wasn't complex was the number of war dead.

As he thought about the war, Joseph circled his spoon around the lip of his soup bowl, then circled the bowl a second time while waiting for the clumps of stale bread to soften. He couldn't figure out why the name of the soup was beef, when it smelled like chicken. Using his spoon, he scooped up pieces of soaked bread, and let it continue to soften in his mouth. It did not taste too bad for the Vulture, Joseph thought.

He was just finishing his soup when a young man, maybe four years his senior, got up from another table, walked over to Joseph and sat down across from him. Joseph was familiar with the men from the other table; they would frequent the Vulture occasionally for a couple days at a time. His head tilted over his soup he lifted his gaze toward the stranger. The young man was a friendly sort with lots of red hair and pale white skin.

"Hey kid, want to earn some extra money?"

Joseph, with his mouth full, nodded.

"Meet me at midnight tonight, this is private, keep it to yourself ..."

Joseph shook his head in agreement, acting nonchalant as he swallowed the soggy bread. He was trying to appear calm, while a celebration played out in his mind. Maybe the redhead was about to take him into the underground world of smuggling.

Chapter 13

June 1778: The Smugglers

Joseph ordered another bowl of soup, thinking he should eat more so he wouldn't get hungry in the middle of that night's job. He took a deep breath, his anxiety was palpable. He knew what to do. Just listen to what the redhead said. Do not ask questions.

Naturally, Joseph was curious to know more, but he would have to learn by observation, a most valuable tool when undercover. If they wanted him to know something, they would tell him, and he left it at that. When at the Vulture, Joseph was now routinely included. Finally, he was getting a close glimpse of the underground operation.

After a few missions, consisting mainly of running weapons, he could not understand why Colonel Barnes and the British Navy had not figured out how these ships, loaded with muskets, ammunition, boots and blankets, were able to get by the British blockade. The ships he unloaded at night did not dock at the long wharves. They stayed quietly moored in the bay like dozens of other ships. One morning you would see a ship peacefully moored and the next morning it was gone, vanished without a trace, as if swallowed by a sea serpent.

Under the cloak of night, a couple of nights a week, Joseph hauled crates from ship to shore. The money he made in one night was about equal to five days of working on the wharves. Once the goods were safely stowed for the next leg of the journey to the Continental Army, payment was made and the redhead and Joseph simply faded back into their everyday life.

As the redhead was counting coins to give to Joseph, he suggested, "Kid, if you aim to live to do more smuggling you would be smart not to flash your gold coins around, especially in this area." The redhead waved his arm toward the waterfront. "This place is full of bottom-feeders." The redhead, in a tone of warning, added: "Some men around the waterfront would cut your throat if they didn't like the way you look."

Joseph replied, "Yes, sir, I understand. I stay to myself."

The redhead began to walk away, then stopped, turned and in a whisper said, "Don't forget, if anyone caught on to what you are doing, they would hang you from the nearest tree."

Joseph nodded.

The nighttime rendezvous were becoming routine and Joseph was amazed at the easy money he could earn by smuggling. During the day, their dory was hidden under the scrub brush at the edge of the marsh.

One night, Joseph and two other men had brought their cargo to shore, where they opened one crate of muskets at a time. The air was still, no sound to be heard but the lapping of the water on the shore. Once each crate was opened, they transferred as many muskets as would fit into new pine coffins, already occupied with the bodies of young rebels who had died on board British prison ships. These ships of death were moored off New York. It was a routine sight, a flatbed wagon piled high with rebel coffins. They did not draw suspicion; therefore they were not searched. Joseph was impressed by the cleverness, and thought how these soldiers, even in death, continued to help the revolutionary cause.

Joseph laughed to himself about what Barnes had told him, that things are not always as they appear. An example of that was right in front of him. Coffins were an unlikely hiding place for contraband, including muskets, powder, balls, bayonets and even French brandy.

The next day would be Joseph's first information drop. He jotted down what he had observed and learned during the first month. Of course, it was all in code. From then on, the drops would be every two weeks and always in a different place. Each drop location he had committed to memory. In his first report he summarized his work, including the macabre way the muskets were getting past British guards along the route to New Jersey. Writing about that, in a coded manner, was difficult. He finished the letter and took it to the drop location.

He felt good. A month's work on the Flushing waterfront had revealed valuable information and now the report would get to those with a need to know. Joseph's mind burst with confidence, as his work would surely save lives, and perhaps this could mean the end of the war and victory for the King!

After a few long days on the wharf, Joseph walked to the Vulture . He was tired, wishing he could skip that night's job. Working day and night was wearing him out. After a modest meal of soup and bread, he left the tavern in a hurry, his mind tired. Heading for the waterfront, he noticed fog moving into the shallow coves. The entire bay was soon covered with a veil, sliding softly over the still surface of the dark water. He paused, watching the fog with its hypnotic powers, magically softening all it covered and making Joseph's world smaller.

He identified with the fog and chuckled. Fog, he said in a whisper, you would make a good spy, you move with complete silence. You, like myself, wait and watch. Fog he thought, you have your own clandestine talents.

Joseph was growing impatient. The appointed time to meet was fast approaching. He sat, crouched on the bank of the bay, a mixture of mud and clay coating his leather boots. The combined smell of wet grasses and salt air soothed Joseph's thoughts while he waited for his co-conspirators to join him on that late June evening. He had a gnawing feeling that he was being watched; he had felt this for most of the day.

Still no sign of the redhead and their other cohorts. Things were supposed to work like a well-oiled machine. With the fog, he could barely see the single lantern's glow, the all-clear signal, from the rogue ship. The cargo waited. Joseph waited. Unlike other nights, Joseph was haunted by an odd feeling. But, why would anyone go to the trouble of watching him? No one knew him; he was undercover. He sat hidden on the shore in the brush.

Suddenly he heard the sound of a flatbed wagon approaching. He was not alarmed because it was a familiar sound every hour of the day and night. The wagons carried the dead rebel soldiers from the death ships. He was gazing into the fog when he heard the other two smugglers arrive. The lantern still glowed softly, barely visible. Without a word, Joseph and the two others pulled their dory out from underneath the brush, the boat's hiding place.

The lantern signal grew less visible. The three smugglers swiftly launched their dory, shoving off from the muddy shore. Without a word, they placed the oars in the oarlocks and rowed in the direction of the lantern. Quietly, the dory glided on the water without a sound, except for the soft sound of the oars disturbing the water's surface. Joseph feeling feeling that someone was watching, combined with the other two being late, irritated him.

He knew the drill: unload the illegal cargo from the ship into their dory, get back to shore, open the crates and transfer the cargo into coffins. The flatbed driver would leave his horse and wagon in an agreed location while he visited a house of ill repute and enjoyed a good meal.

Ever so quietly, the dory continued to glide closer to the ship. With no one speaking, the dory pulled up alongside a large schooner. A big man was there to meet them with a hand signal, meaning they did not have much time. Wooden crates filled with weapons were lifted over the edge of the deck and passed down to Joseph and the two other men, several feet below in the dory. The heavy crates, long and awkward, were packed with gleaming French-made muskets and bayonets.

The redhead gave the signal that the dory was full. The big man on the schooner either ignored or overrode the signal and a few more wooden crates were added to the dory. Joseph was worried about the weight. They gradually got the dory pointed in the direction of the shore. With some difficultly, they began to row but the weight in the bow was too much. The distance between them and the ship widened but Joseph noticed the bow was barely above the water line. Water had begun to lap into the boat, pooling on the boat's floor. There were too many crates in the bow.

The redhead stopped rowing and stood up. He ever so gingerly eased himself near the bow and pushed one crate of muskets overboard into the water. The dory seemed more steady but the other smuggler protested the dumping of the muskets. The two exchanged blows, the boat rocking wildly. Joseph pointed for them to sit down. He thought the two were going to capsize the dory. The redhead lost his balance and the other man did too and both fell overboard. Both men came to the surface and grabbed the same side of the dory, frantically trying to pull themselves back into the dory, causing the cargo to shift. In a flash, the boat capsized and the cargo sank.

Startled by the frigid water, Joseph quickly came to the surface, spat out water, and took a deep breath. The dory had turned upside down and he didn't see either of the other men. He waited and they didn't come up for air. He began to swim toward shore, his heart pounding. He glanced back, hoping to see the others but there was no one. He continued to swim, and feared his cohorts, like the cargo, lay at the bottom of Flushing Bay.

Joseph's coded message had found its way to Colonel Barnes and the young lieutenants. They were impressed by all of the information that Joseph had gathered in only one month.

Barnes had spent many years undercover and missed the action. He decided to visit Flushing Bay, hoping for a chance meeting with Joseph. He could not stop thinking about what Joseph had said about the coffins filled with contraband. He wanted to get a closer look at the smuggling operation and the flow of contraband, which he now thought he could stop.

Dressed as a merchant, Barnes arrived at the bustling waterfront. There were only a couple more hours of daylight. He walked the wharves, glanced at the shoreline and was stunned to see the great number of ships. He then walked up the hill to where the street was lined with one tavern after another. Barnes knew from the coded letter that Joseph frequented the Vulture.

Barnes did not see Joseph in the tavern. The stench of the place was overpowering, but he forced his way to the keeper and ordered a whisky and ale. He described Joseph to the tavern keeper asking if he had seen the kid lately. Barnes said that he was his maternal uncle, having just arrived from Richmond to take the boy home.

The barrel-chested tavern-keeper knew exactly who the stranger was talking about. "You know, sir, I have not seen the kid in a few days, which is not like him, he is a daily patron of the Vulture. I bet he moved on, kids do that you know, and especially now with the fighting." He poured a couple more whiskies for two men sitting next to Barnes. "Shame if I say so, no kind of future here for such a bright kid," said the keeper.

Barnes nodded. He knew Joseph would not have moved on, he would not have gone anywhere. The colonel had a twenty-four hour leave from the encampment and planned to spend the night at a local boarding house, hoping he would not catch lice. Before Barnes left the Vulture, he told the tavern keeper where he was staying, asking him to give a message to the kid if he showed up.

After a restless night, disturbed by street noise from flatbed wagons, carriages and loud people, Barnes rose at dawn and walked down to the waterfront hoping to encounter Joseph. The robust activity all around him was like a giant bee hive; hundreds of people carrying, stacking, loading, and unloading. Wooden crates, barrels and sacks of grain, flour and rice were stacked high. Behind him, he saw an endless line of flatbeds, pulled by teams of horses, patiently waiting in lines to pick up or deliver shipments.

Barnes turned and walked up the bank between two building and onto the dirt road full of seafarers thirsty for ale, hungry for food and yearning for a woman or conversation. He entered the Vulture, again almost choking from the smell of the place.

His eyes met briefly with the tavern keeper's. He had a worried look.

"Any news about my nephew?" Barnes asked.

The tavern keeper was silent.

Barnes grew uneasy. "Is there something wrong?"

"I am sorry, sir, your nephew was found last night."

Barnes was confused. "Found? What do you mean, he was found?"

"I am sorry, but your nephew has been found murdered." Barnes was visibly shaken. He tried to pull himself together. He was on assignment.

Barnes repeated, "Murdered? How could that be?" Barnes felt as though he had been kicked in the gut. His head was spinning. What the hell happened? Had the rebels suspected him? Barnes didn't think so. Joseph was too damn good at what he did. Who were his enemies? Barnes knew of only one person who didn't like the kid, and that was Krumb. Perhaps Joseph had gotten too close to the smuggling operations.

The tavern keeper took Barnes by the arm, pulling him to the side "Your nephew's body was found near the wetlands on the shore. His body was hidden in the thick underbrush. They think he had been there a few days. I know this must be a terrible shock."

The keeper paused to pour a couple ales, and continued, "Stabbings are not uncommon on the waterfront; we have at least a couple a month. But the killing of a boy his age doesn't make sense."

"You saying the kid was stabbed?" Barnes dropped his head. The kid's loss was hitting Barnes hard.

"I took the liberty to have his body brought to the Vulture's cellar."

Barnes could not believe what he was hearing. He didn't say a word.

The tavern keeper told Barnes, "Let me show you the way to the cellar. We have to go outside and around to the back of the building." The keeper yelled to his helper to keep an eye on things.

The cellar door opened with a creaking noise, it was cool inside. Barnes saw a soiled and torn piece of sailcloth draped over a body. He hesitated for a moment, hoping it was a mistake, hoping it was not Joseph lying there. His hand lifted a corner of the sailcloth, just enough to see the victim's face. It was Joseph, his hair encrusted with mud and sea grass.

"Sir, would you like to be alone with him?" said the keeper.

"No, please stay." Barnes paused. "I am his only family; I will make plans to take him home. The boy will be taken home and buried near his mother."

"He was a good lad," the tavern keeper said, "on the shy and quiet side. He visited the Vulture daily. Even though I would like to think we were like family, I didn't even know the lad's name."

"His name is James," replied Barnes.

The keeper then said, "We could give him a proper burial up at the Hillside Cemetery. There he would be with all the seafarers, master mariners and drunks who arrived at Flushing Bay and never left. You can see their graves dotting the hillside."

"Kind of you to make the offer."

The keeper lifted the sailcloth revealing the stab wound. "The boy was stabbed and bled to death. The knife went right through his vest and into his heart." The keeper's voice filled with sadness as he continued, "I just can't imagine who would have wanted him dead. He minded his own business, and from what I saw, he did not have an angry bone in his body."

Barnes could hardly speak. A lump of guilt and anguish lodged in his throat. He just nodded his head, holding back his rage.

The keeper noticed Barnes' face full of anguish, and he suggested, "Let's go upstairs and get you a whisky, it will ease the pain."

Barnes nodded, "Perhaps it will. That might do me good, thank you."

Before leaving the cellar, Barnes examined Joseph's fatal chest wound. Then he eased the sailcloth back over Joseph's young body and followed the keeper outside to go back inside the Vulture. Barnes tried to maintain a stoic exterior, so as not to draw attention to himself. He sat on a bench putting his elbows on the grimy table. He put his face in his hands.

The tavern keeper handed Barnes his whisky, and in a whisper told Barnes of the latest rumors. "Some say your nephew was involved with the dory that was found floating bottom-up in the bay."

Barnes, stunned, dropped his hands from his face. With a bewildered look he scanned to see who was sitting nearby. He then whispered, "A dory flipped over, what are you saying?"

"Well, like so many young people today, maybe the kid needed money to eat and maybe he got involved with nefarious activities."

Barnes tried to look surprised, "Nefarious? What are you telling me, do you think he was doing something illegal?"

"I don't mean to offend you sir, but word is, a couple nights ago a boat capsized. Rumor has it that the boat was full of French-made muskets in route to the rebel army."

Barnes began to picture the likely sequence of events. The smugglers ran into trouble, the dory capsized, Joseph swam to the shore, only to be stabbed to death the moment he stepped out of the water.

"I would like to ask a favor," Barnes said, sipping his whiskey. "Would you find me a coffin for my nephew?"

"Oh, sure, I can get you a coffin. A workshop just down the road makes coffins; they work around the clock trying to keep up with demand. They owe me a couple favors."

"I will send a flatbed this evening to pick up James." As Barnes turned and exited the Vulture, he was so deeply devastated that he feared his legs might buckle. He walked to the livery to get his horse and once on his way back to Harlem Heights, he allowed himself to cry.

Just as the tavern keeper promised, Joseph's body was placed into a coffin. A man with a flatbed picked up the coffin and brought his body back to Harlem Heights. Colonel Barnes saw the irony. A sarcophagus that may have been used to hide smuggled weapons became Joseph's casket. At Harlem Heights, Colonel Barnes, with the coffin in sight, walked to a cooled campfire and picked up a piece of blackened charcoal. He printed on the top and side of the pine box: Private Joseph Holmes, L.A.R., Middle District, Died: 30 June 1778, aged 14.

Barnes brushed the black charcoal from his fingers and left instructions for the coffin to be taken to the Holmes family in Middle District. He went to his office and reread Joseph's last information drop, seeking a clue to explain his murder. He was a kid who joined the L.A.R. at the age of thirteen with hopes of working in the stables and serving his King. One year later he was dead. Barnes thought about the murder again and again. Something was amiss; it didn't make sense. Perhaps someone had let the word out, exposing Joseph's cover. Disgusted, he thought there was no way to prove anything. After all, they were fighting a war.

He wondered if Joseph was the target, or someone else? Joseph was not a complicated person, but his death seemed riddled with questions.

At dawn the next morning, a lone soldier on horseback headed from Harlem Heights to the Holmes family farm in Middle District. A short distance behind the soldier was a flatbed wagon carrying Joseph's body.

Later that morning, Colonel Barnes met with his two junior officers,

Lieutenants Krumb and Worthmore. They had taken their usual places across from Barnes at the table.

"I have unfortunate news from Flushing Bay to share with you."

Krumb rolled his eyes and sighed. His immediate response was a smug look, followed by a cutting comment. "That kid has disappeared on us before, so there is no new news from Flushing Bay. There that kid goes again, making us look like fools. It is a disgrace and he should be imprisoned!"

Barnes was startled at Krumb's remark, turned to Krumb asking him with a stern and penetrating voice, "Lieutenant Krumb, who is talking about Joseph? I didn't bring up Joseph's name."

Worthmore watched, confused at Krumb's remark, "Would someone explain what is going on?"

Krumb looked nervously at Barnes, then at Worthmore. The lieutenant had become fidgety. He snapped at Colonel Barnes, "Well, that is what I thought you said—I thought you said Joseph."

"Give the kid a break, Krumb, you know this situation is entirely different compared to the kidnapping." Barnes was growing more suspicions of Krumb, but he doubted that Krumb would have gone so far as to have him killed, even if he hated the boy.

"Several days ago sometime after his drop, Joseph was murdered."

Krumb was not able to keep his mouth shut, "He is dead, are you sure? How could that be, I bet it is a hoax; I never trusted that ..."

"Lieutenant Krumb," Barnes interjected, "as your superior officer I am sentencing you to your tent for seven days. Your meals will be brought to you and during this time you are to have no communication with anyone, no books, no booze. You are to sit with yourself and think about your heinous attitude toward a fellow soldier who is now deceased. Next you may be looking at a demotion and a new assignment in the field."

Barnes dismissed his two Lieutenants and began to think about the valuable information Joseph had gotten for them at such a critical time. The surreptitious movement of guns and ammunition was at a peak. The running of contraband had to end; winning the war was at stake. Joseph's information gave the British army a chance to stop at least some of the smuggling. He died a hero.

⋘⊙

129

Magdalene picked up the wooden bucket, with the ash from the hearth, and walked to the kitchen garden. There, she mixed in the ash with the soil. Using a pitchfork, she then mixed the vegetable compost into the ash and soil mixture. Leaning on her pitchfork, she stopped to get her breath. With her left hand, she pushed hair out of her eyes. She was thankful for another beautiful day. For more than a year, their home had been so quiet with only her and Jonathan. She wondered if she would ever get used to the silence.

That was when she noticed a soldier on horseback coming up the long drive connecting the house to the town road. Her immediate thought was that Joseph was home. Magdalene dropped the pitchfork as she ran down the road to meet him.

As she got closer to the man on horseback, she realized he was not Joseph. Magdalene's moments of euphoria came to an abrupt end. She looked aghast at the young soldier who politely greeted her.

"Is this the home of Mr. Jonathan Holmes?" asked the soldier.

"I am Mrs. Holmes, may I be of help?" The soldier dismounted and introduced himself. Magdalene saw he was tall, as tall as Obadiah. She watched as he turned to his saddlebag and lifted the flap. He pulled out several letters.

"Mrs. Holmes, where might I find Mr. Holmes? Is he nearby?"

Just as the soldier asked the question, Magdalene saw Jonathan in the distance coming in from the fields. Once he was by his wife's side, the soldier introduced himself again and then presented Jonathan with a letter addressed to him.

Magdalene became light-headed, and her body crumbled to the ground like a rag doll. The soldier and Jonathan carried her into the house. Once Magdalene was comfortable, her husband went to his desk to get his letter opener. He sat next to Magdalene as she wept.

With her face streaked with tears, she asked her husband, "Which son have we lost?"

Jonathan placed his letter opener under the flap and broke the wax seal. He unfolded the paper, read it silently to himself; folded it and placed it on his lap. He breathed in slowly, held the air in his lungs for a moment then exhaled. Magdalene watched her husband as his tears began to run down his cheeks. He took his wife's hand and wrapped his arms around her.

As he embraced her, he said, "Magdalene, we have lost Joseph."

She shook her head, saying, "No, it can't be my youngest, he is fourteen, No, please tell me this is a mistake." Magdalene repeated that one word, mistake, each time louder. "I am certain there is some mistake!" She then began to wail, nearly hysterical. Jonathan had never seen his wife so distraught. He desperately tried to give his wife comfort.

While weeping, her words filled with grief, she tried to say, "Joseph my youngest, my lovable and smart young man. Now, his life is gone."

The young soldier stood near the hearth, Jonathan sat by Magdalene's side. He stared out the window. In a soft tone of voice, he repeatedly asked himself: "How could this have happened? Joseph was not in combat, how could he die? How could this have happened?"

He turned his head and asked the soldier, "Our youngest son is just a lad, like you; there is no word in this letter about what happened. What was the cause of his death?" Jonathan dropped his stare to the letter on his lap.

The soldier walked across the room to Jonathan and placed his hand on his shoulder. Meanwhile, Magdalene's distress seemed to be worsening.

The soldier took Magdalene's hand. "Mrs. Holmes, I am sorry, truly sorry for your loss." Any attempt to provide Magdalene and her husband solace was a insurmountable task.

Her thoughts began to whirl, seeking something or someone to blame. She grew angry thinking about the British monarch, for whom she was indifferent. The loss of their youngest son revealed the ruthlessness of war. With war came unmeasurable grief and endless amounts of sadness that were surely not meant for any parent to suffer or endure.

Jonathan asked if it could be a clerical error. He left Magdalene's side and asked the young soldier again, "Could it be a misidentification? We have five sons fighting for the King and the war is becoming a very risky and deadly endeavor."

He wiped the tears from his wife's eyes and took her into his arms to comfort her and himself. As they embraced, Jonathan's eyes were drawn to the window. In the distance, a flatbed wagon was slowly making its way toward their home. He closed his eyes tightly. As the wagon approached the house, Jonathan whispered in her ear, "My dear Magdalene, Joseph would want us to be strong."

The soldier saw the flatbed wagon approaching the dooryard. Without saying a word, the soldier turned and left the room to meet the driver. On the flatbed was a single pine coffin. With reluctance, Jonathan and Magdalene followed the soldier outside. In front of them on the flatbed Jonathan saw the black lettering, spelling out his son's name and date of death, regiment and age.

Magdalene saw her husband was in agony and she took his weather-beaten hand in hers, held it tightly and whispered, "Joseph is at peace."

Early the next morning, Jonathan was awakened by the crowing of King George. His muscles ached as he got out of bed. Must be from the digging, he thought, as he recalled his neighbors coming to help dig Joseph's final resting place. In silence, he began to recall the events of last evening. Once the neighbors had gone home and after Magdalene had fallen to sleep. Jonathan followed his urge to see his son's body before burial.

He entered the barn and knelt down beside the coffin, removed a couple of the nails from the lid and whispered, "Son, I don't mean to disturb your peace, but I want to see you one last time."

Slowly he lifted the lid and carefully slid it onto the barn floor. Jonathan saw his boy's face, hair combed back, eyes closed, the face of an angel. Jonathan's eyes moved from his son's face to his chest and he gasped at the sight of his son's blood-soaked vest. With one hand, he lifted Joseph's vest to see the fatal wound. It appeared that whoever had killed his son, had aimed for his heart. Jonathan sobbed, his body trembled and his gut filled with rage.

He raised his eyes toward the heavens, and saw the hayloft where Joseph once played. He yelled, "Please tell me, why someone would kill my boy, why?" After a few moments, Jonathan stood on his feet and walked across the dirt floor of the barn to where a horse blanket was draped. He picked it up, gave it a couple shakes and embraced the blanket closely to his chest. After several moments, he laid the blanket lovingly over Joseph's body and he tucked in the sides to make a snug fit.

Again with his eyes lifted to the heavens he demanded, "What in God's name happened to our boy? How could they bring him back to his mother and me like this! Joseph was killed, a fatal stab wound in his chest! How could this be, he was a fourteen-year-old stable boy!" Jonathan spent several more minutes by his son's side.

"Please forgive me, Joseph, it is my fault." He continued to moan, a low painful moan. Tears saturated his face as he bent over and kissed his son on his forehead. His tears fell on his son's face.

A small gathering congregated around the freshly dug grave. Magdalene stood stoic next to her husband near the pile of freshly dug dirt. The wholesome aroma of the soil soothed her, while at the same time the sweet earthy smell often accompanied final farewells. The service was short.

After the few friends there left, her eyes focused on the wooden cross at the head of her son's grave. She knew her suffering had no bottom. She asked herself, "Why wasn't I more assertive? Why didn't I stop Joseph? I am his mother and I should have said no, I failed to protect my boy." She shivered at the thought that she never again would hold her son in her arms or behold him with her eyes.

A short time later, Jonathan returned to the gravesite with two bowls of tea, a few small biscuits and smoked meat. They shared no conversation, only tea, biscuits, meat and touch. She picked up her bowl of tea, held it gently in both hands and gently sipped it until it was gone. "I am ready to go home; we can walk home in the twilight."

Jonathan thought Magdalene would benefit from a visitor, so he asked Martha Brouwer to come. He hoped that one of Martha teas or many remedies might help Magdalene. Magdalene told Martha about not being able to relax or sleep. "Martha, I am unable to stop thinking about Joseph." She paused and began to weep. "What about my other sons, will they return home in a wooden box on a flatbed wagon, too? This fighting is ruining everything that is good about who we are and what we do. The war is destroying the lives of our children, the hopes and dreams we have for them are drowning in bloodshed."

When Martha took Magdalene's hand and listened, she was surprised to hear Magdalene's strong opinions, especially about King George. Soon a sad silence fell on the two women and the room was still. Martha noticed the dark circles under Magdalene's eyes. She gently laid Magdalene's head on a bed pillow and then went to the kitchen to make her some tea.

Martha Brouwer, also of Dutch ancestry, was known across Middle District for her abilities to cure illnesses and comfort the sick. She was a master of the powers of herbal plants and she could harness an illness with the simple things that grow outside.

Once the tea steeped, she returned to Magdalene's bedroom. "Here, I have some tea. I think it should help you relax and help you sleep."

Magdalene took the bowl of herbal tea and sipped with pleasure.

"I will return tomorrow with a blend of herbs for other teas, and a tincture to be taken daily. I am certain my remedy will give you some peace of mind."

Martha Brouwer's herbal concoction enabled Magdalene to sleep, and with the rest came what she referred to as a productive day. Within a few short days, Magdalene was on her feet again. The first item on her list was to write her four sons and two daughters to inform them of Joseph's death.

Chapter 14

July 1778: Stony Point

J.R. was only half listening when mail call began. When the name Holmes was called by the young private charged with disseminating the mail to the Fort Washington troops, J.R. picked up the letter and recognized his mother's handwriting.

The name Holmes was called again and J.R. smiled as he took the second letter and saw that it was from Abigail.

It had been more than a year since he had seen Abigail, the woman he loved and planned to marry the moment the rebels were defeated. When J.R. last saw Abigail, he never imagined that he would be gone this long or be so homesick. When he enlisted a year earlier, he had been confident the fighting would be over before the harvest. He laughed at his naiveté. News from Abigail was good. She and her parents were as fine as one could expect.

Next, he unfolded his mother's letter and began to read. He stopped, narrowed his focus and read the first couple of lines again. Under his breath he said, "No! This could not have happened!" His voice grew louder. "No, this cannot be possible, not my kid brother! It just can't be, Joseph can't be dead! What the hell happened?"

J.R. was immobilized, refusing to believe what he had read and unwilling to grasp the cruel reality. Bewildered, he thought that he must act, and act now. He must ride to Harlem Heights and demand answers from the British commander. However, that was not possible. He could not leave Fort Washington. He stood up and walked to his quarters; he was dazed and filled with disbelief. Then as if some kind of crazy person, he began to dig through his old letters to find the one that Joseph had sent him. Joseph had written about his kidnapping and the type of work he was doing. At the time, J.R. found the letter confusing, but now in hindsight, things were making sense.

He searched everywhere for the letter but was unable to find it. He became irritated beyond reason; he kicked the leg of his bunk and slammed his fist on the wall. A couple of his bunkmates heard J.R. and went to him but he waved them away. That was when he remembered hiding Joseph's last letter to him in a place where it could not be found. He was not sure just where he had stashed it.

Joseph's rather bizarre letter began to come back to J. R's mind, line by line. It was in that letter that J.R. learned that Joseph was not working at the horse stables. He recalled that Joseph had warned him not to share that information with anyone, not even with his parents. Joseph referred to something about "new assignments," risky scouting missions, behind enemy lines. Joseph conveyed that something sinister might have been happening. J.R. was disquieted as he created a better understanding of what his brother was doing. It is no wonder Joseph lost his life. To him it sounded as if he was a spy for the British. Joseph working as a spy seemed so very unlikely.

Beads of perspiration formed on his forehead as he thought about Joseph. He knew that Joseph had a free-spirited attitude and sense of humor. Initially, J.R. thought the kidnapping story was some kind of joke. Now he painfully realized that it was no joke at all. More of what Joseph had written in the letter come flooding back. It was a relative, a cousin named Poore, who had kidnapped Joseph. And what did he mean when he said a lieutenant loathed him?

The meal bell began to ring, and he heard soldiers lining up. He remained behind, his stomach in knots. If he wrote a letter to Harlem Heights, asking for an explanation, would that tarnish Joseph's record for not following his superior's gag order? He thought long and hard. What would Joseph want him to do, how would he want him to react?

ↄᔆ

Nearly a year later, J.R's company left Fort Washington after two years there. The company boarded military vessels for the thirty-mile trip north on the Hudson River to their new assignment, defending an important ferry crossing at Stony Point. Because of its high elevation and broad views of the Hudson, both north and south, Stony Point was considered critical for the British to occupy.

After being at the physically commanding Fort Washington, J.R. was surprised to find that Stony Point was not a stone fortress, with high ramparts and towers. Stony Point was just that, a stony point, perched 150 feet above the Hudson River with grand views in all directions. It was a natural fortress with water on three sides. The fourth side was a deep, swamp leading to a steep rocky incline.

At Stony Point, J.R. and other soldiers constructed abatis, sharpened wooden obstacles made of felled trees. Among the Hessian soldiers who worked with J.R. on that project was Heinrich With. Heinrich didn't speak a word of English, but they gained a good understanding of their job and each other.

In a short time, the few hundred men from Fort Washington made modifications to enhance the natural defensive protections of Stony Point. The top and sides of the fortress were guarded by a gunboat and an armed sloop sitting in the Hudson River. At the top of the point were numerous iron and brass cannons, four mortars and four howitzers, not to mention a detachment of the Royal Artillery, the LA.R. and a small Hessian brigade.

By the end of June, 700 soldiers were garrisoned at Stony Point. The soldiers bunked in large tents. J.R. liked the location. He thought that if he could ease his grief about Joseph's death and not worry about his two sisters being married to rebels, maybe he could find peace at Stony Point.

Two weeks later, in the middle of a moonless night, J.R. was awakened by voices. The noise got louder and soon a number of voices were yelling. Then he was jolted by the sound of clashing bayonets. There was no musket fire or cannon fire. It did not make sense; he wondered what was taking place. J.R. woke his fellow bunkmates, pulled his breeches on and grabbed his musket. He lifted the flap of his tent and he and his bunkmates exited to be greeted by Continental troops, who took their weapons and ordered them to surrender.

Like his fellow soldiers, J.R. was bewildered. A rugged group of rebel soldiers surrounded them. Many were not in uniform and most were bearded. In the distance, he saw the lowering of the British flag and heard cheers.

Later that day, J.R. learned that Stony Point was captured almost without a single shot being fired. The rebel army was under orders not to attack with muskets. They were to use only their bayonets to ensure the element of surprise. J.R. was beginning to grasp the rebels' hard-as-nails mindset. The rebel army was already in control of West Point and now they had Stony Point. J.R. was speechless when he learned that the Continental troops had taken Stony Point in less than thirty minutes.

The Continental troops stood guard over the several hundred men they had just captured. J.R. sat with a few dozen others, while the number of prisoners at Stony Point was tallied by rank. At 2:00 a.m., J.R. heard the count was over five hundred. Later some of the British officers would be traded for rebel officers being held onboard the prison ships anchored off New York.

Since his enlistment in early 1777, J.R. had not seen combat once, and now he was captured by the element of surprise. How were the rebels able to reach the top of Stony Point when some considered it impregnable? He watched rebel soldiers tell everyone to prepare for departure. When one rebel soldier walked past, J.R. asked, "Sir, where are you taking us?"

The answer was a cold look. Then the soldier barked: "On your feet, Tory, shut up and do what you are told!"

The defeated soldiers, after eating a semblance of breakfast, learned their official status. They were prisoners of war. If anyone attempted to escape, he would be shot.

Just after sunrise, a few hundred American soldiers loyal to the Crown and a handful of Hessian troops were ordered to gather their few belongings, and they began marching to a prison several hundred miles away in the Colony of Pennsylvania. They were ill prepared for the grueling march; they had poor footwear and took barely any water or food. It was hot and humid, the middle of July. A long row of guards marched or rode horses along each side of the long row of prisoners. The wounds, and men with fevers and infections, were forced to walk. The number of men dwindled as those who could not keep up died where they dropped.

After several days of marching, J.R. noticed Heinrich and they exchanged glances. After a time, they walked together. The two men did their best to keep each other focused. Once they reached their destination, J.R. checked around him. It seemed as if nearly one-third of the soldiers had died along the way.

At Easton, in the Colony of Pennsylvania, the prisoners learned of the overcrowded condition at the prison. When the guards told the Stony Point prisoners about the lack of space, Heinrich was perplexed and anxious.

J.R. talked slowly to Heinrich, while using his hands to help express what he wanted to say, "Stay close to me." Heinrich understood that some prisoners were to continue marching.

The guards walked through the few hundred prisoners, looking for men who appeared healthy enough to continue marching to another P.O.W camp. J.R., Heinrich and a few dozen other prisoners from Stony Point were ordered to stand near the prison's interior wall and wait. Heinrich did as J.R. suggested and he stayed close. J.R. was growing uncomfortable standing against the wall. A thought haunted him, were they going to be executed? A new group of prison guards was assigned to them, and J.R. thought they might be executioners.

Then from out of nowhere, a large cauldron of watery soup appeared, along with cornbread infested with the tiny white eggs and larvae of the Indian-meal moth. J.R. was relieved and gave Heinrich an encouraging look. Heinrich was repulsed by the appearance of the cornbread. J.R. s concern was that if they didn't eat it, they might not have the strength needed for the next march. Soon they were ordered to fall in line. Guards on horseback flanked the line of more than a hundred prisoners. J.R. hoped they would make it to the destination alive.

Chapter 15

August 1779: Prisoners of War

The Continental officer in charge eventually told the marching prisoners that their destination was a remote camp, Albemarle Barracks in the Commonwealth of Virginia. To J.R., Virginia was a world away from Middle District. To actually know their destination filled him with relief. At times, it was easy to imagine the rebel guards were going to march them until they all dropped dead.

As the prisoners approached the entry gates of Albemarle, many of them were exhausted and thirsty, but they could not help noticing the beauty of the Virginia hills. The view reminded Heinrich of his home in the Principality of Hesse. Heinrich's gaze brought a smile to his dust-covered face.

A sudden yell from a guard cut short his smile. "Hey, let's move it, you will have plenty of time to take in the scenery later!" To spur them along, the guard nudged several prisoners with the end of his musket.

Albemarle Barracks was perched high on a hill, on the north bank of Ivy Creek. The creek was an oasis for the fatigued prisoners of war. So was the prison camp. As J.R. walked through the entry gate, he noticed a complete lack of guards. He entered the interior prison yard and he was amazed at what lay before him. Everywhere he saw vegetable gardens. Before him was an assemblage of plantings: red tomatoes, carrots, cucumbers, corn, potatoes and squash growing in mounds of dark rich soil. Each garden plot was arranged in straight and tidy rows. J.R. heard the surprised gasps of the other men, as they too beheld the sight of greenery. J.R. thought this Garden of Eden was surely a good omen.

J.R. smiled and his heart was at ease, a feeling he had not felt in a long time. He studied the men who were busily tending to the numerous plantings. They were a hearty bunch, well-nourished and appeared to be humble farmers, while the rows of plants stood as if they were standing at attention. However, they had no superior officer, no battle to fight, no blood to lose and no war to turn their lives upside down. J.R. laughed to himself; the gardens were the only thing that exhibited militarism in the entire place; a quality in complete contrast to the prisoners tending them. No one, not even a war-weary soldier, would guess those casually dressed men, pulling weeds around the squash plants, were trained officers of the King of England!

The prisoners were soon addressed by Continental officers, who said they were allowed them to write letters home and accept money from family members. The hard currency that families sent could be used by the prisoners to buy needed items from local merchants, helping the local economy. Perhaps the greatest restriction placed on the prisoners was that they had to promise to never pick up arms to fight against the Continental Army.

Everything J.R. heard and saw provided him with simple comfort. Both he and Heinrich had been highly anxious when they arrived at Albemarle. Now J.R. couldn't wait to write to Abigail. He wanted to relieve her fears of his capture, and give her a description of this Eden, incorrectly named a prison. J.R. smiled at Heinrich. They could rest easy and recover from the long march from Stony Point to Albemarle Barracks.

J.R. and Heinrich settled into life at Albemarle, and sometimes they received word of the fighting. The latest news was that the front lines of the war were shifting southward from the colonies of the Northeast to the mid-Atlantic colonies, where battles waged more fiercely than ever. Many thousands of young men enlisted on both sides creating a lack of men to work the fields. This had a grave impact on food production across every Colony. As young men abandoned the cultivated fields for the battlefields, keeping the troops fed became a serious problem. The Holmes farm was an example of labor loss due to the war. Five hard-working brothers had shared the chores, where now, all of the work rested on the shoulders of their father and mother.

Enormous demands were placed on the farmers because they were unable to cultivate enough crops to feed the troops. Washington's army, unlike the Loyal American Regiments and British troops, could not depend on imported food and supplies. If Continentals could not feed their army, the army would desert.

The war also triggered a growing need for tradesmen, such as blacksmiths, wheelwrights and coopers. The monumental problem was how to keep an army fed and supplied without tradesmen. For example, coopers made casks for the storage and transport of gunpowder. The lack of something seemingly as ordinary as a barrel could immobilize the rebel army.

The Continental Army came up with an ingenious solution to the labor shortage by putting prisoners of war to work on farms and in trades. A couple weeks after arriving at Albemarle, new prisoners were gathered for questioning about their knowledge of planting and other trades. A Continental officer called for J.R. and Heinrich to meet with him in his office.

"So tell me soldier, what did you do before enlistment, do you have a trade?" the officer asked J.R.

"I am a planter and harvester,"

The officer responded with a broad smile. "With which crops have you experience?"

"I have planted and harvested a variety of grains, oat, wheat, barley and rye. I maintained my family's fruit trees, mostly peach and apple."

The officer looked at Heinrich, and then back at J.R. "And, what about your friend? He doesn't speak English?"

"His name is Heinrich With and he too understands farming."

The officer impatiently asked: "Understands farming? Has the young man gotten his hands dirty behind a plow or harrow?"

J.R. sat quietly for a few seconds reminding himself that he had no idea what Heinrich knew and what he didn't know.

The officer's eyes darted back to Heinrich saying, "Stand up boy and let me see what you have to offer the revolution."

Heinrich had a vague idea of what was going on as J.R. motioned him to his feet.

The officer saw Heinrich was tall, but a little on the thin side but that was no matter. "Heinrich, I see you are a young man with a good strong back." He motioned Heinrich to sit down. There were a few moments of silence while the officer shuffled some papers and dabbed his pen into the ink well. He scratched something out on the paper in front of him and said, "You will hear from me about your assignment to a farm."

J.R. heard those few words and feared the worst, it sounded as if their stay at Albemarle might have come to a quick end.

The officer continued, "You have two options, you are required to choose one of the two. I suggest you to think each option over carefully." J.R. sat and thought that when the enemy offers you options, it cannot be good.

The officer said, "First option: I am giving you an opportunity to fight with the brave Americans of the Continental Army; to fight with young men like you, who love this land. Brave men, just like you are needed. With this offer, you will be deeded 30 acres when the war ends. This great opportunity gives you a chance to fight on the side that will win. Mark my words, we will be victorious!" J.R. had a good idea about the second option. He thought they would be working like slaves who labored in the cotton fields fourteen hours a day, with no break and little to eat. J.R. cringed.

The officer continued, "The second option is forced labor on a farm. If engaging in the fight for freedom from the tyrannical King is not your choice, you will serve out your time as a prisoner of war doing forced labor. Let me remind you, with either choice you will be supporting Commander George Washington, his Continental Army and the goals of the revolution."

"Sir, as prisoners of war, we choose forced labor."

"So that it will be, forced labor." The officer scribbled a few notes in a document and added, "My corporal will be in touch with you with the details."

J.R. and Heinrich walked back to the barracks. Heinrich was confused. He began to speak excitedly in German. In response, J.R. spoke slowly while using his hands to enhance what he was saying. "We are going to work on a farm." J.R. repeated, "Work, soon you and me will leave here." J.R. figured that Heinrich understood the basics. Heinrich grimly nodded; he was anxious about making another change. He didn't want to leave Albemarle Barracks.

The officers of Albemarle assigned J.R. and Heinrich to a Mr. Soule, who had written a couple times expressing his dire need for laborers. A few weeks later, Soule received a response from Albemarle Barracks. He was thrilled to hear that two prisoners of war would soon be ready for him to pick up. He could not have received the news at a better time, as harvesting was on the doorstep.

A few days later, Soule hitched two horses to the wagon and waved goodbye to his daughter, who stood at the kitchen door. As he headed down the carriage path toward the dirt road, he waved to his one laborer in the field.

With his two sons and his other young farmhands all off fighting for independence from the King, Soule saw his farm slipping further and further into debt, sliding into the hands of the bank. Some relief came in the spring of 1779 when his first prisoner of war arrived at the Soule farm just as planting season began. He was as hard working as two men, but Soule needed more hands or he would run the risk of losing the crop in the fields, the crop they had labored long and hard to plant.

At Albemarle Barracks, Soule saw a long line of Virginia planters, all there picking up prisoners. The activity lifted his heart and he was growing confident that the Continental soldier and Virginia regiments would indeed have bread on the table this winter. Everyone there, from cobblers to innkeepers, were abuzz as they picked up prisoners to fill their particular labor need.

Soule climbed down from his wagon, watered his horses, hitched them to a post, then walked toward the commander's office. A crowd of men gathered near the office door, waiting their turn. Soule watched the young prisoners as they were led to waiting flatbeds and carriages. He noticed that most were about the same age as his sons. Getting a closer look, he saw some of the prisoners were thin, maybe malnourished. He immediately hoped his own boys were safe and out of the enemy's hands. Soule heard his name called and took his letter of notification to the officer in charge, then he waited outside next to his horses and flatbed. After several minutes the two prisoners were brought to him.

A Corporal Villian introduced himself. Soule learned that Villian would visit and check Soule's paroled prisoners monthly. During that time, the officer would address discipline problems "I will be making sure those Tories stay in line. You know you cannot trust their kind, not for one moment."

"I currently have a prisoner working for me," Soule said, "and no one has come to check on him, is this a new procedure?"

"Certainly not. What is this prisoner's name? I will add him to my roster."

"Ned Lawson,"

Villian wrote Lawson's name in his book. "Before I forget, I have one final suggestion, if you find the need to whip your prisoners, don't hesitate to do so. I encourage people to exercise a stern discipline when, and as, you find it necessary. If they attempt to escape, and you are able to stop them with a gun, then use it, or let me know. I will have them hanged." Villian chuckled, then noticed the two prisoners were being led toward them. The corporal gave the two prisoners a look of mistrust.

J.R. and Heinrich were now officially the responsibility of Mr. Soule.

The corporal told J.R. and Heinrich, "I will be stopping at the farm, unannounced, and expecting to find no problems. You will be working diligently to support the Continental Army, our grand revolution. Do you understand?" Without giving them time to respond, Villian continued. "Oh, I almost forgot, if you try to escape, we have dogs and you will be caught and hanged. Those bloodhounds never miss catching a Tory or a nigger—one in the same wouldn't you say, boys? Am I making myself clear? You will—

Soule with a disapproving look interrupted. "We really need to be leaving now." He then motioned the prisoners to climb up onto the flatbed wagon. "It is time we get on the road back home." They tossed their knapsacks onto the flatbed wagon.

Soule felt a weight lifted off his shoulders. His farm would soon be producing again and he would be able to pay off his loan from the bank. "The sight of the two of you makes me one very thankful man! I felt fortunate to have gotten one prisoner earlier this spring and now having the two you is wonderful!"

Both J.R. and Heinrich understood Soule. The man was full of smiles. J.R. thought that even a blind person could see the joy and excitement this man carried.

By the time they neared the farm, Soule said, "Ned, arrived here last spring, and did the work of three men. Dozens of cultivated fields are plentiful, just bursting with what looks to be a very healthy harvest."

J.R. listened and noticed how Soule's voice was soft and calming while being excited about the upcoming harvest.

It was clear to J.R. that Soule was giving them both a hearty welcome to the farm. "You know, if not for the two of you, much of this abundant harvest would die in the fields. J.R., does Heinrich understand any English at all?"

"No, sir, he does not. There was little reason for him to learn English because he served in an all-Hessian regiment. He will pick it up once settled at your farm. After all, farming, like music, is an international language."

Soule smiled at J. R's comment. "Yes, I suppose you are correct.

Farming is a language understood by all farmers who share common methods and practice, all over the world." He scratched his head and asked, "If Heinrich knows no English, how did the commander know he was a good farmer?"

J.R. tilted his head, shrugged his shoulders and replied, "I really don't know. My guess would be Heinrich seemed like he could do lots of farm work."

"We have to give that much to the commander, he know a good worker when he sees one."

Heinrich, in silence, listened to the words and laughter being bantered between Mr. Soule and J.R. He liked the soothing sound of Soule's voice, which continued as they went over bumps, around hills, and along the streams. Soule talked to the two of them as if he had forgotten that Heinrich did not understand a word. He told them how all of his former farmhands had gone to enlist and fight against the King. They rode past a farm and J.R. could see two women working the fields, a job once exclusive to men.

Soule broke the short period of silence with comments that weren't in his usual upbeat tone. "Times have changed. It has become more common to see women doing the hard labor of farming. I am a widower, with one daughter. She has her hands full taking care of the domestic chores, but I have had to ask her a few times to help with the farm work. It is not easy for anyone during a time of war."

J.R. listened as Soule gave a brief summary of his life and his farm. Every so often J.R. turned to give Heinrich looks of encouragement. It did not seem at all likely that they were heading to a place where they would be treated harshly with whips, chains or daily beatings. As the flatbed rattled and bounced along the long drive to the farm, J.R. and Heinrich's eyes gleamed with the sight of the large two-story home and the even larger barn, along with several out buildings. It was a welcome sight for the two weary prisoners.

Soule climbed down from the flatbed and called to his daughter. She came out of house and wrapped her arms around her father. J.R. and Heinrich nodded toward her. Soule introduced J.R. and Heinrich to his daughter, Comfort.

Within a moment of meeting each other, Comfort and Heinrich were mesmerized. Heinrich tried to hide his attraction. He spoke in his own language, telling Comfort that he found it very good to make her acquaintance. As if in a daze, Heinrich stopped, realizing that he was

145

speaking Deutsch. He blushed, embarrassed. All the while, he thought he would be the luckiest soldier in the world to get a glance of Comfort's loveliness every day. He was infatuated by her wholesome appearance. Her fair skin, deep blue eyes, long neck and feminine curves intrigued him. He never imagined women of the British colonies could be so captivating, so lovely.

J.R. saw the chemistry between the two and smiled as he watched Heinrich go weak in the knees. Comfort was more prudent. She judiciously watched him while maintaining her distance. She thought he was devilishly good looking. She sized him up as a strong man with a gentleness about him. She noticed he had not said one English word and she thought he might be shy.

To break the silence, Comfort asked a question. "Where are the two of you from?"

"I am from Fishkill, Middle District, New York. Heinrich, who does not speak English, is from the German principality of Hesse." With an astonished expression on her face, Comfort is baffled.

"He doesn't speak any English?" How would she ever get to know him if he doesn't speak English?

"I have a feeling he will learn quickly," her father said.

Her father's words gave her hope. Again, Comfort gave him a welcoming smile. This time she blushed. Their brief encounter lasted but a couple minutes, before Soule took the two prisoners of war, to show them the bunkhouse.

Reflecting on the noticeable attraction between Comfort and the blond-haired, blue-eyed Heinrich, J.R. thought about the first time he met Abigail, the woman he loved, the woman he had not seen in more than two years. Comfort and Heinrich's encounter was a painful reminder to J.R. of how much he missed Abigail.

As they entered the bunkhouse, J.R. saw a hearth, writing table, wooden chest, a couple of benches and several bunks. The large room was as accommodating as almost any inn.

"Ned is out in the field working, his bunk is over there," Soule said. "Why don't the two of you pick the bunk you want and make yourselves at home, the blankets are in the chest. I have things to do so we will catch up later."

Soule, about to leave, paused. "Oh, I expect Ned will be back soon." He excused himself and was gone.

J.R. and Heinrich each picked a bunk and rolled out their blankets. J.R. saw that there was more than one small writing table. He emptied his knapsack putting his corked inkwell, pen, paper and sealing wax on the table closest to his bunk. Picking up the sealing wax and holding it in his hand, he recalled the day he and Joseph were packing to leave for Harlem Heights. He could almost hear Joseph ask him if he had enough sealing wax to share. J.R. felt a tear run down his right cheek.

After they were settled, they sat down, waiting for what might happen next. Then, J.R. stood up, feeling compelled to write a letter to his mother. Heinrich watched him go to the writing table and realized that he should be doing the same thing.

"It has been nearly two months since we were captured," said J.R., "and my family has no idea where I am. They may not even know if I am dead or alive. I have to let them know I am fine." Heinrich was smiling as he stared out one of the three windows. J.R. said, "I know you can hear me, but you don't understand a word I am saying. I don't know why I am talking to you as if you do."

Heinrich saw a dark-skinned man walking toward the bunkhouse. J.R. heard the lifting of the door latch; he turned his head and saw the door swing open. He was a bit startled to see a Negro man, a man who was obviously tired from working in the fields all day, but not too tired to greet the two with a nod and a smile.

Ned Lawson introduced himself to J.R. and Heinrich. It took Ned a moment before he realized that Heinrich was a soldier of the Hessian regiment.

"I am pleased to meet you and greatly relieved you are here. We have a bountiful crop to harvest. Are either of you farmers, or have you done any planting and harvesting?"

"I have and Heinrich, well, time will tell. Let's say he is a fast learner."

Heinrich nodded his head smiling. Soon the door opened again; Soule brought a tray with a variety of smoked meats, cheese and bread for the three men.

Within days, Comfort offered to teach Heinrich English, and he eagerly accepted her offer. He would rush through his late afternoon chores around the barn, never wanting to miss one moment of lesson time. They would often meet outside in the shade of a tree, or on the porch. He quickly absorbed what she taught him and he found that English was slightly like his own language. Comfort took her teaching seriously and every day she held certain expectations for him. She would slowly say a word and he would repeat it back to her. She would introduce a noun, and she would point to what the word meant.

Heinrich had an intense desire to learn, especially so he could talk with Comfort. He also wanted to learn English so he could be a more effective worker with Ned and J.R. His pronunciation improved daily and his mastery of verb tenses was impressive. Comfort got J.R. and Ned involved, asking them to reinforce the new words and to continue reinforcement in the field while they worked.

During Heinrich's lessons, their joyfulness was often heard in the bunkhouse. Ned and J.R. would smile when they heard the merriment. J.R. was glad for Heinrich but it also reminded him of Abigail and he was sad they weren't able to be together.

Within several weeks, Heinrich had acquired some fluency in English. That was when he realized if he learned too quickly, the lessons would end. When Comfort told him that they could now begin to focus on reading and writing, he was thrilled. Comfort told him that learning to write was more of a challenge than learning to speak or read. He found it curious that after spending an entire day speaking English, his dreams remained in German. Heinrich dreamed in Deutsch and whether dreaming that he was with Ned, J.R. or Soule, they all spoke German.

Comfort would sometimes enhance her lessons by walking to many different areas of the farm, teaching words that had real-life meaning. One day they walked to the brook and another day to the apple orchard. They visited the pond and watched as the polliwogs hatched and scooted away. Heinrich's confidence grew when he could pronounce and easily identify common Virginia plants, trees and insects.

Once Heinrich grasped nouns, he conquered prepositions, pronouns, adjectives and adverbs. Heinrich did not have much cause to write English, but he followed Comfort's instructions. J.R. and Ned both kept journals, sometimes writing in them at night. Heinrich's new assignment was to keep a journal in English. He began nightly to write short journal entries. He wrote about the weather, the length of the day, phases of the moon, and what crops were being harvested. He also kept a record of the farm production, and the repair of the several plows on the farm. He also began to make critical comparisons between the older team of oxen and the younger team. Every week Heinrich would give his journal to Comfort, for review and grammatical correction.

Not everyone found happiness in the joy of the two young people. When Corporal Villian arrived for his first visit to check on his three prisoners, he saw Heinrich sitting on the porch practicing English with Comfort. He dismounted from his horse and strode quickly across the grass to where they were sitting.

"I demand to know what you think you are doing?" he said.

Comfort took one look at him, turned her head, and ignored him. She continued with her lesson. Heinrich understood every word that came out of Villian's mouth. He was appalled at the way Villian spoke to Comfort and restrained himself back from teaching Villian how to speak to a lady.

"Young lady," Villian said, "I asked what is going on? Why isn't this prisoner working?"

Calmly, Comfort stood, faced the corporal and said, "I suggest you get on your horse and leave this property, I do not take kindly to men who bully and don't have manners to introduce themselves."

Villian was shocked by the young woman's bold and disrespectful reply, but before he was able to say another word, Comfort continued,

"You would be wise to start over. I repeat, get back on your horse and don't dismount until you apologize, introduce yourself, and tell me what business you have here." Villian was taken aback, and rage was building inside him. He saw the young woman's audacity as insubordination. He stood there growing increasingly angry. After a few moments of silence, it appeared to be a standoff. Then Villian budged.

"Young lady, I am Corporal Villian. I am here is to oversee the three prisoners of war who are paroled to Mr. Soule." He paused, then said, "I, let me repeat, I am in charge of the three prisoners."

Heinrich, using every ounce of his willpower to hold back, continued to watch and listen. He repeated to himself, do not get involved. You are the prisoner and Comfort is doing very well handling this on her own.

"I am Mr. Soule's daughter," Comfort said. "What is your business here today?"

Villian was filled with anger for being treated this way. "What is this prisoner doing, sitting with you when he should be working? He is a forced labor prisoner!"

"I am teaching him to speak English, is there something wrong with that?" Comfort said calmly.

Villian, who was turning red in the face, shouted, "Yes, there most assuredly is something wrong with that! This man is a prisoner of war, our enemy. He is not a scholar in school. Can you get that into your head?" Corporal Villian was out of control and he continued to rant, "If you want to help soldiers, I suggest you help those men who are fighting and dying for your freedom and independence! Do you understand me?"

Comfort made no reply. She continued checking her list of nominative-case possessive pronouns. Heinrich sat there in admiration of Comfort's assertiveness.

Meanwhile, Soule was walked from the barn, having heard parts of the exchange between his daughter and the corporal. He was pleased that his daughter held her ground with the man in uniform. Soule coldly acknowledged the corporal and pointed out. "I see my daughter has everything under control." He looked at Villian. "First apologize to my daughter, and then we will talk."

Villian ignored Soule and began a diatribe, "So let me guess, are the men who are paroled to your farm working to produce food for our Continental soldiers, or might this place be some kind of school to teach our enemies how to speak English?" Villian paused. "From what I see, you are running the risk of losing your prisoners and to hell with your farm!"

Soule did not say a word. Corporal Villian inhaled and paused. Then pointing at Comfort and at Heinrich and back to Comfort, he blurted, "The next time I come here, I do not want to see this traitorous behavior of teaching the enemy English! Am I making myself clear?"

The corporal's thundering remarks carried all the way to the bunkhouse. Ned and J.R. came out to see what was happening.

At the moment J.R. saw Villian, he slowed and said quietly to Ned, "Watch out, this guy can be a problem."

It was clear Ned understood.

Villian noticed the two other prisoners approaching. He stopped talking and took one long look at Ned. The corporal had a change of mood and began to grin. "Well, well, today, Mr. Soule, you are full of surprises." Attention was drawn to Ned, and Soule was prepared for trouble.

Corporal Villian walked across the front yard to Ned and checked him over. "My, my, what do have we here; an escaped slave perhaps? I am certain your master is missing you bad. I might recommend to my commander that we immediately sell you back into slavery." Villian added: "I see three prisoners, none of whom seem to be doing any work. My report about today's visit is not going to rest well with the commander."

Not another word was spoken. Soule was not going to defend himself or explain how he managed his farm to an uncouth and vulgar excuse for a soldier.

Corporal Villian eyed Comfort and then Soule. The corporal wanted someone to argue, but to his disappointment, there was only silence. He then mounted his horse and left the farm.

As the Corporal rode away, a worrisome feeling crept into the five of them, but it was Ned who was especially disturbed.

Comfort began to weep, and she ran to her father's arms. "What kind of monster is that man?"

"Daughter, please don't pay him any mind. He enjoys being pushy and dictatorial."

"But Father, can that man take Ned, J.R. and Heinrich away from us?"

Her father wanted to be honest and did not sugar coat his reply, "Yes, my dear, the man might have that power, but he would need the support of the commander at Albemarle. I would be surprised if he got it. Remember, we are in the middle of a war and people in places of decision-making have more important affairs to handle."

Soule stopped, and in an attempt to lift his prisoners' spirits, said, "Let's not give that man a second thought; he has already taken up too much of our time today. And lastly, Comfort, you continue your instruction with Heinrich. To hell with what Villian thinks!"

A month had passed since Corporal Villian's visit, but he certainly had not been forgotten. Soule was proud of the work being accomplished on the farm. Harvesting was moving along with great speed. J.R., Ned and Heinrich pledged they were not going to let Villian get under their skin. The three men loved the work they were doing and where they were doing it.

J.R. was grateful to be on Soule's farm; fate had served him well. He could not have asked for better friends than Ned and Heinrich. He thought what an odd group they were. Ned was a former slave who was fighting for his freedom, Heinrich a Hessian soldier who willingly decided to leave his home and fight for the British empire with no promise of a wage or land; and himself, a third-generation American colonist fighting to preserve the British colonies and their way of life. Only a war, he thought, could bring these three very different men together.

Comfort continued to read Heinrich's journal once a week to review his progress. She noticed that Heinrich's writing revealed a strong curiosity and keen thinking when it came to improving farm production. At the same time, she knew she was falling in love with him. The love she carried in her heart lifted her to new heights; a joy no one could take from her, not even the corporal.

After much hard work, the farm's harvest was on its way to market. Soule gathered J.R., Ned and Heinrich to share some great news. "This year's harvest has given us an abundant yield. I am now able to pay the bank loans for seed and have enough money left for next year's seed!" Soule was triumphant with the successful turnaround of his farm and he knew who deserved the glory. "I want you to know that we have three reasons for this good fortune, Ned, J.R. and Heinrich. I am indebted to each of you. Your hard work has not only saved the farm, you three have brought joy to my life." He paused as tears welled in his eyes.

Soule left his three workers and returned to the house to pay his accounts. He gazed out the window, and as far as he could see were empty fields, once full of barely, oat and wheat. He felt satisfied. In the distance he saw a lone man on horseback riding high in his saddle. Perhaps it was Corporal Villian, stopping by to brighten our day, he said, smiling to himself. Or maybe the man was a weary traveler. He noticed the rider now was coming up their drive. He wore a Continental Army uniform.

Soule thought there were only two reasons a soldier would be coming to his farm. Those two reasons were his two sons, Solomon and Oliver. He felt an ache in his heart that got stronger as the rider and horse got closer. The rider was now directly in front of him. He halted his horse, saluted Mr. Soule, then dismounted. The soldier handed Soule a letter. As he took the letter, his eyes seemed frozen on the name written on the cover. Yes, it was to him, but he preferred not to open it. Comfort watched her father, and she feared the worst. She went to stand beside him.

"Young man, I would rather not read this letter." He knew what heartbreaking news was in the white envelope. He knew he had lost one of his sons and he kept wondering, is it Oliver, or is it Solomon? Which of my boys is dead?

The soldier watched Soule as he hesitated. "Mr. Soule, I think it would be best if you read it."

With that, Soule unfolded the envelope and peeked at the beginning of the letter. In bold, black ink he read the words, 'Solomon Soule'. He fixed his eyes on his son's name and began to weep.

"Solomon, my eldest, our first-born son!" He felt weak all over and without reading the rest of the letter, it fell from his fingers onto the ground.

The soldier grabbed Soule as he too crumbled to the ground. J.R. and Ned ran to help Mr. Soule into the house and sat him in a parlor chair.

Heinrich was outside to console Comfort. She picked up the letter from the ground and read it. Heinrich took her arm and walked with her to the house. As they entered the parlor, she ran to her father, yelling, "Father, this can't be!"

The letter said Solomon lost his life on October 9, in the battle to recapture Savannah from Loyalist and British troops. The young soldier remained standing next to Soule, his eyes filled with compassion. There was a silence in the room, Comfort at her father's knee. The soldier glanced at the three men and Comfort, thinking how good it was that Soule had so much support. The soldier knew the poor man would need it.

"Excuse me, Mr. Soule," he said. "I have a second letter for you."

Soule was confused. For a moment, he thought it was the same letter, the one he dropped outside. After a short silence, he realized there was indeed, a second and separate letter. He tried to say something but he could not speak. He was bewildered, wondered why he would get two letters. He began to feel a tightness around his chest, like he was suffocating. Comfort asked him to breath slowly. She took the second letter from his fingers.

Utter disbelief, agony and confusion filled her heart. With Heinrich by her side, Comfort opened and read the second letter to herself. Unable to say a word, her facial expression was absolute and all-telling. She felt all of the blood leaving her head and felt faint. She knew she had to be strong for the sake of her father. She regained her composure and went to her father's side. She took his hands in hers. "Father, Oliver is missing in action." But there was more, the Army thought Oliver had drowned in that the same battle to retake Savannah.

The news could not have been worse for either Soule or Comfort. Solomon and Oliver were now both considered dead, and they never would return home. That evening, Soule shut himself in his library. He withdrew from all work and other activities, and remained closed up in his house for nearly the entire winter.

∽

The new year began with more snow as Soule continued his solitude. He had become a rare sight to Ned, J.R. And Heinrich. The tremendous loss of Solomon and Oliver had sent him into a deep depression. Month after

153

month went by, and Comfort saw no improvement. She took what little food he ate to him in the library. His face was thin and he appeared to be without hope. Comfort was always her father's ray of sunlight, but even she was unable to bring her father out of his grief and misery.

The winter months lagged but not because there was a lack of work. J.R., Ned and Heinrich always found something in need of repair or replacement. Ned had willingly taken on Soule's work as best he could. Comfort began to manage the books and accounts, while J.R. and Heinrich spent weeks fixing the plows and harrows. They made new shovels and different kinds of rakes. All of their hard work was in preparation for the spring planting.

Soule's anguish overpowered him as he struggled to rise from the depths of despair. He thought about the war and all the torment that accompanied it. He thought there must be another way to get to the same desired result. But man chose war to solve a problem or reach a goal. Solomon and Oliver believed the war was worth the fight for freedom from the Crown. In that equation, he did not define the word worth and failed to mention the word loss. He did not want to give up, but it was just too painful for him to accept the fact that his sons were dead.

He told himself repeatedly that he needed to carry on with life, no matter how deep his sorrow. He wondered if he would ever feel joy again. Then he remembered his daughter. He realized he needed to continue being a loving father to Comfort. She needed him; now more than ever. Comfort could not imagine never seeing her brothers again. Now she felt as though she had lost her father along with her brothers. She feared that she could get lost in her own sorrow, but too many people depended on her, so she could not allow her anguish to control her. People needed her, especially her father. She feared that if she gave up, he would too.

Comfort busied herself with her father's bookwork and her cooking and housework. She believed her strength of mind would help her heal. At the same time, she could also help lift her father's spirits. Despite her sorrow, she was also grateful. Ned, J.R., and especially Heinrich, were her cornerstones during the long winter months. But no one could fill her father's shoes. She needed and wanted him to be there for her, to leave his library and come back to life.

Day after day, as she took him his meals, she would enter the library with a positive attitude laced with kindness and love. But, as she opened the library door, she would find him slumped over, unshaven, in his robe, and he wouldn't talk or make eye contact. Just the sight of him was disturbing. She tried to encourage him by telling him about her day. She also tried to cheer him with a humorous story about something J.R. and Ned had done. Her father had no reaction and he barely ate. She had confidence in both herself and her father. When the weeks became months, she did not give up.

ᴇᏜᎥ

After a long day spent repairing the barn's north wall to keep the snow from blowing in, Ned returned to the bunkhouse feeling tired and uneasy. The winter-long absence of Corporal Villian was a welcome surprise, but it was eating at him, something just did not seem right. Ned's worrying was interfering with his work, his sleep and his thoughts. Every morning he thought, this might be the day. Villian will show up with shackles and take me to the deep south. He expected any day to be dragged off the farm and sold to the highest bidder at a slave auction. Ned was not doing a good job trying to hide his feelings from the others. They knew Villian had gotten under Ned's skin; he had gotten under everyone's skin.

Soule had once tried to assure Ned. "Such an act of cruelty would not happen on my land or on my watch." Ned had confidence Soule would do his best to protect him. But now the poor man was in mourning. Ned thought seriously about his one and only option, to make a run for the northern colonies. Late at night when lying awake, he could not make sense out of the contradiction of the revolutionary talk of freedom. They wanted their freedom while at the same time the same men wanted to deny him freedom. He could only hope that answer would come sooner rather than later, but, after all, most of the Continental Congress members were slave owners themselves!

Chores were done and Ned returned to the bunkhouse. He knelt next to his bunk, and from underneath he withdrew a wooden case. He opened the case, and pulled out his most cherished possession. This will cheer me up, he thought. With gentle fingers he lifted his violin as if it was his first-born child. Then, with his long fingers, he picked up the violin bow and tucked the violin under his chin. The bow glided smoothly across the strings like a swan over still water. A beautiful melody came forth surrounding Ned like a secure cocoon. As his bow slid over the strings of the violin, he felt calm, his heart felt joyful, but only for a short time.

Ned's violin solo filled the bunkhouse with the grandeur of Vivaldi.

155

It was sweet and soothing and as he played, his eyes closed, his tall body hypnotically swaying. He stood with his back straight and the bow feverishly gliding over the strings. He recalled how grand the music made him feel as a child, like a monarch wearing velvet trimmed with ermine and jewels.

After years of fighting and a year being a prisoner of war, Ned had lost all his sheet music. He played everything from memory. Johann Sebastian Bach was one of his favorite composers. For anyone within earshot of the bunkhouse, the violin made music so beautiful you would think it could end all hatred and war. The first time Heinrich heard Ned playing, he was tearful.

Ned lifted his bow when he saw Heinrich smile with happiness while tears seemed to well-up in his eyes. "Heinrich, I am sure you familiar with Bach?"

"Yes and please play more. The violin music reminds me of my family and makes me homesick. If I was home, I would have begun my apprenticeship by now."

"Did your apprenticeship have to do with music or violins?"

"Yes, it did. I beg you Ned, please play some more." Heinrich didn't want to talk about his apprenticeship; he wanted to listen to the violin music.

As Ned played, Heinrich would sit on his bunk, close his eyes and think of his good fortune in Virginia. Listening to the music from the land of his birth helped diminish his feeling of being homesick

⁊⊙

During the winter months, while Soule secluded himself with his grief, the three prisoners of war shared their own stories about their past. Throughout the cold months, the chores were few. When they ended, Ned, Heinrich and J.R. returned to the bunkhouse, made a fire in the small hearth, and enjoyed their free time while waiting for Comfort to call them for the evening meal.

Heinrich's English had improved greatly since he had arrived and he talked about home whenever J.R. and Ned were willing to listen. After Ned had played a few pieces of music, he stopped and asked Heinrich, "How did you end up here in Virginia; it is a long way from Hesse."

"I was to begin my apprenticeship to study to be a Luthier, a violin-maker just like my father and grandfather," said Heinrich. "And then word was spread, Frederick II was in need of volunteers to help England. I put my apprenticeship on hold and volunteered to help put down the rebellion.

"Why would Frederick II get mixed up with Britain's problem?"

"You see Frederick II is related to King George III, who has his soldiers spread thin all over the world. He needed men who would go to North America to put down the rebellion." With much enthusiasm Heinrich said, "I wanted to go to America!"

"Do you think your choice was a good one? Do you get paid well?"

"Yes, a good choice, but, no pay. We are not paid."

"No pay at all for your service?" Ned asked.

"No, nothing for me, but Frederick II is paid and paid well for each enlistment."

Ned exclaimed, "My word, sounds like slavery to me!"

"Now that you mention it, perhaps so, but not really, I wanted to travel and have adventures, so, here I am. Before coming to the British colonies, I read about the greatness of North America. I read about the tall, thick virgin forests, lakes as clear as crystal, and the abundance of wild animals." Heinrich paused and thought Ned and J.R. come from the British colonies, and they may not fully realize what they have, how good life can be in the colonies. "Once I arrived and saw the abundance of land, I understood King George III's determination to keep his colony from falling into rebel hands."

One evening, Heinrich asked Ned if he could hold his violin. Heinrich's fingers gently ran over the violins curves and long neck, and his face beamed as he said, "Ned, your violin, it is a very great violin, a German-made violin."

"No wonder you know so much about violins! Your family makes them!" Ned said.

Heinrich modestly nodded and smiled.

Another snowy afternoon, Heinrich drew a few illustrations of the various Italian, German and Bohemian violins. Then he showed them to Ned, explaining the sometimes hard to see differences between them.

Heinrich was as curious about Ned's musical talent as Ned and J.R. were curious about Heinrich's enlistment. "Tell us how you became such a masterful violinist."

"You two don't want to hear about all that." Ned hoped they would not press him to talk about days he would just as soon not talk about.

"Ned, I think it is your turn to tell us a little about your story," suggested Heinrich.

Ned took a deep breath, laid his violin back into its velvet-lined case and began to share just enough information to make his bunkmates happy. "I am going to start with events most recent, and go back in time, until you both become bored beyond reason! When I left the plantation, I began to learn less formal, free style music and playing. I picked up tunes and songs played by folks I had met; they did not have my particular classical training."

J.R. was not surprised that Ned had begun his life story talking about his music.

"During my first few months in my regiment," Ned said, "I learned to play gigs and reels. What fun it was! People would jump to their feet, grab their sweetheart, and dance endlessly. They would dance with hoots, howls and a steady chapping would come from those few sitting and watching. It was a tough time and music made us all feel better."

For a moment, Ned's eyes went to a window covered with frost. "Since the first day of my enlistment, I played to entertain the other soldiers. I will tell you, I saw first-hand the power of music as a healing medicine. For those men who were homesick and war weary, I played and played. Spirited music, with an upbeat sound, brought life to a bunch of war weary souls. The last piece I would play was a song with the melody of a serene lullaby."

"Who was your teacher?" asked Heinrich.

"Mr. Lawson taught me to play."

"Was that your father?"

"Well, I guess you could say that." Heinrich and J.R. were puzzled by Ned's answer, but didn't ask for clarification.

"Mr. Lawson had told me, 'Ned, my son, you are a gifted violinist and it pleases me to have taught you to play and love this instrument, just as I do.' Since the day I joined the Ethiopian Regiment, my musical horizons changed into a new form. I guess you could say my violin-playing morphed into fiddle music, using the totally different bowing patterns for southern fiddle tunes. I learned how to imitate other fiddle players. The soldiers enjoyed listening to everything I played. Bottom line, I simply loved to play, to help make the sad faces of war smile and forget the death and misery surrounding them."

J.R. was in awe of Ned's articulate speech and the depth of his knowledge.

૭

Signs of spring abounded. Flocks of geese were headed north followed by flocks of wild ducks. Croci were showing off their vibrant colors, with dandelions not far behind. Spring grasses and wildflowers covered the fields like a magnificent tablecloth and birds filled the air with their song as they busily built nests.

Comfort was in her glory. She loved the sunlight and the longer daylight hours. The sun was growing more intense, drying up mud puddles. In spite of all the natural wonders awakening from a long winter, Soule was still reclusive and despondent.

As Soule peered out the library window and noticed his own reflection in the glass, he barely recognized himself. His face was thin, unkempt and pale as if he had barely survived the winter. Beyond his frail reflection in the window, he saw Corporal Villian standing in the dooryard. Soule knew he had to force himself to go outside and confront the corporal. If he didn't, he could never face his workers again.

Comfort heard the library door open and thought it strange that her father was leaving the library.

Soule exited the house and walked toward Villian. "Where have you been, corporal?"

Villian ignored the question and asked one of his own: "I want the farm's yields from last year's harvest. I want those numbers now!"

Soule gave him the counts and told him that it was their best harvest ever.

The corporal simply snorted, as he recorded the numbers in his book. "Where are the prisoners?"

"The men are in the fields planting oat seed today."

Villian continued to look around, then he went into the barn. Soule knew he was bent on finding trouble. Villian wanted to bully and he wanted an argument. Villian saw Ned entering the rear of the barn, to get another sack of oat seed.

"Get over here, prisoner, right now!" Villian shouted.

Ned was shocked, first to see Villian and second to see Soule was outdoors. Ned's first thought was Villian had brought shackles with him? Ned slowly walked toward Villian. He tried to hide his nervousness and fear that this man could sell him into slavery. Ned held his head high, even though every bone in his body trembled.

"You salute me!" barked Villian.

Ned saluted him.

Villian seemed pleased to see Ned, as if he had not been able to browbeat anyone for some time. Soule, still watching, was not about to leave Ned alone with the bully. Villian barked orders to Ned to care for his horse.

At that moment, Soule went into the house to tell Comfort to load his musket and bring it to him. Ned noticed that Soule had disappeared, but he didn't want to appear panicked. He tried his best to remain calm. When Ned finished caring for the corporal's horse, he asked, "Corporal Villian, is there anything else you want me to do?"

"In fact my boots need a good cleaning and polishing," Villian replied as he walked through a small pile of fresh horse manure and mud. Villian appeared to want to push Ned closer to his breaking point.

Ned had enough of the fool masquerading as a corporal. Of all the years he lived on the Lawson plantation, he never had to clean anyone's boots but his own. Villian, sensing Ned's reluctance and irritation, was savoring the moment. Villian was certain Ned was one step away from insubordination; it was written all over his dark face. Villian walked to his horse and reached for a leather whip hanging from his saddle, he grabbed the whip and he snapped it on the dirt, then once more. Ned stood stoic.

From the kitchen window, Soule watched in horror and yelled to Comfort to hurry. Comfort returned to the kitchen with her father's loaded musket. He grabbed it and headed outside just as Villian raised his whip to strike Ned's back.

Soule startled Villian by shooting into the air and yelling, "This sick game of yours, corporal, will stop right now!"

Villian turned and stared at Soule. "It is your fault that this boy needs to learn a lesson, so don't yell at me, old man."

Comfort came running out of the house carrying her father's loaded pistol, and pointed it at Villian, "Unless you want a ball to lodge in your gut," she said, "you best drop that whip."

Villian did not drop his whip.

Soule ordered, "Corporal, if you don't get on your horse and get off my property, I will personally take you back to your commander and tell him of your abusive treatment and threats toward my men!"

Comfort stood firm with the pistol pointed at Villian. "I know how to use a pistol! If you try to swing around and hit anyone with the whip, you will be a dead man."

After a period of silence, and without saying a word, Villian rolled up his whip, kicked the bucket of water over, then mounted his horse and galloped off.

The look on Ned's face went from horror to relief. He shook his head, "I don't think I have ever seen a man who was filled with such hate."

Soule agreed. "Ned, you can be sure he won't be spreading his hate around here. I intend to write to his commander at Albemarle."

Ned looked at both Comfort and Soule. "I am grateful for your quick action to stop what was about to be unleashed on me."

Later that day, as Soule recalled the early morning events in the dooryard, he felt more alive than he had in months. His months of seclusion and heartbreak had come to its end. He felt relieved and strangely free, realizing that he could again interact with others. His two sons were lost in the Battle of Savannah and it was now time to let them rest in peace.

Chapter 16

October 1781: Expressions of Love

Fourteen months had passed since J.R. and Heinrich arrived at the farm. During those months they worked long hours, dawn to dusk. The result of their hard work was evident with two years of high crop yields. The labors of the three prisoners did not go unnoticed by Mr. Soule.

Before dinner one evening, Soule invited Ned, J.R. and Heinrich into his library. There they shared a port wine imported from Spain. Together they lifted their cups into the air and Soule made a toast. "To the three men to whom I owe much." He referred to them as his adopted sons and he saluted them for what they had done for him. "I am in your debt."

The men heard Comfort knock on the door. It was time to eat. At the table, Soule's settled on his daughter and then on to Heinrich. He thought no political ideology, no Crown or bloody rebellion could defeat or conceal the power of love. Nothing could impede that which was growing in the young couples' hearts.

As dinner came to a close, Mr. Soule said, "Gentleman, may I suggest that we return to my library for a cigar." With nods of agreement, J.R., Ned and Heinrich accepted Mr. Soule's invitation. Before the four men left the table, like the gentlemen they were, each one thanked Comfort for the delicious dinner that she had prepared and helped her clear the table.

Comfort stacked the dishes for washing. Looking at the massive pile, she shook her head, figuring that she would be cleaning up until midnight. She could not sleep anyway; her mind was occupied with thoughts of Heinrich. It was good to hear her father's laughter; a sound she had not heard since the deaths of her brothers had brought both horrific sadness and good fortune to her and her father.

∽⊚

Comfort closed the hatch to the cold storage in the floor of the kitchen. She had her apron filled with carrots, squash and turnip. Her eyes traveled across the room to where Heinrich's journal lay, waiting for her weekly grammar check.

Having a few minutes to relax, she wiped her hands on her apron, settled into the wooden rocking chair near the hearth and picked up the journal. As she read his writings, she thought about all she had learned about the man with whom she wanted to spend the rest of her life. He wrote: "In this country, farming is satisfying to my heart and mind. The soils are rich and fertile for crops of all sorts. I think this dirt has been waiting thousands of years for planters. The weather in Virginia could not be better with early spring, moderate winter and long summers with plenty of rain."

On another morning he dropped his journal off at the house for Comfort to review. By late morning Comfort would begin preparation for the mid-day meal. She had a few minutes and began to review his writing. She thought she would focus on his sentence structure. Sitting at the worktable, across from the hearth, she began reading a sentence that seemed alive. She was captivated by the lightness of his words. They were like calm clouds. She felt a sense of wellness, in her heart and mind. Half startled, as if awakened from a deep sleep, it hit her. She was reading a poem. He had written a poem for her.

Heinrich's poem flowed with expressions of love. This work was not characteristic of Heinrich's journal entries, or his other writings. She felt awkward and hesitated to continue reading. She wanted to read more but she was in a quandary; the poem seemed too intimate and she was a little embarrassed. She opened the journal again, but immediately closed it. Confused, she sat in the rocker. She needed a few moments to calm herself, then she would begin to sort out what was tumbling around in her mind.

She picked up the journal and turned a few pages, and there it was. She slowly viewed each fragrant word, as if in her vivid imagination she felt him gently caress her hand. Was she dreaming? Should she force herself to open her eyes? She could not be dreaming; the warmth and touch felt too real. Why was her head resting on the pages of the opened journal? Startled, she opened her eyes and there was Heinrich, standing with Ned and J.R. They apologized for waking her.

She was embarrassed and said, "I dozed off, would you … please, would you give me a few minutes and food will be on the table."

Ned and J.R. went to the well to wash their hands. Heinrich remained in the kitchen. "Forgive me, Comfort," he said, "if I have caused you any embarrassment. My poem is about you and my feeling for you."

She pushed back her hair. She was disconcerted about her untimely nap and she stood up to begin preparing the mid-day meal. Once she felt composed, she smiled and said, "Heinrich, your poem is beautifully written. Now, you must excuse me, I must get our meal ready."

Heinrich stood back and watched Comfort hurry this way and that, as she prepared lunch. He noticed that she fumbled with everything she touched. She was disoriented in a kitchen where she could work blindfolded. While slicing bread and putting plates on the table she said, "Heinrich, your poem is beautiful."

She paused. "You express the same affections for me as I have harbored for you." Abruptly, she placed her hand over her mouth. Her eyes widened, shocked at her own confession of love!

Heinrich joyously hooted and howled. He picked up Comfort and carried her outside, twirling her around. His shouts of happiness brought Soule running to the dooryard, to see what was causing such excitement. He stopped in his tracks when he saw Heinrich and Comfort romping around like school kids, both of them wide-eyed and smiling. When they saw him, they stood at attention, arms at their sides, as if they were caught sneaking apples from the orchard. Soule, with a grin, asked about the noise, trying to hide the fact that he knew exactly what was going on.

"Father, we are fine, nothing is wrong, in fact it could not be better!"

Heinrich, filled with excitement, composed himself and asked, "Mr. Soule, may I speak with you privately sometime?"

"Certainly, Heinrich, you are welcome to my library when you finish the evening milking."

The news about Heinrich and Comfort was not really a surprise to anyone, least of all Soule. But, all the while, he remained hesitant to encourage or discourage them. This was not simply love between two people. After all, Heinrich was a prisoner of war; perhaps easy for them to forget, but no one else would forget he fought for the enemy!

Soule thought about the grief and pain that he and Comfort had suffered during the past several years: his wife's death in 1777, then his sons' in 1779. He wanted his daughter to experience something other than loss and death. He was unsure how to go forth; what solutions could be suggested to alter the reality of the situation. He wanted his daughter's happiness and security. He did not want her judged by people because of whom she loved. He had spent most of the afternoon in search of a solution, asking himself time and time again, how could their young love get beyond the barriers?

By late afternoon Ned and Heinrich had completed the milking, cleaned out the cows' stalls and given them fresh hay to eat and straw for bedding.

"You get along now Heinrich. I will finish up here." said Ned.

With confidence, Heinrich knocked on the library door and a cheerful voice from the other side asked him to enter. The room was just as Heinrich remembered from his last visit to enjoy cigars. It had two windows and three walls of books. He walked over to Soule and shook his hand. Soule offered him a seat. Once settled, Heinrich was struck by the number of books. The shelves reached from the floor to the ceiling. Many of the books were bound with beautiful leather, or tree bark.

"You like our literary collection?" Soule asked. "It has taken us years to build it."

Heinrich said, "I cannot imagine being the proud owner of such a collection. Each book offers knowledge for the fortunate one who might open the cover."

Soul smiled, "How right you are. This is a collection, son, of which we are very proud. My wife and I found many hours of pleasure in these books. You can take one to read if you would like."

"Thank you, sir. Learning to read and speak English has given me endless opportunities."

Heinrich's eyes slowly perused the shelves near him. He saw works by the great orator, Patrick Henry. He saw book of poetry. He saw books with writings by Francis Hopkins, the poet and humorist. He noted the book, *Traveller* by John Ledyard, and political writings by John Jay. John Trumbull's *The Progress of Dulness,* grabbed Heinrich's immediate interest. He removed the book from the shelf, then turned to Soule,

"Sir, what is Mr. Trumbull's work about?"

"Oh, yes, that is a satire about the British way of doing things. Not about the Crown, but satire in verse about the methods of British schoolmasters and education."

The young man showed a keen ability to think, in depth, about a wide range of topics. He had the practical ability to repair equipment and resolve problems. The thought of Heinrich as his son-in-law pleased Soule. The thought of his farm someday being in Heinrich's hands gave him a deep feeling of satisfaction and peace of mind. But that would have happen in an ideal world, a world that was then out of everyone's grasp.

Soule watched as Heinrich's eyes darted to a neatly piled stack of pamphlets. On the top was a work by Thomas Paine, titled, *The American Crisis.*

"I am slightly familiar with Mr. Paine. I've listened to Ned and J.R. discuss the writer in depth," said Heinrich as he lifted the pamphlet just enough to get a peek at another revolutionary pamphlet under it.

As they continued to talk about authors and their works, not for a second did Heinrich, or Soule, forget why he was there. Even though Heinrich's thoughts were captivated by the large assortment of books, he wanted to get to the purpose of the meeting. He was there for a reason.

In the kitchen, with her daily tasks almost complete, Comfort rested in the rocking chair. She was anxious to learn the outcome of the meeting between her father and Heinrich, but it was getting late. She quietly crept down the hall to see if they, indeed, were still in the library. She heard their voices and saw the oil lamp's soft glow under the door. Her morning would come early, so she went to bed.

Heinrich was waiting for the right moment. During a pause in the conversation, Heinrich sat with his backbone straight, his shoulders back. He took in a breath of air and exhaled it slowly. "Excuse me, sir, I mean, Mr. Soule, I mean, I would with great respect like to ask you, sir, for your permission to marry your daughter."

There was a long silence. Heinrich was not expecting this pause, which seemed to have no end. Although Soule was not surprised by the question, he took his time to answer. "I would be a proud father to give you my daughter's hand in marriage," he began. "You are a fine young man, smart and hardworking."

Again silence. Heinrich sensed that Mr. Soule had more to say, but what might it be? How many other ways could Soule tell Heinrich he liked him? What else might he say? The pause didn't seem to end. The room was soundless, a haunting stillness. Heinrich could not imagine what he might hear next.

"There is one regrettable issue we need to discuss," Soule said, his voice gently breaking the eerie silence.

Heinrich took a deep breath when he saw anguish on Soule's face.

"There is one more thing. Son, you have made me a proud man with all the work you have done on the farm. You, J.R., and Ned have saved me from ruin and for that, I am forever in your debt. But on the other hand, Comfort's security and happiness is my highest priority." He stopped, paused again as Heinrich waited. "Son, might you think about how my daughter's life would be very difficult if she were married to a soldier of the Crown? Both of you would be labeled as traitors to the revolution."

Heinrich understood all too well what Soule was saying. Yes, he was a soldier whose enlistment was to suppress the rebellion. Soule's statement assumed the British would not win.

"Sir, what if the rebel army lost the war, how might that impact my marriage to Comfort? If the British won, wouldn't my marriage to your daughter have the opposite effect?"

"Yes, it would, but that is not what is going to happen. The French are now completely supporting the war. They are sending thousands of men to fight the British and Loyalist troops. The French Alliance will end the war and the British Empire will suffer a costly defeat."

"You seem so sure about this. How can you be so confident this is how the war will end?"

"From all my reading, I believe the men who hunger for freedom from a tyrant King will have victory."

Heinrich tried to understand what Soule was saying. He was saying the Continental forces would beat the British and others would not accept his marriage to Comfort. Or even worse, the young couple could be forced into exile. Heinrich sat speechless. With his confidence gone and his hopes dashed, he felt defeated.

"This marriage," Soule said, "would not be in the best interest of my daughter. It would be a marriage filled with huge challenges that no young couple should endure."

Heinrich watched Soule rise from his chair and somberly walk across the room to a cut-glass decanter that rested on a small pedestal table. He poured some wine into a small pewter cup. After filling the cup, Soule turned to Heinrich and asked, "Son, would you like a taste of dandelion wine? It is Ned's own recipe. That man is a master at wine-making!"

Heinrich, although heartbroken, said, "Please, I would like that." He was thinking that it was odd that the war had brought Comfort and him together and now it seemed the war would keep them apart.

Soule poured wine into a second cup, placed the glass plug back into the decanter and turned to Heinrich. He was pained to see so much sadness on the young man's face. He handed Heinrich a cup of wine and put his hand on his shoulder. Heinrich thought that maybe their conversation was not over, which gave him a grain of hope.

Soule took a seat and both men raised their cups of dandelion wine to each other.

Heinrich said, *"Prost"*

"Cheers," Mr. Soule responded as they both took sips of the wine. Attempting to be cheerful, hoping it might help Heinrich out of his somber mood, Soule remarked, "Our Ned makes a fine wine from those weeds doesn't he!" Ned has an endless array of talents,"

Heinrich nodded, "Ned is indeed remarkable. I could listen to him play his violin all day and night."

Taking another sip of wine, Heinrich sat in abeyance on the edge of an upholstered chair. At that moment, he felt like a document waiting to either be signed or tossed to the wind. The small talk was fine, but all the while, he worried about how this news would impact his relationship with Comfort. No matter who was victorious in the war, their married lives would be difficult. If the Continental troops won, they could be exiled. If the British won, the Soules could be forced to forfeit their farm for their allegiance to the rebellion.

Soule broke the silence with a serious tone. "Son, I will, with great pride and confidence, give you my daughter's hand in marriage if ..." Then came another pause, giving Heinrich enough time to repeat to himself what he had just heard. His hopes were lifting, but cautiously. Heinrich waited for Soule to finish his sentence, to finalize his thought. He waited to hear what followed the word if.

Mr. Soule lowered his voice, leaned closer to Heinrich and quietly told him, "I beseech you to stand and fight with the Continental Army."

Heinrich did not know the English word, "beseech." He recognized how similar it sounded to the German word, *besuchen*, meaning to visit, but that surely was not what Soule meant. Was he to visit the Continental troops? He was certain beseech was similar to the German word, *ersuchen*. That made more sense to him.

So, if he understood correctly, Soule was pleading with him to join the Continental Army, to actually change sides in the war and fight against the British and American Loyalist troops! In Soule's view, the winning side.

The request was an option that had not crossed Heinrich's mind. Nonetheless, once he got over the initial shock of what he was being asked to do, he sat quietly for several minutes. His considerations of the request kept circling back to the woman he loved. He could think of nothing he wanted more than to share the rest of his life with Comfort.

Soule sat across from Heinrich and contemplated the request that lay before him. Heinrich's mind drifted as he pondered his initial enlistment as a volunteer from Hesse to suppress the rebellion. He was a soldier but had no strong sense of loyalty to the British. His loyalty was to the other Hessian men with whom he fought. His loyalties had never been with the Crown. Heinrich was wracked with confusion, unsure if he could fight with the rebel army. After all, not so long ago, it was the enemy. He began to understand his loyalties now were with Comfort and her country; a country that he hoped would become his country, too.

Fearing his request might be unreasonable, Soule softly broke the silence, "I am aware, son, that you are considering a massive decision. But, let me remind you that the tide of the conflict is changing as we speak. Washington's army is showing remarkable promise. Mark my words, the Continental Army will succeed; the war's days are numbered."

Heinrich wished he was as confident about that. Heinrich cleared his throat. "Shortly after our capture at Stony Point and the march to Pennsylvania, the Continental Army asked me to enlist and join them. Their request for me to change sides came with a promise of thirty acres of land. I chose to remain as prisoner." It was then that Heinrich realized so much had changed since that day.

With conviction, Heinrich exclaimed: "I think we are going to need a preacher!" Mr. Soule jumped to his feet with joy. Heinrich continued, "I will do as you request. I will enlist and be proud to join the Continental Army. I will do my part and victory will be ours. I will then return to Comfort, the woman I love."

Soule was thrilled. He lifted his pewter cup of dandelion wine toward Heinrich and said, "Cheers, my soon-to-be son-in-law."

The following day, Heinrich woke to do the morning milking and swung his feet out of his bunk and onto the cold floor. It was a snowy January morning. "Put your feet on the floor and you will wake up with a jolt!" he said to anyone who might be listening.

Heinrich, sitting on a three-legged stool with his hands being warmed by the cow's udder, rested his head against the cow's belly while he squeezed the milk into a bucket. Ned was cleaning the goat pen, and once one bucket was full, Heinrich called out, "Hey Ned, you want to take this bucket of milk to Comfort?"

"Be right there." Ned replied.

As Heinrich continued to milk, he heard the sound of the squeaky barn door. A blast of cold air filled the barn. Heinrich heard soft footsteps approaching. Comfort had come to the barn to fetch the morning cream for the butter churn. She was bundled warmly with a large cloak and a tightly wrapped scarf around her head and neck. Only her eyes were exposed.

The bundle of clothing couldn't hide her unsettled expression. "Father told me. I think he is being unreasonable," Comfort said as her breath hovered in the air between them. She appeared on the verge of tears, not knowing if she was angry, hurt or confused.

Heinrich stood up. "Comfort, your father is right, there would be no peace in your life if you married a prisoner of war, a man who was a soldier for the King, like those who took the lives of both your brothers."

"I don't want you to go back to war. I don't want you to return to fighting. You should not have to risk your life for me."

As she spoke he noticed she carried a newspaper under her arm. "What are you reading?" he asked.

To his shock, she began weeping as she tried to answer him. She waved the paper above her head and said, "I am reading the news about the damn war!" She threw the paper onto a pile of cow manure. "The reports are tragic. Continental troops mutinied just outside of Morristown, New Jersey." Comfort composed herself and began to summarize the article. "Can you imagine, Pennsylvania soldiers under Washington, in the dead of winter, wearing only rags with no shoes and no food, killing their officers!"

Granted, he thought, the news was horrific. How could Washington's men expected to fight with no shoes in the dead of winter. Could this be accurate or simply propaganda?

Comfort forced herself to continue, "Heinrich, it says starving soldiers were demanding the Continental Congress to give them their back pay, food, shoes and clothing. What is going on? What has happened and who is responsible for this horror? We treat our prisoners of war better than we treat our soldiers! How could the Congress or General Washington allow this to happen? What kind of men are they? These are the men who are supposed to lead us to victory and they can't take care of their troops!"

Her eyes locked with Heinrich's. She saw his anguish and he saw her fear. He put his arms around her, held her close and whispered in her ear, "All will be fine, I promise. We may hit some bumps, but we will get through this."

Without a doubt, the news was not indicative of an ultimate Continental victory. He did not show Comfort how alarmed he was to hear about the soldier mutiny. He wanted to soothe her and show her he was not afraid. Comfort, still weeping, begged him not to enlist.

"We must cancel our wedding plans, not postpone them, but cancel them! Heinrich, we have no choice; the wedding is off! I refuse to marry you. I do not want you to suffer or die because of our love for each other. It makes no sense at all. Father surely did not understand what he was asking of you."

"Comfort, I assure you," Heinrich said, "I will be fine. I will not end up like the soldiers in New Jersey." He put his arms around her. The smell of lavender soap was intoxicating. Even if it appeared that the rebel forces were struggling to survive, he was more determined than ever to hold to his marital agreement with her father.

One month later, the printed news and word of mouth about the war was more of the same. Continental troops continued to take a beating. Losses, defections and a second mutiny ended with the execution of the two ringleaders. For the Continental Army, the print news was often grim. Heinrich wondered if Soule was still as confident of a Continental Army victory as he was that evening in the library.

One night Heinrich got out of his bunk and walked to the window in the bunkhouse. It was covered by frost that had an intricate design that the full moon brought to life. It glittered like the hand-cut crystal that his mother cherished. All these elements have a purpose, he thought. And was there a reason for his existence? He began to feel comforted and went back to his bunk and pulled the covers to his head. He lay there, thinking. He was going to enlist.

Soule and Heinrich went to Charlottesville, where Heinrich enlisted. Whether it seemed real or not didn't matter; his enlistment was a done deal. Not only was he a soldier again, he was no longer a prisoner of war. The idea of not being labeled a P. O. W. gave him an emotional boost.

That evening, he wrote this in his journal: "I, Heinrich Helmut With, have joined the revolutionary effort to free the colonies from the tyrant, King George." He read the sentence a few times; it was still hard to believe. Everything was changing; he was excited to know what he was fighting for, Comfort and their future together. Now, he would be assigned to the

2nd Virginia Regiment, which was charged with clearing the British out of South Carolina.

A couple of weeks later, he received his orders. He would muster out on the 15th of March. Comfort and Heinrich quickly chose the first Saturday in March for their wedding day. He would return to battle as a married man.

∽

Soule and his daughter had arranged a small wedding ceremony at their home. Details were made and plans streamed forth for Heinrich and Comfort's consideration. A small number of neighbors would attend. Heinrich asked J.R. to be his best man, and Ned was asked to provide the music.

From her mother's trunk, stored in the third-floor attic of the large farmhouse, Comfort had chosen a delicate light blue dress to wear. Heinrich picked early blooms of wildflowers for her hair. She tied and knotted the stems together creating a garland of yellow and violet flowers to crown her golden hair.

Ned's violin music played softly in the background as Heinrich stood proudly in the front of the room. With the music, those at the wedding were able to stop thinking about the war for a day, and to remember that love and life goes on.

With her hand on her father's arm, Comfort entered the room. Soule looked proudly at his only daughter as he placed her hand softly in Heinrich's open palm and turned away, to wipe a tear from his eye. A second later, he faced Comfort and Heinrich and quietly wished them marital felicity. It was not long before the reverend said, "Mr. and Mrs. Heinrich Helmut With, I now pronounce you man and wife."

J.R. had not been to a wedding since his sister Elizabeth had married Nathaniel Beardsley in five years earlier. His thoughts were of Abigail, hoping that someday they too would marry.

Chapter 17

March 1781: Off to War

S oule thought about how wrong he had been to make such a demand. He lay in bed with darkness surrounding him; his stomach tied in knots. Regret covered him like a blanket. He kept repeating to himself, "Why did I consent to the marriage?" He realized how terribly his daughter would suffer if Heinrich didn't come back to her.

He could have explained his reasoning to them and simply said no. Heinrich could end up dying just like Solomon and Oliver; and his beloved daughter would be a young war widow. Would she then hate him for forcing Heinrich off to war?

The young couple had everything they could ask for, except time. Their short time together as husband and wife gave each of them many good memories to recall during the upcoming separation. The day of Heinrich's departure started like any other day. Heinrich woke early and smiled while he gazed at his sleeping wife. He kissed her on her cheek, got up, dressed, then went out to the fields to work alongside Ned and J.R. for the last time.

The kiss from Heinrich gently awakened Comfort. She wasted no time getting up and dressed and made her way downstairs to the kitchen. She grabbed the poker and jostled the embers in the hearth, giving them some air. The fire began to burn and the warmth felt good on that cold March morning. She got busy preparing tea, cheese and jam, to be accompanied by bread. From deep within, a sadness began to overwhelm her. The dreaded day had arrived. She dropped her head, her chin quivered and she thought about him not being in their bed that night, or the next night. She did not know when she would see Heinrich again.

She glanced at the small cloth bag on the table waiting to be packed with bread, dried fruit and smoked meat. She wished she were small enough to climb inside the bag and go with him. The bag signified reality. Her beloved was about to reassume the life of a soldier.

Her excitement of the past several weeks and the planning for the wedding day had vanished. Her mind conjured up terrifying thoughts of the danger Heinrich would soon encounter. She felt weak, grabbed the back of the rocking chair and took some deep breaths to soothe her anxiety. Tears began to slide down her cheeks. It was as though she couldn't catch her breath.

Soule was startled to hear his daughter crying, and he sprang to his feet fearing she had cut herself. He found his daughter kneeling on the floor, with her face and hands wet with tears. He bent down, pulled her to her feet and held her tightly. All he could do was to try and assure her that all would be fine, but the words rang hollow.

Heinrich returned from the field earlier than usual. He had some last minute packing to do. His leather saddlebag was almost full except for his wedding gift from Comfort—a new journal. He went to the kitchen, where he would be alone with Comfort, to say good-bye. They embraced and kissed, neither could hide their sorrow.

Outside, after saying his farewell, J.R. held the horse's reins while Soule and Ned said their goodbyes.

Ned gave him a hearty handshake. "Heinrich, you best get back here to the farm darn soon, for I will need to have my violin bow re-haired." And with that, Ned smiled and gave Heinrich a hearty pat on the back. Heinrich gave him a hug.

Finally, Mr. Soule approached Heinrich, patted him on the back and said, "Son, please come back to us safe and soon."

Heinrich smiled and with a glitter in his eye replied, "I don't plan to be gone too long."

Last, Heinrich went to Comfort. He took her hands in his and kissed away her tears, whispering, "Always remember, how much I love you; I will be back soon."

As Heinrich mounted his horse, Soule shouted, "Godspeed, son."

J.R. shook hands with Heinrich one last time before letting go of the bridle while Mr. Soule stepped back to put his arm around his daughter. The four of them stood and watched while Heinrich rode down the path to the dirt road. There was not a dry eye.

The truth was, Heinrich was joining some of the bloodiest combat the war had seen. The latest news about the war was grim. General Benedict Arnold and his British troops had torched Richmond, Virginia, burning it to the ground. But word of defeats, casualties, ambushes and hangings was destroying morale on both sides as the battles intensified in the Carolinas, Georgia, Virginia and southern Pennsylvania.

Heinrich had been a brave and skilled fighter right up to his capture at Sandy Point in July of 1779. Even though he had not loaded a musket in two years, he felt sure that he would still be the sharpshooter he had once been. He remembered that just two years ago, he could fire and reload a musket in less than 15 seconds. Timing could mean the difference between life and death.

Heinrich's 2nd Virginia Regiment joined with General Nathanael Greene's men for a march to push British Brigadier General Lord Rawdon and his men out of South Carolina. Heinrich was relieved to see how well the men in the 2nd Virginia accepted him. He thought his new fellow soldiers were happy to have any new enlistment.

General Greene's plan was first to take back Camden in South Carolina, where Lord Rawdon's primary post was located. By late April, Greene and his troops arrived in the thick forest at Hobkirk Hill, close to Camden. Greene was not ready to attack; he was waiting for reinforcements. Camden, their target, was a mile and a half away.

While waiting on the hill, one of General Greene's soldiers deserted to Lord Rawdon's side. Soon, it became too obvious that the deserter had shared strategic information about Greene waiting for reinforcements. At dawn, Rawdon's army attacked General Greene's men and the 2nd Virginia. The attack caught the rebel troops by surprise as they were preparing for the day, shaving, drinking tea or washing clothing in the river. The British broke through the rebel line, forcing Greene's men and the 2nd Virginia to retreat.

Several hours after the battle ended, Lord Rawdon and his men and returned to their encampment in Camden. This gave Greene's men a chance to go back for the dead and wounded. It was almost dusk, and finding the casualties was a challenge in the thick forest. More than one hundred of Greene's men were wounded that day, forty men were captured and early estimates were that at least a dozen men died. About four-dozen soldiers were considered missing.

໖

Six months after Heinrich mustered out with the 2nd Virginia there still was no word from him. Comfort struggled to remain optimistic, hoping to hear from her husband. She was not getting any information from the 2nd Virginia, except that he seemed to have disappeared during the surprise attack near Camden.

Soule tried to appear optimistic in front of everyone, especially his daughter, but silently he worried about Heinrich's well-being. Although she didn't tell her father, Comfort knew every bit of pessimistic news; she would read the print news even before her father got it. Perhaps she appeared too busy to be carrying such a burden, but she wasn't. Day after day, she imagined Heinrich as the victim of the most perilous hand-to-hand combat while fighting off surprise attacks by the British. Comfort felt she had grieved enough with the loss of her two brothers. She wanted to see the war end and Heinrich to come home.

One cool, late-September day, Comfort was sitting by the kitchen hearth. She placed her hand on her belly and whispered, "Oh my little baby, don't cry, your daddy will return." Her condition was beginning to show through her petticoats, skirt and apron.

That evening Comfort sat in silence with Ned, J.R. and her father. She ate her dinner thinking about the possibility she could be a widow with a child. She thought about, her having no husband and her baby no father. Her heart ached every moment she was without Heinrich. She refused to talk with anyone about her feelings. She needed every ounce of her strength to maintain hope. And when that seemed impossible, she would go to their bedroom, weeping tears of anguish.

Chapter 18

October 1781: War's End

One crisp, late-October morning, Soule finished his morning tea and was ready to take another flatbed of grain to the mill, but put it off. The monthly visit from the Corporal Villian was long overdue, and he hated to think what might happen if he left the farm and Villian showed up.

The following day Soule spotted him on horseback in the distance heading toward the Soule farm. Soule walked outside as Villian arrived and led his horse to the water trough.

"Have you heard the news?" Villian asked Soule. When Soule didn't respond, Villian asked again, "Have you heard the good news? Oh likely not, living way out here."

Soule finally said, "No, I have not heard good news for quite some time."

Villian smiled, waited for a few minutes, keeping Soule in suspense.

Soule went back to preparing rope to tie the harvest down on the flatbed.

Villian, hating being ignored, exclaimed, "That British devil Cornwallis and his soldiers surrendered!"

Soule heard the corporal, but figured he was playing some kind of game.

"Yep, just last week, the damn bloody Brits gave it up at Yorktown. Those British bastards had no choice; well I guess they are no longer the mightiest military in the world." Villian laughed. A long silence followed.

Soule wondered whether a surrender really had happened. He had not heard a word about a British surrender in Yorktown. But, then again, they had been busy with harvesting the crop and had not been off the farm for a few weeks.

Giving Villian the benefit of doubt, Soule asked, "What might this mean regarding …"

Villian quickly interjected, "Regarding your two remaining prisoners of war?" The corporal snickered and then began to laugh before answering. "Let me see, what impact might the end of the war have on your two Loyalist soldiers? Well, first off, your boy will be sold back into slavery. I will be sure to sell him in the deep south, as he would get a better price down there. Plus, he will have some masters who will teach him a few lessons on how to be an obedient slave. Your boy has the odds stacked against him. First, he is a runaway slave, and also a bloody traitor! Damn stupid of him to have fought for the King!"

The corporal laughed again. "I tell you, you can mark my word, he will have a hell of a time just staying alive on those plantations." More laughter as he rambled on, "I can see it now, your boy might think fighting for the King was some kind of paradise with a promise of freedom. The real paradise is waiting for him. His new lot in life will provide him with plenty of time to think over his previous bad decisions! But, why would I care, his sale will bring a pile of cash to put toward the war debt. In fact, today I am taking the boy back to Albemarle; don't want to waste any more time. I gotta get that slave on the damn auction block! He will bring an excellent price, in part due to your superior care. I must thank you for feeding him so well."

Soule hid his shock. He was disgusted at the idea of Ned going to auction like some kind of chattel. It would have to be over my dead body, he thought. Ned wasn't going anywhere! Feeling anxious, he had to think fast.

Calmly, Soule said, "You may not be aware, corporal, but we are in the middle of reaping the oat and barely fields. Ned Lawson cannot leave this farm just yet. The earliest you can have him would be early November, then he will be all yours."

Villian was sorely disappointed. He began pacing back and forth. His silence was worrisome to Soule.

"I am a very busy man," Villian finally said, "with responsibility for dozens of prisoners. I have a few other boys I can put on the auction block before I come back for him. I will concede and let you keep him until then, but not any longer. The plantation owners and growers in the southern colonies are clamoring for labor!"

Soule was surprised Villian did not insist on taking Ned immediately.

"Damn," Villian mumbled, "I have been waiting to sell the black one back into slavery for a heck of a long time but I guess I can wait a couple more weeks." Villian thought Ned would fetch enough money for him to live like that fat old fool, King George himself!

Villian stopped pacing and said, "Oh, and by the way, have you heard anything from your third prisoner, that Hessian?" Villian paused. "I mean that son-in-law of yours."

Soule had a one word reply. "No."

Once Villian was gone, Soule took a seat on the bench outside the kitchen door. He mulled over all the news. First, he spoke with his daughter. He would talk with J.R. and Ned once they came back from the fields. He dreaded the idea of sharing the news with Ned.

He thought to himself, the British surrendered, those words lifted his spirits. Finally, some good news, but how could he feel relieved with Heinrich apparently missing in action. And Villian will be coming back to take Ned into the deep south. His life would not have a chance to get back to normal until those issues were resolved. He then remembered that back to normal was impossible, with the deaths of Solomon and Oliver. Things would never be as they once were.

The kitchen was quiet, then he remembered that Comfort had taken a nap. He did not want to disturb her rest. He figured it would be best to get back to his work. Soule went to the barn to bundle and stack the shafts of the freshly cut grains.

Before too long, Ned and J.R. came back to the house to have something to eat and drink. Comfort had left them some black bread, butter and smoked ham on the kitchen worktable. J.R. fetched the food and took it to the barn, where they enjoyed a couple minutes of relaxation. They noticed Soule must have been busy stacking grain.

Just as Ned was about to ask J.R. a question, they heard the squeak of the barn door. Soule entered the barn, and J.R. and Ned immediately noticed the forlorn expression on his face. They feared the worst, thinking it was bad news about Heinrich. They immediately got to their feet.

J.R. asked, "Sir, what is the matter? Is … it Heinrich?"

"No, still no word about Heinrich, but I do have some important news for you both. I have just received word that the war has ended."

J.R. and Ned were dumbstruck. They repeated together, "The war is what?"

"The war has ended; it is over," replied Mr. Soule.

They could not believe what they had just heard! The war was over. It really did not seem possible. For several fleeting moments, the war's end seemed more important to Ned and J. R, than asking who won! Both men began to jump with joy. J.R. immediately thought of Abigail. He could go home and they could be married. Soule watched as they celebrated. After a moment, Ned saw that Soule was standing solemnly, with no interest in joining the merriment. J.R. became uneasy.

"Sir, is there something you haven't told us?" Ned asked.

When Soule didn't say a word, they realized that there was, indeed, more to the story.

Ned became still and said, "It just occurred to me that we are celebrating the end of the war, not knowing who surrendered. The expression on your face gives me the impression that the Continental Army surrendered to the British and Loyalist side. Is that what happened?"

Soule shook his head, saying, "I am afraid not."

A dark silence enveloped the three men. J. R's head dropped into his hands. Ned was trying to figure out how this would affect his life. Soule began to tell them what he knew. "The British have indeed surrendered after a long battle and siege at Yorktown. I cannot imagine how much of a disappointment this is for both of you."

"The British have surrendered? J.R. said. "What in hell happened? The mightiest nation in the world surrendered to a colonial militia; it makes no sense!" J.R. turned to look at Ned, whose face was full of concern.

Ned turned, rested his head against the barn wall and moaned loudly, "Oh, no, please, it can't be the British who surrendered. The British were to win this war. They were supposed to suppress the rebellion and I was to be free."

Soule wondered when he should tell them the rest of the news, although Ned seemed to have an understanding of what it was. He walked to Ned and he placed his hand on Ned's back. Soule gave voice to the words he had to share with Ned. "I regret to tell you this. Villian expects to sell you into slavery."

"Mr. Soule, I know what was in my future if the British lost," sighed Ned. "I know all too well what tragedy is awaiting me." Ned knew that with a British surrender, the Continental's would sell every black man who fought for the King. It did not matter if they were former free men or former slaves, they were all to be auctioned into slavery to help pay the debt of the war.

Soule said, "Corporal Villian told me that he will be handling your sale."

When Ned heard that, he shook his head in amazement and said, "Just when you think it can't get any worse it does. Villian ..."

Ned sat down on a wood box, put his head into his large dark hands and ever so slowly began to hum a spiritual hymn while he slowly rocked himself back and forth. Soule and J.R. listened to the spiritual's soothing power.

Then, unable to hold back the tears, Ned stopped humming. He lifted his large brown eyes to Soule's face and said, "I think it is time for me to thank you for being such a kind and just man. I will fondly remember these years I have worked for you. You gave me freedom, responsibility and dignity. Working on your farm with both J.R. and Heinrich filled my heart with brotherhood and has given me memories no one can take from me, not even a beating with a whip. Even if they try to whip the memories out of me, they won't be able to do it, they are mine and I will take them with me to the grave." A large teardrop traveled down Ned's high cheekbone, leaving a shiny wet streak on his smooth dark face.

"You don't need to thank me Ned," Soule said, "I want to thank you. Men, will you please excuse me; I am going to talk with Comfort." As he approached the barn door and began to lift the wood latch, he stopped and turned around. He walked back to where Ned and J.R. were sitting. "Ned," he said, "I refuse to allow you to be put into slavery. I will help you escape."

Ned thought he had misheard Soule. "Pardon?"

Soule repeated his words. This time louder and with more emphasis. "I will help you escape!"

Ned shook his head. "I am grateful for your support Mr. Soule, but I could not place you and your daughter at such risk. The penalty for aiding slaves to escape is harsh. It would be seen as treason; you could be sentenced to death by a firing squad."

Soule interrupted Ned, "Son, there is no way I will allow you to be sold into slavery and that is final." Both Soule and J.R. were already thinking about how they could pull off an escape in the middle of the post-war confusion that likely was spreading throughout the colonies.

Ned spoke up, "I could not put you and Comfort in such peril. If I was to attempt an escape, I could not involve anyone else. I would do it on my own."

Soule quickly replied, "An escape like that would be very risky for you. You would be more successful if you accepted my help."

J.R. had an idea. "What if we disguised Ned as a woman and smuggled him to the British-controlled Colony of New York. Ned would be safe there!"

Soule exclaimed, "That is an ingenious idea, J.R."

"We could hide him in the next wagon of oats heading to Philadelphia," J.R. said, beginning to flesh out his plan. "From there, he could either travel by foot, eluding others by passing himself off as a slave woman purchased by a rebel family moving to Queens, New York. Or he could be smuggled on board a ship heading to the port of New York."

Soule liked J. R's idea, "This will work. I will wait until Corporal Villian's next visit and then I will file the report of Ned's disappearance. That will give you time to get closer to your destination."

"What about his disguise, how do we make him look like a woman?" J.R. asked.

"That is a challenge we can give to Comfort," Soule said smiling. "She can find the necessary clothing and make the alterations needed." Soule's face lit up. "My wife, bless her heart, was a tall woman. We have a trunk of her things in the attic, hats, shawls, dresses, and petticoats, everything we will need."

Ned's head was spinning. All he heard was woman's clothing, hiding in the oat shipment and Comfort making alterations. Nonetheless, Ned was willing to risk being caught, anything for a chance to be free.

Ned had fought for the Crown for one reason, for the promise of freedom. He enlisted and fought with confidence that the rebellion would be defeated and as a result, his freedom would be forthcoming and would be protected.

Several years earlier he had left the plantation to enlist in the Loyal Ethiopian Regiment. The regiment's first fight was the Battle of Great Bridge. That battle resulted in the British troops losing control of the Virginia Colony. He remembered it was a huge loss for the British and American Loyalist troops. If that defeat was not tough enough, then came a smallpox breakout. Most of the men of the Loyal Ethiopian Regiment died, so Ned and the other survivors joined a British unit and continued to fight.

Ned's Loyalist support eventually lead him to Kettle Creek, in the colony of Carolina, and again the Loyalists were defeated in mid-February 1779. All the men lucky enough to survive the fighting were taken prisoner. Ned thought that in many ways, being captured and ending up on Soule's farm was the luckiest day of his life.

… Ned's life story was something J.R. knew little about. While they were planning his escape, their evenings became a time to share their boyhood memories, the days before the war. J.R. was engrossed with Ned's stories; Ned's life was so different and, J.R. had to admit, far more interesting.

"Going back to the beginning," Ned said. "I was born in Virginia, southwest of Richmond on the huge Lawson Plantation., where I spent my life until I finally left. The Lawson family owned my mother and me. We lived in a room attached to the back of the main house."

Ned stopped for a moment. "I need to clear this up first. When I left the plantation, it was not an escape." Ned continued, "Mr. Lawson, told me how he had become deeply depressed when my mother died. He would sit in his chair for hours, rocking back and forth, with no interest in anything. That was when I began to understand the bond between my mother and Mr. Lawson. They were in love." He paused.

J.R. said, "If this is too painful for you to talk about …"

Ned interrupted, "No it isn't. So, as I was saying, I remember their laughter and how joyful they were together in the privacy of his home. He would sing a song, gently hold her hand and dance her around the room, step by step, over the beautiful hand-woven carpets. He played his violin and watched her dance as if she was the Queen of Spain. The joy on both of their faces was love. What puzzled me was that their relationship would dramatically change when someone else was present. They did not look each other in the eye. When they were together in public, they didn't even touch. Their change in behavior seemed odd.

"Now, of course, I understand it. My mother and Mr. Lawson, when in public, were behaving as the norms of society dictated. They were hiding their true feelings. After my mother died, I encouraged Mr. Lawson to get out his violin and play, but he didn't. He simply sat and mourned for her."

Ned's voice picked up; he became more enthusiastic. "Several months had passed, and finally Mr. Lawson opened his violin case. I was outside reading in the shade of a huge chestnut tree when the sounds of his violin drifted out the opened window of his study. He played each note as if it was a butterfly taking flight; the music flew past me, over the fences and into the fields. After that day, his violin was never far from his side.

"It was curious that when he played a waltz, he smiled, even winked while fixing his eyes on a spot where no one stood. It took me a minute or two to realize that he was thinking back to when he played for my mother and she would twirl and dance. I believe he felt my mother's presence every time he played her favorite melodies."

Ned cleared his throat. "You know, J.R., I think love is painful sometimes. There are situations you have to accept. Despite the kindness of Mr. Lawson, the family owned my mother and me. She was born on that plantation. As a child, she worked as a servant, cleaning and helping in Mrs. Lawson's kitchen. From what my mother told me, Mrs. Lawson died suddenly at a young age. At about that time, my mother was in her late teens and her servant position was changed to become Mr. Lawson's private servant and companion."

With a tone of happiness he said, "I recall how kindly my mother and I were treated by Mr. Lawson. It was in stunning contrast to how the other slave children were treated. They were forced to work long days in the fields, while I had a privileged life with proper clothing. I learned mathematics, grammar and history. I remember how Mr. Lawson took an interest in my childhood and young adulthood. While some boys my age were sold at auction, never to see their parents again, I lived in a protected world."

J.R. was captivated. Slavery and the social behavior behind the scenes were new to him.

"In 1774, I turned twenty years old and it was also the year Mr. Lawson died. I felt abandoned, alone." Ned fell silent.

"Why did you feel that way?" J.R. asked.

"I knew why," Ned said. "Mr. Lawson was my father."

J.R. repeated Ned's words, "Mr. Lawson was your father?"

"Yes. But I didn't know that until my mother was dying. I grew up thinking that my father was a slave, and that sometime after my birth, my father was sold to another plantation. Most slave children were lucky if they knew one parent.

"The truth eventually presented itself. I was just about eighteen when my mother died. She was the only family I had or at least the only family I was aware of having. On her deathbed she told me my father was Mr. Lawson." Ned's eyes teared up and he wiped them away with the back of his hand. "My Mother apologized to me for not sharing that information earlier. The evening she died, I lost my mother and learned who my father was.

"You can't imagine how confused I felt. Just as Mr. Lawson had done when feeling lonely, I too cheered myself by playing my violin. It took me to another world, a brighter and happier time. I would then stop and try to accept the truth and all of its complications. Knowing who my father was was even more difficult than not knowing. I felt like a person with no clear past and no sense of who I was. As a kid, I noticed how different I looked from most other slave boys. My color was a lighter shade compared to the others. I noticed, too, that my mother was much fairer skinned than most slaves were. Her eyes were a bluish-green and she referred to herself as a quadroon."

J.R. asked, "A what?"

"A quadroon. A quadroon refers to a person who is one part African and three parts Caucasian. To say the least, I was disappointed about the insensitivity toward women like my mother. A white man loved my mother, but he couldn't take her in marriage."

"How were you treated by the Lawson family?"

Ned smiled, "The Lawson family did not treat us like their other slaves, but we most certainly were not family. My mother was there to serve Mr. Lawson, and he had to live by the dictates of society. Perhaps he was a slave to the expectations of society. Even though most people on the plantation knew of their arrangement, he could not verbalize to anyone that he was my father. After my mother's death, my life was filled with confusion and shame. I think she kept the truth from me hoping to spare me the pain."

J.R. interrupted, "Didn't you tell Heinrich and me that Mr. Lawson taught you how to play the violin?"

Ned brightened. "Yes, perhaps my most gratifying experience was when I began to learn to be a violinist. I spent hours every day learning to read sheet music and I practiced until my fingers hurt."

Ned told J.R. about when he was given his first violin. On the day he turned twelve, Mr. Lawson gave him a fine German-made violin. That was the most wonderful gift he had ever received. He never treasured anything more than his violin.

"Whenever I played, my mother's face glowed with pride and when she watched Mr. Lawson teach me, I could see tears of joy in her eyes. Growing up with a man like Mr. Lawson was my good fortune! He not only taught me to play, but he taught me mathematics, about nature and the planets, the sun and the moon. My mother taught me to read and Mr. Lawson made sure there was never a shortage of books from which I could choose. Finally, when Mr. Lawson died, he left me the signed, dated and witnessed paperwork documenting that I was a free man. This document was his last and most enduring gift to me."

J.R. shouted and nearly fell out of his bunk. "You say you have paperwork declaring you are a free man?"

"Yes, I keep it with me, it is hidden in the silk lining of my violin case. Why?."

"You will not have to smuggle yourself to New York, or risk your life. We will show your document to Villian."

The bunkhouse was silent. Ned was shaking his head, distressed. " J.R., I do wish your assumption of my freedom was correct. My document signed by Mr. Lawson is not valid any longer."

"What do you mean not valid?"

"During times of war, all the rules change and there is no way to get around those changes. Regardless of my papers, I fought on the side that was defeated."

J.R. sat on his bunk with his mouth open, but nothing came out. He felt like someone had just belted him in the stomach. "Ned, I am sorry for getting so excited. I wish I could take some of your disappointment away."

"J.R., you, Comfort and Mr. Soule are doing just that by helping me get to New York, and for that I am grateful."

☙

The shipment of oats was leaving the farm with Ned hiding in it. Soule usually hired a man to take the oats to Philadelphia but this time, he was taking the loaded flatbed himself. Soule had a friend south of Philadelphia and this friend would see that Ned got to the port of New York.

Comfort had risen earlier than usual that day. She had a short list of things to do before Ned's departure. The skirt Ned would eventually wear needed lengthening and widening. She found a woman's casual straw hat in the attic along with a shawl to cover Ned's head when he changed into his disguise after he arrived in Philadelphia. Comfort and J. R also had come up with a plan for Ned's violin. It would be wrapped and held in his arms, as if it were a small child.

The farm was quiet and the sun had not yet risen when J.R. heard the noise of the flatbed's wheels fading away down the farm road. Soule and Ned were on their way. Everyone was cautiously optimistic. Ned knew this was his best chance for freedom.

As J.R. heard them leave, he felt a deep sadness, thinking about how much he would miss Ned. J.R. was the last one remaining. Heinrich was still missing.

During the early part of the trip, Soule was careful to maintain the appearance that he was traveling alone. At any point along the road near Albemarle, he could bump into Corporal Villian, riding through the country to check up on other prisoners. His nerves on edge, Soule tried to prepare himself for the unexpected. It would take them nearly three days to reach Philadelphia, if they had no problems. The flatbed was stacked full and the load of oats was tied down as Soule worked the wagon around the deep ruts in the road, fearing a broken wagon wheel or axle. If the wagon broke down, he would be prey to lawless gangs.

After Soule and Ned left, J.R. did the morning milking, cleaned the stalls and gave the animals fresh bedding. After breakfast, he began cleaning and sharpening tools. He still technically was a prisoner of war, even though the war was over. J.R. had read that the several thousand British and Loyalist soldiers captured at Yorktown were being held as prisoners of war. He hoped his brothers were not among them. J.R. also learned that the post-war negotiations were going to be complicated and he began to realize that finding agreement between all parties could take a very long time. Until numerous issues were resolved, he would not be going home.

After a while, J.R. stopped working to check on Comfort. Entering the kitchen, he saw her sitting near the hearth in the rocking chair. She was close to giving birth and she was exhausted.

"Today would be a perfect time for you to get off your feet and rest," he told her. "You don't need to cook for me; I know how to manage on my own and I can maneuver in your kitchen quite well."

With amazement, she asked, "Are you serious? Honestly, you really would not mind if I went to lie down? I am just worn out; there has been too much going on all at once."

"These few days your father is away may be your last days of peace. Please leave me to fend for myself. Usually you are taking care of everyone else, go rest and take care of yourself."

After an uneventful trip, Soule and Ned arrived in Philadelphia. No one could have been more thankful than Ned. Their contact in Philadelphia was a Quaker family who had been helping slaves for several years. Ned promptly got into his disguise, and as Ned was about to leave, Soule handed him a small green velvet bag. Inside were several gold coins.

"Ned, this is a token of my appreciation for the years of labor you have given me, Comfort and the farm. Thank you. "I could never pay you in full, so let's remember that I owe you." Soule wiped tears from his eyes as he gave Ned an embrace.

Ned held the bag in his large hand and thanked Soule for his friendship and generosity. Quickly, Ned turned to leave with a Quaker man. They walked out into the night and disappeared. Soon he would be at the port of New York, where he would have the protection of the British. Soule knew only Ned's general destination after New York and he was comforted to know that he would have a new beginning.

When he left, Ned also carried his disguised violin "baby." In the case, Ned were two letters: One showing that he was a free man, and the second a letter of introduction from Soule about Ned's character, his military service to the King and his abilities, including reading, writing and music. It noted Ned's enlistment with the British Army, his enduring allegiance for the King and his capture by rebel troops in 1779 at Kettle Creek.

As Mr Soule left Philadelphia, the sun was low in the eastern sky. In the early morning light, he saw for the first time that burnt-out buildings lined the road. Battles had been fought in cemeteries, backyards and on main streets. There was destruction of homes and businesses everywhere.

Soule traveled through the war-torn cities of Philadelphia, Richmond and Charlottesville and it was unnerving to think that the war had come so close to his farm in Albemarle County. To think that the destruction of home and property reigned from New England to Savannah was numbing. He said to himself, we won the war, but at what cost?

The closer he got to the farm, the more he dwelled on Heinrich's fate. He had to find Heinrich. Each time his flatbed wagon passed columns of sad, war-weary men, he would look at their faces, hoping that one might be his son-in-law. Their faces showed no expression; they were simply blank. It was unsettling to see that some of the soldiers were just kids, now prisoners of war. Column after column of British soldiers captured in the battle of Yorktown walked past. They would be held until a peace treaty was agreed upon.

They had received no definitive word about Heinrich from the 2nd Virginia Regiment. Records did list him before the battle at Camden, but there was no record of him since. As the flatbed wheels turned over bumps and around ruts in the road, he felt sadness and responsibility for Heinrich's disappearance. After all, he had made the request for Heinrich to return to battle.

He played out the sequence of events surrounding the disappearance of his son-in-law. Nearly seven months had passed since the battle of Camden. After the battle, the army said that about fifty men were missing. Could Heinrich have been one of them? Was he a deserter? That thought gave him shivers. Mr. Soule continued to ponder each possibility.

Nightfall came quickly. The days were getting shorter. He rode onward, pleased by the thought that he would soon be home; a place removed from the physical destruction of war.

After several days on the road, he could finally see the farm. Comfort greeted him at the door. He was happy to see her so cheerful. She hugged him tightly, and once again he felt the fullness of his daughter's pregnancy between them. He smiled, thinking that soon he would be holding his first grandchild.

During their evening meal, Soule told Comfort and J.R. about the trip to Philadelphia and what he had learned. "The British plan to provide transport to Nova Scotia for all the former slaves who fought for the King. He is giving them land on which to live free and in peace."

J.R. replied, "Imagine, former slaves having their own town. It would be the first such town of its kind in North America." The three praised the King's progressive stand.

Soule asked if Corporal Villian had paid a visit. Comfort smiled. "Good news father, no sight of the evil man." Soule then reviewed with Comfort and J.R. their answers to the questions that Villian would ask once he arrived and found Ned missing.

Nearly a week after Soule's return from Philadelphia, J.R. saw Corporal Villian enter the farm's front gate. The corporal was leading a second horse and J.R. could see two pair of shackles draped over the saddle of the second horse.

Villian saw J.R. and yelled out, "Hey prisoner, I am here for the slave." Villian spat to the ground a blend of chewing tobacco and saliva. The concoction just missed J.R's boot.

J.R. ignored Villian's arrogance and said, "We have some bad news for you."

Villian's eyes darted to J.R. "What the hell do you mean, bad news?"

J.R. casually stated, "What I mean is, the prisoner ran, he is gone."

With that remark, Corporal Villian jumped down from his horse and grabbed J.R.'s shirt. The corporal, seething with anger, violently shook J.R. while spitting words at J.R's face. "I don't believe you. You double-crossing sack of shit. I don't believe one word, and if he isn't here, perhaps I best sell you into slavery!"

He continued to shake J.R., then pushed him to the ground. "You best tell me where the boy is hiding or I will return with several men and we will do a search of this place, up one side and down the other. Maybe set it on fire, that would bring the boy out."

J.R. got back to his feet, and brushed dirt off his beeches. At that moment Soule walked out of the house and demanded the corporal to get off his property.

Villian told Soule, "If I don't leave with the slave, then I will leave with this prisoner."

Soule replied sternly, "That, corporal, is out of the question. Who do you think you are? J.R. Is a prisoner of war and his army surrendered. You would be in violation of several agreements pertaining to the status of prisoners and the peace treaty negotiations. If you try to carry out your threat or if you attempt to take this man, I will make sure that the authorities know what you have been up to."

Villian scowled and spit, with his face twisted in anger. "Oh, you think so, huh? You don't know what you are talking about, old man ..."

Soule interrupted, "I know your intention was to sell Ned Lawson and pocket the money. Apparently, something you have been doing rather often. Then you tell your commander that the slave escaped or died of fever." Mr. Soule had no such proof of his accusation. Nonetheless, it got Villian's attention.

Villian shut his mouth, mounted his horse and promised, "Trust me, I will be back to search your farm and I will put out word about the escaped slave. Once I find that boy, he will wish he was dead!" The corporal turned his horse and left the Soule property.

Villian was gone. Soule was confident he would never see him again.

In December, Soule got his first look at someone else when Comfort gave birth to a beautiful baby boy. She named him Henry Christian With

Chapter 19

Early winter 1782: Return from War

When Obadiah returned home from the war, he was the grand age of thirty with graying hair around his temples and a look of maturity that surprised his parents. They were relieved to find that he was the same curious, friendly and well-read son who had enlisted nearly five years earlier.

Obadiah had immediate and heartbreaking business to which he needed to attend. It was a promise he made to his best friend, Charles Chambers. He had to tell Charles' wife, Charlotte, that her husband was dead.

He and Charles were close friends; a friendship that began during their childhood. They enlisted together in the Loyal American Regiment. The two friends fought side by side, battle after battle, year after year and had made an agreement that if anything happened to either one of them, the other would be there to support and comfort his family.

It happened after the surrender at Yorktown when Charles and Obadiah were on their way home to Middle District. Bunches of vengeful hooligans, well aware that the British had surrendered, continued killing Tories. The roadways were now more dangerous than they might have been during the war. Rebels perched in trees and hid behind stone walls. As Charles and Obadiah rode home, a shot came out of nowhere. The musket ball just missed Obadiah's shoulder and struck Charles' chest. The ball blew open his heart and killed him instantly.

Obadiah grabbed Charles as he began to slump and fall from his horse. He pulled Charles to the ground and grabbed his musket, loading it with a ball and powder. He remained crouched near Charles' lifeless body. His eyes peered along the top of the stone wall and darted up to the trees, as he searched for the culprit. He saw and heard nothing as he knelt over Charles.

Charles and his wife, Charlotte, had one daughter, Isabelle, who would soon be turning four. She was only a few months old when her father mustered out.

Within a day of arriving home, Obadiah paid his visit to Charlotte. He knocked on the door and Charlotte, immediately smiling and welcoming, looked around and asked, "Where is Charles?"

Obadiah had to tell her that, after having waited four years for her husband's return, he was killed on the way home. Weekly he visited Charlotte through the winter month of January. He helped her gather wood and go to town to pick up provisions. She was grateful. Charlotte and Obadiah were not strangers; they had known each other for half of their lives. During one visit to her home, Charlotte was busy cooking chicken soup while Obadiah taught Isabelle how to play the board game, checkers.

January faded into February and Obadiah's weekly visits became more frequent. About that time, Charlotte and Isabelle had made their first visit to meet Obadiah's family. Magdalene was especially happy as she gazed at the two of them and saw her son was in love.

As Charlotte spent more time with him, she began to see all the good in him, all the qualities her Charles was drawn to. She realized that she had feelings for Obadiah and tried to suppress them. Were her feelings for Obadiah a betrayal to Charles? After a few months, she told him that they would have to stop seeing each other.

He could not believe what she was saying, but he agreed. "If that is what you want, I understand."

She began to weep and told him the truth. "I have been confused and do not want to betray my love for Charles by falling in love with you."

When Obadiah heard that he said what he felt in his heart." Your love for Charles will never be compromised, and the love you carry for him will be forever enduring." He wiped a tear from her cheek. "Charlotte my feelings for you go beyond love, and I wish you would consider my proposal of marriage."

"Whenever you have something to say," she said, "I listen because you always make such good sense. May I have some time to consider your proposal?"

Obadiah left Charlotte that afternoon disheartened, but also, oddly enough, hopeful. He longed for Charlotte to give herself permission to move on with her life. He knew that Charles would approve.

On the second day of April 1782, Obadiah and Charlotte were married. Their marriage helped mute the post-war chaos for a day. Their marital union had given the family hope of rejuvenation.

The newlyweds moved into a small room on the first floor. In time, Charlotte knew her way around the kitchen and she was a tremendous help to Magdalene. Everything was beginning to feel good. Charlotte and Isabelle brought vitality to the war-weary family.

By April, Elijah and Jacob had also returned from the war. One unseasonably cold evening, the wind was blowing and snowflakes whirled and tumbled with the brisk wind. The three sons and their father were talking quietly by the burning hearth when Elijah asked his father question that was also on his brothers' minds. "Father, what is wrong with Mother?"

Jacob added, "Is it the war that has taken the life out of her? She appears to be ill; is there something you are not telling us?"

Jonathan was not sure what to say, "I understand your concern, but I am not sure what is causing your mothers exhaustion and discomfort. Within the last several months, your mother has lost weight, and has become more dependent on her pain medication. Yes, there is no doubt that the war has worn her down. Then, of course, the horrid news of Joseph's death seemed to kill her spirit. I don't know what to say."

Mrs. Brouwer continued to provide Magdalene with teas, tinctures and compresses every week."

Obadiah then asked, "Father, what about melancholia?"

Just in case their mother was still awake, Jonathan replied very quietly. "She did never seem to get past Joseph's death. I think she buried a part of herself with him. All I can say is the war has taken a toll on her."

Jonathan had never felt so unsettled, he did not trust the new government and he had lost confidence in the Crown. A peace agreement had not been reached and everything in the colonies was chaotic. There was no common currency, no common laws, and no one to enforce the laws. And he thought his wife was dying.

Much to Obadiah and his father's chagrin, talk of giving Loyalist men and their families amnesty appeared not to be important to the negotiations. Obadiah wondered why people's lives seemed incidental when compared to compromising on boundaries, fishing rights, paying creditors, and releasing prisoners of war. Obadiah thought that the King had forgotten about the sacrifices the L.A.R. had made.

About one month later, Obadiah and Elijah made a visit to the Bull's Head Tavern. They watched as tempers erupted among the patrons. Theories were being debated about amnesty. Hot-headed men got into fist fights and some patrons were cursing the King.

A middle-aged man said, "Of course the Crown won't support amnesty. It is not in the King's interest!"

Obadiah asked, "Why would it not be?"

The man answered, "The King has this crazy idea to send the Loyalist men and their families to the forsaken place of Nova Scotia. I hear it is a pile of rocks with a thin layer of poor soil. It might be fine if we were fishermen." Several men laughed and others shook their heads in discouragement. "But we obviously are not fishermen; we are planters and farmers."

Chapter 20

January 1782: Vanished

Soule held Henry in his arms and thought back to the love and pride he had for his own two sons, Solomon and Oliver. Mr. Soule remembered the hope and promise his sons had offered. Now they were gone. He whispered to the baby, "Your father will be home soon and he will be so proud and happy to meet you, little one."

Comfort walked into the room. "Well, father, it is Henry's time to eat."

He gently handed Henry to his daughter. "You must be very proud, my dear."

"Yes, I am father, very proud." Her smile melted away. "Father, where can he be? Do you think I will ever see him again? I just miss him so." Her tears began to fall, landing on Henry's blanket.

"Daughter you are a strong woman and you must continue to be. I will do all I possibly can to find Heinrich. We must keep in mind, with the surrender of the British just three months ago, chaos and uncertainty still reign. I believe Heinrich is alive and will come home to you and your son."

After two attempts to find Heinrich, Soule planned to take advantage of the mild January weather and travel again to Camden. Once there, he would knock on doors, ask more questions, and scour the updated lists of soldiers missing in action. Reviewing the casualty lists and Continental records of the battle of Camden should reveal something. Mr. Soule was determined. It had been nine months since records had shown Heinrich With present and accounted for.

During morning breakfast, Soule told Comfort and J.R., "I don't know how long I will be gone, most likely a couple nights. There must be some updated records, or new information in Camden, that will help us find Heinrich. Perhaps I have missed something, or maybe I have not spoken to enough people. I will also pay a visit to the Continental forces headquarters." He paused. "I will not stop searching for him."

His first stop was the Continental Army headquarters. There, he reviewed the updated list of men who were missing in action. The list was long; why wouldn't Heinrich at least be on this list? Next, he scoured the long list of dead, and thankfully, once again no Heinrich With. Several names on this list were smudged; some names barely readable. But nobody with the last name With.

He thought about the events of Heinrich's last battle, on the ridge outside of Camden. It was a surprise attack by the British. The British were under the impression that the Continental Army's artillery had not yet arrived. Initially there was a fierce fighting and the Continental troops left the ridge, retreating to a safer area. If Heinrich survived that battle, he was one fortunate soldier. Soule repeatedly asked himself, could Heinrich have been wounded, but escaped capture? If that was the case, then what? Would he die in the field from his wounds, or would someone find him? But if he was found, they would have notified someone. By dusk he returned to the Burr House Inn to eat and rest.

The following day he returned to the army headquarters. He asked to see the list with the names of the British soldiers' who were captured by the Continentals in the battle of Camden.

The soldier assisting Soule said, "Yes sir, but I thought you said you are looking for a Continental soldier."

"Yes, I am, but I would like to review the list of captives held by the Continentals," replied Soule.

The soldier, a little puzzled said, "Sir, the Continental troops didn't capture any British troops during that April battle. Records show there were none, likely because of Greene's hasty retreat." The young corporal continued, "During that battle, the British captured about 40 of our Continental troops. But, like I said, the records show the Continentals did not capture one Brit or Loyalist."

Soule had not learned anything more about Heinrich. Then he thought of another possibility. Perhaps Heinrich left his Virginia regiment and fought with the Hesse-Kassel troops in the British Army. Thus, Heinrich might have been part of the thousands of British troops who surrendered that October in Yorktown. The corporal informed him that there were no Hessian regiments in the Camden battle.

Soule thought, maybe Heinrich went to the British side, leaving his Virginia regiment. He then could be a prisoner of war held by the Continental Army. That possibility was not a good one, for as soon as the 2nd Virginia noticed him, they would have shot him for being a traitor. Soule dreaded to think about such a possibility.

He would not likely be informed of that answer until finalization of the peace agreement. Even though that idea pained Soule, he knew it could have happened. Perhaps Heinrich began fighting with his Virginia regiment, but did not feel comfortable there.

The next day Soule knocked on doors and asked questions. He described Heinrich dozens of times to people. He rode his horse out to the ridge where the battle had been fought, to the place where Heinrich was last known to have been. The only sign of life was the sound of woodcutters and their axes a short distance away. He found nothing.

❦

With the longer days, Albemarle County planters had begun cultivating their fields. In town, seeking to hire a couple of men to help with the planting, Soule was fortunate to find two brothers wanting work. Their mother was a war widow barely able to keep food on the table.

No one wanted to say so, but hope was waning for Heinrich's return. The first of March, Comfort and Heinrich's first wedding anniversary, came and went with little notice, except Comfort wondered if she was a war widow. She tried to dismiss that thought. She didn't want to give up hope.

The workday began at six in the morning and did not end until eight o'clock at night. They used two plows and the tilling was accomplished rather quickly. More than a year earlier, Ned had rebuilt both plows. They were rugged and fast, pulled by two of the best workhorses J.R. had ever seen. The plow cut through the sod like butter. J.R. followed the plow with the harrow and the aromatic smell of the soil again reminded J.R. of Middle District. The mixed fragrances and scents made him homesick.

Chapter 21

December 1782: Long-Awaited Reunion

A damp, raw December day cast a gray gloom over the fields of Fishkill. Rain welcomed J.R. back to Middle District and as he walked the last couple miles, he was in disbelief that took him more than five and one-half years to get back home.

It had been fourteen months since the British surrender and just two months since Soule picked up the letter addressed to him from Albemarle Barracks Headquarters. Soule thought the letter could mean a date for J.R. to return home. Or it might be news about Ned. Soule thought, his pulse quickening, what if it did have something to do with Ned? Soule was hesitant to open the letter. He could not bear the idea that Ned had been caught, sold or hanged. Soule finally sat down and read the letter. It was good news for J.R.

The familiar scenery brought back so memories of J.R.'s life before the war; especially the memory of when he first met Abigail. That was six years ago. It did not seem possible. But he could not think of Abigail without thinking about the treaty. His thoughts about the treaty were as dark as the clouds above him. He had many questions. Would he and his fellow Loyalist soldiers be accepted by the new government? Would amnesty be a part of the peace? J.R. could only hope that provisions would be made for the thousands of Loyalist colonists to remain in their homes. He was perplexed as to why it was taking so long to finalize the treaty.

The treaty was of vital importance to everyone's life and future. It would determine where he might be living one year from now! Would he and his family be exiled from the land and the home they loved? Would they become refugees? After all, many men of the L.A.R. picked up their guns not for the King of England, but to prevent a rebellion, to keep the colonies from falling into mob rule.

J. R's mind raced. The revolution had ended, the fighting was over and there was a clear winner. He hoped he was wrong, but he felt the struggles of those who fought for the King were not even close to being over.

He tried to walk near the side of the road, to avoid the ruts and puddles. With blistered feet and worn shoes, his pace slowed. He sat on a mound of dried grass, closed his eyes and took several deep breaths, trying to clear his mind. He heard what sounded like horses in the distance. He could see two men with horses pulling a flatbed. It was the first time, in several hours, that he had seen anyone. The team of horses got closer and the two men pulled up alongside J.R. and stopped.

The one holding the reins mumbled something.

J.R. did not hear what he said.

Then the man shouted at J.R., "I said, where you headed, stranger?"

"I am on my way home."

"Where's that? Where's your home, boy?" the man asked.

"Middle District."

As soon as the two men heard the words Middle District, they perked up. The second man said to the one holding the horse's reins, "You know what, we found ourselves a Tory. Middle District ain't nothin' but a hot-bed of Tories, all of them traitors!"

J.R. didn't want to pose a threat. "Gentlemen, I have spent the last three and one-half years as a prisoner of war and I have been freed to go home. I have paperwork, the war is over, and the British surrendered."

"What the hell is this traitor talking about, surrendered?" The two men on the flatbed laughed. One of the men climbed down from the wagon, walked over to J.R. and grabbed him. He flipped J.R. onto the ground. The guy holding the reins told his partner to forget the Tory and climb back up on the wagon.

J.R. did not feel relief that they were gone. He was struck with a realization that as a Tory, his life was in danger. The hate for Loyalists was a harsh reality.

He thought about how war had taken a toll on him. Then, he identified his nagging anxiety. He felt responsible for Joseph's death and had not seen his parents since Joseph was killed. Would they treat me differently, J.R. wondered. The wind picked up and carried with it small pieces of hail that stung J. R's face. Low clouds shrouded tree tops.

Memories of his enlistment surged into his mind. He found it curious that he was walking the same dirt road that he and Joseph had ridden on horseback, that day in June 1777. The two brothers proudly rode with their orders neatly folded and placed in their saddlebags as they headed to the British camp located in Harlem Heights. They believed that victory was ahead of them. Today he walked home, not as a hero, but as one of the defeated. He walked home without his brother; he was one of the dead. As he walked, he tried to ignore his aching feet, worn boots and weary heart.

The hunger in his stomach caused him to stop and rest. He placed his knapsack on a stone wall, and then made himself comfortable on the edge of the wall. The hail had changed to light rain and the rocks were wet and cold. He opened his knapsack, searching for the hardened bread. He tore off a bite-size piece and his saliva softened the crusty morsel. It tasted fine to him and he felt fortunate to have traveled with food from Comfort's kitchen.

The second bite of bread was beginning to soften in his mouth. He could taste the yeast and whole grains of the rye. Then, it began to hail again. With a firm footing, he got to his feet, grabbed his knapsack and continued his journey.

J.R. looked off into the distance at the brown fields, crisscrossed with a lattice-work of rock walls and cedar rail fences. Each field boasted a large royal oak tree for shade. These majestic oak remained, while all the other trees had been cut down and cleared away. The lone surviving trees now served as shade-givers for grazing farm animals. He accidentally kicked a stone and broke his thought. He saw the sun breach the clouds, and for a moment, sunshine lifted his spirits.

His mind grew more burdened the closer he got to home. Much had changed, would the sight of him provoke mournful memories of Joseph? His guilt came to the fore. After all, he was at Bull's Head Tavern when Joseph enlisted in the L.A.R. at the age of thirteen.

He was too young to grasp the responsibility and the risks of what he was doing. J.R. blamed himself, he should have put an end to Joseph's idea of enlistment. He was assured he would be a stable boy. He stopped walking and attempted to calm his feeling of responsibility for Joseph's death.

ஒ

J.R. saw the outline of the stone chimneys that towered over the rooftop of his home. They were his beacon, like a lantern hung off a ship's mast. His journey's end. The chimneys rose majestically at each gable end of the house. Magnificent bookends holding his post-war world together.

As his mother worked in the kitchen, sunlight broke through the clouds. A beam of warmth penetrated the glass window, filling the room with light. Like magic, the dark clouds vanished, blown away by the wind. Magdalene was churning the morning's cream into butter. She sat on a bench near the window, so she could easily glance out to see if J.R. was walking up the long dirt road to the house. She and Charlotte had just finished baking biscuits after going to the root cellar to get some peach preserves.

Two weeks earlier, Magdalene had received the long-awaited news, a letter from J.R. saying if all went well he would be home during the first week of December. She squinted as she peered out the window, the sun catching a bubbled imperfection of the window pane. She stopped her churning, placed a hand to block the sun's glare, to get a better look. She thought she saw him. Yes, it was him. She blinked. Could it really be him? She began to tremble with excitement. One thing was sure, someone was walking up the carriage path. As he got closer, she could see it was a tall man coming toward the house. She continued to look out the window, for fear that if she stopped, he would vanish.

The butter churn caught on her long skirt, and fell to the floor on its side as she bolted out the kitchen door to the porch. "John Roger, you are home!" The commotion startled the chickens, creating a duet of both the joyous welcome from Magdalene and the chickens clucking. King George joined in. The barn door flew open and Jonathan emerged, wondering what was causing all of the noise.

John Roger saw his mother and father running toward him, his mother's skirt flowing in the wind and her shawl flying around each arm. She flew into J. R's arms, almost knocking him off his feet. His father embraced them both with a hug. J.R. was instantly reminded of his mother's love; a powerful, yet gentle force, and he felt a calmness surround him. He had not experienced this feeling in over five years. He was home, he was truly home, and the war was over! He wept tears of relief and thankfulness.

J.R. stepped back from his mother's long embrace. As he looked at her, he tried to hide his shock, hoping it was not showing on his face. He hid his distress, and held back the urge to ask if something was wrong, if she was ill. He walked with his mother and father up to the house and into the warm kitchen. In all of the letters that he had received while gone, no one had mentioned that his mother's health was failing. He knew she was getting older but, in his gut, he knew something else was going on.

His mother's hair was now gray, but still worn gracefully high on her head, giving way to loose stands that curled around her neck and face. His mother was thinner and frail; she had lost the color in her cheeks. He was sure his father would have written to him if she were ill. J.R. smiled at her, wrapped one arm around her shoulder and held her tight thinking of all the years that had passed since he had seen her last.

J.R. asked his father, "Where are Obadiah, Elijah and Jacob?"

He father replied, "Elijah and Jacob are in the barn, Obadiah is out to the lower twenty, resetting stones in the wall."

With excitement, Magdalene went to the porch and briskly pulled the frayed rope attached to the dinner bell, ringing it feverishly. The loud clear rings gave a fast traveling message. Elijah and Jacob raced from the barn to greet their brother. They yelled repeatedly, "John Roger.

Once Obadiah heard the bell, he stopped his work. His brother was home! He nearly fell, as he rushed from the field, jumped the brook and ran to the house.

J.R. saw his brothers and was suddenly speechless. They had grown, matured by the war and the years. They were thin, but muscular. He felt comforted, at ease to see that their faces carried the same smiles they took to war. The rest of the day and into the evening, their home was filled with hugs, smiles and tears of thankfulness. He could not believe that Obadiah was thirty years old. Obadiah introduced him to his wife, Charlotte, and her seven-year-old daughter, Isabelle. He glanced around the room. Everyone was there, except for Joseph.

J.R. braced himself for the time Joseph's name would be mentioned. Then it happened. His father mentioned Joseph when he talked about the horse stable. J.R. became anxious as his eyes darted from his father's face, then to his mother's. He immediately realized that there were no blank stares, dirty looks, or blame towards him for allowing Joseph to sign up with the L.A.R. Relieved, he watched everyone talk about Joseph with smiles on their faces. He sat and listened as they all spoke lovingly about Joseph. It was then, at that moment, he felt comforted by his family's willingness to talk about Joseph as if he were right there with them.

J.R. did not mention Joseph's last letter to him. He recalled how Joseph's letter tore him apart inside, leaving him bewildered. Joseph wrote that he was not a stable boy as he was initially promised when he enlisted. His stomach muscles twisted in a knot when he thought about Joseph's risky scouting missions behind enemy lines. And what about Joseph's kidnapping by a gang, the leader of which was a man named Salem Poore, who claimed that he was a cousin. J.R. knew that he could not have made the story up; it was too strange to not be true.

For now, the letter was his secret. He would not broach the topic of Joseph's apparent undercover work. He figured there would be a time to share that information, certainly not then. There was no talk about how Joseph actually died. J.R. was curious to know how the death of a fourteen-year-old kid could be so shrouded in mystery. There was much more to the story of Joseph's demise. He wanted answers and feared Joseph had taken those secrets to his grave. Unknown to him, the only family member with any knowledge of Joseph's cause of death was his father.

Charlotte set the table with bowls for drinking tea and in the center of the table she placed a carefully stacked pile of biscuits. They were arranged on one of Magdalene's most beautiful serving dishes from France. At each end of the table were placed small bowls filled with jam, lemon curd, wildflower honey and freshly churned butter. J.R. watched his mother, Charlotte and Isabelle, as they did the final fixings for the family's first tea in several years.

Magdalene went to the cherry cupboard and with a long reach, gently removed two of her largest tea pots. Both had been resting on that top shelf, undisturbed since Joseph's death. Holding one pot in her hand, her thoughts focused on Joseph's burial, the last time she used the teapots. She grew silent.

Everyone was seated and J.R. had his eye on one particular bowl with dark-ruby-colored black raspberry jam. The contents of that bowl had his undivided attention. He had not had any black raspberry jam in years and it was his favorite. To add a little citrus flavor to the teapot, Magdalene added dried lemon rind to her brew. As the fragrant tea steeped, it infused the water with tastes from half a world away.

One by one, piping hot bowls of tea were poured and passed around the table. The warm biscuits were sliced open and lathered with butter, honey or jam. Jonathan and Magdalene sipped their tea, while their eyes met. So much of their happiness was with them, right there, right then.

The conversations between the four sons began as a robust attempt to catch up on all the years of separation caused by the revolution. J.R. counted three other matters that were best not discussed: The treaty negotiations, Joseph's death and his mother's frailness.

While chomping down on biscuits, J. R's eyes darted from his parents, then to his siblings. They were almost carefree in their conversations and laughter. They carried on as if their lives were going to continue on, undisturbed, as if they were frozen in time. They must be in denial, or were the past several years so painful and so destructive that they could not bear any more bad news? Perhaps they were just happy to be alive, maybe the defeat had not sunk in yet, or were they merely enjoying the moments together before the approaching storm arrived?

J.R. could not help but see how tired his mother looked. She appeared worn out, weak, and at times seemed to suffer from pain or discomfort. He knew the war had taken a toll on her, but he was concerned that something else was going on. Later that evening, he learned that his concerns for his mother were shared by his brothers.

"How long has she been like this?" asked J.R.

"We think mother does not want this to be a topic or burden," Obadiah answered, "we are simply following her wishes and not breaching her privacy. If she wanted to tell us, she would have. If she is more comfortable this way, then that is how it will be."

"What about father, have you spoken with him?" asked J.R.

"No, father is following her lead. Mother's illness is her private matter. All we need to know is what we see. She is very weak and may not be with us too much longer," sighed Obadiah.

Elijah tried to reassure J.R., "Father has taken steps to help mother feel better. He contacted Mrs. Brouwer and she has visited mother regularly providing herbal teas and giving her concoctions for her discomfort and pain. Also, Charlotte has been invaluable, helping mother with chores and cooking."

His brothers had validated J. R's worst fear; his mother was terribly ill. What might that mean for her and for the family?

Obadiah, Jacob and Elijah were burning with curiosity. They wanted to know about their brother's years as a prisoner of war. They had heard horrible stories about captured loyalist soldiers, but J.R.'s appearance discredited any stories they heard. He did not look as though he had been mistreated.

That evening the four brothers gathered around the hearth and listened to J.R. speak affectionately of his years at Soule's farm. And J.R. was equally curious to learn more about how his three brothers' spent their enlistment years. The four brothers told about things they saw, people they met, and places they went, along with the horror, tragedy and destruction they had witnessed. They were not stories of mystical events but of bloodshed and loss.

They talked about Stony Point and the attacking rebel forces crossing deep marshes of muck in complete darkness and silence. They talked about Ned's escape to avoid being sold into slavery.

Jacob said, "So, Ned was going to be sold to a slave owner by the army of men who boasted that they were against oppression and were fighting for freedom and self-determination?"

They talked and talked until the fire began to die. Obadiah went off to bed hoping not to wake his wife. J.R., Jacob and Elijah took their weary bodies to the attic bedroom, where waiting were their straw mattresses on frames of wood and rope. As J.R. tried to get to sleep, he thought about Joseph. He missed his kid brother so much it hurt.

J.R. awoke with a jolt; it sounded as though a herd of horses were loose downstairs. J.R. heard Charlotte's soft voice as she welcomed everyone to the mid-day meal. Had he slept that long? Now awake and wide-eyed, he stretched his arms to the ceiling and got to his feet. He was a bit embarrassed and hoped no one noticed he had slept until noon. He listened to the lively chatter of his brothers babbling on about the weather, as they hung their coats on wooden pegs. He then heard a voice he could not mistake. It was Mr. Brouwer, sounding as jolly as usual.

"Abigail is expecting J.R. to share dinner with us on Sunday," he said. Then, Brouwer handed Charlotte a small package of herbal remedies for Magdalene. He visited for a minute and then was off to the post.

On succeeding evenings, the four brothers warmed themselves at the fireside sharing stories. While in the middle of telling his brothers about Soule's kindness and generosity, J.R. said, "I believe Mr. Soule saved my life. Being sent to work on his farm was my best fortune. I spent three years on the farm, during which time I was in the company of two soldiers with whom I have enduring friendships." J.R. paused. "One might think nothing good could come from war. I am happy to say there are a few exceptions."

❦

On Sunday, Jonathan had one of his best horses saddled up for J.R. to ride to the Brouwer home for dinner. J.R. dressed in his Sunday best, wearing boots that were new to him. J. R's boots had literally seen hundreds of miles and they were deemed past the point of repair.

On Saturday, J.R. had been given a pair of boots, which fit him best when he wore thick socks. The boots were a gift from a neighboring family, the Tuckers. They had lost a son at Yorktown. J.R. pulled the boots onto his feet and they felt so comfortable he stood up, grabbed his mother by the hand and danced her around the kitchen worktable. He twirled her around while he hummed a tune he had learned from listening to Ned play his violin.

"These boots fit great!" he said. He bowed to his mother, kissed her hand and thanked her for the dance. When he led her back to her chair, he noticing how winded she was by that short dance. Even her smile couldn't hide her dull complexion and the dark circles around her eyes.

On his ride to the Brouwers on Sunday, J.R. was feeling confident and could not wait to see Abigail. And yet, going to see Abigail did not seem real to him. After being apart for so long, the idea seemed like a dream. As he rode, he wondered if he was the same person with whom she had fallen in love so many years earlier. He thought back to when he first saw Abigail, in December 1776. It was a time when he was so happy, he was almost carefree.

He grew uneasy. Life had become so complicated and nothing seemed to be as it once was. He wondered if that might include their love for each other. He reminded himself that having doubts was normal. Soon he planned to ask Mr. Brouwer for his daughter's hand in marriage; but not that Sunday. First, he wanted to cherish the day of their reunion and make sure their flame still burned.

❦

The winter snows were relentless. In January and February of 1783, snow blanketed the fields, and drifts climbed the sides of the Holmes barn and house as if trying to race to the roof. The harsh winter did not keep J.R. from the Brouwer home, though. He had been paying Abigail regular visits since mid-December. He was determined to receive assurance of intentions from Abigail, before going to Mr. Brouwer for permission to marry his daughter.

In February, in the face of the cold winds and deep snow outside, the Brouwer home was celebrating. Mr. and Mrs. Brouwer had given their permission for J.R. and Abigail to marry. The wedding date was set for the seventeenth day of May. Along with his blessings, Brouwer gave some advice. "It may be a good idea for you to consider to have your wedding ceremony sooner rather than later."

Abigail asked jokingly, "Father, you aren't trying to get rid of me?"

Brouwer replied, "No, my dear, it is not that. I want to marry you off, but I am concerned about the coming Preliminary Articles of Peace that will soon be policy. There may be some unknown hardships coming our way." Abigail was puzzled by her father's remark, and she looked at J.R. who appeared to be in deep thought.

"We have no idea how these articles may impact all of us," explained Brouwer.

J.R. assured her father that the wedding date would be flexible.

Regardless of the Preliminary Articles or peace treaty negotiations, February was a month of other new beginnings for the Holmes family. Obadiah and Charlotte, who were celebrating their first wedding anniversary, announced that they would be adding another Holmes to the family. Charlotte was expecting in September.

The month of March arrived along with the Preliminary Articles of Peace. Regardless of the document's name, the articles were not considered helpful to the Loyalists. There was no mention of any form of amnesty for the Loyalist population.

In J. R's estimation, the articles expressed Britain's decision to recognize the sovereignty and independence of the thirteen colonies. Protecting the property rights of Loyalist families was mentioned in two of the articles, but J.R. noticed that the negotiators gave each colony the power to resolve issues about reimbursement of confiscated Loyalist property. But more important, there was no enforcement or consequence if any colony decided to simply ignore compensation for confiscated property. J.R. reread the material and saw that the articles were vague at best, with no accountability. J.R. and his brothers were outraged.

During his next visit to Abigail's home, her father discouragingly admitted, "It is a kick in the teeth. Loyalists will most likely not be compensated for their loss of property."

Her father added: "Do they think we are stupid? The way the articles are written promise us nothing. The individual states will do what they want and there is no way to hold them accountable. There is no mention of Loyalist recourse and no penalty for those states that don't follow the articles of the agreement that make the states accountable."

"I have heard numerous rumors," J.R. said, "about the exodus of Loyalists. In truth, many began to voluntarily leave the thirteen colonies seven and eight years ago. Many left with hopes of returning once the war ended."

Abigail looked at her father. "Yes, just like some of our family who left the Colony of New Jersey for a small community located at the mouth of the Penobscot River."

"The Crown is granting tens of thousands of acres to be divided amongst all who fought against the colonial rebellion," her father said. "Some who had seen the land complained of rocky soil, isolated wilderness and shorter growing seasons. We are being told there are no churches, shops, taverns, inns or homes, nothing! An enormous task lies ahead for those settlers, with untold obstacles and enormous hardships."

Chapter 22

The Woodcutter's Wife

In the Carolinas, a woodcutter's wife knew nothing about the Continental Army soldier she found lying face down in her vegetable garden. The soldier was bleeding from a deep wound on his head. A ball had ripped across right side of his head just above the ear, the gash nearly penetrating his skull and just missing his eye.

Mrs. Robinson was alarmed when she bent down and saw his blonde hair matted with blood. It appeared that part of his scalp was missing. She was amazed he was still alive. She looked around to see if anyone was watching her. The rebel uniform he wore was disconcerting, but he needed immediate help. She shouted for her husband. The Robertsons carried him into their small home and placed him on the bed of their son, who had been killed fighting for the British in the Battle of Waxhaw Creek.

Scottish immigrants, the Robertsons were a Loyalist family, but not because they were devoted to the Crown. They took the Loyalist side because they had a strong dislike for the horror that came with war. They vehemently opposed the rebellion and the death and destruction it was causing. When their son died, they felt they had suffered enough and hoped the rebels would leave them alone.

While tending to the soldier, Mrs. Robertson noticed his head wound was especially deep. Through a gap between the dried blood and torn flesh, she could see his skull bone. She thought it would be a miracle if he survived. She gave the young man around-the-clock care the first few days.

The woodcutter's wife felt the lingering presence of death and waited for it to come while continuing to clean and bandage his wound. Days became weeks and the young man, although still alive, had not opened his eyes. All the while, she made sure to get fluids into him, starting with drops of water and herbal tea. Mrs. Robertson used herbal remedies to treat the wound. Slowly the head wound began to heal.

In late October, the Robertson's heard the news; the war was over. The British had surrendered at Yorktown. The woodcutter's wife continued to care for the soldier. She thought he could hear because he reacted slightly to noise. When she read Bible stories to him, he appeared soothed and relaxed. His family will be missing him, she thought, while missing her own son. In early December, the young man opened his eyes for the first time.

Mrs. Robertson was stunned to see his radiant blue eyes. She smiled and quietly talked to him. She told him about his arrival and that he was safe. She said they would take care of him and he need not worry. But there was no response. The soldier did not talk. The woodcutter and his wife thought that his speechlessness must have been a result of battle trauma or the deep wound to his head. He never spoke a word to them.

Late that same month, the young man was well enough to go into the forest with the woodcutter, all the time never talking. The woodcutter watched him work with the axe; he was a natural. They spent the next spring, summer and early fall going into the forest looking for felled trees, then cutting the trees and stacking the wood. When snow arrived, they took a smooth-bottom flatbed into the woods and hauled out the wood. Most of the wood was taken to town to sell or barter. The remaining wood was used for their own heat and cooking.

A year passed from the time they began going into the woods. It was December 1782. The Robertsons and the young man were sitting quietly enjoying a bowls of mutton stew and bread when they heard a loud knock on the door. It was a knock that they had been expecting. They had heard that Loyalists were receiving visits from military agents, carrying notices of eviction.

The woodcutter opened the door. There stood two imposing soldiers dressed in Continental Army uniforms. One soldier told them they were there to inform them they had to leave. He explained that the Robertsons' names were on the list of people who had refused to pledge support to the rebel cause. The woodcutter invited the two soldiers to step into their home, so he could close the door and keep the cold wind out.

The young man stopped eating and was startled by the appearance of the two men in uniform. He abruptly stood up and saluted the two soldiers. The Robertsons were dumbfounded.

One of the soldiers asked, "What do you think you are doing? Who do you think you are saluting?"

The young man didn't answer.

The soldier walked over to the young man, got in his face, and said, "You better answer me, who do you think you are?" The soldier became annoyed at getting no response, carelessly shoved the man out of the way. "You sit down, boy. You don't salute me. You are a traitor, and traitor are not welcome here."

He shoved the young man back toward his chair, but the young man missed the chair and went to the floor, hitting his head on the hearth. He tried to get to his feet while the soldier grabbed the young man by his hair.

Mrs. Robertson yelled for the soldier to stop.

The soldier said, "Maybe I will stop. I'll stop to take this pretty boy to the Camden jail for assaulting a man in uniform."

"Assault? He didn't assault you," Mr. Robertson said.

The soldier sneered. "You are a trouble maker too. No one cares about your opinion, old man. And you," he said to the young man, "what do you have to say for yourself? You better talk or I'll …

"Wait!" Mrs. Robertson shouted. "Just wait one moment, please, I must get something."

The other soldier drew his pistol, not sure what the woman was getting.

She soon returned. In her hands was the Continental Army uniform the young man had worn. She pushed the uniform into the soldiers' faces. "This is his uniform. He was wounded in battle, a severe head injury and he cannot speak; he is not able to answer your questions."

The two soldiers immediately changed their tone and began talking among themselves about a mix-up of paperwork. They didn't ask them any more questions. The assumption had been made that this was the Robertsons' son and they were not Loyalists. One of the soldiers apologized for disturbing their meal, placed the uniform on the table, and they left.

Mr. and Mrs. Robertson sat back down, relieved. The young man just stood there, staring at the uniform he once wore. "Yes, son," she said, "that is your uniform. It was the only thing you had when we found you in the garden." The young man's blue eyes were glued to the uniform, his uniform.

Small pieces of his memory began to return. He remembered marching with other men, the loud sounds of cannon and gunfire, orders being shouted, men yelling, musket fire and commands to retreat. He recalled screams and calls for help. He saw several men fall. He was beginning to remember. It all began coming back. He could picture it. His head felt as though it was going to burst with all the information coming back to him. But who was he and where did he belong?

He urgently tried to put the fragments of his past together. It was as if he was looking into a kaleidoscope, seeing jumbled and vivid reminders of his past events, one moment colliding together with others and then things falling apart. In a daze, he heard someone calling, he recognized the voice, it was his voice. He realized he was calling the same name over and over. He felt dizzy and sat at the table.

Just then, the woodcutter's wife placed her hand on his shoulder. He lifted his face toward her and said one word, "Heinrich."

Both the woodcutter and his wife watched the young man's expression; he was coming to a most joyful revelation! And then he repeated his name, "Heinrich, Heinrich Helmut With."

The couple began to cry tears of joy, thinking only of young man's well-being. Later, they would realize they were not being evicted. The woodcutter told his wife, "Thanks to Heinrich, we will not be exiled. The Continental soldiers think he is our son. He and his uniform saved us."

⁊⊚

That same month, in Virginia, Soule was hoping that by early spring he could find a few hardworking men who could take on the many challenges of planting. After Ned and J.R. left, Soule had struggled to keep good workers on the farm. There was a critical shortage of labor, with thousands of soldiers dying in the war and thousands more being exiled. Many of the men who did return from the war were not healthy enough for strenuous labor. Some were battle worn, others malnourished and many had wounds. Then there were those who had lost interest in working for someone else, setting out to claim free acreage in newly settled territories.

Even more than his labor problems, Soule thought about Heinrich. He needed to know what had happened to him. Not a day passed that he did not wish he would look up and see Heinrich riding his horse down the long road to the farm. His heart would break every time he saw Comfort and his grandson. Comfort might be a young war widow and Soule felt responsible.

Henry was a year old and a handful for Comfort. He was walking and wanted to run. Comfort was only partially content sharing her life with

Henry and her father. Nearly every night Comfort cried herself to sleep. Her heart ached for Heinrich, and tried not to think the worst. What also pained her was that her father lived in deep regret about having asked Heinrich to fight with the rebel forces.

Soule had traveled to Camden three times in the last year. He would review all the lists of soldiers who were killed, missing in action, or captured by the enemy. No one with the name Heinrich With appeared on any of the lists.

Each journey to Camden seemed more confusing and created more questions. Was the record keeping accurate? Might the spelling of Heinrich be changed to Henry; did Heinrich go by a nickname; was his name misspelled? In four months, it would be two-years since Heinrich's Virginia regiment mustered out. Something was amiss in the records, and he wracked his brain to figure it what it was.

ॐ

Soule put the final bag of flour on the flatbed. He also had sugar, molasses, spices, ale, brandy and one orange. He checked his list and was satisfied. He had the provisions Comfort requested and he had picked up material for repairs on the plows and harrow. The flatbed also carried fabric for Henry's new breeches. It was about mid-afternoon by the time he left Charlottesville.

The December day was sunny, unseasonably warm, with a breeze coming out of the West. He smiled when he thought of Henry and the orange he had requested. As Soule drove the flatbed toward the farm, he saw a lone man walking in the same direction along the side of the road. Soule figured he would offer the stranger a ride, and he pulled back on the horses' reins as he came alongside the man.

"Whoa, boys, whoa!" Soule shouted at his horses. He turned to the man and asked, "Would you like a lift?"

Soule stared at the man and blinked his eyes. "Heinrich? Heinrich, is it you? I don't believe my eyes!" Soule blinked his eyes again. "Heinrich, my God, I just don't believe my eyes!" Soule jumped from his seat on the flatbed and wrapped his arms around Heinrich. "Welcome home, my son! Damn! Welcome home!"

Heinrich's joy was hardly containable. He had recognized the kind, gentle voice the second Soule had asked him if he wanted a lift. Heinrich

213

climbed onto the carriage and said, "You can't imagine how happy I am to finally be coming home. I can't wait to see Comfort."

As they finished their ride home, Soule and Heinrich talked non-stop. Heinrich told Soule about his war wound, how he was nursed back to health by a woodcutter's wife, his inability to speak and how he had remembered his name earlier that month. After that, Heinrich said, everything started falling into place, even his memories of Comfort and the farm. He was on his way home when Soule saw him.

The flatbed wagon turned off the road and onto the long drive that ended near the farmhouse and barnyard. Henry was anxiously waiting for his grandfather to return. He knew he would bring him back an orange. He kept looking out the window for the wagon.

When Henry spotted the flatbed, he cried with glee, "Bampa! Bampa!" Comfort, in the other room mending, smiled as she heard her son's excitement. Henry left the house and stood on the porch, dancing as his "Bampa" brought the horses to a halt.

Heinrich's mouth was wide open in disbelief. "Yes, Heinrich, you have a son." Soule was able to keep the best until last.

Both men got off the flatbed and Soule picked up Henry, gave him a kiss on the top of his blonde head, handed him the orange and said, "Henry, this is your father." A little shy, Henry waved at Heinrich and offered to share his orange. After a while, Soule handed Henry to his father, who gazed at the young boy's face in wonder.

Heinrich's eyes met Soule's and they both smiled. "I am a father!"

"That you are, my son, you most certainly are."

Carrying Henry like he wouldn't let him go, Heinrich began looking around.

"She's in the house," Soule said with a wink.

Heinrich and Henry went inside and Heinrich called Comfort's name. She heard someone call her. That voice! Could it really be? The voice called for her again.

Comfort rushed into the kitchen, and there he stood with Henry in one arm, a sight she thought she would never see. With her heart full, she ran into Heinrich's free arm. Happy beyond belief, they held each other tight, with Henry giggling between them.

Chapter 23

March 1783: Another Loud Knock

The March winds in Middle District lashed out across the fields, waking them for planting season. A southwesterly gust swept around the farmhouse, causing the wooden shingles on the roof to flap. Magdalene lay peacefully in bed, having just finished tea laced with pain relief. She listened to the howling wind. The vigor of nature soothed her while she lay warm and safe in her bed.

It was early morning and the sun bashfully hid behind large clouds. She, like the sun, would hide. She was under her feather comforter, her cloud. She closed her eyes and thought it must be a good day for someone, or something, somewhere. She figured that it was a good day for a rabbit, a squirrel or a beaver. Any well-mannered animal would be snuggling with their family in the place they called home. Magdalene then fell back into a sound sleep.

She woke again, but this time from a dream about Virginia. She enjoyed her dreams about her sister. In a strange way, the dreams provided her with a chance to visit with her. In this particular dream, Magdalene and Virginia were well, in good health, and they walked along a stream, taking turns identifying each wildflower they passed. They came upon a group of pink lady slippers, and Virginia spoke with excitement in her voice. Magdalene gazed upon the soft pink of the flower and told her sister how precious and delicate these flowers were. Magdalene told Virginia that she too was a fragile flower, so delicate. The girls both laughed as they continued their walk. Holding hands, Virginia full of warmth and happiness, and Magdalene, pain-free and full of laughter. Suddenly her dream ended.

Magdalene woke, startled and wide-eyed. Who on earth could be at our front door, she thought. It was highly unusual to receive a guest at this time of day. The repeated knock had disturbed her dream.

The knocking grew louder. Obadiah had just come in from milking when he heard the determined rapping. He opened the door to a cold blast of wind. A well-dressed young man about his own age was standing there. Two other men, in Continental Army uniforms, were a few steps behind.

Obadiah began to feel uneasy as he greeted them politely. "Hello gentlemen, how might I be of help to you?" All the while, Obadiah knew exactly why these men were there. He hid his distaste for the uniforms and had to force himself not to tell the three men to get off his property. He expected that he and his family were about to face the ugly consequence of being on the losing side of the war.

The well-dressed man said, "I am an agent of the new republic, representing the local governing body of New York for the interest of Middle District. We are here to provide you with important and urgent papers." The man held out his hand holding a folded piece of paper as he continued, "This is for Mr. Jonathan Holmes, would you make sure these documents are given to him?"

Meanwhile, as the man spoke, J.R. and Magdalene had both made their way to the front hall to see what was going on. J.R. supported his mother's arm and she stood between him and Obadiah. She curiously studied the tall man.

Obadiah stood as still as a rock while trying to maintain his composure. "Mother, these men represent the new government." Magdalene invited the men inside.

The tall one said, "Thank you, but we don't have the time."

As he spoke, he seemed familiar to Magdalene. Odd, but there was something about him that reminded her of her father. She smiled at him and his bright blue eyes were stunning. They reminded her of Virginia's eyes. Magdalene quietly asked, "Excuse me, young man, would you state your name?"

The well-dressed man replied with a slight, almost crooked smile, "Mr. Poore, ma'am, my name is Salem Poore." When she heard the name Poore, she felt as if each and every bit of life was being drained out of her. She felt light-headed; her fingers grew cold and trembled. She told herself, this was no mistake. He must be Virginia's son. Did he really say Poore? Maybe he said Moore?

J.R. broke the silence, asking his mother if she was feeling okay. There was no response. It was as though she was not there. Her eyes remained fixed on the man with the blue eyes. Meanwhile, Poore gave Obadiah an envelope with a waxed seal with the mark of New York pressed into the wax. New York was no longer a British colony. New York had a new identity, and the wax seal was a vivid reminder of that.

Obadiah saied, "My Father, is in the field, I will go and get him."

"No, that will not be necessary. We have numerous homes to visit and I cannot waste time waiting for your father to return. Just see to it."

Obadiah nodded his head. "Certainly, I will see my father gets this."

Magdalene, acted as though she had not heard a word of the conversation. She stepped closer to the tall man and again asked, "Son, would you tell me your name again please?" His intense blue eyes focused on her as he coldly articulated his name. "S-a-l-e-m P-o-o-r-e." As abruptly as the three men arrived, they mounted their horses and departed.

J.R. thought about his mother's unusual reaction to the man; asking him questions about his name. He helped her back into the bedroom and back onto her bed. He placed a pillow near her, suggesting she get comfortable and then sat silently on the foot of her bed. He was thinking about his mother's reaction to the man, and realized that both he and his mother were familiar with Salem Poore.

In his heart, J.R. felt that this man had kidnapped Joseph. Magdalene felt in her gut that he was her sister's son. Neither of them had spoken to each other about the man.

J.R. knew about Joseph's experience with Salem, but he kept it to himself. He turned to his mother and quietly asked, "Mother, do you know the man who brought the documents for father?"

She softly replied, her voice weak and emotional, "Yes, I feel very certain I know that man. He looks just like her and he resembles my father." She paused for a moment and repeated in a whisper, "He looks so very much like her." She turned to J.R. and asked, "Son, would you hand me the medicine bottle from the table." Her voice was almost breathless and her thoughts dazed from the shock of the sight of her estranged nephew.

J.R. asked, "Mother, he looks like whom, whose mother?" He handed his mother the amber bottle and she swallowed a large dose of the tincture.

Moments later, her voice lowered and she answered, "Dear, he looks like his mother. He has those unmistakable Poore blue eyes. He is my sister's son, the baby she gave away."

J.R. sat there, trying to sort out what was going on. He recalled his last letter from Joseph with his claims of having a cousin with the same name as the man at the door. He did not know what to think but he wanted his mother to rest so he said nothing more. He sat close to her and placed her hand in his. Her fingers were soft and warm, just like her heart, he thought.

Could that man be Aunt Virginia's son, my cousin? Neither he nor his brothers, except for Joseph, had ever seen this cousin. Could mother be mistaken? Possible, but not likely. The man does have the family name, Poore. If this man is a cousin, might he be aware of his own connection to the Holmes family? Not necessarily, he thought, but then he recalled what Joseph had written in his letter. The man told Joseph he was indeed their cousin.

Obadiah peeked into his mother's room and saw J.R. sitting at the edge of the bed holding his sleeping mother's hand. He entered, saw she was asleep and whispered to J.R. "It is good to see mother sleeping soundly. She seemed upset or puzzled by that man."

J.R. could see confusion on Obadiah's face. Unlike his mother and himself, the name Salem Poore apparently did not mean anything to him.

Obadiah looked at J.R. "I have a great deal more concern for the letter in my hand than for the name of that man representing the new government." After a few moments, Obadiah added, "Our poor mother, what was she doing asking the man about his name?"

J.R. smiled and shook his head, as if to say he did not know.

Obadiah continued, "This man was delivering an official document of grave concern, and mother wanted to know his name, is there something here I am missing?"

"Mother seems to think we are related to him. He has her maiden name of Poore."

Obadiah responded, "Oh, why sure, that is likely it. Mother never hears of anyone with her Dutch family name. It must have been a surprise, a surprise for her to hear this man had her old family name of Poore."

"Yeah, I think so."

Obadiah now seemed satisfied with his mother's mild interrogation of the man. He left the room, still holding the parchment envelope.

J.R. continued to hold his mother's hand while listening to her breathe. Each breath was shallow and each breath took effort. They all knew her health was failing but all they could do was be there for her, comfort her, and remind her how much she was loved. During the four months he had been home, he noticed a remarkable decline in her stamina. He tucked her hand under her blanket and left the room.

In the kitchen, he found Obadiah helping Charlotte with the hearth fire. The document lay on the edge of the worktable. "I will hold off disturbing father from his work and will give him this information once he returns for dinner," Obadiah said. He appeared uneasy. "We should all be present when we open this letter."

"I agree," J.R. said. "Let's wait until father, Jacob and Elijah return from their work. It's not like this letter is holding any great secret."

Hours later, Magdalene woke with a gnawing pain. She opened her eyes to see her husband had kept her company while she slept. He smiled at her as if they had not a care in the world; as if all was good now and forever. She returned the smile, trying not to worry him; she did not want to worry anyone.

Magdalene knew the letter's purpose. She might be sick but she had not lost her hearing. While her husband did not say a word to her about the letter, it was clearly understood by the Holmes family that they supported the losing side and would be punished for supporting the King. And today the delivery was made. The only thing they did not know was the detail in the evacuation orders. Magdalene's body began to ache. Her pain seemed lodged in the lower part of her back and up along her spine. The intensity of the pain and discomfort overwhelmed her. All the while, she knew there was something she would have to do, something that was more painful than her sickness. She understood she was not well enough to travel and the thought of her illness separating her from her husband and sons was unimaginable.

She squeezed Jonathan's hand and whispered, "My dear husband, trust me, I am fully aware of the challenges we face. All will be okay. I am not afraid." She paused and repeated, "I am truly not afraid." Her large pillow cradled her head and she closed her eyes for a moment.

Charlotte quietly entered the room carrying a small tray of herbal tea that Mrs. Brouwer had prepared.

"This bowl of tea will help you relax and reduce your discomfort."

Magdalene sat up and thanked Charlotte for the tea. She took a sip and smiled, "Oh, this tastes wonderful. You added the perfect amount of our delicious honey."

As Magdalene lay on her bed, her thoughts drifted from what may happen in the future and back to the present. Her failing health was unspoken; she preferred that. She thought that she was silly, but believed if the topic of her health came up, it would confirm her illness, validating the way she felt. As if the pain she lived with daily, was not validation, speaking about it would confirm that it was a reality.

Magdalene knew she was not going to get better and did not want

❧

Magdalene poured herself another bowl of tea and thought about the virtues of being tolerant. She, however, had no memory of acceptance for King George III. And, there was no doubt that after the past several years, she had no tolerance at all for the Crown.

The King's practice of oppression of the Colonists spurred the civil disorder. The Crown betrayed its subjects, the very people it vowed to protect. It broke laws against mankind and the dignity of people. As she sipped her tea, it felt soothing and she relaxed. Glancing out the window, she thought about the beautiful day and the awakening of spring. She hoped she would be able to see just one more.

She believed that, compared to the obstacles and injustices her husband and sons would soon confront, her own death would actually be welcoming. Magdalene thought that death was an easy way to freedom from the invidious order of evacuation.

The new thirteen colonies were not wasting any time unleashing their ill will toward Loyalist families who had been in the colonies for generations, longer than many of those who wanted the revolution. The love of the land was not the cause of war; it was disagreements about the King's treatment. She knew her husband and sons would soon have to depart and she doubted she would be traveling with them. She would be strong and accepting of her fate; she wanted her family to remember her as strong and proud. She thought that it would make their journey easier if they knew she was not afraid. Her children had a lifetime ahead of them and she had given them many gifts, but this one final gift would be her last, and likely her most enduring.

Nonetheless, being human, she worried about what tomorrow would bring. She took comfort in knowing that she raised her children with the knowledge and the wherewithal, to deal with whatever came their way. Her sons were strong, hardworking and unified, providing her with invaluable peace of mind. If she had one wish, with every ounce of her being, she wished that she would die before her family scheduled to sail.

She could barely hear the soft chatter of voices coming from the dining room, where her husband shared the mandate with the family. She remained in bed, feeling too drained to get up and join them. Lying still, she heard only her husband's voice, his voice was calm and steady as he prepared to read the details of their fate.

Magdalene wept, not only from her physical pain, but also from the pain of knowing not going with her family would cause her to die not once, but twice.

↶⊚

Everyone was gathered around the large walnut table. On the table was the letter with Jonathan's name written in large dark ink. Then, he simply waved his hand toward the envelope as if to say, this is not important right now.

"Son," Jonathan quietly said to Obadiah, "at this moment I cannot bear to read this order. Please hold it until I am ready. After all, we know what it means; we know all but the details." Obadiah knew that the most important thought on his father's mind was his mother.

Jonathan slowly walked outside to the well where he poured fresh water into the basin and washed his face and hands. For several moments he stared at his calloused hands; hands toughened from a lifetime of work on his beloved acreage. Each callous had a reason to be there; that one was from plowing the soil, this one from the barley harvest and these from cutting oats. He mused about his love of the soil; it was magical, the life sustaining substance on which all life depends. Then, like a cannon shot, the March wind slammed the barn door shut and jolted Jonathan back to the present.

He realized that he had to read the letter and he would do it now. He returned to the house and once again gathered everyone around the dining table. Their father seated himself at the head of the table and, with trepidation, Obadiah handed him the letter. Obadiah, Jacob, Elijah, J.R. and Charlotte waited. He took the envelope, and looked at each family member with assurance and confidence. He gathered all his strength not to appear unnerved as he read the evacuation mandate.

The clock ticked and the hearth fire in the kitchen snapped; they were the two singular sounds in the room. The tick-tock resembled the beat of life, steady, trusting and enduring.

Jonathan began to read silently. Suddenly, the sound of a child's laughter came from the kitchen. The joyful sound of Isabelle reminded Jonathan of just what is most important. He thought to himself, land and house may come and may go, wars may be lost, but the importance of family continues.

The letter was penned in dark ink, with large script. As his eyes moved smoothly down the page, his sons waited. Jonathan folded the letter in half, then placed it back into the envelope. With his hands resting on the table, he tried to gather words filled with fortitude and firmness. His sons watched and waited.

Jonathan put his shoulders back, cleared his throat and, trying to be stoic, said, "We will need to plan for drastic changes. The new republic requires us to leave our home, our farm and our land with no option to return. Because of our dedication to maintain the colonies for the Crown, we will forfeit our property and material possessions. The new government will confiscate everything. They intend to auction our farm, home, animals and acreage. They will take those funds from our lives' work to pay down their war debt."

Their father continued, "We in the past we have survived adversity and this time, again, we will overcome the challenges that lay ahead of us. We will face hardship together."

Jacob waited for his father to pause and asked, "What if we do not leave, if we pledged to live in peace?"

"Son," responded Jonathan, "refusal to follow this order of evacuation would mean we could be tried for treason, followed by imprisonment or execution."

Jacob could only shake his head in bewilderment. "Are you saying they would execute us? The war is over and the treaty signed. Why, sake's alive, we surrendered!" He repeated even louder saying, "We surrendered, which means we will live in peace and respect the laws and become contributing citizens for the new colonies Our beliefs would blend with the new political ideologies. After all, the only area of disagreement was over how to react to the actions of the King, and now he is not a player anymore. I swear, I just don't get it!"

Elijah said, "Jacob, listen, you do get it and I get it too. Give me one reason why the King would negotiate for our amnesty?" Elijah paused, giving Jacob a chance to respond, then continued. "It is as plain as the crown on his head. The King wants us to settle the British lands to the North. With the tens of thousands of refugees, the King will now have part of British North America settled by some of his most faithful supporters. Don't be mistaken, King George III thinks of only what is best for him and his empire, and maybe in that order. Rest assured, he doesn't wake up in the morning thinking about what is best for his subjects!"

Jacob angrily slammed his fist on the table. "That son of a bitch! We fought bravely for King and Country."

"Son, you may be correct on all points," Jonathan said, "but that is not the issue. Since there will be no compensation for our loss of property from the new republic, it is said that the King will do all he can to provide us with land grants for all who fought for him. Plus, building materials, tools, and livestock will flood our way by the shipload, from England. You will be granted your own tract of land. They are surveying thousands of acres while we speak."

Jacob, clearly frustrated, sat in deep thought.

"To attempt to make sense out of this is a waste of time, brother" Elijah said. "Who knows the answer to the question, why do things have to be as they are? You know, this is how I see it. Look at it as an opportunity. Change is sometimes a good adventure, new and exciting. Perhaps, like our great grandfather sailing from England to settle in the Colony of New York, nearly a hundred years ago."

Obadiah spoke up. "Remember what grandfather Obadiah told us. He said people move far away, and they never come back. We are not the first people to say goodbye, to give up the land on which we were born."

Once Obadiah finished, his father continued to summarize the letter. He informed his family, "The British fleet and soldiers will, for the next several months, continue to occupy the port of New York. During this time, they will provide refugees in the area with safe transport to Nova Scotia. These ships will be protected by a British Navy man-of-war. We will be given more details in time."

Jonathan told his family, "The auction is scheduled for June 17, we have about two months."

Obadiah said in disbelief, "Nothing sounds more final than an auction date, having a date to be out of our home makes the evacuation so tangible."

J.R., Elijah and Jacob were stunned; they were at a loss for words. The date, June 17, crashed onto the table like an axe being wielded by a giant.

Jonathan lifted his chin, wanting to appear stalwart in front of Charlotte and Isabelle and his sons.

Obadiah needed to let some steam escape. "So, we will pack up and leave because we must, but the new government is blatantly stealing. This new republic is no better than a den of common thieves or a ship of pirates!" He wrung his hands, feeling as though he just woke up from a nightmare. He shook his head, while muttering, "Will these men of the new republic not be satisfied until they have destroyed us? Does surrender not have any meaning to them? Is their revenge so hateful, so destructive that they would demand us to leave with our pockets empty? What is the matter with these people?"

Soon everyone left the table and tried to carry on as usual. J.R. began to build a fire in the living room hearth with Jacob's help and Obadiah came in with an armful of wood.

Jonathan stood up, his face worn and pale, and slipped the letter into the desk drawer. He walked to the living room, where his sons were now gathered, and said, "We will do, what we must. Whatever we need to, we will do."

Elijah agreed, "If we must leave by mid-June, so be it."

Chapter 24

April 1783: Port of New York

A May wedding was being planned for J.R. and Abigail. During one of Mrs. Brouwer's weekly visits, she asked Magdalene, "Is there anything in particular that you might like for the wedding day?"

Magdalene smiled and graciously replied, "I would like to see J.R. and Abigail married by Reverend John Beardsley of the Anglican Church. I realize I am making a big request, with clergymen being so difficult to find since the war." Mrs. Brouwer smiled and told Magdalene that she would do her best to have Reverend Beardsley perform the ceremony.

A couple weeks later, Mrs. Brouwer left the Holmes farm with deep concern. Magdalene was growing more frail. Once she returned home, she shared her concern with her husband.

Brouwer dropped his head in dismay. "I cannot imagine the stress she is under. The family is facing numerous hardships including the evacuation and the auction. Combine that with Magdalene's health and it is too much for anyone. In addition, there is the fear that she may not be able to travel. What will they do? I just don't know how dear Mrs. Holmes is holding up as well as she is!"

⨏⨏

Obadiah and J.R. finished an early morning meal and packed their knapsacks for one night. Charlotte had provided an ample amount of food for them to eat, including apples from the root cellar, bread, cheese and smoked ham. The two were heading to the Port of New York to meet with their regimental leaders at the British Army Headquarters. The purpose of their trip, was to pick up transport information for the Holmes family and for the Brouwer family.

The British headquarters was charged with overseeing the complex logistics of the evacuation. Tens of thousands of Loyalists found themselves in the position of being war refugees. British ships were to depart from every port from Savannah to Portsmouth, taking Loyalist families to places that many referred to as wilderness and frontier. A soldier's military company and rank categorized each refugee's departure date. The transport information included the boarding date, the ship's name and approximate dates of departure and arrival, the latter dependent on the winds. No one wanted to miss his specified boarding date. The choice was simple: be on the ship or run the risk of being arrested and thrown in prison.

Soldiers of the Loyal American Regiment of New York would be boarding ships and making their way to the mouth of the Saint John River, in an area of British North America called Nova Scotia. The ships carrying any and all war refugees sailed with protection of British warships. Protection of the fleets was critical. The fear of an assault on a ship loaded with Loyalists could not be ruled out. Revengeful rebels, pirates and privateers were a real threat at sea.

The British would continue to occupy the Port of New York until the last Loyalists set sail. The projected deadline, as stated in the treaty, was late November 1783. The massive exodus, and coordinating tens of thousands of men, women and children, with several dozen ships, was an unforgettable undertaking.

As the sun rose up from the eastern horizon, Obadiah and J.R. rode south on the old Post Road. As the two rode, they were often in silence. The closer they got to the Port of New York, the more eerie the surroundings became.

It was a sorrowful sight. They saw people of all ages walking slowly along the road, people who knew that once they were at the port, they would be safe from mischief. As they walked, they were also aware they were one step closer to uncertainty. Women, both young and old, walked alone. Children with dirty faces and unkempt hair ran alongside carriages asking for something to eat. Three-generation families walked along the road dreading the prospect of living in unsettled wilderness, a wild frontier, where they could face plague, wild animals and dangerous people. J.R. saw it as a flood of discouragement, flowing with all of its debris to the harbor. One more cold reality of war, he thought, the destruction of family, community and the individual.

Obadiah shook his head as if just awakening from a dream. "I cannot believe my eyes. The number of men, women and children is shocking and disturbing."

Both of them scanned the seemingly endless line of refugees. Some walked as if in a trance while others appeared to have nearly given up hope. Older brothers or sisters tended to the younger children in the family, often carrying them. They saw women who seemed about ready to give birth.

The farther the two brothers rode, the more crowded the road became. Obadiah saw a number of women with small children who were coping alone, without a husband. It pained him to think that Charlotte and Isabelle would have had to suffer the same fate if she had not married. He was puzzled that these women and children were being exiled. They were not a threat to anyone or anything.

"It seems inhumane," J.R. said, "to force these broken families onto ships and endure risky voyages only to begin life in an unknown frontier. These woman have small children, no money, and no husband. They have no one to depend on."

Amid such bleakness, J.R. began to think about facing this challenge with hope. What lay ahead depended so much on one's ability to adapt to the new life. Sure, he felt nothing made much sense, and sure, the disappointment of defeat would endure long after the rebels' celebratory bells stopped ringing, but without optimism, defeat would hang over them like a dark venomous cloud. Some refugees were fortunate and did not have to walk. They had carriages or wagons to get them to the port.

It came suddenly. J.R. had a startling flashback to the forced march he had endured as a prisoner of war. The death march from Stony Point on the Hudson River to the prison in Easton, Pennsylvania. It was the vision of men, sick and hopeless. He looked away from the refugee families, toward the horizon. The never-ending trail of sadness had triggered thoughts of the overwhelming despair that he witnessed and felt as a prisoner of war, marching with a long column of defeated men, men with no shoes, others in pain, and others who fell to the road like a burlap bag of bones.

The brothers heard little except for the rhythmic sound of the horse's hooves and the cries of babies and small children in almost every direction. Obadiah ended their silence, saying, "J.R. you hungry? Let's rest the horses and stop to eat some lunch." They got off their horses and led them to a brook for a drink. J.R. and Obadiah went upstream and scooped up handfuls of water for themselves. The horses splashed in the water up to their knees, while the brothers sat on a mossy patch eating bread and cheese.

Obadiah took out his knife and sliced an apple into four pieces. One for him, one for J.R. and the other two for the horses. J.R. bit into his apple wedge and the smell and taste woke his memory to the sights and sounds of Albemarle Barracks and his life at the Soule farm. It was a good memory, but it left him with a feeling of melancholy. They finished lunch, mounted their horses and continued toward the port.

J.R. remained quiet. To Obadiah, he appeared troubled. "What's up, brother of mine?"

"Oh, nothing, I am just thinking."

J.R. was thinking about going to live in some unsettled backwoods at the mercy of the Crown until they could manage on their own. He imagined he would soon be taking his family to lands with extreme hardships. A dreadful notion, but it would soon be his reality. Awaiting the exiled refugees was the austere, remote wilderness of coastal British North America.

When they arrived at the headquarters, J.R. and Obadiah met with a series of officers and clerks. They followed the instructions they were given, that included waiting for longs stretches of time in several different lines. They overheard conversations, some of interest, others heart-wrenching. Evidently, the British arranged the complete evacuation with three fleets of ships. Each fleet took Loyalists to places with names that many had never heard: Port Roseway, Saint John River, Annapolis Royal and Port Mattoon.

Outside a tent, they stood waiting in a line that backed up against the wharves. J.R. saw countless ships, moored and waiting. After standing in a few lines, he felt just like those ships, moored and waiting. There were thousands of people and everyone appeared to be surrounded by chaos.

They couldn't help but notice people were finding shelter of all sorts, from torn sailcloth tents, to huddling in corners of burned-out brick buildings. Many hundreds of people lived in shanties on the waterfront, all waiting. It tormented J.R. to see people living in such squalor, while their own homes in Scarsdale, New Rochelle or Trenton were auctioned to pay off the rebels' war debt. The entire area smelled of human waste and the poor sanitation conditions made a perfect invitation for the spread of disease. There was no way his mother could survive such a journey, J.R. decided. It would be more than she could possibly endure.

The two brothers collected every detail: date to embark, name of the ship, port of arrival, approximate sailing time and how many personal items they could transport, and preferred ways of packing and labeling. The helpful officers and soldiers processed their paperwork and answered all of their questions except one.

Obadiah had asked it. "Our mother is ill, quite weak and we cannot imagine how she could endure traveling. What are her options? Are there accommodations on board ship that we don't know about? Could she board a ship later in the year, once she feels better?"

For the answers they had to go back into another line. After another long wait, they learned that their mother had few options, and they were offered little encouragement about her leaving at a later date. "I am sorry gentlemen," an officer said, "but our last ships leave New York this fall. If your mother is well by then, let us know and we will see what we can do. But, after that, there will be no more ship transports."

෨

Obadiah was eager to return to Middle District, but J.R. had one more thing he wanted to do. That was to try to find Ned. "He is like a brother to me, and I know he has got to be here." J.R's voice trailed off, then he continued, "At least I hope he reached New York. He was traveling during a chaotic and uncertain time. We need to ask around for the location of the free blacks waiting for transport to Nova Scotia. I can't leave the port without knowing if he reached here as a free man."

There were still several hours of daylight left. They were told that the camp for free blacks could be found in the south end of the port. The two brothers struggled through the narrow, crowded streets noticing that much of the port was lined with burnt out buildings. Obadiah followed J.R. past ruts, puddles and trash.

When they arrived at one of the many tent cities, J.R. could hear someone singing a song, the lyrics sounded anguished, but uplifting at the same time. Obadiah was struck by the beauty that rose above the hapless living conditions. The song was bursting with a myriad of emotions, concluding in a passionate plea for peace and freedom.

J.R. smiled at Obadiah. "That song reminds me of the songs Ned would hum or sing while we labored in the fields. If he made the trek from

Philadelphia without being arrested and sold back into slavery, I think he would be here, or close by."

They were approaching a large encampment and entered another burnt-out area. Charred beams hung loosely from the interior of some buildings and the stale smell of ash and soot permeated the air. Finally, they were at a camp for black Loyalists. J.R. approached the guards at the gate and they were ordered to halt. After a few minutes of questioning, they were led to the officers in charge. J.R. and Obadiah noticed there were dozens of well-armed guards outside the perimeter.

"Why is this camp so highly protected? What is that all about?" Obadiah asked.

"It must be for protection. Maybe the British are hoping the guards would deter anyone from trying to take these people from the protection of the British Army. The slave market is at an all-time high, each one of these people in this camp would fetch a terrific sum. That makes them an easy target for pirates, gangs, or southern militias looking to make a pile of gold. The people in this camp are worth more than gold to a group of hooligans."

The camp had tens of hundreds of free black refugees waiting, many for months or even a year, for their date of embarkment. Many lived in fear of being captured and sold back into slavery. They wouldn't feel safe until they set foot on the soil of Nova Scotia. And their safety also was a concern of the British. Any British vessel carrying free blacks was heavily guarded by warships. They were guarded not only because of their value, but because the peace agreement stated the British were required to give all blacks back to the new nation so they could be returned to their rightful owners. This is one treaty agreement the Crown ignored.

Once in the officers' tent, they were asked what they needed. J.R. explained that he was a prisoner of war with Ned Lawson and was looking for him. "I am hoping he is here. Do you know of him?"

The officer smiled. "Follow me, please."

They walked a short distance and the officer pointed down a narrow dirt path, lined with tents. "You will find Mr. Lawson down there to your left. Lawson is practically running the entire camp. He is assisting others with their forms, and teaching them to read or spell their names. A man like him is a gift."

J.R. and Obadiah thanked the British officers, turned and walked through the row of tents, where they heard men singing what sounded like songs you would sing in church. Then, they walked through a yard where dozens of children were playing tag. J.R., followed by Obadiah, entered a tent. There in front of them was Ned.

Ned had his reading spectacles on, a pen in his hand and was sitting at a desk covered with papers and large hardbound ledgers. Hunched over stacks of papers, he was reviewing and recording names, along with brief descriptions, into the pages of a book. Ned was dipping his quill into the ink well, and didn't notice his visitors. J.R. watched Ned work without a care in the world. Ned had truly arrived safely to the city of New York. Totally absorbed with his work but sensing someone's presence, Ned queried, "How might I help you?"

J.R. waited a second and replied, "Do you have a moment to say hello to an old friend?"

Ned's eyes left the pages of the ledger in disbelief. Dropping his pen, Ned said: "I don't believe it! I just don't believe it! Is it really you?" Ned got up, walked to J.R. and wrapped his big arms around him. They hugged as tears filled their eyes. J.R. and Ned stood back, and Obadiah came forward with his hand out to introduce himself.

"I am honored to meet you, Obadiah. I feel that I have known you for years."

"And I feel the same. J.R. has told me some good stories about you."

"Tell me," Ned asked, "how are Mr. Soule and his daughter? I think of them and their kindness daily. They saved me from a life of slavery."

J.R. smiled and replied, "Mr. Soule is now a grandfather of a baby boy. Comfort named the boy Henry Christian With. I left the farm in December."

Ned noticed that J.R. didn't mention Heinrich. "Still no word about Heinrich?"

J.R. lowered his head, "No word, nothing. Mr. Soule has made a number of trips to Camden, searching for him. It's as though Heinrich With never existed; he seems to have vanished."

"You mean to say Heinrich has been missing in action since April 1781?" Ned shook his head in disbelief.

"Comfort said she would post me letters to keep me informed, but I have not heard from her. I hope all is well."

Changing the topic, Ned asked: "Tell me, what are your plans for evacuation? When and where are you going?"

"That is exactly why we are at the port today. All day we have been collecting information. Since my three brothers and I were spread between two different New York regiment and three companies, we will be sailing on different ships, at different times. We are all headed to the same place, the mouth of the Saint John River, Nova Scotia. And what about your evacuation arrangements?"

"I will be sailing to Shelburne, Nova Scotia, to ultimately settle in Birchtown. It will be the first black Loyalist settlement in all of North America. The Crown should be proud. They may not have won the war, but they kept their promises to their black recruits and their families." Ned paused. "I worry, though, because farming experience is all we have ever done. I have heard the land in the area called Birchtown is not too great for planting. The soil sounds like a rock pile. I just don't know what to think, but at least we are free, and hopefully we will have the opportunity to better ourselves."

"Ned, let's stay in touch, we won't be too far from each other. Well, not far by boat."

Ned smiled and replied, " I will see you soon, I hope, in Nova Scotia!"

Chapter 25

April 1783: A Family Reunion

King George woke J.R. He smiled, thinking that at Soule's farm the roosters weren't nearly as ornery as George. As he pulled on his breeches, he could smell bread baking. In spite of their busy day and late return home from the port, J.R. felt surprisingly well-rested. Obadiah was in the kitchen and they immediately headed to the barn, where their father was skimming the cream off the milk.

Jonathan saw his two sons bore anxious looks. "I know what you need to tell me." He paused. "I know we have heartbreaking matters to confront. Especially about your mother. I don't know exactly what illness afflicts her, but I can see its finality. She's getting weaker and weaker to the point where I have doubts she will survive the summer, let alone an evacuation."

Although J.R. and Obadiah wished that reality could somehow go away, they were relieved to see their father understood the seriousness of their mother's situation.

Their father lowered his head and rubbed his eyes as he began to weep. Watching his wife's illness take all the life out her was more than he could bear. "My sons, I know that once I board the ship, I will never see Magdalene again. I will never hold her, never see her smile or hear her voice. I would rather die than leave her. But at this point, I want us to proceed as if she is going with us."

Obadiah and J.R. were at a loss for words. J.R. told his father that he would finish the chores and take the cream to Charlotte. Within a few minutes, Charlotte rang the breakfast bell. Jonathan washed up and joined his four sons along with Isabelle and Charlotte for the morning meal.

Isabelle was delighted to see everyone at the table eating the food she helped her mother prepare. She stood up, walked over to Jonathan, who she called Papa. With a child's compassion and innocence, she asked, "Papa, why are you sad?"

Jonathan smiled at Isabelle. "My dear Isabelle, I am sad because sometimes things happen and I cannot do anything to change them."

"Those things make you sad?"

"Yes, my dear, they do."

Isabelle gave him a hug, "If you need help I will help you. I help Mother with cooking, I can help you too!"

Charlotte entered the room and took a seat next to Obadiah. She asked, "What was that all about?"

Jonathan smiled at Charlotte. "That was all about companionship, kindness and the importance of family."

Later that morning, Mr. and Mrs. Brouwer and Abigail arrived to hear the evacuation details. Obadiah helped his mother into the dining room, where she sat next to her husband. Obadiah and J.R. began with summaries of their day at British Military Headquarters at the port. Obadiah then provided some of the details, such as who would be taking what ship and when embarkation and departure were scheduled. "We will be traveling in two different groups. This has to do with the military company in which we served." He paused and asked if there were any questions. There were none.

They then divided into two groups. Those traveling with Obadiah's company and those traveling with J.R.s. Obadiah said, "Father, mother, Charlotte, and Isabelle, will sail with me. We embark June 15, our ship's name is *H.M.S. Generous Friends*. With favorable wind and weather, we could expect a two-week sail."

J.R.'s group included Mr. and Mrs. Brouwer, Abigail, Jacob and Elijah. They were to board *H.M.S. Montague*, on July 8. Jokingly, J.R. told the other group, "Those of you sailing on board *Generous Friends* will have a three-week head start on the rest of us, so by the time the *Montague* arrives, I expect our houses to be built." Everyone had a needed chuckle.

After all of the questions were answered, J.R. nodded to Abigail, and taking her hand, they stood up to make an announcement. "Abigail and I changed the date of our wedding, we will marry April 26." Conversation about a wedding was a welcome topic change. Jonathan glanced at his wife; she was radiant. The upcoming wedding had lifted her spirits, of that much was certain.

೧ⓢ

The morning of the wedding, Magdalene awoke afflicted with pain and she gathered all of her strength to get out of bed. Soon she must get dressed. She glanced at the medicine at her bedside and she hesitated—it made her so sleepy. She did not want to fall asleep during the ceremony.

Magdalene was bursting with joy, knowing that for the wedding the Holmes and Beardsley families would once again be united. Sarah and Beach soon arrived with their children, Magda and Cicero, and Elizabeth and Nathaniel with their daughter, Emma. It had been years since they had all been together. They shared hugs, conversation, excitement and tea before leaving for the Brouwer home. Jonathan was happy to notice the relationship between his sons and his two sons-in-law didn't appear to have been damaged by the war. It was a bittersweet reunion, though. It seemed likely that this would be the last time the Holmes and Beardsley families would be together.

During the war, Sarah and Elizabeth had been able to visit their parents only once in Middle District, but they wrote regularly. The sisters settled were settled in the colony of Connecticut. They were several hours' ride away and the roads were not safe for traveling during the war. Plus, their husbands were away, fighting with the Continental Army.

In a letter written in early 1778, Sarah told her mother that Elizabeth and Nathaniel would soon be moving closer to her and Beach. Nathaniel had made a successful bid on a farm in Sandy Hook, near the Housatonic River. Sarah's letter asked her mother not to let the circumstances of the farm's acquisition upset her. The farm was auctioned after being confiscated by rebels. A family of Loyalists had abandoned it, wanting to get away from the fighting.

Although disturbed by the story, Magdalen knew in her rational mind that it was what it was. She tried to feel happy for Elizabeth and Nate having their own home and farm. Yet she was haunted by the word confiscation. Quickly, she folded the letter and tossed it into the flames in the hearth. She did not want anyone in the family to know what was happening with Loyalist properties. Weary, she sat in the rocking chair while she watched the flames devour the letter.

As the ceremony began, Magdalene stood stoically as J.R. watched Abigail walk on her father's arm to be given to him in marriage under the royal oak tree on the south side of the Brouwer house. The list of guests was short, very short, as many of their friends and neighbors had left during the war. Other friends were scheduled to depart that day with the Spring Fleet.

Abigail's short-sleeved dress was made of blue satin with ivory lace adorning the neck. The soft blue of the dress matched the color of her eyes and the lace matched her white porcelain skin.

Much to Magdalene's satisfaction, the couple began to exchange their vows in front of Reverend Beardsley, uncle of Beach and Nathaniel and a familiar sight when a Holmes family member married. Jonathan gave Magdalene's hand a squeeze as he heard the reverend say forever. He thought about how short forever really was. It seemed only a few years ago that he and Magdalene made the same vows to each other. He was overwhelmed with both sadness and joy. He gazed at Magdalene's face, and for a fleeting moment saw the face and eyes of the beautiful girl he had fallen in love many years ago.

In front of their families, J.R. pledged his love to Abigail, the woman who kept his heart alive while he was a soldier and a prisoner of war. As he made his wedding vows, he felt his anxieties about moving to a virtual wilderness melting away.

J.R. and Abigail were now husband and wife. As Beach and Nathaniel congratulated J.R., he introduced them to Abigail. Together they talked about family, farming and each other's goals. J.R. listened as his brothers-in-law talked about the current planting season, the crops that were in most demand and their interest in being part of local town and state governments. J.R. couldn't talk about the planting season because he had no land to prepare. But he did tell Beach and Nathaniel that he had begun to feel more confident regarding the adjustments facing them.

"The King is surveying the land into 100 - 200 acre lots along the east side of the St. Croix River and the land on the banks of the Saint John River. And loyalists from Castine, in the District of Maine, have already settled a small town along the St. Croix."

Beach and Nathaniel were finding it difficult to grasp the concept of the Holmes family sailing to a wilderness and leaving life as they knew it behind. Beach said, "It is difficult to imagine our families will be divided by such distance. It saddens me to see Sarah's family treated in this way. I was hoping for amnesty for the Loyalist families."

Nathaniel nodded in agreement and added, "The thirteen colonies are about to lose some of the most knowledgeable and hardworking people. I just don't get it."

J.R. saw the troubled expression on the faces of his brothers-in-law.

Nathaniel said, "We will miss all of you. It is heartbreaking, especially for Sarah and Elizabeth. They are having a tough time understanding that their family is exiled and will not be allowed to return. Yes, you were part of the opposition, but our families go back nearly ninety years and no war will break that bond. Personally, I think it is senseless."

The fiddle music began and J.R., with a sparkle in his eye, said: "Hey, what do you say we go ask our wives for this dance?"

"Great idea," replied Nathaniel. Beach went to his wife, and he waved for Obadiah to join in. Suddenly, four couples were having a first and maybe final dance together.

Fatigue had conquered Magdalene. With the help of Mrs. Brouwer, she retreated to a comfortable chair that offered her a view of the celebration. Mrs. Brouwer provided her with medicine and she fell asleep listening to the violin music. She drifted off to a place of where there was no pain and, in the distance, she saw her sister, Virginia, who seemed to be getting closer each time she saw her.

Chapter 26

7 June 1783: Sandy Hook, Connecticut

Jonathan Holmes was astonished; all of a sudden it was June. He had spent the entire month of May with Magdalene, making every moment count. They picked flowers for Virginia on the first day of May. They had basket lunches beside Joseph's grave. On those days Magdalene was unable to leave her bed, he sat by her side and read her some of her favorite poems. He also gave her foot massages.

Jonathan smiled when he thought of the memories he had stored. She could always make him smile and once they were apart, she would continue to make him smile. During the month together they talked about everything, including death and her inability to go with him to Nova Scotia. He was overcome with emotion to see Magdalene open up to him. She spoke of her illness, their children and their years together. He was comforted when Magdalene spoke about going to Sarah's homes in Sandy Hook, where they would have their final goodbye. Her eyes brightened when she spoke of seeing her three grandchildren, Magda, Emma and Cicero.

The reality of the last six years had come to a crescendo, not to be ignored. Jonathan dreaded having to face what would be the most heartbreaking day of his life. He walked to the kitchen door, went outside and heard a dove calling for his mate, all the while thinking he soon would have to say goodbye to his.

It had been two years since he began to notice his wife's gradual decline. Her appetite became almost non-existent and her strength had waned. The rose from her cheeks was replaced by alabaster white; dark half circles appeared under her tired blue eyes. Her loss of weight and frailty were harsh and constant reminders that she was gravely ill.

Each night, Jonathan lay beside his wife hoping the warmth of his body and his own good health might reduce her pain and miraculously be absorbed into her body to make her well again. A strong-willed malady conquered Magdalene. He remembered when she barred any discussion about her fading health. She kept her illness to herself, not willing to burden her loved ones.

This morning was just like all other mornings. Charlotte entered Magdalene's room, and Magdalene gazed at Charlotte's long golden hair as she opened the curtains. Charlotte then helped her sit up in bed, fluffed her feather pillow, then set a bowl of herbal tea in her frail white hands. The chamomile tea gave the room a fragrance of flowers. Charlotte would sprinkle just a pinch of lavender in the tea, hoping it would help calm her for what lay ahead that day. Isabelle entered the bedroom and cuddled near Magdalene.

"I remember the days when I had your energy," Magdalene told Charlotte.

Charlotte said softly, We need to find some of that energy for today's travel."

"Yes, I know, dear. Today we travel to Sarah's home in Sandy Hook."

Charlotte began to pack a few things in a bag, as Magdalene cradled her bowl of tea in her hands, noticing that her thin fingers were nearly the color of white bone china. She took another sip thinking how happy she was with her two oldest sons' marriages.

As Charlotte brushed Magdalene's hair, Magdalene looked at Isabelle and said, "June is my favorite month. Do you have a favorite month?"

Isabelle asked, "Why is June your favorite month?"

"Because of midsummer's day, when the sun stands still."

Isabelle's eyes opened wide. "The sun stands still, really?"

"Well, no, not really, but the day is so long, it seems as if the sun does stand still. When I was about your age, I loved going with my grandmother on midsummer's eve to gather some of the herbs she used for healing. Those plants were said to possess strong healing powers, stronger than plants picked during the other nights or days."

Isabelle smiled and said, "I would like to go out on that night and find plants. Would you take me?

Magdalene smiled and kissed Isabelle on the head. "My dear child, I would love to spend a midsummer's evening with you, but I fear I can't. I am not well enough."

"You must have learned a lot from your grandmother," Charlotte said.

"Oh, yes, I did learn much from her. We went on many adventures together."

As Magdalene's eyes swept around the bedroom, she recalled, to herself, that it was in this bedroom she gave birth to her seven children. This was where she mourned for her youngest son, Joseph. This was where she spent every night close to her husband. And now she had to say goodbye to the room.

"You know Charlotte," she said, lowering her voice, "I am fully aware I will not be leaving aboard any sailing ship in the fall, but I must keep my spirits up. I must keep everyone's hopes high."

Charlotte took Magdalene's hand in hers, "Your family takes much comfort in the love you have for them and in the love they hold in their hearts for you. I hope you take comfort in knowing that they love you dearly and will forever have you in their hearts."

Magdalene smiled. Then she groaned. A prolonged dull ache was radiating from her spine. Charlotte returned to her side with a spoon of pain medicine. After swallowing a teaspoon of the liquid, Magdalene soon found solace, listening to her own breathing. "Charlotte, would you please get the two tea pots on the top of the cherry cabinet and pack them with my things going to Sandy Hook?"

"Certainly, is there anything else that you would like to take?"

"Yes, no one would notice if some of my Irish linen tablecloths were missing and two pairs of silver candlestick holders." She wanted her daughters' to have them.

Jonathan had prepared the back of the flatbed wagon for his wife's journey. Worried the trip might be too much for her, he tried to make it as comfortable as possible.

Meanwhile, Mrs. Brouwer was busy preparing and packing herbal medicines for Magdalene to take along. Tears ran down her cheek. It was sorrowful to pack only enough opiates for two months, knowing that was all she would likely need.

Jonathan recalled the last time he spoke with Sarah and Elizabeth. He confirmed the family's evacuation plans with his daughters and their husbands during their visit for J.R.'s wedding. He told them about the auction, but most importantly, that their mother's illness would not allow her to sail with the rest of the family.

The roads were still badly rutted and the journey would be bumpy, so

Charlotte gave Magdalene a couple extra drops of herbal tincture. They stopped at the Brouwers to drop off Isabelle and pick up the medicines that Magdalene needed. Jonathan was thankful that Magdalene slept most of the way while Charlotte sat with her in the back. Jonathan and Obadiah rode upfront, taking turns with the horses' reins.

After they arrived at Beach and Sarah's home, Elizabeth and Nathaniel came from a short distance down the road and together they shared tea and biscuits. Sarah had prepared a room for her mother and because of the long ride, Magdalene was resting in a soft, warm bed.

Nathaniel said to Obadiah. "I am sincerely disappointed from what I hear about the Treaty of Paris. The needs of Loyalists were ignored by both the Crown and by the new independent colonies."

"Well, I am sure the Crown might disagree with you, Nathaniel," Obadiah said. "The Parliament can boast about the free land they are giving to Loyalist families, not to mention, transport to a godforsaken frontier where these land grants are for the taking.."

Beach added, "I did not risk my life fighting for freedom for this to happen to our family. We could all live together in peace."

Jonathan said, "Generations of our family will be born and will die before all the scars of this war are healed. My grandchildren and their children will suffer from the sins of both the war and the final negotiations of the peace."

Elizabeth brought the harsh reality back to everyone's mind when she asked her father, "When might we see you again, father?"

"My dear, Elizabeth, you ask me a question for which I don't know the answer. The new group of colonies have made it a crime for Loyalists to return. If we disregard their dictate, we could face trial and imprisonment."

Elizabeth's eyes filled with tears. Nathaniel walked to her side and put his arm around her as she wept. As Sarah watched her sister weep, the reality of their final farewells sunk in. It was something for which none of them was fully prepared.

After tea, Sarah packed food for the return trip to Middle District. She had a linen sack in which she placed apples, dried meat, cheese and a couple small loaves of oat bread. Beach went to the stable to harness the horses. Charlotte helped Elizabeth clear the table and stack the dishes for washing. Obadiah went to see his mother one last time.

Finally, Jonathan slipped into Magdalene's room. She was sleeping deeply and he took her hand, held it tightly, kissed her on her white cheek, then again on her forehead. Into her ear he whispered, "I love you, my Magda, my love."

She showed no response; she was still sleeping from the pain medication. Jonathan touched her hair, and gently tossed a sole curl that was determined to hang over her eyelid. He touched the outline of her cheek with his finger. He then kissed her lips. If only I could stay with her, he thought. She is very ill and needs me near. He did not want this moment to end, but he knew that it had to end. Jonathan let go of Magda's hand after placing it next to her side, above the colorful quilt.

At that moment, Magdalene opened her eyes reached for his hand. She gathered her strength and focus before whispering, "Jonathan, I am not afraid; I know we will not see each other again but I will be fine. Our daughters are here for me, and our sons are there for you. Please go, knowing that our love for each other is everlasting. All earthly things must come to an end, but our love is eternal."

Almost like magic, Magdalene fell back to sleep. Jonathan kissed her lips and his tears fell from his eyes onto her closed eyelids, as if she too were weeping. He slowly let go of her hand, remembering the feel of each finger. He left the room, looking back but once.

Obadiah, Charlotte, and Jonathan climbed back onto the flatbed and left the Beardsley farm. Jonathan had gotten strength from his wife's last words to him. He had gotten to see his daughters and his grandchildren, and all seemed well and happy. He admired his sons-in-law Nate and Beach Beardsley. Both men were hardworking and quick-thinking. He was especially pleased that his daughters would be caring for their mother. He sat on the flatbed, picked up the worn leather reins and handed them to Obadiah.

As Obadiah headed the flatbed back home, Charlotte sat between her husband and father-in-law. She noticed Jonathan's head tilted down, tears forming in the corners of his eyes. One tear, as large as an evening star, fell from his face onto his hand. Charlotte took his hand in hers, not saying a word, and gave it a squeeze. Jonathan looked up at Charlotte and saw the same smile that had cheered Magdalene every morning.

To his father, Obadiah said, "As Elijah often says, all will work out." Jonathan nodded, yet he was certain that his Magda would be resting in peace before the *Montague* dropped anchor at the mouth of the Saint John.

Chapter 27

14 June 1783: Embarkment

The wooden chests were nearly packed. Charlotte slipped the sterling silver flatware and a crystal pitcher into the blanket chest and Obadiah nailed it shut. Even though they were about to have their last breakfast in their home, they were so busy they hardly gave it a thought. There were big holes in the Holmes household with J.R. living with Abigail's parents and Magdalene staying with Sarah.

J.R. and Abigail arrived; he would be taking them to the port, then return with the horses and flatbed wagon until it was time for his departure in July. He reminded his father and brother they needed to be on their way by noon. J.R. hitched the horses to the flatbed. He and Obadiah loaded several canvas bags and several wooden chests onto the wagon. The chests and bags were filled with clothing, wool blankets, down filled quilts, kitchenware and pots for cooking. Jonathan packed his canvas bag and before tying it off, he realized that he had forgotten something—Joseph's knapsack. It was his only material connection with his son and he could not leave without it.

Charlotte packed a teapot that had belonged to Magdalene's mother, and some of the families' platters. Once she felt she had all necessary items, she thought about what she could pack into the little space remaining. In her mind, she sorted through the many things being left behind.

Earlier that week, Obadiah had constructed a wooden crate in which he and J.R. packed hand tools and a couple of axes. Charlotte found a spot for a large array of dried herbs for cooking and for medicinal purposes. These herbs grew in abundance in Middle District, but she wasn't sure if they grew in the climate of Nova Scotia. In the crate went lanterns and candles and a pair of sterling candlestick holders that had belonged to Magdalene's mother. Almost everything Magdalene and Jonathan possessed was handed down from her parents. Much of that had to be left behind. They had limits on how much they could take.

Obadiah packed a couple pair of horse harnesses and reins. Finally, J.R. placed a couple large bags of his seed collection into the crate then he nailed on the lid. With charcoal, he wrote his name and military company as well as Obadiah's name and company on the outside of the crate: John Roger Holmes, Captain Randall's Company, L.A.R. Obadiah Holmes, Captain Finaly's Company, L.A.R.

For the last time, Jonathan tended the few cows, horses, chickens and sheep that remained. He reminded J.R. to care for them until the auction. Jonathan thought it was a blessing to have been so busy those last few days, otherwise leaving would have been even more difficult. Nonetheless, he grew more restless as embarkment time approached. Jonathan and Obadiah felt some comfort knowing they would be away, on board *H.M.S. Generous Friends,* by auction day. Everything was happening so quickly. It didn't seem possible that this would be the last time they would see their home.

At noon, J.R. took his father, Obadiah, Charlotte, Isabelle and their packed bags, chests and crates to the assigned meeting place in the Port of New York. They arrived by late afternoon, as requested, one day prior to boarding. At dockside, stevedores helped unload the wagon and made sure each chest or crate was clearly labeled. Within minutes of their arrival dockside, Obadiah saw some of his buddies from Captain Finaly's Company. Seeing them lifted his heart. He felt fortunate to be reunited with them.

Jonathan was astounded by the sights and sounds of the port. He had never seen so many ships. His eyes darted from the tall, regal masts to the tall chimneys on shore. The chimneys jutted up into the sky surrounded by nothing but burnt rubble; the remains of war's destruction.

J. R's voice rang out, above the street and wharf noise. "Well, this is where we say goodbye until sometime in late July."

Jonathan turned from the busy waterfront, with sadness. He walked to J.R., gave him a hug and said, "You have a long ride ahead of you son, you best get going."

J.R. replied, "Not as long a ride as you have in-store for yourself, father."

The goodbyes were brief. They were about to embark on a voyage, whether they were ready or not. In one sense Jonathan felt leaving was so final, while at the same time embarking on *Generous Friends* had everything to do with a new beginning. Once under sail, the ship was expected to arrive at the mouth of the Saint John River by early July, winds permitting. It was part of the second spring fleet, consisting of about a dozen ships, carrying about two thousand loyalists to a wilderness

⁂

J.R. walked into the barn. He wanted to check the property one last time before the auction. He climbed the dusty old ladder to the second floor loft. It was nearly empty of hay. It was almost eerie. The barn was abandoned except for a few animals. It was in this loft where he stored his prized seed collection.

The sacks of seeds were exactly where he had left them after the harvest of 1776, except for the bags he packed in Obadiah's cargo. He opened the linen bags, dug his hand down deep into the seeds and smiled; the seeds felt cool and dry. They caressed his skin and felt like silk from the Orient. He thought it a miracle that his carefully selected seeds survived the war, no small feat, with the number of Loyalist barns that were torched.

He had packed some of his seeds in Obadiah's crate, for insurance, not putting all his seeds in one basket. Next month the remaining seeds would board the ship with him. These bags of bounty represented food for his family for many years to come, perhaps for generations.

Outside the barn, he stopped to look around. The house was void of all life and the fields lay fallow. No soil had been plowed, no seeds had been sown. There was no longer a reason to ring the bell and no smoke was coming from the sturdy chimneys. Everything was peaceful.

That silence was broken by the boisterous voices of Jacob and Elijah, who were walking up the carriage path. The two suddenly quieted as they looked around at what had been their home.

"Without our family living here," Elijah said, "it is nearly unrecognizable."

J.R. added, "Odd isn't it, to realize just how much the loved ones in your life make your house a home."

Jacob nodded and added, "With Mother at Sarah's and Father onboard the *Generous Friends*, our home appears different."

"Yeah, I get it now," Elijah said. "Our real home is with our family."

245

"I hope that whoever buys this house," J.R. added, "will have at least half the happiness that we had making this our home."

The three brothers walked over several acres of the property. The fallow fields bloomed with wildflowers where grain once grew. Over the hill, near the cemetery, the peach tree and apple tree bore budding fruit. A tranquil blanket of grass covered the family cemetery, and the path beyond the cemetery, to the ruins of the Mohegan roundhouse, was narrowing from lack of use.

J.R. lifted the latch on the cemetery gate and his two brothers followed him. From the grave marker, be it a large stone, a piece of slate or a wooden cross, they knew who was where and when they were born and died. J.R. paused in front of Joseph's grave and spoke to him, as if he was standing there. Finally, single file, the three brothers followed the path from the cemetery to the house, as they had done hundreds of times.

Chapter 28

17 June 1783: The Auction

The auctioneer's agenda was full. Loyalist home, after Loyalist home was being sold to the highest bidder. Homeownership for many young rebel families was becoming a reality with the thousands of properties confiscated from exiled supporters of the Crown. At the Holmes farm, the long path leading to the house was clogged with carriages and flatbed wagons. The bidders were anxiously waiting for the auction to start. It was a dreary morning and low clouds hung over the farm. Planters with money wanted this prize, some of the best dirt in the Middle District.

Many of the bidders wore cloaks that matched the dark gray sky. The group that gathered seemed fitting to be attending a funeral, not an auction. From where J.R. stood, the bidders appeared to resemble oversized vultures. They stood almost motionless, waiting in silence for their turn to pick the bones.

A low murmur of men's voices lingered heavy in the damp air. Excitement grew and suddenly the muffled muttering came to an abrupt halt with the sound of the gavel. Before the bidding began, the auctioneer gave a final sales pitch. He briefly described the home and some of the farm equipment, but said much more about the 400 acres of prime farmland.

Then the bidding commenced. J.R. felt a sudden pain in his heart. He watched and listened as the men furiously shouted out their bids. The atmosphere was tense, the bidding went higher and higher with no sign of stopping. Finally the number of men trying to buy dwindled from twelve to seven, then to five. The auctioneer spoke so quickly he sounded like a hundred bees buzzing. Everyone was intently watching, listening and wondering how high the bidding would go.

J.R. moved closer but was unable to see the faces of the men intent on making sure their bid was heard. The bidding was reduced to three men. The price of the farm had reached a record-breaking sum and the bidding was still feverish. J.R. thought about how the home was full of memories and how no deep-pocketed bidder could ever buy those. Those memories were his to keep. J.R. tried to get a better look at the last two men still bidding. A startling chill went through his body when he saw the face of the last bidder.

The voice willing to pay almost anything was that of the man who his mother said was his cousin, the man who had visited their home in April. The man who served them with papers directing them to leave the colonies would be buying their home and property. He was not puzzled as to why anyone would desire the farm, but why would he pay almost anything for it? It seemed odd. The sound of the gavel hit the wood and, then a loud "Sold." It was so loud and with such gusto, that it startled the chickens. King George echoed the resounding sold from the top of the hen house. The bidding was over. And his estranged cousin, his brother's kidnapper, had become the new owner of the Holmes farm.

Salem Poore's final bid was for everything, including the 400 acres, the house, barns, the plows, stables, horses, cows, sheep, chickens, and one noisy rooster with a Loyalist name.

J.R. watched the men as they mounted their horses or climbed up on their carriages and wagons to leave. All those men in dark overcoats, after seeing who bought the best dirt in Middle District, were moving to the next auction like a flock of famished vultures. As some discouraged bidders walked to their carriages, a few of them asked each other about how that young lad had acquired so much money. J.R. wondered the same thing.

His mother had called that man her sister's son. As J.R. looked at Salem from across the yard, he thought, he is my cousin. My cousin now owns the Holmes family farm. This prompted many questions.

J.R. had little knowledge of Salem or his life. While J.R. fought in the Loyal American Regiment, he assumed Salem fought with the Continental troops. And, most of those troops did not get paid; they were lucky if they were fed.

He replayed in his mind the crack of the gavel and the loud, "Sold!" followed by "Sold to that young man." Only moments after the bidding was closed, J.R. watched as Salem as he took a small bag from a pocket inside his cloak. He poured the contents on the table. There was a small pile of gold and silver coins, gold necklaces and precious stones. Salem pushed the pile across the table to the bookkeeper who represented the Continental Army. The new government's agent counted out a proper amount of gold coins, then shook Salem's hand and returned everything else to Salem, while thanking him for his contribution to pay down the war debt. A few men walked up to Salem with admiration and congratulated him on the purchase. J.R. thought perhaps Salem was a war hero. But what kind of hero got rich on the war?

∽⃝

Not in his wildest dreams would J.R. have thought that Salem bought the Holmes farm with gold stolen from Loyalist families. Salem had indeed become a wealthy man, one of the wealthiest in the district. But at that point, the question of how he obtained this wealth was pure speculation to most.

Salem was one of many who had first-hand experience in the shift of money and power during the war. The rebellion had brought about a monumental transfer of wealth from the Loyalists to the revolutionaries. In his delusional mind, Salem thought he was an heir of his own making, yes, a self-made man. Nearly his entire life he had made his own decisions and one of his best decisions was not enlisting. He established himself as a Son of Liberty. That position, combined with his generous contributions to high-ranking officers, paved his road to respect from some of the most powerful revolutionaries in the area. He could not lose. If the rebellion failed, he would still have his stolen treasure.

Salem burst with pride as he signed his name to close the purchase. He stood back and gazed at his new home. He felt like a king. He did not waste any time getting familiar with his new property. He blinked as if not believing his eyes. All of this was now his! He walked into the kitchen; it was large and inviting. He peered out the door at the empty yard. The auctioneer had gone.

His eye followed the hedge down the drive and there he saw the royal oak tree. This was the tree that held so much pain from his youth. This was where he would sit, marveling at his cousins and fantasizing about their utopian lives. His thoughts suddenly froze in uncertainty. He went back into the house and slammed the door so hard the frame splintered.

He kicked a leg of the kitchen table and slammed his hand against the neat row of cooking pots, several hitting the floor with a clatter.

In those gloomy days, those desolate days of being alone, he had no hope and no one to support or nurture him. In that time in his life when he longed to be in a family with sisters and brothers, the pain was unbearable and it scared him to death. The pain was greater now, and he was confused. He asked himself, why would the pain be greater now, I own everything, I have lots of money. I finally have what I have been wanting all my life.

Later that day, two flatbed wagons pulled into the yard loaded with imported furniture of the finest quality. Tables, chairs, stuffed sofas, mantle clocks, dressers and wardrobes were just a few of the things delivered. A week earlier, Salem attended auctions in Marshfield, south of Boston. One Loyalist home after another was liquidated. It was Salem's good fortune to buy furnishings that he now was able to use in his new home in Middle District. Four men unloaded the wagons and placed the furniture in the specified rooms. Salem was so proud of himself, he relished the thought he might even be the wealthiest man in the district. He smiled to think of the power he would now be able to impose upon others.

Then from out of nowhere, came the thought of what if. What if he lost everything; he would be back under that tree, homeless, penniless and unloved. He was beginning to have tremendous doubts about where he might be a year later. Salem talked to himself, mumbling unintelligibly. He marched to the splintered kitchen door, opened it and yelled, "Tomorrow I will hire men to cut that damn tree down! Do you hear me, do you?" Again, he slammed the wooden door, knocking off splinters of wood.

Anger and hatred were his dominate emotions and they were the only emotions he allowed himself to have for many long years. He clung to those feelings during his years with the Sons of Liberty. It helped him get the cruel job done. His dark side controlled his thoughts during his life of plundering. He wanted to rid himself of those emotions now but was doubtful he could.

At night, his sleep was usually fitful and he often would awake screaming one word, "Why?" He always asked the same question but never received an answer. He had seen these people in his dreams for years, and his mistrust dominated his thoughts. Were these people trying to destroy him? When he was sleeping, they chased him for miles. He always found himself at the end of the chase standing alone by a freshly dug grave. When he was awake, he could hear their voices. He would ask them, why are you here? The only time they were quiet was when he asked them a question. He knew why he was being haunted. He was the bastard son of a British merchant who violently raped his mother.

He yelled at the people, "I beg you to let me be, leave me in peace. Can't you see that I am in anguish? In pain like my mother, a pain so severe that she took her own life." Salem began to wail. Leaning against the wall, he slid to the floor begging the invisible fiend to leave him.

As quickly as the haunting torment appeared, it was gone. His eyes darted cautiously from the kitchen window to the sitting-room hearth. He yelled, "Are you really gone?"

There was no answer and Salem sat with his legs curled to his chest, afraid of what they might do to him. He was somewhat satisfied to know they were listening to him, that he would ask them to be gone and they would leave. But what he didn't know was when they would be back and how long they would stay. The last time he looked out the kitchen door, no one was there. The yard was empty, but now a lone man, about his age was standing there. Salem left the window, returned several minutes later, and saw that the man was still there. Salem grew more uneasy. Looking at the kitchen ceiling, he asked, "What the hell does that fellow want? Perhaps he needs work. Maybe he was wounded in the war and is sick in the head."

Salem's eyes went to the well-organized kitchen hearth and he saw a large knife. He smiled and thought, I can use that to protect myself. His eyes darted to a row of wooden bowls, all placed according to size. Next, he walked into the dining room, all the while knowing he had to calm himself. After all, he had been waiting years to call this place his home, and now he would have everything his cousins took for granted. He wanted to be happy and he said to himself, the house will make me happy.

He ran his fingers along the top of the dining table. The sun finally appeared from behind a dark cloud. The room suddenly became radiant and filled with light. He noticed the large fireplace in the sitting room and smiled. It was a dream come true, Salem thought. That large part of him that was lost after the Gates died and when he learned of his mother's death.

About half an hour had passed and Salem went to the kitchen to see if the lone man was still standing in his yard. He eased his head to the edge of the window to get a peek, hoping not to be seen. To his horror, the man was still there, sitting on the grass with his back against a fence post gazing at the house. He was suspicious. Who was that man? Was he one of them? Or, he might be some deranged soldier, injured in the head by a cannon blast or a musket ball. Salem didn't have his pistol for protection. His eye darted to the kitchen knife.

J.R. now was standing by the fence post in the yard, not understanding exactly why he felt so compelled to be there. He was not even sure Salem was there. But he had a driving need to find out how this orphaned kid could manage to buy such a costly piece of property. He tried to understand that how the property was bought should not matter. He knew, especially in that day, that any wealth of that size often was an ill-gotten gain.

Of course, no one knew for sure, not the banker, not the auctioneer. Only a few select people knew the real story behind Salem and his new-found wealth. A few knew how to work the system, and to hell with virtue.

Salem slowly opened the kitchen door, watched the stranger and yelled, "You best get off of my property!"

Instead of leaving, J.R. walked slowly to where Salem stood. As he got closer, Salem recognized the man; his face began to twist into a scowl. "Aren't you gone yet? You know you are trespassing. What do you want?"

J.R. was certain Salem recognized him. As he got closer to Salem, the twisted look evaporated from Salem's face. Salem looked at J.R., nodded his head and turned his eyes downward.

Clearing his throat, J.R. said in a strong voice, "If you grow to love this farm, this land, this home, one-half as much as I love it, you may become a happy man." J.R. turned and walked toward his horse.

Salem watched him. Then J.R. remembered that he had one last thing to do before leaving the property. With Salem's eyes glued to his every move, J.R. walked past his horse and headed up a narrow path toward the peach grove. Salem wondered where he was going and figured he was up to no good.

J.R. followed the path that led to the family graveyard. Salem, curious, followed him over the knoll and then toward the cemetery, which was surrounded by a stone wall and latched wooden gate. Salem stood along the path, not taking his eyes off J.R. He watched as J.R. kneeled, bowed his head and said a final goodbye to his kid brother, Joseph. J.R. then moved to the graves of his grandparents, Holmes and Poore. J.R. noticed that Salem was approaching the cemetery with a puzzled expression. Salem entered the cemetery, stood by a grave, then collapsed to his knees as if he had been shot. J.R. rushed to Salem, asking him if he was okay. Salem cursed him and told him to get off his property.

J.R. quietly said, "I would be grateful if I could have a few minutes to say goodbye to my family."

Salem's response was a loud, gruesome sound. A bellow from hell.

J.R. stared, thinking Salem was possessed by rogue spirits, or an insidious beast. His estranged cousin, now rolling on the ground, was bawling high-pitched shrieks. Them, with his eyes closed, Salem barked, "Leave me alone. All of you go away, leave."

J.R. didn't see anyone else. Concerned for Salem's safety, he stayed, but kept his distance. Next, the jumble of words making no sense simply got louder, as Salem's sobs and cries of confusion filled the air. That was when J.R. noticed that his cousin was at his mother's grave. Had he noticed his mother's name carved into the rose-colored slate headstone? He watched as Salem, now quiet and exhausted, lay on the grass.

Salem was curled in a fetal position, crying, "My mother, my mother." He said, "I have finally found my mother, she is here! I have found her."

J.R. then heard Salem, curled near his mother's headstone, beg his mother for forgiveness. He was astonished at Salem's sudden childlike grief. J.R. wanted to get away but thought Salem should not be left alone. Without saying a word, he put a hand on Salem's shoulder.

Salem briefly gazed up at him, then said, "I am her ... her son, Virginia is my mother!" J.R. simply listened and said nothing.

Salem repeated, "Virginia is my mother. I did not know that they found her body and buried her here. No one told me anything, nothing at all. She has been waiting for me to find her." Salem went silent.

J.R. sat on the grass near Salem, "I am sorry for your loss. I don't remember Aunt Virginia. I was only five months old when she died, but I do remember all the wonderful stories my mother shared with us about when she and Virginia were children." Salem's eyes were red. His eyes grew wider as he listened to J.R.

Next J.R. pointed to the Poore headstones. "Here are your maternal grandparents." Salem's eyes grew large and a smile came to his face as he slowly said, "They are here with their daughter. I never knew them, but at the same time I feel close to them."

J.R. felt tremendous sympathy for Salem, apparently a young man with little knowledge of who he was and little knowledge of his mother or his grandparents. Salem was truly a child with no family.

Salem then saw the headstone next to his mother, a smaller shiny black slate headstone that read:

Joseph Holmes
Born March 1765. Died June 1778.
Aged 14 years

Salem read the name on the gravestone. He turned to J.R. and said with a whisper, "Your brother is dead?"

"Yes, he was my youngest brother."

Salem was emotionally overwhelmed; he lay crumpled on his mother's grave. He did not move, lying on the grass with his arms outstretched. J.R. was jolted as he watched Salem begin to beg for answers from his mother's headstone. "Why mother? Why did you take the easy way out? Why did you leave me by taking your own life?"

J.R. watched as Salem's frustration morphed into uncontrollable anger. His facial muscles grew rigid and his hands rolled into tight fists as he wailed, "I demand to know why you gave me away! How could you leave me? You handed me off to strangers! I was your child, your only child." Salem paused and his anger melted into a torrent of tears.

Watching helplessly, J.R. did not know how to console Salem. His mother, the one person expected to love him unconditionally, had abandoned him. J.R. again placed his hand on Salem's shoulder. Salem knocked the hand away. Salem spat out in a rage, "You, you had it all. You had a mother and father. You had a family that loved you. Don't try to comfort me and don't touch me. You have no idea about the hell my life has been. You have not a clue, you pampered son of a bitch!"

J.R. stepped back. He did not know what to do so he decided to leave. He headed toward the small gate. Looking back, he saw Salem hugging his mother's gravestone. J.R. stopped at the gate and sat for a moment on the stone wall. He watched as Salem still was clinging to his mother's cold headstone.

Going back to Salem, J.R. was able to help him back to the house, where he made a fire in the hearth and heated a small kettle of water for tea.

A few minutes passed and Salem asked, "Why are you here and what the hell do you want?"

J.R. was slightly bewildered by the questions. "I don't want anything. I am here because of the auction and I want to wish you well in your new home."

"Sure," Salem said sarcastically. "You want to wish me well! What kind of fool are you? Or perhaps you think I am the fool!"

"I am the type of fool who looks for good in everybody," J.R. replied. "Salem, if you need me for any reason, I am staying with my wife's family, the Brouwers. They are good people, and if you need anything, please come by. We should be here for another couple of weeks. After that, I have two sisters in Sandy Hook, Connecticut, Sarah and Elizabeth Beardsley."

Salem nodded in understanding. J.R. sat with Salem for a while longer, then he said goodbye.

J.R. mounted his horse and trotted back to the Brouwer home. He thought only of the very odd sequence of events that had observed that day. Unbelievable events and yet they had happened right before his own eyes. The new owner of the Holmes farm continued to puzzle him. Salem obviously had serious problems, and J.R. wondered if he ever could rid himself of his demons.

Abigail gave J.R. a hug was he got home. Noticing that he appeared shaken, she asked him how things went at the auction. He bore a perplexed expression and after a moment said, "I think today has been the most bizarre day of my life."

"Was there a problem?" Abigail asked, now full of curiosity.

"No, well, not a problem. Oddly enough, my estranged cousin bought our farm with a fistful of gold."

Abigail first appeared delighted that the farm would remain in the family, then her look turned to one of shock when she heard his comment about a fistful of gold. He had some explaining to do.

Chapter 29

Late June 1783: One Last Visit

As J.R., Elijah and Jacob rode into their sister Sarah's yard, she and Beach came out to greet them. J.R. got right to the point of their visit. "How is mother?" he asked Sarah.

"Mother is doing okay, some days are better than others but she isn't getting better. I wish I had better news."

Elijah, eager to see his mother, asked, "Is she sleeping?"

"Mother is awake." Sarah continued in a softer, lower voice, "In all honesty our mother's health has worsened since she arrived, perhaps due to the long ride to get here."

Jacob noticed that no one wanted to talk about the real issue and it annoyed him. "Our mother is dying," he said quietly. "We all must prepare for her loss." His bluntness startled, Sarah, J.R. and Elijah. "Why are we afraid to admit our mother is dying? We all know it but we don't talk about it with each other. To embrace what is happening is to embrace her."

After a moment, Sarah said, "I agree with you, Jacob. Mother seems to be the only one who is not in denial."

Seeing his mother lying in bed, J.R. did not know what to say. He didn't want to talk about the evacuation, the auction, or their estranged cousin, Salem. He certainly did not want to talk about his father and older brother, who were soon to disembark at Saint John. He was almost speechless. Elijah's face was glum, and Jacob, without saying a word, gazed at his mother with love.

Magdalene spoke up with a weak voice and carefully chosen words. "Please don't worry about me. I am not afraid and I am ready to be relieved of the pain my body has suffered." Magdalene had one more thing to share with her children. She asked if someone would get Sarah.

When Sarah came into the room, she smiled through her obvious pain. With a soft voice, she said, "I want the four of you to know my final wish. Please bury me near my parents, my sister Virginia and my beloved son Joseph in the Holmes family cemetery." Her words were scented with the lavender aroma that rested over her tired body.

J.R. began to speak. "Mother, we will see that your wish is honored and I promise that arrangements will be made before we board the *Montague*."

His mother smiled in her weakened state. Her eyes closed for a few moments and then she suddenly opened them as if not wanting to miss one fleeting moment with her children.

Sarah suggested, "I think it would be good for our mother to spend a little time alone with each one of us." Elijah was first to say his goodbyes.

During that time, J.R. asked Sarah if she might go outside with him. As they walked toward the Beardsley apple orchard, with its trees heavy with apples yet to turn from green to red, he told Sarah who had bought their family farm. "The farm has been sold to a Mr. Poore."

Sarah quickly replied, "Poore, that is our mother's name. Is this person related to us?"

"Yes, the man is our cousin, Salem Poore."

Sarah laughed and said, "Okay, you say our cousin bought our farm. That would be all well and good, but my dear brother, we don't have any cousins!"

His lack of knowledge about Salem led Sarah to further frustration and disbelief. But, as J.R. continued talking about Salem, she began to realize that perhaps it was true. He suggested that Sarah write a letter to Salem regarding their mother's wishes. He told her that Salem knew about the sisters in Connecticut. J.R. said he would make sure that Salem expected her letter. He would talk to Salem before he boarded his ship in July. "I think it is best if we don't let our mother know who bought the farm. It may be upsetting to her."

Sarah was nodding in agreement when she exclaimed, "No, I think not!" She paused. "On the contrary, I think mother might want to know. Perhaps knowing who bought our farm will give her some comfort."

He thought about Sarah's desire to be open with their mother. He was abashed. "Sarah, you are right and I apologize. Creating another family secret won't be good for anyone. I'm confident Salem will honor our mother's wish. After all, mother is his aunt and only sister to his mother, Virginia."

Sarah recalled that every year on the first day of May, she would gather flowers with her mother and sister to place a spring bouquet on Aunt Virginia's grave. Now she learned that Virginia had a son; a son about the age of J.R.

"This doesn't make any sense," Sarah said. "Why weren't we told about this cousin? I did not know that Aunt Virginia had a child. I didn't even know she was married!" Sarah's curiosity made her dizzy as the number of questions grew." "This feels like good news, knowing that we will have a little bit of family left in Middle District. But, why have we not met this cousin and why was he never invited to our home? Was he living in some far off country, raised by his father? Why the secrets?"

J.R. listened and watched as Sarah spouted one question after another. He wanted to give her answers, but couldn't. He watched as she was overwhelmed with tears.

He wrapped his arms about her. "Sarah, the only thing I can say is sometimes things are complicated. Sometimes matters are out of one's control, leaving us with little understanding of what may have happened. Decisions are made not knowing what the future might hold. I have similar questions, but there doesn't seem to be anyone who could provide an explanation."

"What about Mother?"

J.R. took a deep breath as Elijah came out of the kitchen door and walked over to where Sarah and J.R. stood. "Mother is in pain, but refuses to take anything because she doesn't want to miss one minute of our visit."

J.R. decided that it was time for him to visit with his mother. He found it impossible to think that this would be that last time he would sit with her, chat with her and kiss her goodbye. His heart was heavy. He thought about how the war had offered nothing more than loss; loss of life, home, family, and tradition, all culminating in a loss of hope. He sat on his mother's bed and she reached out for his hand.

After several moments of silence, he began to tell his mother about his hopes for his and Abigail's future. She smiled with pride as she listened to him. Then he wanted to ask her a question.

"What is it, son?

His heart rate increased; it worried him to bring up the topic. "Mother, I want to tell you about the person who purchased our homestead." She was puzzled as to why the new owner would be a topic for them to share. "Mother, a man about my age, purchased our farm; his name is Salem Poore."

Her eyes opened wide and she could not believe what she heard and asked, "Are you quite sure this man purchased our home and property?"

"Mother, I have no doubt. I was present at the auction and I watched him bid on the property and buy it with a handful of gold coins."

She tried to make sense of it. "You said gold coins?"

"Yes, Mother, that is how he paid for the property. How could he have amassed such a fortune?" J.R. thought he knew the origins of the loot, but he did not want to share his speculation with his mother. The spoils of war were not the topic.

He listened to his mother as she quietly began to speak. "After my sister died, I regret I didn't go and look for Salem and invite him to live with us." Tears welled up in her eyes, but she held back her emotions just long enough to tell her son about the tragic events that led to Virginia's death.

"My sister's suicide was more than I could comprehend and knowing she had given her baby away to strangers was more than I could bear. I was grieving her loss and my heart was crushed that she didn't ask me to raise her baby. I should have told all of you a long time ago about Virginia's cause of death and about her son, your cousin, Salem Poore. I regret my actions, there is no excuse, please forgive me."

"Mother, you have done nothing wrong, there is nothing to forgive."

She suddenly tensed her muscles as pain shot up her spine. J.R. still holding her hand, asked Sarah to fix her a dose of herbs and opiate for her pain. Within minutes, their mother was sleeping peacefully.

J.R. looked at her frail body and lily-white skin. Her hair encircled her head like a halo. This was his last memory of his mother.

ఌ

No one answered the door. J.R. continued to knock, but the house was silent. There was no one there and he did not know what to make of it. He had to talk with Salem about getting permission to use the family cemetery for his mother's burial. He decided to leave Salem a note. He hoped his note along with Sarah's letter would reach him. He had no time to waste; they were scheduled to leave for the port early on Thursday, they had to have the flatbed packed by Wednesday night, and this was Monday.

He was not surprised that his acquaintance with Salem would end as strangely as it had begun. He had hoped to see Salem that one last time, but he felt solace just to say goodbye to his home. As if guided by years of habit, he wanted to walk around the house and barn taking in the sounds of nature and the sight of lush greenery. He wondered if it would be anything like this in Saint John. He walked to his mother's kitchen garden and was not surprised to see that rabbits had settled in.

J.R. was startled by King George. The rooster jumped up on the roof of the hen house and voiced his dislike for being disturbed in the middle of the day. J.R. ignored George and walked to the barn and opened the squeaky barn door. The place was empty; the animals were out enjoying the July weather.

He turned and headed to the back door of the barn, while looking up into the hayloft's tall ceilings. The loft was still bare to the walls and probably would remain so until fall. There appeared to be a shadow at the far end of the loft but he couldn't make it out in that darkened area. He began to climb the wooden ladder and it began to appear that something was attached to one of the large beams. As he got closer, it appeared something was hanging from it. In horror, he saw it was a body. He could see blond hair over the man's face. It was Salem!

J.R. wasted no time climbing up to cut the rope from around his neck. As he lowered Salem's body, he noticed Salem was no longer warm to the touch. He placed his fingers on Salem's neck to see if he could feel a pulse.

Kneeling over Salem's body, J.R. began to weep. He felt such sadness because no one could save him. His cousin must have taken his last breath several hours earlier. No one was there for him, to help him, to protect him from himself.

He asked Salem, "Why didn't you come to me at the Brouwer's home? I would have helped you, you know I would have helped you." He found Salem's death particularly difficult. He thought there was nothing, not the war, not his forced march, or even the loss of Joseph that could have prepared J.R. for the sight of Salem's body hanging from a rope.

∽

The next morning Mr. Brouwer and Jacob rode into town to notify the authorities. That afternoon, Elijah and J.R. dug a grave next to Salem's mother's. Only J.R., Abigail, her parents, along with Jacob and Elijah attended the burial. J.R. thought that after all these years Salem and his mother would be together again. There were no flowers, no minister, but for perhaps the first time Salem had a family who prayed for his soul and grieved for him.

After the burial, they went to the house. Abigail and J.R. walked into the dining room and J.R. noticed all the new furniture. Abigail remarked how the house smelled musty and how the windows needed to be opened.

"Abigail, let's leave that to whoever owns this place next."

Abigail smiled back at him. On the dining room table, he saw a letter, neatly folded and noticed his name was written on the outside. He nervously picked it up and began to read. It was Salem's will. Feeling uncomfortable, he put it back on the table and told Abigail that it was too private for him to read.

Abigail said, "The man wrote a will, then hanged himself, and he wrote your name on the outside. He intended for you to find it."

J.R. reopened the document and read it from beginning to end.

Abigail saw J.R. had a puzzled expression. "What is the matter?"

J.R. was stunned, "Salem left his estate to his next of kin." He repeated, "He left everything to his next of kin, his two cousins in Connecticut."

Abigail tilted her head, "Cousins in Connecticut?"

"Yes, his cousins are my two sisters, Sarah and Elizabeth. I had briefly mentioned to Salem about my sisters."

Abigail perused the document, "Look here, at the bottom, it was notarized by a Middle District attorney, Samuel Morgan, Esquire."

J.R. was stupefied. Time was not waiting for anyone. J.R., Abigail, her parents, Elijah and Jacob were to leave Middle District two days. They now had only one full day to make all their final preparations. They were running late, never expecting something of this magnitude to happen. They made it an early night, knowing they would need the next full day to pack and load the flatbed.

It was a hot July morning. Jacob and Elijah were outside with Mr. Brouwer loading wooden trunks, crates and cloth bags onto the flatbed wagon that would take them to the port. Regardless of everything needing to be done that day, J.R. had to take time to meet with Mr. Samuel Morgan, Esquire, to provide him with all the necessary information about the sole heirs of Poore. Morgan was an older man and seemed highly irritable. Morgan said he would send a letter of notification to the heirs today. He had only one question.

"Are your sisters Tories too?"he asked, with suspicion.

J.R. was taken aback. "Excuse me sir. Did you ask if my sisters were Loyalists?"

"Yes, indeed I did. If they are Loyalists, as you put it, your cousin's will would be invalid. His entire estate would become property of New York."

"My sisters live in Connecticut and both are married to soldiers who served in the Continental Army. Does that answer your question sir?"

"Oh, indeed it does, they will have to show proof of such when the time comes."

J.R. thanked the attorney and left his office, thinking Mr. Morgan was not the most accommodating man he ever met.

Next, J.R. had to go to the post to mail Sarah a copy of the will. As usual, the post was the busiest place in Middle District. He waited in line to be served, paying little attention to the gossip and rumors. Finally, he reached the front of the line. J.R. handed the letter to the man behind the table, and the man handed J.R. a letter in return. J.R. was in such a hurry he stuffed the letter in his pocket without looking at the return address. He needed to get back to the Brouwer's home and he rode back in haste. The rest of the daylight hours were spent nailing down crates and chests, labeling containers and loading up the flatbed wagon.

Chapter 30

7 July 1783: H.M.S. Montague

orning arrived abruptly for the tired household. J.R. and Abigail, for the first time in weeks, stayed in bed just a short while longer. They cherished their time alone, having no idea when they would see privacy again.

Finally, the six of them climbed onto the flatbed for the ride to the harbor of New York. A clear day with light winds accompanied them all the way to the port, where a long line of flatbeds waited to be unloaded at dockside. As J.R. stood up to see where the line began, he saw dozens of ships anchored at the harbor's edge. Most of them belonged to the summer fleet waiting for a new group of refugees to transport to British North America.

They slowly edged their way to the waterfront. As time went by the line of flatbeds got longer. J.R. and Abigail shared an air of excitement as he held her hand and gave it a little squeeze. There were hundreds of people, going in all directions. The air was filled with Loyalist farewells.

J.R. and his family were allowed to board the *H.M.S. Montague* a day early because the captain gave him the responsibility of maintaining the ship's manifest. He had to log each passenger to include the full name, age, place of birth, employment and place of destination. Also included in the log was the number of bags, crates or chests that were stowed onboard and in the ship's hold. In addition to keeping the manifest, J.R. kept his own personal journal, a daily record of progress, weather and events.

The ship's captain was a man with a big smile, a man characterized by his love of the sea. He greeted J.R. and his family as they boarded the ship, introducing himself as Captain Tucker. He did not have a British accent and later, as the captain showed them where they would bunk, J.R. learned he was a Loyalist from New Jersey.

Several steps down from the main deck were several cabins that could each accommodate up to 24 people. The modest accommodations stunned Mrs. Brouwer and Abigail. Their cabin had 12 berths made of wood planks. The cabin was small and offered little to no privacy. A few berths had a piece of torn canvas draped in front. Abigail noticed the potent smell of mold along with a few other odors she preferred not to identify. She was thankful that the voyage had a beginning and an end, ten to maybe sixteen days. She braced herself to deal with the circumstances.

They were all embarking on their first voyage; none of them had ever been on board a ship. They, unlike their ancestors, never had to endure an Atlantic crossing. As the captain showed them around, Mrs. Brouwer could only smile encouragingly at her daughter, and her daughter did the same to her. They both knew this voyage was going to be a challenge.

Overall, Elijah and Jacob saw the evacuation as an adventure of a lifetime. They were excited about the much-talked-about receiving large parcels of land where they could begin new lives, land without anarchy like their soon-to-be neighbors to the south and without lawless thugs roaming around. Elijah thought their situation was similar to that of Grandfather Obadiah. He had embarked on an Atlantic crossing to New York, leaving England for land in the British colonies.

That evening the ship lay at anchor in Oyster Bay. J.R. woke, climbed out of his berth, and as he pulled on his breeches, something fell out of his pocket. He immediately recognized the letter he had received from the post a day earlier. He then noticed it was from Mr. Soule. He proceeded to climb to the upper deck and finding two lanterns aglow, he walked to the brighter one and read his letter. As he read, he had to sit down. Soule wrote that Heinrich had finally come home. Tears of joy gathered in his eyes as he read the details. It could not have been better news. His first thought was that he must find Ned and share the fabulous news with him before the hundred-plus people began embarkment.

A British Navy sailor, on watch, arranged for two sailors and a boat to transport J.R. to shore, and it was getting light by the time they arrived. The sailors agreed to wait for J.R. to return after his visit with Ned.

J.R. quickly found Ned in the same place, and he was already at work at the table, filling a large book with information. Ned was shocked to see J.R. and he feared bad news until he saw a smile on his face. J.R. handed

Ned the letter and as he read, he cheered at the top of his lungs. Ned could not believe his eyes: Heinrich was safe. Hearing of Heinrich's injury and the care he received from Mrs. Robertson seemed like a miracle.

J.R. had no time to waste; he had to get back to the ship before it docked at the wharf to bring on board its passengers. By the time his transport could see their ship, J.R. could see Abigail at the stern searching for find him among the dozen three-masted schooners, cargo vessels and other ships of the summer fleet. He waved to Abigail. When he boarded, he saw Abigail was upset. She didn't know why he had disappeared during the night. She calmed down after he explained about the letter and its fabulous news and how he had to share the news with Ned.

Abigail smiled, "J.R. you have perfect timing, my dear. Breakfast is just about ready to be served." They held hands and joined their family at the table for breakfast.

After they had finished eating, Captain Tucker provided J.R. with a tentative list of those who were to embark. J.R. skimmed through the names and he smiled at each name he recognized, men from his company. There were several soldiers' widows listed as head of their families. He was saddened by their losses. Most of the men coming abroad the *Montague* that day were attached to Captain Randall's Company of the Loyal American Regiment. Some were troops from Jacob and Elijah's Beverly Robinson Company.

The sound of heavy chain being brought up from the depths of Oyster Bay jolted J.R. from his thoughts. The crew weighed anchor and the ship made its way to the wharf, where it docked. J.R. could see dozens of people waiting to board the ship. Scattered about the wharf were several large piles of bags, chests, crates, all of which were hauled onto the vessel.

As J.R. began logging each passenger and their particulars into the ship's manifest, he saw first-hand the faces of the war-weary men, women and children. Many were hungry and tired, others appeared restless and anxious about being on board a ship for two weeks or more. Most of the children carried a toy, a rag doll or a small carved farm animal. The children held onto their toy tightly, a cherished possession and their link to the only home they had known. There were people of all ages, from a baby boy only days old to a woman in her eighties. J.R. learned that she had lost her husband during a raid by a rebel gang.

In just that day alone, more than one thousand people embarked on nearly two-dozen ships. Those who came aboard the *Montague* were not familiar with life at sea; they had never met a sailor or a ship's captain. They were predominately farmers, planters, people of the soil. Many fearful about what the next two weeks might hold.

Captain Tucker tried to do all he could to ease his passengers' fears. He was the kind of ship's captain who was never far from his crew or passengers. His love for the sea was evident in his leadership and in his tales about pirates, gales, rescues of ships in distress and of course incredible stories about sea monsters. J.R. had heard that when the ship was under sail, the first mate would take the helm and the captain would entertain anyone who wanted to listen with yarns laced with howling winds, dense fog, phantom ships, and a peg-leg ghost.

The ship's quartermaster was a fountain of facts. The children asked him many questions about the *H.M.S. Montague.*

"Our vessel is about 170 feet in length, it has a broad beam, allowing for plenty of sleeping space. It is called a full-rigged ship and boasts four tall masts. If you look up this mast," the quartermaster said, "you will see what we call the crow's nest."

Some of the kids laughed at the name, crow's nest.

"Crow's nest does sound unusual, but the view from way up there is like having the eyes of a high flying bird and you can see far ahead of the ship. The view from there tells us of what may lie ahead of us, enemy ships, a storm or a whale." The children found the quartermaster equally as entertaining as Captain Tucker.

In J.R., they had picked the right man for the job of deputy agent. He knew the importance of record-keeping. He laughed to himself when he compared the boatload of war refugees to his collection of seeds. Each person had his or her attributes, be it profession, talent, knowledge or ability; they each had a quality that would benefit the whole, just as his seeds, alone unique, but together they could fill fields with oats, wheat and barley.

With paper, inkwell and quill, he immortalized each and every soul who embarked that warm sunny day in July. All the while, the words goodbye, write, and God be with you echoed from shore. After J.R. logged in each passenger's name and information, Abigail helped them find their bunks. It took J.R. all morning to process the passengers, while stevedores stowed their belongings. Once all the passengers and their belongings were aboard the ships of the Summer Fleet, the fleet awaited orders to set sail.

Captain Tucker told J.R. that the *Montague* would be making a stop at a coastal town in Connecticut to bring on board a number of Loyalists from Stratford. Most of the people being transported to Nova Scotia were from the five former British Colonies of Connecticut, New York, New Jersey, Maryland and Virginia. Many Loyalists from the Massachusetts Bay Colony had been leaving the colony since 1775; they relocated farther north and east, away from the conflict.

While they waited to set sail, that first night on the ship was not easy. Abigail barely got an hour's sleep. Some young children were crying, while others fussed and whined until the early morning hours. The sounds of child after child filled the night with their frustration and unhappiness.

J.R. knew the next couple of weeks would be tough on the young. There would be no yard or garden in which to run and play, no soft bed and the food would not be their mother's cooking. Perhaps worst of all was the threat of sea sickness or measles.

With J.R. hoping for an early departure, he didn't get much sleep either. To get a break from sleepless babies, he left his cabin and climbed the ladder to the upper deck. Once there, he marveled at the nearly full moon. He breathed in the salty sea air. The sea's surface sparkled as it reflected the moon's glow. The summer sky and its constellations were the only thing familiar to him. It was the same night sky he remembered from Middle District, the same sky he gazed at in Virginia. He knew the same sky would be waiting for him in Nova Scotia.

From the ships stern, J.R. looked toward the eastern horizon; it was beginning to show a slight glimmer of light. He heard a couple crew members talking as they walked to the ship's bow to weigh anchor. J. R's heart began to beat faster, their journey was about to begin. After weighing anchor, the ship caught a favorable breeze. Soon the entire fleet, hoisted sails bulging with wind, began the journey.

Departing the comfort and security of Oyster Bay the *Montague* slowly left the harbor of New York. Many of the passengers, some half awake, were on deck to watch their colony disappear into the horizon.

Mrs. Brouwer stood next to Abigail at the ship's railing as they sailed farther and farther from the land they knew as home. Mrs Brouwer sadly watched the land fade into nothingness, the land soaked with her son's blood, the land to which her ancestors had sailed from the Netherlands to find opportunity in New Amsterdam.

It was common knowledge that the Crown had made generous promises to those who were relocating to Nova Scotia. These promises were encouraging to the Loyalists who had to leave farms and tools that had been in their family for generations. Many were excited to begin to build homes, cultivate the land and rebuild their lives. They believed as they sailed north, ships were leaving Great Britain for Nova Scotia with warm clothing, farming tools, seeds, livestock and ammunition. With the refugee's expectation that these promises would be kept, the bleak rumors of poor soils, rocky coastal lands and cold climate did not seem as daunting.

On the other hand, J.R. had become a skeptic when listening to the promises made by the Crown. It sounded good to be true. If it sounded too good to be true, he thought, it likely was exactly that. Realistically, he had found, much was beyond the Crown's control.

If just one person in the long process of carrying out the pledges was inept, many people in the new settlements would suffer, or even die. J.R. noticed how each and every man aboard had a different idea of the Crown's commitment. He heard other men aboard the Montague talk excitedly about the Crown's agents surveying massive tracts of land to grant to every former soldier and his family. But since the Crown had failed to give the Loyalists protection during the war and in the peace agreement, J.R. was not going to set his hopes too high.

He understood he could only depend on himself. He wanted to clear the land, build their home, cultivate the fields and live in peace. At least the assurances of the Crown kept most refugees' spirits up during that unpredictable time under sail.

Journal of John Roger Holmes

Voyage of Exile to Nova Scotia

8 JULY, DAY 1

Before dawn, the crew weighed anchor in the Port of New York. The winds were good, visibility was clear. Captain Tucker assured us of a pristine day for sailing and he was accurate. The sailors raised the mainsail and the ship gradually began to feel the force of the wind. I had never put much thought into the astounding power of wind. My knowledge of wind power began and ended with the windmill. Now that I see it first hand, I am reminded how the wind has taken people around the world!

Within no time, the *Montague* was on course, with the ultimate destination the mouth of the Saint John River, Nova Scotia. Several of us watched as Sandy Hook Light disappeared into the horizon. An excitement filled me, I had temporarily forgotten the reason I was aboard such a magnificent ship, I had forgotten about leaving the only home I'd known.

My imagination bursts with questions about life at sea, The excitement I feel is like how I felt after I found my first arrowhead, when my imagination went wild with visions of Mohegan people.

The wind's work keeps me humble, it is effortless compared to the work of the ship's crew, they never stand still. I found it hard to believe when Captain Tucker told me we were sailing to the same waters Samuel de Champlain, a navigator and mapmaker, visited nearly two hundred years ago, in 1604.

Captain Tucker said Saint John is the distribution point for thousands of war refugees and it is one of several ports that will become home to the tens of thousands of people from the three fleets sailing out of New York.

It will not be long before we realize that these exiles are the new founding fathers of this rugged, maritime frontier. Not a choice I would have made willingly, nonetheless the decision was made.

Today's meal was steamed green beans, biscuits and a clear-broth fish chowder.

9 July, Day 2

I try not to dwell on something I have no control over, but I can't stop thinking of Mother. I miss her terribly.

A large number of passengers, both adults and children, are suffering from sea sickness. Last night many woke to the sound of vomiting. Poor Jacob was plagued too. The captain said it will be short-lived, thank goodness. Mrs. Brouwer had just the right tincture for Jacob.

Winds continue to blow in our ship's favor. The ship's crew knew just how to rig the sails for the changing wind as we began to set our direction toward Connecticut. The crew showed mastery of those complicated tasks and used words that were foreign to this observer.

Once we arrived at New London, in the former British Colony of Connecticut, we learned the 18 additional Loyalists had grown to 31. The ship dropped anchor off the shore, and a transport was sent for the new passengers and their belongings. It took several hours to get the new passengers and their baggage aboard.

When ready to leave New London, a sailor raised a flag, which meant the crew could weigh anchor. If the captain needed to hurry passengers not yet on board, a shot was fired. Next the crew opened the topsail. The routine and speed of the crew was impressive, and they all worked together with precision.

I logged the new passengers' names and information in the manifest. Much to my astonishment, Reverend Beardsley boarded the *Montague* in New London. Abigail made sure the reverend and his family found a comfortable cabin.

With favorable breezes, it might take us until tomorrow to rejoin our fleet. As the sun set tonight, I soon noticed the moon rising, a commanding appearance, I went down to our cabin to ask Abigail to join me on deck to see the grand sight. Captain Tucker told us the moon was in perigee. Along the horizon it appeared monstrously large and so beautiful. I suddenly thought of Mother, and I had a strong sense she was no longer in discomfort. I felt her so close to me, I could almost imagine I heard her voice.

Evening meal: Beet soup and black bread and domestic fowl.

10 July, Day 3

During the early hours of the morning, a fierce thunderstorm tossed us around like rag dolls. I was awakened each time a child rolled out of his berth and onto the floor. It happened several times. Each tumble out of the berth sounded like a bag of bones crashing to the floor. That sound was immediately followed by a child's cry. The poor children had no idea what had happened to them. The winds howled all night into the early morning hours.

Dawn brought a dense fog. I could barely see the top of the masts. The only way we knew we were still with the fleet was by the blasting of small cannons or the ringing of a bell. Having this communication with the other ships was comforting.

With the morning on our third day came more sea sickness, which we attributed to the rough seas last evening. At mid-day the fog lifted. The warmth of the sun cheered most everyone.

Most comforting is the British warship that is traveling with us to protect the fleet from any uninvited guests, like privateers or pirates. Both are a real threat.

By early evening Capt. Tucker said we were about 140 miles from Sandy Hook Light. With favorable winds we sail all day and all night.

Today's meal was not worth mentioning.

11 July, Day 4

When I woke, Captain Tucker was beginning to change our course eastward. Shortly before noon, the ship's direction shifted to north by east. By day's end, we had sailed a total of about 200 miles since we left Oyster Bay. I had no idea how the captain knew where he was going, when he could see but twenty feet ahead of him. Captain Tucker said the currents and winds are the two factors that dictate the routes ships follow. The North Atlantic currents go easterly.

Soon our captain heard the blast of a gun, the frigate's signal ordering the fleet to lie to for two ships of our fleet to catch up. With the threat of pirates, or worse, the sight of a rebel brig, the ships needed to stay together for protection.

Evenings have become a time to have tea and tend to the bedtime for the children. We all hope the nights will become quieter once the children are more familiar with their surroundings. But it is not happening yet.

Abigail's parents are taking one day at a time. The Brouwers are getting to know the others on board. Which is good. After all, my military company will be some of our neighbors.

Elijah and Jacob spend much of their day on deck working with and sharing stories with the sailors, or maybe it is more appropriate to refer to them as the crew. An exceptional group of men. I had never seen such cooperation of men working together in rhythm.

12 July, Day 5

A couple days prior, I thought a sudden stomach sickness was due to the ocean swells from the thunder storm. Unfortunately, it isn't seasickness, as a couple of the children have a cough and a fever and their faces are covered with a red rash. Mrs. Brouwer said it is the measles, and it is spread through coughing. With such close quarters, the illness will likely sweep through all the children before we see Saint John.

Today when Captain Tucker looked to the east, where a fog bank was heading toward us, I saw him pick up his spyglass. He had spotted a privateer ship coming toward us. He said it was no doubt a rebel privateer vessel, with an hour glass on its flag. Captain Tucker told me the hourglass flag meant our time was running out!

Within a short while, we heard the blast of a cannon, which was our frigate firing a warning shot over the privateer's bow. The cannon blast was so loud, the napping children woke up crying. Tucker said that rogue ship now knows the Montague is voyaging with protection.

Capt. Tucker said privateers are endorsed by their nation to cause havoc on the high seas. They strip ships of guns, cannons, cargo and rigging, then sink the ship or take it back to their port as a prize. Jacob's response to all that was as I expected, "Those rebels love their anarchy on land and sea."

13 July, Day 6

Today was uneventful. We are wrapped in fog, it couldn't get any thicker, and we are unable to see even one ship of our fleet. All the ships rang bells and fired guns to let each other know they were not far away.

The bell ringing was comforting, especially knowing the fog could cause us to get lost or collide with another vessel. Since the maps were not terribly helpful, the ships were always taking celestial reading, but of course even those important readings were put aside until the fog lifted.

By the end of day, the Captain told us we were 240 miles from our destination. This news was met with joy and excitement.

Our meal was baked fish. Our catch came from right off the bow.

14 JULY, DAY 7

The fog continues; no ships in sight. The poor visibility poses risks. We continued the ringing of the bell to let the other ships know of our location. Winds are minimal, and the Captain is relying on the current to give us some progress today.

I am growing weary of being at sea. I have taken the opportunity to pay our Reverend Beardsley a visit or two. Of course he asked about Mother; he is keeping her in his prayers. He spends all his time reading and writing, such a scholarly man.

Abigail yearns for the voyage's end. I reminded her that once the voyage ended, there will be no one serving her dinner as we are all enjoying now.

Our meal: Salted beef, bread and tea.

15 JULY, DAY 8

We were joyous by day break. The fog was gone, which gave everyone reason to celebrate. The sun and blue sky were back!

Abigail and I dined with the captain this evening. I watch Jacob and Elijah mingle with the crew and wouldn't be surprised if one or both of them decide they might make their home on the high seas.

This afternoon a few men were bickering, no doubt some are anxious about being at sea and still no land in sight. I hear several women are tense about the sighting of the privateer ship a couple days back. It wasn't taking much to ignite clashes between passengers.

Captain. Tucker kept a steady watch for the privateer ship. It has been tailing our fleet for a few days now. He said the privateers are likely just being nosey.

Today's meal: A clear-broth cod and potato chowder.

16 JULY, DAY 9

Another morning with abundant sunshine, with the water reflecting the sunlight with sparkles for as far as you can see. The children on board seem to be over the worst part of the measles. Mrs. Brouwer feels certain other ships met with the same misfortune. Today some of the men dropped lines over the gunwale hoping to catch fish for dinner.

The captain has not given us any new information on how much farther we must sail. I am hopeful tomorrow he will give us an update. Too tired to write much tonight.

As I write, I can hear thunder in the distance. I hope it is thunder and not blasts of cannon fire.

17 JULY, DAY 10

The day began lovely, with sun and some clouds. Captain Tucker said we will likely wake up to clouds and rain tomorrow. The days are becoming repetitive so I attempted to engage the captain in conversation. At the helm, he was an optimistic fellow, giving orders to his first mate and chatting with the quartermaster. He performed all his duties to sail the ship from the helm. I marvel at his proficiency.

I have never known anyone who has his unique wealth of knowledge about everything from navigating, weather, tides, currents, and the rather complicated process of hoisting the correct sail for the particular wind and the desired direction.

While watching the moonrise this eveing, I had thoughts of Mother. She always found such comfort with the heavenly bodies, the moon and the stars.

Tired, should sleep well tonight.

Today's meal: salted pork, potatoes and biscuits, with tea and wine.

18 July, Day 11

The fog has returned, obscuring our fleet. But we can hear the bells, so the ships are out there. Interesting how sailors use every sense available to them to detect and determine. I suppose farmers and planters do also.

Captain Tucker said we are about 140 miles from Saint John. He cautioned us, though, saying if the fog doesn't blow out of here, it will be a long 140 miles. This voyage is testing many virtues. Patience is one we will need to master.

19 July, Day 12

We woke to clouds and rain with strong gusts of wind. Not a good day to be up on deck. We were told by Captain Tucker that once we enter the Bay of Fundy, Saint John will be about one day's sail! This was great news for everyone on this damp and breezy day. Abigail said we need some sunny days to dry our wet clothing. Nothing is drying and we are running low on clothing.

By late in the day, there was great enthusiasm expressed about the sightings of shore birds. Everyone's heart is lifted. We are getting closer to our destination.

When the weather is poor, we eat our meals in shifts at a table below deck, about twenty people per shift. This takes several hours to get everyone to the table. The crew always eats first.

Tonight more salted pork with beans and biscuits

20 JULY, DAY 13

Sun and a dry breeze were with us most of the day. Abigail put some items of clothing on deck to dry. We can see almost every ship in our fleet, a breathtaking view. Today is the first day in over a week, we could see land. I never realized it is such a powerful feeling to see land!

Captain Tucker tells us we will enter the Bay of Fundy the day after tomorrow. With that news, spirits are high. Some of the men in my company are ready for a mug of ale. Once we enter the Bay of Fundy, Captain Tucker may bring out a keg to share.

21 JULY, DAY 14

I woke early as usual, up before the sun. I almost fell over when I stepped on the deck. I could see land on both sides of the ship! Jacob and Elijah joined me for the early morning sighting. The sun was rising over a mass of land or island. Later that day several men dropped a fishing line over the side for cod. If someone had a net, they could pick up hundreds of fish.

Fish will be on our dinner plates tonight. The ship's cooks were happy with the haul.

Word is we are running low on flour.

22 JULY, DAY 15

How fortunate we are. Another sun-filled day. Everyone is joyful, today we sailed into the Bay of Fundy. All I can say is that this has been a very long voyage. I can't imagine how Grandfather Obadiah managed a voyage in ships of the last century across the entire Atlantic Ocean.

Today's meal: cod cakes. For the men, a keg of ale was shared.

23 JULY, DAY 16

Favoring winds gave the Montague good sailing today as we sailed north into the bay. Since we last saw the light at Sandy Hook we will have sailed about five hundred miles once we get to Saint John. It has been a long time to be at sea! Captain Tucker said we will reach the mouth of the Saint John River during the early hours of this coming morning. I, like most, have been anxiously waiting for this day, after sixteen days onboard ship.

The sun is out, the breeze is warm. Bickering between two men got the attention of the quartermaster, who confronted the two and defused the situation.

Boiled cod and potatoes was the fare today.

24 JULY, DAY 17

A few hours before sun rise, I heard the heavy chains as the crew dropped anchor. We have arrived. I fell back to sleep until dawn. Once awake, I was eager to get up on deck. My first look at the shoreline caused me to wonder if this is the right place, there is nothing here! We lie at anchor at the mouth of the Saint John River. Since the rest of our fleet lies at anchor with us, my immediate thought is that this must be the correct place.

From the ship, I see a very rough coastline blanketed in a heavy mist, not a welcoming sight. And not like any coastline we have around the port of New York.

To my amazement, there is nothing here! No wharf, no pier, no structures. This place, Saint John, I am told is to become our city. There is nothing here!

Jacob and Elijah joined me on deck. They too were stunned to see there was nothing, nothing at all. Jacob figured there would at least be a pier. Elijah, trying to be humorous, said this place has one thing, a name. Jacob is hopeful there is a settlement closer to Fort Howe, a short way up the river.

Abigail came up on deck and took one look at the shore and with much bewilderment began to weep. She said this was what she expected, but to expect it and then see it were two very different notions. She scanned the shoreline once, twice and a third time remarking there was no waterfront with warehouses or wharves or businesses. Abigail was not alone in her reaction. Many of those on board were startled to see the place the Crown said was to be our city and our home.

Very surprised to see not one wharf, virtually no buildings, or the bustle of trade from here! This place where we have arrived is starkly different from where we came. I can't fully describe my first impression, the land is nothing more than a rugged and rocky coastal wilderness. As my eyes scanned the shoreline, I could not see even one shelter.

The fleet was welcomed to Saint John by what Captain Tucker referred to as "Scotch mist." He described it as a combination of a fine vapor and relentless drizzle with lingering fog. Anyway, after noon I and several other men will board a transport and go ashore. I look forward to getting my land legs back. I hope it all looks better once the mist is gone. Trouble is, Captain Tucker told us Scotch mist can hang around for days at a time.

Epilogue

Letters of Correspondence 1783-1784

(From Sandy Hook, Connecticut, to Saint John, Nova Scotia)

19 July 1783

Dear Father,

I don't know where you may be or what you might be doing when this letters finally is in your hands. I hope you are all in good spirits and fine health. I must begin this letter with mother. I am full of sorrow and grief. Mother died the night before last, July 17, the night the moon was in perigee.

I can assure you, she left this world peacefully. I will always remember her for her strength of mind. Her last words were, "Be kind to each other." She was always full of kindness.

Yesterday mother was buried in the family cemetery, which was her wish. She now shares the same soil with Joseph, her sister, mother and father, all in the sweet earth of Middle District.

I think of you and the family daily. I worry the living conditions are primitive. We occasionally hear word from others who have family in Nova Scotia, and regrettably the stories are of challenge and difficulty. With the lack of shelter, other than tents, I am unable to understand why the Parliament was not better prepared for the war refugees.

I want to thank J.R. for his attention to detail. As you might very well know by now, Elizabeth and I inherited the family farm. Sister and I were speechless to have gotten the news. The great sadness surrounding our inheritance is unfortunate. Our cousin Salem also left us a significant amount of gold and precious stones. After much thought, Elizabeth and I will forward this to you with one desire. We would like these funds to help orphaned children. I think cousin Salem would have wanted something like that to be done, helping orphaned children.

It appears Nathaniel and Elizabeth are keenly interested in returning to the farm. They have plans to bring the family homestead back to its original glory. They are going to have a barn raising early next spring. Nathaniel hopes lumber will be more available by then. Nathaniel's entire Continental Company has pledged to help build the new barn. Elizabeth is enjoying motherhood, Emma is a sweetheart.

Finally, please share this letter with the rest of the family. I miss you all, and I refuse to accept I may never see any of you again. Nonetheless, you are with me spirit and memory. Beach, Magda, Cicero and I are fine and our family continues to grow. We will be adding a new baby to our family soon. Be well and we send our love to all of you. Your loving daughter, Sarah

(From Saint John to Virginia)

5 September 1783

Dear Heinrich,

Such great news to hear you finally made it home! I was on board the H.M.S. Montague when I learned of your good fortune. I then immediately took a transport to the shore to share your good news with Ned. He was so happy, he couldn't keep his tears back! He had been worried sick over your disappearance.

And you are a father! What do you think of that! I can only imagine the relief Comfort felt when she saw you. She never gave up hope. She knew you would be coming back. Even when prospects of your return seemed gloomy, she tried her best to remain positive.

I am doing well in spite of the wilderness conditions in which we find ourselves. No supply ships from England yet. Winter could be here before the promised supplies arrive. That could mean the winter may not be survivable. Food is sparse and shelter is flimsy.

Thank goodness my father packed small hand tools. We have been able to build a small log structure that will be our protection against winter wind and snow. The native people say the winter season can be long and very cold, with strong winds coming off the ocean that seems almost to surround us. We are smoking meat and salting fish for winter. Deer are abundant year-round, and rabbit too. I don't think we will go hungry, but I am not as optimistic about not freezing to death.

Ned is nearly running everything at the encampment for free black Loyalists in New York. There are about three thousand who will be boarding ships this month for Nova Scotia. He will be a distance from me, but we promised each other to get together soon after he arrives this fall.

Oh, I almost forgot, Abigail and I finally married! I am the happiest man in the world. Give my best to Mr. Soule and Comfort and don't forget a pat on young Henry's head for me.

J.R.

(From Saint John to Sandy Hook)

10 October 1783

Dear Sarah,

The arrival of your letter lifted our spirits!

First, I must tell you, regardless of the numerous hardships with which we are confronted, we are all in good health. It appears we will be spending a cold winter in a small house made of logs. It has no windows. We will have no floor either, so we will cover the earth with pine tree needles and leaves to keep some of the cold away. Many will be living all winter in long tents made of old sail cloth Some tents will have several families living together. We have been at the mouth of the Saint John River for nearly two months. We continue to wait for supply ships from England. Since our arrival we are living in a large tent, it gets very cold at night and it is still October. Fort Howe is nearby, and the fort is also waiting anxiously for supply ships from England.

We have a new family member, Obadiah and Charlotte have a son. He was born about four weeks ago. His name is Jonathan, after our father, of course. Isabelle is thrilled to have a brother. Baby Jonathan is one of three children born since we arrived.

You and Elizabeth have a great idea. To provide assistance to the orphaned children of Nova Scotia is spot on. There are many children here who have recently lost their last living parent. Too many children lost fathers on the battlefield, then their mothers died from the stress and strains of the exile. The most hideous part is many of these children have grandparents in the thirteen colonies, but are not allowed to return, thus they are doomed to an orphan's life.

Currently we are living in a frontier, no mercantile, no blacksmith, no bakery like Uncle Joost and Aunt Sophia's place.

The good news is the surveyors have been working endlessly to ensure we have our own land grants by spring. I will be granted nearly 130 acres inland from the Saint John River. We will be about two hours up the river from Fort Howe. My piece of property is just above the glebe, land belonging to the church.

Your brother, John Roger

(From Virginia to Saint John

January 9, 1784

Dear J.R.

I read your letter with feeling of excitement and disbelief. Your challenges are remarkable. I hope British supply ships found their way to your shores, I am sure the Crown would not leave all of you without supplies until spring.

Here it is the dead of winter, the only thing that moves around here is the wind, snow, an occasional bird or a fast-moving rabbit. To look out and see the well-cared-for fields resting snugly under their blankets of snow, fills my heart with pride. But Henry is the one who is makes me most proud.

He turned two years old last month. I enjoy being a father. Comfort is fine She is my joy. She has a glow about her, maybe a sister or brother for Henry might be in our not-too-distant future. I would like a whole house full of children. Comfort agrees.

Up until a couple months ago I had not been paying close attention to the growing pains of this new country. There is a constant struggle between the different colonies and the idea of a central government, and many don't want to make the central government more powerful than the individual colonies. Everyone has their own idea of how this new nation of ours should be governed. And some of those men who fought for the rebellion are complaining about high taxes. I don't think any of these issues will be solved soon. Mr. Soule tells me the court in Massachusetts has abolished slavery. That is a positive milestone for the new nation.

You know, J.R., I feel like the most fortunate man in the world. The woodcutter and his wife saved me from certain death, I am married to the most remarkable woman and I have an active healthy son. With all of that, I have a father-in-law who possesses wisdom and insightfulness, which he never hesitates to share with me. I am a grateful man.

They say spring will be early this year. How they come up with these ideas I don't know. I look forward to planting and hope for another abundant yield. I guess, when spring arrives to where you are, you will go up the river and begin to clear your land and build a home. I look forward to hearing from you soon.

My best, H.H.W.

(From Saint John to Birchtown, Nova Scotia)

14 February 1784

Dear Ned,

I hope this letter finds you safe, in good health and warmer than I have been these past couple months. Our accommodations are not great, but better than a tent. Our party numbers eight adults and two children. All of us are staying in a small log shelter. Jacob, Elijah, Obadiah, my father, Mr. Brouwer and I worked endlessly during the months of August, September and October to complete our modest shelter with no windows and a piece of canvas for the door. I do believe we have found ourselves in an untamed frontier!

Most families have erected canvas tents. And some of the wealthier refugees have been able to rent rooms or even a modest house. The French, who had lived here up until the mid-1760s had shelters but many of them have fallen into neglect, or the wood has been taken for re-use.

As I write this letter to you, the fire's glow provides me with light. While everyone sleeps, we take turns staying awake to keep the fire burning. I believe if we let the fire die, we could freeze to death in our sleep! I imagine you are experiencing the same thing.

Needless to say, we look forward to spring, during which time we will be given our land grants, ships will be arriving with food, clothing and tools and hopefully we can depart our current humble quarters. I have heard of some men wanting to sell their land grants to move to another town.

Let's make a point to meet toward the end of summer. Think about visiting over this way. My land is about two hours up the Saint John River from here. It is a small community a short distance inland from the river. On the surveyor's map my land grant is just above the glebe property of the church. Oh, one more thing, by the end of the year, we will no longer be part of Nova Scotia, but a new province. I'm not sure yet what they will name this province.

It is my turn to sleep, I will wake Obadiah, it is his turn to watch the fire. Be well, my friend.

J.R. Holmes

(From: Birchtown to Saint John)

March 1, 1784

Dear J.R.

Would you believe, almost all of us survived the winter. The winds have been dreadfully annoying, nonstop over here in Shelburne. Winter was very difficult. No one had ever imagined winter would be so brutal, the cold and strong winds were relentless. But even the harsh winter was not ntolerable enough to encourage anyone to go back to where they came from. So here we stay.

The quality of land is of grave concern. It is not the land a planter would choose. Once the snow melted, I walked the land to be granted to me. It looks as if it might be better for grazing sheep or goats. The property surely is not for planting.

Yes, I have heard that plans are being made to divide Nova Scotia into another province, the peninsula will remain Nova Scotia and the rest will be named either New Ireland or New Brunswick.

I look forward to traveling to see you this summer. In fact I might just want to buy some land out your way. Also I must tell you, I have met a lovely woman with whom I hope to wed.

I feel positive about my new life in Nova Scotia and think my opportunities have no limits. Although, I would not be totally forthcoming if I didn't tell you I have seen some rude and hateful behavior of others toward the free slaves. It is heartbreaking to see such vulgarness, but again, I hope in time we will put all that behind us. Remember what we were doing three years ago? Attending Heinrich and Comfort's wedding!

Ned Lawson

Acknowledgements

I am indebted to Roger Van Noord, who did the first read of *Above the Glebe* and so much more to get it ready for print. Thank you, Roger, for pinch-hitting for my uncle, Alan Noone MacLeese, an extraordinary editor who died in an accident before this book was finished. My thanks also to Roger's wife, Jessica, who read the final version.

I express my gratitude also to Pat Irish, who reviewed numerous drafts and provided me with feedback.

Finally, I thank Bob Thompson. While doing genealogy research on his family, I found a few of his ancestors were Loyalist. I too have Loyalist ancestry. This inspired me to write *Above the Glebe.*

About the Author

Pamela Gilpin Stowe, is a retired teacher. Originally from Connecticut, she taught gifted education in Maine and Arizona. She is graduate of the University of Maine at Orono and Endicott College for Women in Beverly, Massachusetts. She lives in Maine, spending winters in Auburn and summers in down east Jonesport. She lives with her 12-year-old Shih tzu named ChaCha.

Made in the USA
Columbia, SC
01 February 2023

11366407R00181